The Girl and the Moon

Also by Mark Lawrence

The Broken Empire
Prince of Thorns
King of Thorns
Emperor of Thorns

Short stories
Road Brothers

The Red Queen's War
Prince of Fools
The Liar's Key
The Wheel of Osheim

The Book of the Ancestor
Red Sister
Grey Sister
Holy Sister

The Book of the Ice
The Girl and the Stars
The Girl and the Mountain

Impossible Times
One Word Kill
Limited Wish
Dispel Illusion

The
GIRL
and the
MOON
MARK
LAWRENCE

The Third Book of the Ice

HARPER
Voyager

Harper*Voyager*
An imprint of HarperCollins*Publishers* Ltd
1 London Bridge Street
London SE1 9GF

HarperCollins*Publishers*
1st Floor, Watermarque Building, Ringsend Road
Dublin 4, Ireland

www.harpercollins.co.uk

First published by HarperCollins*Publishers* 2022
2

A catalogue record for this book is available from the British Library

ISBN: 978-0-00-828484-8 (HB)
ISBN: 978-0-00-828485-5 (TPB)

Typeset in Sabon LT Std by Palimpsest Book Production Limited,
Falkirk, Stirlingshire
Printed and Bound in the UK using 100%
Renewable Electricity at CPI Group (UK) Ltd

MIX
Paper from
responsible sources
FSC™ C007454

This book is produced from independently certified FSC™ paper
to ensure responsible forest management.
For more information visit: www.harpercollins.co.uk/green

To my readers for sharing the journey.

The Story So Far

For those of you who have had to wait a while for this book, I provide brief catch-up notes to Book Two so that your memories may be refreshed and I can avoid the awkwardness of having to have characters tell each other things they already know for your benefit.

Here I carry forward only what is of importance to the tale that follows.

Abeth is an ice-bound world with a thin strip of land known as the Corridor circling its equator, kept free of ice by an artificial moon. On Abeth there are four old bloods that show in a small minority of children:

- gerant (which means you grow very big)
- hunska (which makes you very fast)
- marjal (which can give you some of a variety of lesser magics, like command over shadows, water, air, rock, fire, etc. – sometimes more than one of these)
- quantal (which can give you major magics, including accessing the vast power of the Path, and the ability to weave the threads of existence to achieve more subtle manipulations of people and things)

The Missing are the people of a fifth tribe that arrived before these four tribes and were thought to have vanished by the time they arrived.

Important figures from Book Two:

- Yaz, ~16 years old, part of the Ictha clan. Yaz has the blood of the Missing and this gives her the special ability to control the stars. She also has quantal skills
- Thurin, ~18 years old, born under the ice, marjal with powers over water and fire
- Erris, ~5,000 years old. As a young man he was lost in the undercity, millennia ago, before the sun weakened further and ice covered the planet. The city adopted him. It's unclear whether Erris is really alive or just a memory kept by the city. He now inhabits an artificial body that he built with the city's help
- Quina, hunska, a quick-witted, sharp-tongued girl, ~15 years old
- Quell, ~17 years old, one of the Ictha clan. Quell was going to ask Yaz to marry him just before she jumped into the Pit of the Missing. He stayed in the north with her brother and clan when she went south in search of the Corridor
- Theus (age unknown), a spirit made from all of the undesirable traits of one of the Missing. His unbroken form came to Abeth from Earth as a simulation that was imprinted on a baby. Currently he's possessing the iron dog, Zox, and was left in the tunnels under the convent
- Taproot (age unknown), an ancient simulation of a man named Elias Taproot, brought to Abeth by one of the four tribes of men that settled the planet together, arriving after the departure of the Missing. Currently he occupies an empty white box that Yaz was carrying when Eular confronted her

- Eular (age unknown), an old, eyeless man who is high priest of the Black Rock but also seems to maintain a role as a very important cleric in a different faith practised in the part of the Corridor in which Yaz has arrived. A now-destroyed Hayes gate (these are also known as haze-gates) in the Black Rock allowed the priests to visit the Corridor
- Jeccis, an old woman who is part of the Black Rock priesthood
- Krey, a young woman who is part of the Black Rock priesthood

Yaz, Erris, Thurin, and Quina journeyed south across the ice and reached the Corridor. The last few thousand miles of the crossing were achieved using a Hayes gate linked to another such gate beneath the Sweet Mercy Convent.

During the journey it became clear that the spirit known as Theus had possessed the iron dog, Zox, that they'd brought with them from the Black Rock to pull their sled. The creature that calls himself Theus is made from all the 'undesirable' parts of one of the Missing, carved out of that person before what was left of him ascended to some other plane/place with the rest of the Missing. Theus's goal is to reunite with the rest of himself and have a reckoning with his fellow Missing who forced this unwanted purification on him.

The Missing came from Earth. They were the first of five waves of humanity that eventually ended up on Abeth as the stars started to die. The Missing were thought to have departed before the other four waves arrived, though a small number, rebelling against ascension, hid out in the far north and later mingled with the newcomers.

The Missing's last instruction to their cities was that none should follow them – an instruction aimed at the city intelligences and their minions, with the intention of gifting them the world. Unfortunately, after the passage of millennia and the unforeseen arrival of more humans, the cities interpreted the order as being aimed at the new people and acted to undermine their civilization so that they wouldn't have the means to follow the Missing.

The leader of the city minds, Seus, is now working to bring down the moon so that the ice will close over the Corridor and reduce mankind to an ever more tenuous survival on the ice.

Theus, like many of the Missing, was born on Earth and brought to Abeth as a machine-hosted intelligence, though as with Erris it's not clear if he is truly alive or a copy of a man who is now dead. Where Erris was eventually downloaded into a realistic but mechanical body, Theus was imprinted on a baby. This was the baby seen in the prologue to Book One, the baby for whom the ice-witch Agatta predicted greatness and fire. The fact that Theus managed to 'pull himself together' and is able to function so well is a clear indication that, whoever he was before, he was an individual of exceptionally strong will and also someone who required the majority of his personality to be purified before he was deemed fit to ascend.

Yaz's group acquired a new member on the ice – Mali, a novice from Sweet Mercy.

Almost immediately after their arrival at the convent, Yaz and her friends discovered that Eular, whom they had known as an elder among the Broken under the ice, and as the high priest of the order that lived in the Black Rock, was also maintaining the role of a powerful cleric in the Ancestor-faith practised in this part of the Corridor. Eular seems to be in charge and has falsely accused them of murder. He told Yaz she had come a long way to die.

CHAPTER 1

Yaz and Mali

Yaz had walked on water her entire life, and now in this place where it fell molten from the skies they planned to drown her in the stuff.

She knelt on the rock, staring down into a sinkhole at the water some forty feet below. A black depth waited for her, unrippled by the wind, untouched by the sunlight that reached only halfway down. The sheer-sided hole might have been poked into the stone by the finger of a god. The far wall lay more than ten yards away and on that side an iron ladder led down into the depths, marking the stone with rusty tears.

Even if the ladder were on her side it would have been of little help to Yaz. Her hands were held out to either side of her neck by a heavy iron yoke that had already scraped her wrists raw. The metal was hot, having soaked in the sun, which seemed to shine more strongly here on Abeth's belt. To her left Quina knelt, similarly yoked, her ankles bound with rope where Yaz's remained free. To Yaz's right, Thurin then Erris wore the same iron restraint and watched the same dark waters.

Throughout all her troubles since dropping into the pit,

Yaz had never come quite as close to death as that day fishing the Hot Sea when the dagger-fish had dragged her brother beneath the waves and she'd gone down with them, unable to let go. Here she was again, facing the same end.

The audience this time was much larger and far less friendly. Nobody would be paddling to the spot where she went down. None of them would try to save her.

Eular, who had been high priest at the Black Rock, was somehow a major figure in a very different faith down here in the green lands. Now he stood with his masked and eyeless face turned towards Yaz and the others from the far side of the sinkhole. Standing with him were the abbess and the two sisters superior: Mistress Path – or Sister Owl as she had first introduced herself – and Mistress Shade. Nuns and novices ringed the perimeter. None of them looked happy about the proceedings.

Yaz kept her gaze on Eular. She remembered the debris in the hidden room behind Arges's statue back in the Black Rock's temple: a shattered gate. It was clear now that the gate had been broken after Eular used it to escape to the Corridor, and that he must have used it many times before that day. His double life between the caves of the Broken and the Black Rock had been a triple life. He'd maintained yet another personality, using the wonders of the Missing to skip through time and space, supporting at least three separate existences. Somehow he'd carved out a position in the green lands among the people he claimed had blinded him. His manipulation of threads could only have taken him so far – the rest must have been down to external help. Seus must have been at work in this place for years.

From her place on the rim of the Glasswater sinkhole Novice Mali watched the four ice-tribers on their knees awaiting execution. Unlike them she had been allowed to stand, but like them she wore the yoke. The device was designed to restrain people with two hands, and Mali would have found it easy to pull her wrist stump clear, but Sister Cup had secured her elbow to the ironwork with rope. In any event, there was little Mali could have achieved with that arm free. The stump ached all the time and became agony at the lightest touch.

Oddly, when she didn't look at the stump Mali could imagine she still had the hand. She could even wave the fingers or make a fist, almost as if there were a ghost hand there, and that in some parallel Abeth an unmaimed Mali occupied the same space. She'd even found that when it came to manipulating the invisible threads that join each thing to every other, it was her missing fingers that were the most deft, capable of feats of dexterity her fingers of flesh and bone were not.

Mali forced herself to look at the four ice-tribers who had saved her. Sister Pine stood behind them in the white habit of the executioner. Yaz and her friends looked so lost in Mali's world, just as she had been lost in theirs. She remembered their tears of wonder when she'd led them out of the cave, as if the trees and bushes had been heaped mounds of gold and gems. Everything had amazed them: chickens, nuns' habits, the archon's horse . . . And now, a day after their arrival, they were all to be killed. Mali's heart hurt worse than her wrist.

The trial in Persus Hall had been a farce. Mali had answered the archon's questions, protested when he called her a liar, and hung her head when he laughed at her talk of gates that crossed thousands of miles in an instant. Archon Eular had called one of his Church guards to the stand, a woman he said had survived the ice-tribers' raid in which

3

the white box, later found on Yaz, had been stolen from a priest named Pather, who had sadly been killed in its defence.

The woman had pointed at Mali and with unwavering conviction had stated before the court and beneath the timeless gaze of the Ancestor that Mali had been with the raiders, though possibly a prisoner.

The tribers had, Archon Eular maintained, captured Mali on the ice, slaughtered her friends, and coerced her to lead them through the empire in search of plunder. Having murdered Father Pather and stolen Church property, they came to Sweet Mercy seeking new things to steal. It seemed, he said, that they had used unknown magics or poisons to break Mali's will. It was the only explanation for her lies, unless of course she had turned willingly to their cause. Eular had produced the handful of stardust taken from Yaz and claimed it as an example of the corrupt magics of the ice they had used to twist Mali's mind. He had snuffed out its light, claiming that he channelled the purifying power of the Ancestor, and had let the lifeless grains tumble through his fingers to the floor.

Yaz and her friends had said nothing during the trial. In fact nobody had asked them to. Sister Owl and the archon were the only ones who could speak to them, and Yaz had told Mali not to reveal that the two of them could understand each other. Sister Owl had watched the whole proceedings, stony-faced, saying nothing despite her curious interest in Erris. Apparently her respect for the office of archon prevented her from contradicting him in court. And, truthfully, what could the old woman say on the subject that did not come directly from the mouths of the accused?

So now Mali stood yoked beside the Glasswater. Her yoke bore a sigil that prevented her reaching the Path. She knew she wouldn't be drowned, at least not today: the sigil made

4

the yoke far too powerful to risk losing it in the mud fathoms down at the bottom of the sinkhole.

Although Abbess Claw had been largely silent during the trial she had been insistent on two points. Firstly, there would be no rush to judgement in the case of a novice of Sweet Mercy. If Novice Mali had been controlled then the means of that control would be identified and neutralized. Secondly, when Archon Eular had called for his men to take the tribers out into the square and behead them Abbess Claw had stood from her chair.

'At Sweet Mercy we drown.'

The archon had raised a brow at that. 'I beg your pardon?'

'We execute by drowning in the sinkhole.'

Archon Eular had shaken his head, the white mask hiding his expression. 'I don't trust that. I want their blood on the ground before me.'

'You don't trust drowning?' Abbess Claw's trilled laugh sounded all wrong. Mali had never heard the abbess laugh before. 'Do you think the ice tribes are part fish, archon? I doubt they can even swim, though that's immaterial; they will be weighted.'

'Perhaps they have powers . . .' Irritation coloured the archon's voice.

'Powers?' The abbess raised a brow.

'You have to ask? In this place where half your novices show the old bloods?'

Abbess Claw pursed her lips. As close to a shrug as Mali had ever seen. 'And we have to scour the empire for them. And even then not one of the girls here can breathe water.'

'I insist—'

'Archon Eular.' Claw lowered her voice though the whole of the Persus Hall could still hear her, its collective breath held as they watched on, amazed that the abbess would defy an archon over so small a thing as the manner of four foreigners' deaths. 'Archon Eular, you are new in your post and perhaps less familiar than you might be with the convents and monasteries that you now oversee on behalf of the high priest. Within the confines of this convent the laws by which we have lived for more than two centuries are paramount. Church law says these four must die. Convent law says it will be by drowning. It would be unfortunate for us to put your authority to the test so early in your new post over such a minor detail. Sister Owl will keep close watch on the prisoners and in the unlikely event that they attempt to use magic to escape their fall she will counter any such efforts.'

The archon drew breath to answer. Abbess Claw beat him to it. 'But I *will* have tradition followed.'

'Fine.' Eular had thrown his hands in the air. 'Drowning it is, then. I will be attending the execution so let's make it as soon as possible.'

'Thurin Ice-Spear!' Abbess Claw called across the sinkhole. 'You have—'

'Not him. Put the girl in first,' Archon Eular interrupted.

Abbess Claw turned her head slowly and gave the archon a hard stare. 'Quina of—'

'The other one! The darker girl.'

Despite her promise to Sister Owl, Mali started to try to force her way to the ice-tribers. She tried to see the Path but instead the damned sigil filled her vision, splitting her head with a wedge of white agony. 'This is murder! These people helped me!'

Someone put a knee into Mali's spine and a gag into her mouth, pulling back until she was forced to her knees. Still she tried to fight them. Yaz was a powerful quantal and when she unleashed her power people Mali loved might die.

Mali could warn the nuns, but even if she was believed Mali couldn't take away the tribers' last remote chance of escape, however doomed any such attempt might be. Worse still was the idea that Yaz's efforts in rescuing Mali, pulling her from death on the ice through that distant gate, had drained her: she'd not used the Path to fight Haydies or his guards, even when the three-headed dog was on the point of slaughtering everyone. And although those events seemed as distant in time as they were in space, they were actually only on the previous day.

The abbess drew a deep breath, fingers drumming on her crozier. 'Yaz of the Ictha, you have been found guilty of the crime of murder by a court of the Church. Sentence is now to be carried out. May the Ancestor have mercy and join your soul to the great tree.' Abbess Claw made the sign of the arborat, one finger starting low, tracing the taproot, another finger joining to trace the trunk, then all fingers spreading as they rose to trace the branches. 'Have you any last words?'

Across the empty yards Yaz frowned, her mouth struggling to shape unfamiliar words. 'Priest . . . Eular . . . lies.'

The abbess gave a curt nod and Sister Pine pushed Yaz forwards. She fell without a scream and hit the water, vanishing before the splash cleared. Quina started to wail.

Mali broke free for a brief moment, howling behind her gag. The abbess glanced her way with an unreadable expression as two nuns wrestled her back down.

Abbess Claw raised her voice to execute a second sentence. 'Thurin I—'

'The other girl next,' Archon Eular cut across her. 'But let's be in no hurry about it.'

Where Yaz had fallen the ripples were still spreading out towards the opposite wall. A scattering of bubbles rose lazily from the spot where she had gone under. For what seemed an age everyone watched in silence as the ripples faded away. One lone bubble broke the surface.

'Making them wait is cruel, archon.' The abbess raised her hand to signal Sister Pine. 'At Sweet Mercy we are not cruel. We are just.'

Eular caught her arm and pressed it down, though Mali had no idea how he saw it. Or indeed how he had known that Yaz's bronze skin was darker than Quina's pale one. 'Indulge me.'

Abbess Claw sighed and stepped back.

On the far side Erris pitched forward without being pushed. He hit the water with an enormous splash.

'Stop them!' Eular roared. 'Don't—'

But Thurin was already falling as Erris hit the water. With a desperate wail Quina fell to her side and rolled over the sinkhole's edge, screeching as she dropped.

'Stop them?' The abbess turned to fix Archon Eular with a curious stare, head tilted to the side. 'It was your sentence that demanded their lives.'

Eular stood staring at the churning water, fists balled at his sides, as if from behind the closed ceramic of his mask those empty sockets might see all the way down into the Glasswater's murky depths.

CHAPTER 2

Yaz

Yaz had fallen much further before and into colder water, but never wearing an iron yoke that weighed half what she did and kept her hands immobile. She hit the water hard enough to leave her head ringing with the impact. In the next moment everything was bubbles and churning light, the yoke swiftly dragging her down. Terror surged, trying to force her last breath from her lungs. The depths into which she was sinking were black, beyond the reach of daylight, and she had no idea how long it would take her to reach the bottom. Already pressure was building around her, pressing on her chest to release its air, weighing against her eardrums and promising to crush her like rotten ice.

Thurin was supposed to go in first. *Thurin was supposed to go in first.* Eular had seen through their plan and now she was going to die.

She hit the bottom unexpectedly and black mud swirled, replacing the weak light from above with impenetrable night. The mud enfolded her in a slimy embrace. She fought against panic. She couldn't tell if she was entirely within the muck or lying on some yielding surface. Somehow drowning in

9

mud seemed worse than drowning in water. The yoke's weight provided a definite sense of down but she couldn't find any footing to right herself. Instead she forced herself to stillness. The air in her lungs would turn sour more swiftly if she struggled.

She lay in the cool embrace of the slime, knowing that the bones of others murdered in this manner must be lying all around her, the skulls of young girls most likely, watching her with blind, mud-choked sockets. She thought of Eular up above in the sunshine and wanted to scream, wanted to fight. Eular's last-moment interference in how the execution was carried out had left their plan in tatters. Holding her breath would only drag it out. She could die now or live brief minutes longer while Eular revelled in her torment. She was glad he couldn't see her. Once he had seemed a kindly old man, wise but vulnerable, a guiding hand. He'd tricked her well then, and once again he'd caught her by surprise in a final, fatal deception.

The air wanted out of Yaz now. It wasn't just those fathoms of water pressing down on her chest: her body had taken what it needed from what her lungs held. It had to be expelled in order to draw another breath. Her heart pounded against her chest. Her blood thundered in her ears. Blind and deaf, out of reach of friend and foe alike, Yaz remembered the feel of her brother's arm in her hands, her utter determination that she would not let go as the dagger-fish pulled them ever deeper. She had no memory of drawing cold water into her lungs, just the fight, the struggle. The end itself had been merciful oblivion. This time there would be no Ictha hauling her to safety as her boat broke the surface.

So many things could go wrong. Yaz was sure that they had. Where was Thurin? She was going to die alone in the dark. Murdered by someone she hated. Air escaped at the corners of her mouth, bubbling away despite her teeth being clamped together so tight her jaw ached. She was going to die. She was—

Strong hands closed around her legs. A moment later they were on her yoke, lifting her. Still she couldn't see or breathe. Erris had found her. Only Erris could lift her and the yoke with such ease. She might still die but at least she wouldn't be by herself. Her body began to convulse, air escaping her in bursts; the terror held at bay for so long flooded through her, blowing reason from its path.

'Arrrrgghh!' Yaz screamed out the stale breath and hauled in a new one.

Somehow she didn't choke on it. Erris held her while she panted and gasped, unable to speak or even support herself.

'Noooooooooooooo!' Quina's wailing suddenly assaulted them, followed by a loud splat that cut it off completely. A few moments later and she was somewhere near, coughing and spluttering, still trying to scream. 'No! What? Urgh! What is this stuff? Hel—' The mud reclaimed her.

A small flame sprang up. Yaz was still too busy panting and wheezing but she was able to get her bearings now. Erris was supporting her with his good arm and in the palm of his other hand he held a flame, just like the one he'd produced long ago in the caverns below the ice. The iron yoke was still around his neck, twisted at an odd angle, but he'd somehow got both hands free.

'Up you get.' Thurin was there too. Still yoked, he couldn't use his hands to help Quina stand but he managed to right her with his ice-work and set her standing in the waist-deep mud that coated them all. A black dome contained them, rather like the one they had found Taproot in, but much smaller, affording only enough room for the four of them.

And it wasn't made of whatever Taproot had built his from. This was just muddy water. Somewhere, although Yaz couldn't see it, would be a narrow vertical tube connecting them to the surface. To bring down more air all Thurin needed to do was push the water back a bit.

'We had to throw ourselves in.' Thurin's voice was thick with strain. 'That bastard Eular wanted to know you were dead before he sent the rest of us down. Probably knows about Erris. Definitely knows about me.'

'He'll wait up there until he's sure we're dead.' Quina sounded as scared now as she had when the plan had been explained to her. Yaz didn't blame her. Quina was clever enough to be scared. Yaz felt that perhaps she herself was not brave, but just stupid enough to be able to fool herself into optimism. Thurin at least had control of the element they were supposed to die in, and Erris of course could stay down here for a month without problems.

'We need to move up higher,' Thurin said through gritted teeth. 'The less deep we are the less difficult it will be to hold the water back.'

'And the more likely those up top will be to spot us,' Erris said.

'Got to do it,' Thurin said, and the muddy water around their waists began to rise.

'We can't swim!' Yaz gasped as the water reached her chest.

'Time for Erris to show us how strong he is!' Thurin snarled with effort.

Erris pursed his lips. 'That would be easier with two good arms.'

'None of this is easy,' Thurin grunted.

Yaz had hoped that Thurin might be able to lift them all, and their yokes, and maintain the bubble around them, but clearly she'd underestimated how hard it was to work against the weight of all those fathoms of water above them. They needed the yokes off, then they could swim up with the bubble to a lower depth. She turned to face Erris. 'How did you get free?'

'Well, I'm not exactly free.' Erris touched the yoke that still trapped his neck. 'But I can do this . . .' He folded his hand in a way in which hands were never meant to bend, narrowing it so much that it was obvious how he had slipped it out. But even if Yaz could get her hands free she needed the whole thing off her if she was going to swim up with Thurin's bubble to a depth where it was easier to maintain.

Erris took hold of the end of Yaz's yoke. She thought he would try the opposite end where the thing was locked closed with a rivet. When they'd hammered it home, hurting her ears with the crash of iron on iron and rattling her teeth, she had thought that it would be harder to remove than to put in. Instead he grasped the hinged end that had allowed the device to be opened then closed about her wrists and neck. He grasped it in his fist, curling his smallest finger around to press against the end of the hinge-pin.

'Hmmm.' Erris showed no strain but he wasn't built like other men. He could exert his full strength and hold a calm conversation. 'It's tight. Are you sure you can't reach the Path, Yaz? It would help a lot . . .'

A fresh wave of panic rose around Yaz faster than the water. If Erris couldn't get the yokes off, and Thurin couldn't hold the water back long enough at this depth, then, like holding her breath, all this was just doomed effort, merely a cruel prolonging of the process of drowning. She'd already come very close to sucking in a lungful of liquid mud and the thought of having to go through it all again made her want to break down in tears. The Path, however, remained hidden from her. She had used its power to forge many small stars into a single larger one, and then very shortly after in conjunction with Mali when pulling her from the ice through the gate. She could no more call on its power a third time in such a short span than she could breathe water.

'Try mine,' Quina suggested. 'What?' She met Thurin's accusatory stare. 'It might be looser. And if he gets one pin free he can use it to push out the others.'

Erris tried Quina's, then Thurin's, then his own. 'The hinge-pins are too thin to press properly and the locking rivets are in too tight to move.'

Thurin looked pale. Small blood vessels had ruptured in the whites of his eyes.

'We need something small and hard,' Yaz said. 'So you can press the pin out.'

But everything had been taken from them, their knives, food, even the stardust Yaz had collected from the miniature demons in Haydies. They were standing in black mud that might hide the bones of previous victims but little else.

'Move to the wall!' Quina started wading towards the black wall of water Thurin was holding back. 'We can use the stone.'

'It's the other way.' Thurin stumbled as he tried to walk and he nearly fell. For a moment the whole bubble was collapsing, the walls falling in towards them. Somehow, gasping in pain, Thurin righted himself and pushed the walls back. Quina, who had been momentarily engulfed, stood coughing and spitting.

The rocky wall of the sinkhole appeared after a few strides, slimy with mud and algae. Erris took hold of the end of his own yoke in one hand and used his inhuman strength to hammer at the wall. Chunks, chips, and shards of stone broke off beneath his blows. He scooped up a useful-looking piece before it sank into the mud.

'Let's try again.' Erris brought Yaz to the wall and anchored the end of her yoke in the small hole he'd made in the stone. Then, using just his good arm, he lined his shard of stone up with the end of the hinge pin and pressed. The shard broke. He tried again with the thicker end, pressing the corner into the pin's end. 'It's not working.'

Quina waded close. 'Try mine.'

Yaz ceded her place, thinking Quina overburdened with optimism. She eyed the walls of water sealing them against the stone. The light of the small flame still flickering in Erris's palm danced across the black and undulating surfaces. Soon she'd be drowning again.

Quina wedged the end of her yoke against the wall and Erris pressed a new stone shard up against the hinge-pin. 'Come on! Come on!' Desperation rather than optimism coloured her voice.

'There!' Erris cried. 'It moved!' He pulled the end of the yoke towards him, raising his flame. The pin's head was no longer flat to the yoke, and beneath it a small fraction of an inch of bright metal showed. 'Keep still.' Erris gripped the pin head between finger and thumb. Slowly, very slowly, and accompanied by a tortured squeal of metal on metal, he pulled the pin out. A moment later Quina was struggling free of the yoke. It hit the mud with a splat and sank from view almost immediately.

Erris took the pin and used it to push out the pins of Yaz's yoke, then Thurin's and his own. 'We're lucky these weren't better built.'

The instant Thurin was free he began to move the bubble up, with Yaz and Quina swimming to keep level with the air. Erris – too heavy to swim – called out before the water engulfed him. 'I'll climb the wall. It may take some ti—' The water covered his outstretched hand, quenching the flame and plunging them into darkness again. Suddenly Yaz was terrified, splashing around blind, worried she might blunder into the bubble's edge and choke.

As they rose a faint light began to finger into the inky blackness. Thurin's expression became less strained. Slowly the disc of the sky made itself known, rimmed by the mouth of the sinkhole.

'Don't go too high or they'll see us,' Yaz said.

'They've got the light behind them. We'll see them before they see us,' Thurin said.

He reduced their rise to a crawl though, and shortly, distorted through the motion of the surface, shimmering figures resolved all around the edge of the circle.

'How long do they need to watch for?' Quina snarled.

'Maybe they'll throw Mali in too,' Yaz said. 'She did speak for us at the trial.'

Yaz trod water with the others, waiting. She looked to see if Erris was making progress beneath them but their legs were churning up too much mud to see anything. Time passed with agonizing slowness and still the audience above remained in place.

'He's keeping them there,' Yaz said.

'He knows about my ice-work,' Thurin said. 'He'll be worried some of us might survive much longer than expected.'

'It doesn't make sense. He should have told them we had marjal and quantal powers,' Quina said.

'He thought he was going to have us beheaded,' Yaz said. 'So it didn't matter. If he said at the trial we could do all the things we can then that might have caused awkward questions. And if he said it afterwards then that could have been even worse. If we're so very rare then killing us might be considered a waste.'

'Are they going to stay there all damned day?' Thurin was hurting, Yaz could tell.

'We could go a little higher,' she suggested.

'They'll see us, catch us, and drown us again properly.' Thurin shook his head.

'Bring up some muddy water to hide us,' Quina said. 'I mean, not just here, but all over.'

'It could work.' Thurin frowned with concentration. 'I doubt they do this often enough to know how much silt four bodies churn up. But . . . if I'm busy not drowning, keeping the airway open, and bringing up mud from the depths . . . this bubble might collapse. Fair warning.'

Yaz swam behind him and put an arm under each of his, closing them around his chest. 'I'll keep you up. You focus on the other stuff.'

'But mainly the bubble not collapsing,' Quina urged.

Erris's head broke the surface some while later. It felt like an hour at least. He reached for another handhold, driving a hinge-pin into the soft stone before he fell back. 'Hello.' He looked up, blinking water away. 'They're still there?'

'He is.' Yaz resisted snarling. She had no proof that the small knot of figures still standing vigil at the side of the sinkhole were Eular and his guards, but she was sure of it even so.

'How are you holding up, Thurin?' Erris asked.

Thurin gave a pained grunt.

'It's getting darker,' Quina said past chattering teeth. 'At least there's that. They won't stay all night, will they?'

Yaz was far from sure how long the old man would stand there just to make sure they had all died. The water wasn't cold. Cold water is called ice. An Ictha could swim in near-freezing water all day, but Thurin and Quina were beginning to suffer with it and even Yaz, to her shame, felt chilly after so long immersed in the Glasswater.

'I don't think there's anything else we can do,' Erris said. 'Except rise higher as it gets darker. I could circle round to that ladder then try to climb up and kill them but doing it one-armed without a weapon could be tricky.' He didn't sound enthusiastic. Erris wasn't a killer. Also, the sinkhole was only a couple of hundred yards from the start of the convent buildings and unless he silenced the watchers quickly they'd have the whole population of nuns and novices on them.

They waited. Erris began the slow climb around the sinkhole to the ladder since he couldn't swim. When he left the air bubble Yaz felt suddenly alone. Thurin was better equipped to keep her from drowning but somehow it was Erris she associated most with safety. She wondered if either of them felt that way about her. She'd saved both of them before. But she'd hardly kept them safe.

Every now and then, as the sky darkened, Thurin would ease up a little closer to the surface to lessen the burden on his ice-work. Yaz trod water and meditated murder against Eular. Of all the welcomes to the green lands Yaz had considered, none of them had come close to being met by Eular and drowned in a hole. Thurin began to pant with the strain while shuddering with the cold.

'We'll have to fight!' Quina stammered past chattering teeth.

'Wait.' Yaz pointed. 'They're leaving.'

Slowly the final group departed. One figure lingered longer than the rest, barely visible against the darkening sky, then at last they too pulled away.

Thurin immediately began to rise to the surface but kept just below it for another few minutes. At last he broke into the air. At first the night sky was a small circle at the top of their broken bubble, then moments later they were swimming at the bottom of a deep bowl-shaped dent in the water's surface, and gradually it flattened out until they were simply swimming. The sky lay full dark above them, crimson stars reflecting in the water.

Slowly, making as little noise as possible, they swam across to where the iron ladder reached the surface. Yaz climbed out first since Erris had not yet appeared and both Thurin and Quina were so cold as to be barely able to grip the rungs. She helped the other two onto the ladder where they hung for a while, letting the water drip from their furs and hoping it wasn't making too much noise.

'Let's go.' Yaz began to climb. She'd reached about halfway to the sinkhole's rim when it struck her that rather than getting darker it was getting lighter. She paused and looked at the sky behind her. A red glow was building rapidly, as if the sun were rising but at ten times its normal speed, chasing the stars from the sky.

'What's happ—' Light reached into the sinkhole, painting the wall, racing down it as fast as Yaz might climb. A brilliant star, a thousand times bigger than any she'd ever seen, moved into view over the opposite rim of the Glasswater.

'It must be the moon,' Quina gasped several yards beneath her.

Moonlight proved warmer than sunlight and its intensity continued to build. The walls and ladder began to creak as they heated up. Yaz's few remaining furs began to steam.

'Keep climbing!' Thurin called from below Quina, sounding somewhat panicked.

The heat hit Yaz like a blow now: her skin felt as if it were on fire. Below Thurin, where the light struck the water's surface, it began to steam almost immediately.

'We should go back?' Quina asked.

Suddenly the coolness of the water seemed inviting, but Yaz climbed on swiftly. The moon was the thing Taproot wanted to save, the thing that kept these lands free of ice. It might be hot but surely it wasn't going to kill them? It might feel as if she were burning but if it really got that hot then surely there wouldn't be trees and grass.

Fast as she was, the fog rising from the sinkhole nearly beat Yaz. She stumbled onto level ground only to be overtaken by a white wave of mist that reduced visibility to just a couple of feet.

Shrouded in the mist and shielded from the worst of the heat, Yaz helped Quina then Thurin off the ladder. A few moments later the wind changed and took the fog with it, leaving them exposed to the moon's full glare. And Yaz, fresh from near-drowning, now hit by the night-time ferocity of a moon ten times brighter than the summer sun, curled up on the rock with her arms about her head.

CHAPTER 3

Yaz lay coiled on the hot rock, sure that her hides were not only steaming but smoking in the intensity of the moon's light. She'd never felt anything like it. The air seemed to sear her lungs with each breath.

The sound of heavy footsteps on the ladder told Yaz that Erris would soon be joining them. She tried to raise her head and squint but even through closed eyelids the light was too intense and she returned her arm to its place across her face. A moment later his hand, already dry, closed on her wrist.

Yaz couldn't tell how long the heat and the light lasted. Like her near-drowning earlier in the day it was almost certainly shorter than it felt and it felt like forever.

Finally the light dwindled and died, departing as swiftly as it had come, and Yaz opened her eyes to see the last of the mist leaving the sinkhole in tatters, stained red with starlight. The rock all around her was hot to the touch and her skin felt burned. Echoes of the moon's light still dazzled her, leaving her vision unable to penetrate the night out on the surrounding plateau.

'Wow.' Quina uncurled and sat, blinking. 'I wonder how often that happens.'

Thurin crouched beside her, massaging his forehead. 'Once a year would be enough for me.'

'Every night.' A new voice spoke from the darkness. 'Without it the ice would join hands across the Corridor and there would be no life save that of the tribes.' Sister Owl came closer and the starlight offered up her outline. 'When I was a child it was a journey of a hundred and fifty miles from the cliffs of the southern ice to those of the northern ice. Now it's barely a hundred. Without the moon we would have been swallowed up long ago.'

Yaz stood, suddenly angry. 'Yes, we survived. Thanks for your concern.' She'd nearly drowned. Thurin's ordeal had been just as bad. 'You couldn't have moved Eular on more quickly?'

Sister Owl spread her hands. 'You told me yourself that he knew young Thurin is water-sworn. Left to his own devices I believe the archon would have stood watch until dawn. In the end Abbess Claw had to arrange for a summons to arrive demanding his presence at the cathedral in Verity. Fortunately the archon's long absence from the city has vexed the high priest and on learning of Eular's proximity she was quick to insist that he present himself immediately. With luck she may even refuse to confirm his appointment. It's rare for archons to choose their successors, after all, and in cases of sudden death these transitions of power come under closer scrutiny.' The nun blinked and widened her eyes. 'Forgive me, I'm rambling. The curse of old age, I'm afraid. Follow me. We must get you out of sight. The archon left three Church guards to watch the Glasswater and the longer I keep them befuddled the harder it is to unthread the confusion without leaving some memory of that lack of memory.

Indeed—' She clamped her wizened lips tight, frowning at her wandering tongue, and turned to lead them away.

Yaz followed. Mali had told her the old woman was a teacher, used to holding forth before a class of novices. Clearly brevity was not her strength. Even so, Yaz had a sudden desire to be sitting among a group of such girls with the time to listen to Sister Owl's ramblings. She was sure Sister Owl had a vast amount of knowledge stored in her head that she desperately needed to learn if she was to survive in this strange iceless land of blazing moons and unknown faiths.

Sister Owl led them through the dark, deserted convent. Yaz saw no one, no lights burned, but she felt watched. Yaz and her friends were, Sister Owl had explained, balanced on a delicate edge in the midst of a hidden conflict. A conflict that would determine the fate of the Church and hence the empire.

Yaz remembered how Sister Owl had come to the prisoners during their brief confinement before the trial and had spoken to them, confident none of the Church guards that Eular had left to oversee them would know the language of the north.

The ancient woman had hobbled up to the gates of their subterranean prison and peered through the iron bars to where Yaz and the others sat in chains.

'The Ancestor is a many that speaks with one voice,' she had said. 'Whereas the Church is a single entity that speaks with many voices.' She had wrapped a gnarled hand around a bar and drawn herself in close. 'I'm not about to wash the Church's dirty . . .' She struggled for the right word in the tongue of the north. '. . . hides in front of strangers I've only just met, but suffice it to say that I have been engaged in a secret war for the heart of our faith since before Abbess Claw was an itch in her mother's belly. There are forces out there' – she waved her arm at the stony walls – 'forces that have long been seeking to infiltrate both the Church and the royal family, seeking to subvert both to ends that I don't yet fully comprehend but which are certainly not in the best interests of our people. I do not trust Archon Eular's motives, no matter what level of support he might have within the highest circles. Long ago Sister Cloud foretold the coming of the made man, a prophecy spoken only for my ears. She left no instructions but I can't imagine she intended for me to stand by idle while he and his companions were put to death.'

'So set us free,' Yaz had said. 'You must know that these bars can't hold us. We're trying not to start a battle. We don't want to fight you. But Eular is our enemy from the ice and we won't let him kill us.'

Sister Owl had pursed her lips and frowned. 'It's complicated. Faith is simple but religion . . . that can become tangled. Abbess Claw guides this convent in service to the high priest. Our laws must be obeyed or chaos will replace them and a much larger battle than the one you worry about will start. Our abbess is a clever woman, though. You might think she chose her name because of the damage a claw can inflict. But in fact it was the ability to cling on to impossible edges and climb despite the odds that inspired her.'

Yaz thought of the hoola that had once attacked them on a tall pressure ridge, navigating the near-vertical ice as if it were flat ground thanks to its fearsome claws. 'And how does your abbess hope to obey the law without killing us?'

Sister Owl smiled. 'The law says that you must be thrown into the Glasswater sinkhole, secured in iron yokes. And the law—'

24

'That's not going to happen,' Thurin snarled from the back of the cave. 'I'd rather die fighting.'

'And the law', Sister Owl continued undaunted, 'must be followed. The made man will not, I imagine, be inconvenienced by submersion in water?' She looked at Erris.

'No.' Erris inclined his head.

'And you, young man, so eager to fight, you share my own marjal talent for manipulating water, do you not?'

'I do.' Thurin still sounded angry.

'As a child I would swim in the Glasswater with my fellow novices on rare occasions when we felt brave enough to dare the cold. On one such dip I amazed and dismayed my fellow novices by vanishing beneath the water and staying there far longer than anyone could hold their breath. It was, on reflection, a cruel trick and I regretted it immediately on returning to the surface . . .'

'You brought air down with you,' Thurin said, uncertain. 'I could do that.'

'The law demands only that you be yoked and thrown in,' Sister Owl said. 'The wording does not explicitly state that you be killed. If you were to emerge unscathed then the abbess would consider justice to have been served and the mercy of the Ancestor to have fallen upon you. It would however be prudent to keep this miraculous salvation a secret for a while.'

And so it was that after their emergence from the Glasswater Sister Owl led them swiftly into the heart of the convent. She took them below ground, passing down a short flight of stone steps and through a doorway into a long, hand-hewn chamber with three windows at the far end piercing a thick wall. Abbess Claw was waiting, seated behind a table on which a single candle burned. The convent's murder teacher, Mistress Shade, stood beside her. Yaz had learned a few things about Sweet Mercy from Mali on the long night before her execution. In addition to Sister Owl's instruction in the ways of the Path, the arts of battle were taught by Mistress Blade. In Shade class the young novices were taught the arts of murder and deception. Mistress Shade was a surprisingly young woman who looked wholly unsuited to hiding in the shadows while waiting to stab someone in the back. Her pale skin seemed to glow, where her very blonde hair escaped her headdress it caught and returned every scrap of light, and she was small, barely taller than Quina. Even so, Yaz sensed something dangerous about the nun.

She wondered if the chamber was a place where novices were taught. It smelled of many strange things, few of them natural.

The abbess indicated that Yaz and the rest take seats at the smaller desks facing hers. Yaz squeezed in, Quina took a chair from behind the desk next to her. When Thurin and Erris had found places the abbess spoke and Sister Owl translated.

'She asks that you tell us all you know about Archon Eular.'

And so for some time first Thurin then Yaz recounted the adventures that had taken them from the distant north to the green centre. Stories for which there had been neither the time nor privacy after Eular had made his accusations. Abbess Claw watched and listened without expression. Even the most outlandish elements of Yaz's story concerning Eular, like his ability to pass decades in timeless sleep and to step across vast swathes of ice using gates left behind by the Missing, didn't so much as raise an eyebrow. When Yaz spoke of Taproot, a man older than the four tribes' existence on Abeth, a man without a body who existed in fragments and partial copies haunting the minds of great cities, then even Abbess Claw's impressive composure was tested. But she made no interruption.

At last, when the tale had been told, Abbess Claw spoke with Sister Owl and Mistress Shade for a while. Yaz understood none of it and had no reason to expect to, but to her surprise their conversation seemed tantalizingly close to making sense. Yaz wondered about the bond she had with Mali, a bond that allowed her to understand the novice without knowing what any of the words actually meant. Maybe this was an additional effect, seeded by that connection. Or perhaps it was just wishful thinking and the others were also sitting there believing themselves on the edge of understanding.

Early on Owl looked up at Yaz. 'If this ancient of yours, this Taproot . . .' She frowned at the name. 'If he says you and you alone can open the ark using four shiphearts – then why did Eular want to see you dead?'

Yaz blinked. She hadn't fully considered the matter. Eular had been furious with her, and Seus was too. That had seemed reason enough. But their anger was a small thing set against the scale and duration of Seus's larger ambitions. 'I can only guess that Seus doesn't know the ark can be opened that way. Eular wanted me when he thought I could help his army take the ark so that Seus could use direct force to break into it. However long it might take. Now that dream is gone they just want to kill me.'

Owl nodded thoughtfully then returned to her conversation with the abbess and Mistress Shade.

Finally Owl turned back to them. 'Much of what you've told us is very strange and surprising. It seems clear, however, that our interests align in terms of our desire to find out more about Archon Eular and expose any hostile power that stands behind his advancement in the Church. This power appears to be the one you name as Seus, a creation of the Missing abandoned to madness when they departed. It seems that this Taproot-in-the-box is vital to disrupting Seus's efforts to seize control of the ark, yes?'

'Yes.' Yaz nodded. She wasn't sure how much the nuns believed but clearly some of what they'd been told accorded with results of their own investigations.

'So the box that Eular took must be recovered before he is able to hand it to Seus.'

'Yes,' Yaz agreed. Though she didn't know if the box would need to be physically placed in the hand of some metal body Seus had made. She also didn't know where the city of Seus might lie, but all Eular had to do was reach one of the gates he used and then distance suddenly became meaningless.

'The abbess says that I have convinced her it's the Ancestor's will that we aid and shelter you as far as our laws allow. Clearly you can't go wandering the Corridor without speaking the language or knowing how our society functions. You and Quina will be able to stay with us in the guise of novices and we will teach you enough that you're not immediately arrested as soon as you step off the Rock of Faith. Erris and Thurin are more of a problem as their presence for more than a day within the convent for anything but official visits is forbidden.'

'*Tarriska entra Eular,*' Erris said.

The abbess and both nuns looked up sharply at that.

'You speak their language?' Yaz gasped, both amazed and slightly annoyed.

'I do now.' Erris nodded. 'It's related to one of the main marjal tongues. It's taken a while to update my database. Millennia of linguistic drift can be hard to compensate—'

28

'I don't even know what language you're speaking *now*,' Quina interrupted. 'What are you talking about?'

'I told them', Erris said, 'that Thurin and I would go after Eular. I can speak the language and have a much better chance of navigating cities and towns than any ice-triber, no offence intended. Thurin can help me. His tricks can come in very handy.'

'You're not going alone!' Yaz said.

'I won't be alone.' Erris smiled. 'I'll have Thurin with me.'

Yaz shook her head, a strange panic rising in her chest. 'That's not what I mean and you know it! We didn't come all this way together just to split up as soon as we arrive.'

Erris said, 'You and Quina need to learn about this empire. You can't be walking around gawping at everything. And the nuns clearly have a lot to teach you both.'

'What? You and Thurin don't need to learn it too?' Yaz was aware she was raising her voice but couldn't seem to do anything about it.

'No boys allowed. Remember?' Erris grinned annoyingly. 'And I already speak the language. You can teach us the rest later.'

'You'll need our help to find the archon,' Sister Owl said, trying to steer the conversation out of the developing squabble. 'He's going to see the high priest, but after that—'

'What do you call the city we can see from your convent?' Erris asked.

'Verity,' the nun answered.

'He's going there,' Erris said. 'Even if I hadn't set up a locator link with Taproot's box before it was taken I would have known that.'

'How could you know?' Yaz turned to stare at him.

'There are only a few arks in the Corridor. Each was at the centre of a great city of the Missing. They were built

29

above ground though time's covered them over since. It seems mankind erodes cities just as effectively as the ice. But the other ark cities – there were over a thousand at one time – are all under the ice, scraped away with the arks they housed. Vesta, my city, the city the Broken scavenge, it used to have an ark, you know? It was there in my time. And the city we saw when we were climbing up to the convent, this Verity of theirs. It must sit on the ruins of the Missing's ark-city of Veritas. On our source world—'

'The source world!' Sister Owl widened her eyes and made the sign of the tree but in reverse, her fingers coming together along the branches to trail a single finger down along the taproot. 'Truly Sister Cloud saw your arrival a hundred years ago, Erris the made man. The Ancestor stands upon the source world. The taproot reaches back through an untold darkness of years to the seed that was planted there.'

Erris frowned, clearly not comfortable with his inclusion in the nun's faith. 'As I was saying, it seems that when it came to naming some of their cities the Missing drew on one of the ancient mythologies from the early civilizations of the source world, a mythos developed by the Greeks and adopted by the Romans. The city minds haven't all renamed themselves after a stolen mythology – some were already named that way by the Missing who were the inheritors of that culture. Your city of Verity stands on the ruins of Veritas. The Romans said that Veritas was goddess of truth, and Zeus's daughter. Daughter or not, the truth is that Seus wants Verity's ark open and under his control.

'Eular is clearly heading for the city, for his audience with the high priest. But when she releases him he won't have to go anywhere else to hand Taproot over. All he'll need to do is reach the undercity and Taproot can be sucked out of that box into Seus's network. It's important that we stop him, and quickly.'

The abbess spoke, having been offered brief translations as Erris said his piece. Sister Owl translated back for the benefit of the ice-tribers. 'You'll get nowhere without knowing the layout of the city and the workings of the Church. The abbess can't commit a Grey Sister to help you without compromising the convent too much. She says that Novice Maliaya has already been accused of being enchanted by your magics, and as such she would be an ideal guide. If caught we can use that excuse and proceed to "cure" her. Additionally, we can say that she was sent alone to visit healers in the city because the loss of her hand requires more care than can be offered in our sanatorium since the death of Sister Hearth.'

'If Mali's going then Quina and I are going too,' Yaz said firmly.

Thurin looked exhausted but still managed a crooked smile. 'Yaz, the fact that we need Mali is the best argument for you staying here. We can't keep on having Mali escort us everywhere. We need you and Quina to take advantage of this place and learn everything in an environment where making a mistake won't get us all killed.'

Yaz opened her mouth to undercut him with her counter-argument. And found she hadn't got one. Instead she folded her arms and gave him a furious stare before turning it on Erris who at least had the grace to look away.

CHAPTER 4

Mistress Shade left the chamber briefly and returned with Mali. Unlike the senior nuns, Mali hadn't been included in the plans regarding the sinkhole, in part so that her unfeigned distress could help convince Eular that the execution had been successful. The news had been broken to her shortly after being dragged away from the sinkhole, and when she walked into the chamber Yaz could practically see the sparks flying from her eyes. To be fair, though, Yaz had had to share the agonies of the amputation and cauterization of Mali's hand. So, sharing the distress of drowning merely balanced the tally. And Mali would have known without being told that Yaz wasn't dead. She just needed time to relax and examine their bond.

Under Abbess Claw's stern regard Mali made no verbal recriminations, and on hearing that she was to guide Erris and Thurin around Verity she recovered some of her good humour. She even smiled when Abbess Claw left the room, and Sister Owl explained that Eular was the target of their expedition. Primarily the return of the box he'd confiscated from Yaz.

'The *surreptitious* return,' Mistress Shade cautioned. 'The archon is not to know who took the box. Neither is anyone else. If you recover it from his smoking corpse, Novice Mali, you will not graduate my class. And more importantly you will plunge this convent into a great deal of trouble, from which it will not emerge unscathed.'

'Yes, Mistress Shade.' Mali kept her head bowed.

Whoever this woman was, Yaz could tell that this chamber was her domain and that she ruled here with an iron rod.

'He'll suspect us as soon as the theft is noticed, and it will be noticed swiftly,' Erris said. 'The only way to delay that discovery is to take Taproot and leave the box.'

'But we need the box. That was the whole point of going into Haydies!' Yaz surprised Erris by understanding him.

'We still have this.' Erris reached out to tap the needle that had somehow not been taken from Yaz's hides during their captivity and attempted execution.

'But the Taproot we need can't fit into it.' Yaz pulled the needle free.

'We'll have to work something out.' Erris took it from her fingers.

Mistress Shade arched an eyebrow at the exchange and then continued, 'If I had a free hand, I would send a Sister of Discretion, but nobody would believe a Grey Sister to be so ill disciplined as to act independently in such a matter. You understand, novice, that if this goes badly I will deny all knowledge of you and support any punishment that your captors deem appropriate.'

Mali nodded. 'I do, Mistress Shade.'

'Good, then at least I've taught you something during your years in my class. Go out there with these tribesmen, Maliaya, and make Sweet Mercy proud of you.'

A moment's silence followed, during which nobody seemed to know whose turn it was to talk.

'You mean right now?' Mali asked.

The nun opened her hand towards the door. 'I believe that was the third lesson in discretion – there are times to hesitate and times to act.'

'But . . .' Yaz tried to think of a reason for delay.

'We'll be fine,' Erris said.

'Probably.' Thurin seemed less confident.

'Probably,' Erris agreed. 'But we've been on a knife's edge for . . . well, ever since I put on this body, if I'm honest. So what's changed?'

'What's changed', Quina announced, 'is that we won't be there to save you if we have to stay here.'

'You're always going to stay with me?' Erris raised an eyebrow, softening the words with a smile.

'I just don't want you to go.' Quina had the courage to say out loud what Yaz was thinking. She was looking at Thurin now. But it was Erris who moved in and hugged Quina. Yaz's father had used the same hug to end similar arguments.

Mali, taking her cue, embraced Yaz, being careful with her stump, which even though coated with the nuns' sweet-smelling poultices, clearly still troubled her. This second hug led, despite Mistress Shade rolling her eyes, to a general hugging where Yaz found herself squeezed in the arms of first Erris and then Thurin. With only scant furs on she could, for the first time, feel the actual shape of them against her, both lean and hard, Erris broader in the shoulders, Thurin narrow-hipped and closer to her height.

'Be safe,' she told him.

In reply Thurin pressed his lips to her cheekbone, just below the corner of her eye. He withdrew without looking at her, and the spot tingled so much that Yaz had to make a conscious effort to keep from touching it.

'Watch over them.' Yaz wasn't sure who she was talking to. Any one of the three had the power to save the other two from a host of evils. But similarly they were all vulnerable to surprises. And Eular had many of those.

Yaz watched as Mali led Erris and Thurin out into the corridor beyond and away on their mission. The feeling that she wouldn't see them all again refused to leave her. Only by bunching her fists against her thighs could she keep from calling out after them.

'I'm going to settle you with the novices,' Sister Owl said. 'Starting tomorrow you'll join my Path class. During Blade, Spirit, Shade, and Academia lessons either I or one of the other nuns will tutor you in our language.'

They followed the ancient nun back up the stone stairs to the surface and through the silent, starlit convent. As they passed along a narrow passage between two long low buildings Yaz spotted a small, fierce-eyed novice watching them from an archway. She vanished an instant later, swallowed by the shadow as if it had bloomed around her. The girl reminded Yaz so sharply of Maya and of how much she would have loved this place that Yaz missed a step. How quickly Maya would have learned to fight like these greenlanders. She stood, her heart hurting, her breath caught around some painful obstruction low in her throat, her eyes misting.

'Yaz?' Quina came up beside her, hand on her elbow.

Yaz shook her head, not trusting herself to speak, and walked on after Sister Owl.

They came to a three-storey building and approached the doors up a short flight of steps. Owl pushed through into a hallway lit by a single lantern turned down low. There was a door to either side and steps leading up.

'I'll put you both in Grey Class. You're too old but you'll benefit more from the lessons. I'd put you in Red Class but I'm afraid there would be mockery. Some of our girls arrive with a lot to learn about humility.' Sister Owl turned to the right and opened the door into an even more dimly lit room, a long hall with beds set along both walls, maybe twenty in total. The nun pointed to three empty ones at the far end of the chamber. 'I'll wake Wenna and tell her to guide you tomorrow.'

While Yaz and Quina made their way between the rows of sleeping girls, Sister Owl shook the shoulder of a fair-haired novice in one of the beds closest to the door and bent to speak to her.

Yaz prodded one of the empty beds experimentally. Its softness amazed her. There was a sort of long thin bag the size of the bed, stuffed with something yielding. And reaching beneath it she found a support of crisscrossing ropes. Covers that were not furs or hides, but soft, thick and flexible, lay on top of the bag, and the novices lay on top of the bag but beneath the covers. Astonishingly, they had undressed to sleep and wore only thin gowns.

'It's so hot!' whispered Quina, looking up from a similar inspection of her own bed.

'I know!' Yaz had to remind herself they were above ground, not hidden in caves miles beneath the wind. She lay on top of the covers, pulling off all her remaining hides and furs until she wore just her mole-fish skins. There was even a smaller stuffed bag to rest her head on.

Yaz lay back, her head sinking into the softness. Despite being practically naked she felt the sweat trickling off her. It was like trying to sleep in the Broken's drying cave. And here there were no stars, no fires, no source of heat save the bodies of the sleeping girls and the pervading warmth of the south. She supposed she would have to stop calling it the south: this was the centre.

'Can we open . . .' Quina pointed to the row of high windows. They already looked open but Yaz made out a lattice of metalwork and, supported in the diamond-shape spaces, small panes of something that glimmered in the starlight. Glass!

She shook her head. The novice in the closest bed was curled up beneath several layers of covers as if she were cold. Quina lay back, blowing a breath slowly out between her lips. Yaz knew how she felt – how could they sleep in this?

The sound of a tolling bell woke Yaz and for the longest time she had no idea where she was, only that she was comfortable beyond reason and as warm as she'd ever been, save for her time cowering beneath the focus moon.

She opened her eyes and blinked away the blurriness. All around her novices were struggling into many layers of unfamiliar clothing, some pulling the robe they called a habit over the top as the last item. Almost all of them were throwing glances her way. In the neighbouring bed Quina, somehow entirely naked now, rolled over with a groan. 'This place . . . if I didn't have to eat I could just lie here all day.' She blinked and noticed she had an audience. Rather than immediately try to cover herself, as Yaz would have, she tumbled from her bed and stood stretching luxuriously, rising to the tips of her toes. The privation of the long march south had whit-tled her down to something too narrow for the northern ice, leaving her whipcord-thin and hard-bodied, much as the green-landers around them. 'Feast your eyes, foreigners, for I am rather fine!'

'Quina!' Yaz gasped, scandalized. She grabbed for her hides, realizing that all she had to cover herself were the mole-fish skins sewn tight around her.

'What? They can't understand me.' Quina bent languorously to pick up her hide underjacket. 'And I'm damned if I'm going to let them stare me down.'

One of the novices, a small, half-dressed girl with brown hair bristling across a recently shaved scalp, said something that seized the others' attention. All of them were staring now with wide eyes. The girl called something to Yaz and held her hands up to either side of her shoulders, mimicking the position that the drowning yokes held them.

A stern-faced blonde girl, fully dressed, pushed past the shorter girl, knocking her onto a bed. She stopped at the foot of Yaz's bed and spun round to face the others, making some kind of declaration in sharp, authoritative tones. Yaz caught Sister Owl's name among the incomprehensible babble. The announcement ended with the girl pointing at Quina and saying, 'Yath.' Then at Yaz: 'Qwimma.'

'Yaz,' Yaz said, patting her chest. This was probably the girl that Owl had woken the night before. Seeing that she and Quina were among the few yet to dress, Yaz offered the girl an apologetic smile and struggled into her trousers, tightening the waist ties. She slipped on her underjacket, leaving her arms bare save for the black mole-fish wraps covering her upper arms and her lower arms from wrist to elbow. It was more than she wanted to wear and less than she felt comfortable in.

'What's she doing?' Quina came to stand by Yaz as she straightened from dressing. Both of them were taller than the blonde girl. In fact Yaz was taller than all the girls save for one red-haired gerant at the far end of the dormitory and another dark-haired one at the opposite end. She realized that most of them were Quina's age or younger. The blonde girl was looking pointedly at the hides and furs still lying on the bed.

'I think she wants me to put it all on,' Yaz said. She turned to face the girl and shook her head slowly. 'Too. Hot.' She paused and then said, '*Tslata.*'

'What's that mean?' Quina asked.

'"Hot", I think.' Yaz wasn't sure how she knew the word.

The blonde girl gave a puzzled look while others nearby giggled. She shrugged and turned to the doors, beckoning Yaz and Quina to follow.

Out in the hall a crush of novices were making for the main doors, smaller girls from across the way, older girls, some looking to be full-grown young women, crowding down the stairs, all of them chattering, laughing, pushing. The great majority proved too focused on their own business to notice Yaz and Quina, but a few threw sharp glances their way, and as they reached the main doors a tall young woman with long black hair and skin the colour of snow came up swiftly behind them and seized both of them around the back of the neck in an iron grip. '*Wachta senee hare?*'

'Don't,' Yaz hissed as Quina made to break free.

The blonde girl explained their presence once more, her tone shifting from one of command to something far more respectful. The senior novice sniffed and released her grip, saying something short and cutting before striding past them out into the daylight.

Yaz and Quina followed, enjoying the relief from the dormitory's heat that the light wind on their bare skin brought. They followed as their guide led them with the general flow. More and more of the other novices were noticing them now, some clearly recognizing them as the girls who were drowned on the previous day. Whispers ran back and forth as answer competed with question.

Yaz felt uncomfortable walking into the crowded hall with so many eyes on her but her self-consciousness vanished the instant she drew a breath.

'Gods in the Ice!' Quina muttered.

'That smells so good.' Yaz gazed in awe at the four long tables, the novices settling themselves into chairs around them, and the food mounded on plates across the length of each.

As one she and Quina moved to the nearest table. The blonde girl was saying something to them but her urgency seemed far off and unimportant set against the tantalizing aromas filling the room. Yaz had no names for the foodstuffs she could see but her nose assured her that they were very definitely edible. She sat before a bowl heaped with yellow . . . stuff. On another platter crinkly slices of brownish-pink. On yet another a multitude of small green balls. A plate sat on the table before her, with metal implements to either side. She could see that the novices already seated had put food on their plates and were using the blunt knife and the tiny forked device to move it into their mouths. Yaz turned to Quina. 'Should we . . .' But the girl had already taken a handful of the yellow and a handful of the slices. Dropping both on her plate she reached for the green stuff.

Too hungry to stop herself, Yaz did the same. Both of them hunched over their plates cramming the food into their mouths.

'Oh gods,' Quina managed past her mouthful.

'I . . .' Yaz chewed furiously. 'I know!' Jezzel, an Ictha girl two years Yaz's senior, had once told her with great self-importance that a pleasure greater than anything she'd known in her short life awaited her when she took a man to her bridal furs. Yaz, with a mouth full of the crackly, chewy, crunchy, juicy slices was fairly sure that Jezzel would kick any man out of her tent if given the chance to swap him for what the green-landers ate.

Yaz and Quina continued to gorge, exchanging occasional grunts of approval. Yaz chewed until her jaw started to ache, and then chewed some more. She reached for second, third, and fourth helpings.

'Yaz?' Quina said, sounding a bit confused.

'Uh?'

'I . . .' Quina reached towards the bowl that still had some of the green stuff in it. 'My stomach . . . it doesn't want any more?'

'That's—' Yaz had been going to say that was crazy. There was food left. The Ictha fished and sometimes there were plenties, but they never gorged. They ate exactly what was required to keep them alive. The cold ensured no fish was ever wasted, and prudence ensured that they eat the minimum needed to survive, so that when one sea closed and they had to trek in search of the next, they had more chance of avoiding starvation. Until she fell among the Broken, Yaz had been on rations all her life. Now she was unexpectedly discovering that a person could eat so much that they no longer wanted to eat any more. 'I think maybe there's no more room inside us.'

'We're full?' Quina asked with evident distress.

Yaz raised her head and pushed back her plate. 'I think we must be.'

A round of applause went up, and with shock Yaz realized that everyone was watching. Among the clapping audience were a few mocking smiles and looks of disgust, but most, especially the younger girls who'd come to stand and stare, seemed genuinely impressed by the two ice-tribers' assault on the food, almost all of which was now gone.

She stood up, wiping her hands on her legs, and looked around for the blonde girl. 'Wenna?' Belatedly she remembered the girl's name.

'Here!' Wenna waved crossly from the doorway, clearly ready to go.

'Come on.' Yaz hauled Quina to her feet, and together they hurried after Wenna, Quina clutching her belly.

CHAPTER 5

Thurin

Mali led Thurin and Erris back through the forest of pillars in the evening dark. Out on the main part of the plateau the wind scoured the bare rock with a ferocity that would have shocked the Thurin who had emerged from the Pit of the Missing. After months of trekking across the ice, though, it seemed a half-hearted effort by the Gods in the Sky. Mali, however, hunched in her thick outer habit, advanced as if fighting some great beast.

'We'll leave by the Vinery Stair,' she said, with Erris translating. 'The Seren Way's too dangerous in the dark. Especially at night during an ice wind.'

The Vinery Stair proved to be a wide path that snaked its way along the plateau cliffs at a much gentler gradient than the one they'd come up by. Part of Thurin wanted the sun back in the sky to show him the green lands again. Another part of him was thankful that for now it was all hidden. He had been shocked by the open spaces of the ice and its distant horizons after a life lived in caves. Now the world had changed again, keeping the wide skies and distance, but filling all that white space with green, and not just green but ten times a thousand curious objects.

'How are we going to do this?' Thurin asked as they approached the base of the plateau.

'I have no idea.' Erris shook his head and translated the question for Mali. 'She doesn't either,' he translated back.

Thurin barked a short laugh. 'Sounds like when I walked up to the Black Rock.'

'And that worked out fine.'

'Well, if you call fine nearly being eaten by Hetta, nearly being drowned by—' He bit off his complaint once he saw from Erris's grin that he'd been joking.

Mali had more to say.

'She thinks our best chance might be while Eular is talking to the high priest,' Erris translated. 'Mali reckons they won't let even an archon approach the high priest without being searched for weapons, and the box is unusual enough that it should be taken from him until he leaves. So that would be the time for us to strike.'

'Inside their temple? Under the noses of their Church guards? You've seen how crowded this place is. It's not going to be like wandering the Black Rock.' As if to prove Thurin's point, up ahead of them where their path joined a larger way a sled on wheels creaked by, drawn by some kind of horse. He stopped dead. 'What in the hells is that?'

'That's a cart being pulled by a donkey,' Erris said. 'The stuff on it is hay, a type of dried grass. And those big round things are wheel—'

'I know what wheels are!' Thurin snapped, still recovering from the shock of the donkey's ears.

'Sorry,' Erris said. 'And yes, it sounds like a crazy plan. We're not even dressed like locals. Every eye's going to be turned our way.' He spoke to Mali in her tongue and received a rather heated reply.

'She says it's a crazy plan. But apparently the abbess's help doesn't extend much past not murdering us on our arrival. Sister Owl's convinced we'll sort it out, but Mali thinks the old woman is putting too much faith in the prophecy Sister Cloud gave her when she was a child. Mali says the prophecy didn't say anything past predicting that she would meet a man who was made rather than born. That's very different from saying I'd be of help to them, which is also very different from saying this specific plan will work.'

They joined the larger road and began to follow it in the direction of the distant city glow. Walls bounded the road to either side but when Thurin walked closer he realized that rather than being made of stone or ice these were living things, like a kind of small tree, covered in leaves, black in the starlight, all of them rustling as the wind pushed through. Thurin had an impression of open spaces beyond these walls, seething with motion as whatever grew there, hay perhaps, danced to the wind's tune. Something hooted in the night; somewhere another something gave a short squeal and fell silent. It seemed that the darkness was thick with life and Thurin felt watched, as if there might be no 'alone' in this place between the ice.

'We should go back and explain the consequences again,' Thurin said. 'Let them know what's at stake if Seus gets hold of Taproot. The moon will fall. All this' – he waved an arm in several directions – 'all this will be lost under the ice. They need to send an army of their best. People who know what they're doing!'

Erris shrugged. 'The abbess is a clever woman operating under many constraints. This is clearly the best she can do given the circumstances. Shouting at her isn't going to make her believe our story any more than she currently does. And to be honest, it's a pretty hard story to swallow.' He spoke to Mali for a while then continued. 'We'll get into the city and see how things stand, then try to come up with a plan.'

They walked on along the road, which ran more or less straight towards the city, curving around a low hill, crossing a bridge over a river, passing several farmhouses. Thurin walked in a daze, fascinated by the glimpses of life in the green lands revealed by firelight slanting through shutters. He could feel each flame flickering in every hearth and had to rein in his fire magic, which had been banked up during their long trek and now ached to be used. He felt that with little effort he could turn one of those flickers into a conflagration that might consume a house.

Every chimney streamed smoke into the wind and Thurin wondered what it was for. Were they all cooking? Surely they couldn't need to heat their homes? If any of the Broken's caverns had been this warm their ceilings would surely have fallen within the hour.

The wind brought all manner of smells but smoke was the only one that Thurin recognized. In places the hedges gave way to wooden fences and the starlight revealed fields of waist-high crops rippling like the waters of the sea Yaz had shown him. Passing one farmhouse, Thurin came to a sudden halt when he saw a multitude of faces peering at him over the next fence.

'A-are they . . . horses?' He tried to steady his voice.

'Cows.' Erris smiled. 'It's been a while since I've seen any.'

Several of the beasts let out low moaning sounds and Thurin backed to the far side of the road before continuing past them. 'Do the green-landers ride them?'

'Eat them,' Erris said. 'Drink their milk. Make shoes from their skins.'

Thurin looked back at the line of black-and-white faces turned to watch him with huge eyes. The Broken ate fish of course, and rats. But these things were as big as people, and their faces, if not showing a great amount of intelligence, were full of curiosity, a desire to understand. Part of him wanted to apologize to them for not opening the gate and setting them free. 'When will they eat them?'

'Not for months yet. Those still have a bit of growing to do.'

'Those were babies?' Thurin asked, shocked. Still, the idea that they had months to live when contrasted to his likely demise within the next few hours at least eased his conscience a little. It seemed as if they might have the better deal.

As they drew closer to the city the road became steadily more crowded. Carts, wagons, people on foot and on horseback, most heading in. Thurin found himself staring at each new person, starting nervously whenever someone came up from behind. But, contrary to Erris's prediction, all eyes were not on them. In fact most people didn't give them a first glance, let alone a second.

'What?' Thurin looked up and another splat of water hit him square in the eye. Then another struck his chin. 'What's going on?' The stuff was pattering all around him now, as if during the night the sky had been replaced with a cavern roof and once more they were back among the Broken being dripped upon by the slow process of melting.

'Rain,' Erris said. 'It's what happens when it wants to snow but it's not cold enough.'

Thurin wiped his eye then blinked. 'I never really thought about that.' A moment later the rain redoubled its efforts but none of it reached Thurin or his companions. A life spent in the Broken's caverns meant that when his ice-work began to flourish he had first turned his skills towards forming an invisible umbrella. He tried to imagine what the rain was falling from and wondered if the dome of the sky might truly be a distant icy ceiling. But his imagination failed him and the constant parade of terrestrial wonder soon brought his thoughts back to ground level.

The city walls loomed, the houses began to cluster along the road more thickly before stopping entirely for the last quarter-mile. Many of those final houses were large and sprawling, with their shutters open and warm light flooding through windows made from leaded diamonds of glass or smaller windows glazed with single thick and puddled panes that distorted the view inside beyond comprehension. Carts and wagons crowded the yards of these establishments and each time the doors opened a clamour of voices and snatches of song escaped into the night. The wind carried a delicious, bewildering cacophony of smells and Thurin's stomach growled its own reply.

'Taverns,' Erris said. 'Beer, whisky, ale, grog . . . You've a lot to learn, my friend. Fried chicken, roast beef, sides of bacon . . . Suddenly I wish I could eat. All these months watching you lot choke down frozen fish and mushrooms, I was glad I didn't have a stomach. But the last laugh's on me.'

Three men who had come down to the road from one such building stumbled along just ahead of Thurin and his friends. They seemed to have trouble walking in a straight line and frequently needed to support each other before bursting out into raucous song. As Thurin passed them he smelled a strong aroma around them, pungent but not unpleasant.

'They're drunk,' Erris said once they were out of earshot. 'Beer, and the other drinks I mentioned, they have an intoxicating effect.'

Thurin didn't fully understand, but assumed that it was something like the sought-after gold-cap fungi that the Broken had long ago found could be dried and made into a powder that gave wild waking dreams and brought into their caverns all manner of marvels that vanished a few hours later, leaving in their wake only a dry mouth and a black mood.

Thurin gave the last tavern a long lingering look before starting on the dark stretch of road up to the great torchlit city gates. If their mission were a hair less urgent he would have let those aromas carry him through the tavern doors and counted it as significant an adventure as breaking from the ice to see the sun for the first time. 'Why don't they build them closer to the city?'

'Ah, well, that's a sign of the flip side of all this plenty. It's for the same reason they have a great big wall around the city. In time of war buildings near the walls would be used by the enemy for cover, and I've a feeling that this place sees a lot of war. After all, we've just come from a place where they train little girls to kill with their bare hands.'

Thurin approached the crush at the gates with his sense of wonder beginning to be coloured by that sense of imminent peril once again. This was a shrinking world. Sister Owl had seen the Corridor lose a third of its width over the course of her century of life. The Broken had never really had an overcrowding problem, what with the Tainted to contend with. But having lived his life in a place with very definite limits on the space available he could understand the horrors that would follow if that space started to shrink.

There were guardsmen at the open gates, controlling the flow of traffic and casting a suspicious eye at anyone who looked too poor or too drunk. Here for the first time Thurin found himself the focus of attention with two guardsmen elbowing their way through the stream of travellers to intercept him. One held a lantern that flared brightly as Thurin's fire magic reached out unbidden to infect it. He bit back on the power.

Erris, for some reason, had not been their target, but on closer inspection they took hold of him too, noticing his hides. Whilst the green-landers demonstrated a bewildering variety of clothing, they all shared one thing in common: they were wearing a lot of it. As the guard clamped a hand on his shoulder Thurin decided that if they were to pass unremarked in future then the main thing was to bundle themselves up as if this were the ice and staying warm were a matter of life and death.

The guardsman began to haul Thurin off, asking unintelligible questions or perhaps issuing threats. Before Thurin could respond Mali was there, pushing in between them, jabbering at the man in the same tongue.

'She's telling them that the abbess sent her to guide us to the cathedral,' Erris said, allowing the other guard to manhandle him. 'Which is both useful and true!'

The men were less apologetic than they might be: no one in authority likes to yield ground to a child. Even so, Thurin and Erris were released and allowed to follow Mali into the city.

Lights burned everywhere and not one of them was a star. It seemed as if a thousand flames were dancing behind glass, illuminating stalls, doorways, and windows. Everything seemed an invitation; green-lander men and women crowded in the streets and within the buildings. The sound of their talking filled the air cut by tradesmen's cries, the shouts of men trying to steer their beasts, bursts of high laughter, a horse braying – Thurin felt at once buoyed by the energy and assaulted by it. A river of sound and smell flowed around him, over him, through him. One part of him wanted to cover his ears and seek solitude, another longed to dive through one of those firelit doorways and immerse himself in whatever fun was unfolding in the rooms beyond.

Music flooded from a doorway, richer, more complex than anything he'd ever heard before. A heartbreak of song lifting him, almost carrying him away; he didn't need to understand the words to be transported, to have his eyes fill with tears. He didn't know what instruments they might be playing but surely something miraculous to produce this intricate, vibrant torrent of notes. The Broken had nothing in their caves to compare, no musician with one-tenth the skill. And already, as his feet carried him away, another wave of melody broke across them from windows overlooking the street ahead. Thurin turned as he walked, drinking it in with all his senses, aware from the ache in his cheeks that he was grinning like a madman, careless of being jostled and jolted by the crowd.

'It's a lot to take in.' Erris caught his shoulder, his own smile sympathetic. 'You've had a very narrow existence. This place . . . it's different. Wonderful, yes, but be careful: it'll eat you alive if you're not careful. Innocence is what cities like this feed on, and this one has been gorging for centuries. And that's just above ground. The city that lies beneath it is far, far older and much more dangerous!'

Thurin tried to focus on Mali's back, to concentrate on following her and not being led astray. They passed so many people. Literally thousands. Men and women, young and old, more varied than the Broken in every regard, skin tones running a spectrum from white to black through shades of pink and brown, hair in every style, eyes of every colour.

A young blonde woman with a heart-shaped face and full lips squeezed past him filling the air with the scent of . . . something good. Thurin had never given a great deal of thought to the gods but he had assumed that the Gods in the Ice had smiled on him the day they had delivered Yaz into his life. It was, he had always thought, impressive how each person seemed to find the one other that somehow fitted them like a puzzle piece, that person and no other. And when Yaz had fallen among them he had felt that click as if two parts, each needing some specific thing from the other, had met and joined. That had been an easy belief to cling to when his world numbered people in the low hundreds and those of around his own age little more than a score. Suddenly, though, in one step, the Missing's gate had brought him within a few days' travel of perhaps a million souls. Could he still cling to the belief that Yaz had been made for him and he for her? Even when the alternatives above and below the ice could be measured in dozens, he'd felt she might pass him over in favour of Quell or Erris. But now? Every new corner revealed the homes of ten times as many souls as huddled within the ice caves. It frightened him. He didn't want anyone else, but what if she did?

'Thurin?' Erris clicked his fingers before Thurin's face.

'Uh?'

Erris pointed over the rooftops to where the spires of some great building challenged the sky. 'The Cathedral of St Allam. It's where Eular will meet the high priest tomorrow – if he hasn't already. The good news is that the box is in that direction.' He pointed down a side street leading the opposite way. 'So we're not going to have to desecrate these people's holiest place. At least not tonight.'

'And the bad news is that he might already have seen the high priest and be on his way to Seus?' Thurin asked.

'Got it in one.' Erris led off, calling to Mali.

'So where is it, exactly?' Thurin asked, using his ice-work to deflect yet another green-lander who seemed set on barging into him.

'Well, that's also a problem,' Erris said. 'There was a time when I could have found out to within a finger's width, but the systems I'm using have degraded. Most of the elements have literally tumbled from the sky. But it's definitely in the city. And it's this way. Pretty sure.'

'What does Mali say lies in this direction?' Thurin asked.

Erris relayed the question. 'She doesn't know.'

'She doesn't know?' Thurin looked at the girl. 'How could she not know?'

'It's a big city. She probably doesn't get out of the convent much. This isn't like the caves. Almost everyone here is a stranger to almost everyone else. Chances are that most of the people who live here can get lost in their own city if they take a few wrong turns.'

They turned another corner, following a narrower, muddy street. The houses here were still tall but looked as if they were divided into many sections. Washing hung from long-neglected stone balconies. Another corner brought them through an area where lean-to shacks crowded together, the huddle of roofs interrupted by the occasional shattered pillar or collapsed arch. Thurin instantly felt more at home. He'd lived almost all his life in a shack like these, built from the ruins of something far greater. Why this area should exist here amid such plenty he wasn't sure.

'This way.' Erris made a sharp left turn. 'Probably.'

He led them down an almost pitch-black alley between two high-sided buildings seemingly lacking windows. Across the rooftops, glimpsed at the far end, a dome glimmered in the starlight. Mali pointed and said something.

'She thinks that's part of the Church rest house,' Erris said. He continued to translate: 'The archons each have a place at the centre of the complex, a private house where they station themselves on visits to the capital.'

'That's where Eular must be.' The closer they got to Eular the less confident about their mission Thurin felt. Eular had been one of the Broken, a trusted constant who had shown himself to be something entirely different. Just thinking about him made Thurin worry about every other thing he believed in. He shook off the feeling and followed Erris.

Ahead of them a single lantern burned, hanging above a doorway, its wick trimmed low. A man with a shaved head stepped out to block the way. He wore a belted tunic and moved with swift grace.

'Who is he? Why isn't he saying anything?' Something about the man made Thurin nervous.

Mali answered. 'He's a Martial Brother, a monk from the Church of the Ancestor,' Erris translated. He said something to the man and the monk responded by altering his stance and raising both fists. The man's habit shifted as he snapped into position and Thurin could see a sword on his belt. Like the ones the Red Sisters had carried, it was shorter and thinner than those the Broken made, but still looked capable of taking off an arm or a head.

'I don't think he's here to arrest us.' Erris sighed and stepped forward. The arm that the three-headed hound had injured was moving better than before but it was still notice-ably stiff.

'You'd think he'd draw his sword if he wanted to kill us . . .' Thurin wasn't entirely confident on this point though. The man carried an aura of competence. He didn't look like someone who made mistakes.

'Mali says she won't kill a monk.' Erris squared up against the Red Brother. 'And I don't want to kill him either—'

The man spun in to attack, sweeping his leg in an attempt to knock Erris's from under him. Both of them became a blur of motion too fast for Thurin to follow. The Red Brother fought in a similar manner to that with which Erris had amazed the Broken, but they were not the same. The monk's movements were somehow more fluid, with each attack or defence flowing into another in a manner that made the whole thing seem one predetermined piece.

Although Thurin couldn't follow everything, there were times, particularly at the end of a lengthy combination of attacks and counters, when he would see a blow struck – a fist finding flesh, a foot striking a hip, a throw bodily hurling an opponent. It appeared that Erris was getting the worst of it, perhaps taking three solid kicks or punches for each glancing blow he landed. On the other hand, his glancing blows sent the monk spinning, whereas the monk's assault had far less impact. The Red Brother looked as if he could put his fist through a man's face, but it seemed as if he'd have more luck punching a tree than damaging Erris.

After an initial moment of surprise the monk was quick to adjust to Erris's unexpected strength and weight, straining his speed to the utmost in order to avoid Erris's grip. Erris managed to grab a handful of his opponent's habit but a flash of steel cut the Red Brother free. Only a few heartbeats had passed before the pair parted, having thrown dozens of kicks and punches.

The Red Brother drew his sword too fast for Thurin to see. One moment it was in its scabbard, the next it was pointed at Erris, the air still ringing with the blade's vibration.

'This could be a problem.' Erris backed towards Thurin and Mali again.

Despite Erris's remarkably quick healing, Thurin knew that with a sword in hand the Red Brother would be likely to disable the 'made man'. After that a single blow would suffice to send Mali and then Thurin to the gods. So he reached out, focusing his will. A moment later the Red Brother hung with his feet a yard above the ground. 'What do I do with him now?'

'More than that!' Faster than thinking, Erris threw himself in front of Thurin just as several silver flickers shot from the monk's left hand. Mali screamed something as the projectiles thunked into Erris.

Shocked and scared, Thurin almost lost his grip on the Red Brother. Before the monk could gather more projectiles from inside his robe where a bandolier stretched across his chest, Thurin gestured sharply to the right and the man slammed into the wall. To Thurin's dismay the impact wasn't enough to knock the monk senseless. He threw the man at the opposite wall but somehow he managed to turn in the air and brace his legs against the collision. This time Thurin slammed him down into the street and the change of direction seemed to catch him off guard. Briefly the monk tried to rise then slumped onto the grimy flagstones.

'Watch out!' This time even Erris was too slow. Thurin felt a sting in the back of his neck and turned to see a grey-clad monk dropping into the street behind them, landing gracefully even though the rooftops were three storeys above them. Thurin pulled a small dart from his neck. The needle point glistened with his blood but it would take a thousand of them to kill him. Several more studded Erris's arm where he'd tried to block them from hitting Thurin. Thurin blinked unsteadily at the dart and let it drop from numb fingers.

Darkness bloomed around the Grey Brother as if he had landed in inches-deep black dust. A shadow-worker, like Maya. A heartbeat later and Thurin could see nothing.

'Damn . . .' Thurin's legs went out from under him, not knocked away but simply failing him, as if someone had replaced his muscles with water.

Thurin collapsed gracelessly, unable to do anything but wait for the inevitable knife between the ribs. The Grey Brother must have watched their fight with the Red Brother in order to assess the danger. As the venom on the dart rapidly pulled Thurin down into an inner darkness every bit as black as the one outside, he tried to lift an arm and failed. He hoped Yaz would be safe in the convent. He hoped she wouldn't be too sad to learn of his death. He hoped she would know that he'd tried his hardest. Quina too, he realized as he sank deeper. He would miss her more than he'd thought.

The brilliance that shredded the night was as painful as it was unexpected. The venom in Thurin's blood had para-lysed the irises of his eyes as well as most of his other muscles and his pupils were unable to contract against the light. One kind of blindness rapidly replaced the other, leaving only a brief impression of a girl's outline filled with a white heat. Mali! Mali must have touched the Path again. She'd said she wouldn't harm the monks but perhaps this would give Erris a chance.

The brilliance dimmed somewhat and, through the after-images, Thurin could make out blurry shapes. One appeared to be clinging to the back of another. When he blinked rapidly, he thought he saw the Grey Brother with both knees pressed between the shoulder blades of the still-standing Erris and that the monk was holding himself in position by hauling on a thin but strong wire stretched across Erris's neck.

Thurin knew that Erris couldn't be strangled, but as soon as the monk also discovered this he would likely stick a knife into one of Erris's ears, and that would be more of a problem. Fighting to stay conscious, Thurin grabbed hold of the assassin with his ice-work and tried to throw him at the nearest wall. Unfortunately, since he was anchored to Erris, who weighed at least three times what a man should, all the effort achieved was to jolt Erris and send him staggering.

Despite the light pouring from Mali's skin, the scene was growing dimmer by the moment. Thurin knew he had little time left before the venom took away his consciousness. With a last effort, instead of hauling on the monk, Thurin threw his own limp body like a missile.

If there was an impact he didn't feel it. Instead he fell a long way into a soft darkness that swallowed him whole.

CHAPTER 6

Yaz

Their first lesson took place at the top of a stone tower. Four doors at the base led into a chamber that accounted for all the ground floor and was hung with strange portraits of nuns. The Ictha decorated their hides with scorch marks made using a wire heated in a lamp flame. The Axit made images, primarily of their dogs, some of them quite realistic. So Yaz was familiar with the concept of representative art. But the idea that such wonders could be worked with pigments and skill was as much a revelation to her as chickens or trees. She stood staring in awe. 'I thought they were real . . .'

'Me too . . .' Quina reached out to touch the surface of the nearest picture but Wenna slapped her hand away.

'No.' The blonde girl shook her head slowly as if talking to a baby.

Quina scowled but had the sense not to start a fight.

Wenna led them up the central spiral stair to a room at the top where most of the class were already seated on narrow chairs. Light and colour streamed in through tall windows where the glass was of many hues and formed geometric designs. Sister Owl was there too, looking very comfortable in a wide padded chair with a high back.

'Yaz, Quina,' she addressed them in their own tongue. 'Take a seat.'

The ancient nun spent some time addressing the rest of the class – Yaz heard her and Quina's names mentioned. Clearly the novices were now getting the official version and being admonished to keep it to themselves. Yaz doubted that would last long, but perhaps Eular would be gone before the news reached the city. In any event Yaz assumed that Abbess Claw must know how reliable her charges were and have planned appropriately.

Sister Owl set the novices to various tasks, most of which seemed to involve staring at nothing and muttering quietly. This done, she came to Quina and began to ask her a series of strange questions about dreams and lines or paths that might run through them, only to have Quina interrupt her.

'They tested me at the Black Rock. I'm not what you're looking for.'

'Who did, dear?' Owl studied her with those dark and overly large eyes.

'Our priests. I mean, they served a false god and every-thing, and they were collecting—'

'Quina!' Yaz snapped. She liked Sister Owl but there were limits to how much she was going to tell her without good reason.

'Anyway,' Quina concluded, looking slightly abashed. 'I've got no quantal or marjal blood. They tested me.'

'Hmmmm.' Sister Owl nodded. 'Likely they were right. Let's start you off with the basics of the serenity trance. You strike me as a young woman who could benefit from a little centring calm in her life.'

'I feel pretty centred today.' Quina rested both hands on her belly.

Sister Owl proceeded to explain the serenity trance and how it could be reached by reciting various mantras or through visualization. Quina started with one of the simple mantras and the nun praised her efforts.

'You're much better at this than I imagined you might be.'

Quina just nodded serenely. 'It's being so full that does it.'

Rather than ask Yaz to attempt the trance, Sister Owl led her to a corner of the room where the windows' coloured light was pooling. The ancient woman studied her closely. The irises of her eyes were so black that they seemed to be part of single, huge pupils, and the effect was unsettling. Yaz was about to say something, anything to break the silence, when at last the nun spoke.

'From what you've told us, you've walked the Path many times, though in a way that's foreign to me.'

'I touch it,' Yaz said. 'I don't have to try to stay on it, to keep my balance the way Mali describes it.'

'Remarkable. I thought all quantals were the same.' Sister Owl peered even more closely but now seemed to be studying the air around Yaz. 'And I've seen many quantals in my time. But nothing like you, my dear.'

Yaz suspected that she touched the Path the same way that the Missing did. She felt safe keeping that to herself for now, though. 'I had nobody to teach me, I guess.'

'That's the other remarkable thing. The quantal girls who come through my class are taught many different techniques to help them survive the contact. Even then we've had unfortunate accidents. When you take power into yourself you have to own it. The more power, the harder it is to own. Every part of you wants to go in its own direction

61

and the net effect can be to tear you apart. It's true in other walks of life too. The Church, for example, has taken more and more power to itself over the years and always the struggle has been to keep it unified despite this. Power corrupts, it demands to be used. Every archon, every abbess and abbot, every priest struggles not to be led astray by it. The high priest struggles to own that power and give the faith a single direction rather than let it be torn into many factions. The Scithrowl heresy stems from a single archon who felt he needed to walk his own path—'

'Scithrowl?' Yaz also didn't know the word 'heresy' but didn't want to show too much ignorance at once.

'Ignore me, dear, I'm rambling again. My mind is old and full of power. It too wants to wander its own paths. But back to the point. Touching the Path in any way is dangerous. Take only what you absolutely need. Take too much and it will destroy you and everyone around you.'

Yaz swallowed. She knew exactly what Sister Owl was talking about and had several times found herself on the edge of breaking apart after touching the Path. 'Maybe you should teach those trances to me too.'

The first steps towards better control turned out to be the same for both Quina and Yaz. Sister Owl began to instruct them in the tricky business of achieving the serenity trance, the clarity trance, and the patience trance. The patience trance, Yaz decided, was something that she would definitely need, because although Sister Owl seemed astonished by her progress over the course of the next few hours it was also clear that these were things that the novices studied for years on end and not skills that could be acquired over the course of a morning.

'Aaaaaaah!' Quina came down the tower stairs clutching

her back. 'I don't think I've sat that long doing nothing for . . . ever!'

Yaz grinned. Quina had also received praise for her aptitude. Apparently life on the ice enforced the necessary traits. Patience was essential when trekking across the ice, and without clarity how would you spot anything in a white-on-white world? Serenity was the hardest but, as Quina had said, there was something in the novel experience of an overfull stomach that promoted serenity.

The girls streamed through the ground-floor chamber hung with portraits and out through the four doors into the day. Yaz and Quina lingered again, hypnotized by the paintings. The way they both showed their subject, so real that you might imagine them actually looking at you through a window, but also straying into the realm of dreams, astounded Yaz. In one a woman's hair was turning into butterflies!

'You could make these of anything . . . creatures and places that don't even exist!' The idea had never occurred to her before. She supposed now that kettan statuettes could also be carved to resemble mere figments of fantasy. But none among the Ictha had ever done it. She wanted to share these paintings with Quell. She—

'Come!' The blonde girl, Wenna, had returned to get them.

'What's the next lesson?' Quina asked. 'I hope it's fighting. I want to learn how to kick like Mali does.'

Wenna led them through the convent, past various buildings whose purpose Yaz could only guess at. One smelled delicious and a burly nun was working with wood and metal at the front of an area filled with large containers made from planks held in curved shape with hoops of iron. Another had an entirely different but not unpleasant aroma and Yaz saw a nun emerge carrying a largish rectangle bound with hide but with a block of whitish . . . stuff . . . exposed between the two covers.

As she stared after the departing nun Yaz became aware of two novices watching from a nearby doorway, laughing at her. She thought they were from her class, Grey Class, and had been in the room in Path Tower. One was small and dark-haired, a hunska perhaps, as pale-skinned as her red-haired companion who stood a head taller than Yaz – probably a gerant. This tall one had broad shoulders and a blunt, freckled face that was, in Yaz's estimation, quite pretty. Her hair bristled from her scalp where her friend's fell around her shoulders.

'Come.' Wenna tugged at Yaz's arm, which alerted Yaz to the fact that she had stopped moving. She'd not been laughed at for a long time. Perhaps not ever. And the discovery of just how much she disliked it came as something of a shock to her.

'Yaz!' Quina turned back. 'Come on.'

'They were laughing at me.' Yaz found her teeth were gritted together. She wasn't sure where the anger was coming from but she hadn't spent months crossing the ice to be laughed at.

Quina glanced at the pair. 'So the green lands have idiots too.' She grabbed Yaz's arm and pulled her on. 'I never told you about my cousin, Quent. Now there's an idiot—'

As Yaz turned away, the redhead began what had to be, from the way she held her hands up beside her neck, and her false high-pitched shrieks, an impression of Quina screaming as she rolled into the Glasswater.

It was Quina's turn to stop and turn back.

'Don't.' Now that it was Quina at risk of a beating, Yaz's sudden desire for violence broke like a wave, dissipating its strength. 'You've seen how they fight. We need to learn first.'

But other novices had stopped to watch the show, and the dark-haired girl joined in the mimicry, jabbering in words that made no sense in either language but were supposed to belong to the ice.

Quina started towards them. Yaz defocused her gaze and saw the threadscape, the translucent confusion of relationships between each thing and every other. Threads bound one novice to the next, threads showed the centre of their attention, threads flexed with their amusement, with Quina's anger, and with the memories that the two novices were drawing on to stage their re-enactment. Those memory threads reached towards Yaz and Quina and were particularly clear. All of them fresh, flexing with use, and bound to Yaz's own still-raw experience of the other side of those events.

Yaz reached out and took between the finger and thumb of each hand the memory thread of the redhead and her companion. She didn't know the tricks that Sister Owl must know, the ones that Eular used to modify opinions and recollections, but she had some sense of what to do, some instinct for it, perhaps stemming from her Missing heritage. The relevant memory threads seemed to glow with activity, calling out to her. She didn't try to change anything, only to add to the memory of Quina's fall her own memory of drowning in the blackness far below the surface of the Glasswater. She added all of it, the unfiltered terror, the thundering of her heart as her lungs demanded that she open her mouth and breathe in the liquid mud, the cold, awful pressure, the blind dark, the brutal despair of it all. She pulsed it at them along the threads of their memory.

Both girls' eyes widened with terror and a moment later they fell to the ground, bucking like fish in the bottom of a boat. Somehow their silence was more frightening than if they'd been screaming. Both of them locked into Yaz's memory, fighting not to draw the breath they so desperately needed.

'What did you do?' Quina looked at her, horrified.

'I showed them what it was like.' Yaz turned and walked away, pulling back on the threads as she did, releasing the pair, and was relieved to hear them gasping behind her. The impact of her actions had been more effective than she'd intended. Maybe memory was her speciality.

Quina and Wenna hurried after her.

'I just wanted to give them a slap,' Quina hissed.

But Wenna surprised Yaz by saying something short and unintelligible, all save one word that she understood and which summed up the other words too: 'good'.

'How much trouble are we in?' Quina asked.

'I . . .' Yaz glanced at Wenna. 'I think we're doing fine,' she said. This was, after all, a place where the green-landers taught the children to fight. And though the Ictha did not make war, they knew enough to know that often the best way to prevent one starting is when struck to hit back harder.

Wenna led them on, leaving the 'drowned' girls in their wake, and came to a halt at the end of a line of novices filing into the hall where they had gorged themselves that morning.

'We're doing it again?' Quina gasped.

Yaz touched Wenna's shoulder and held up two fingers. 'We eat twice?'

Wenna seemed confused. She held up three fingers. 'Breakfast, lunch, dinner.'

Somehow Yaz's bond with Mali gave the words meaning. She turned back to Quina in astonishment. 'They eat three times a day!'

'Gods in the Ice . . .' Quina clutched her belly. 'I love this place.'

CHAPTER 7

Thurin

'Wake up!' Another slap. 'Thurin! Wake up!'

Thurin blinked and rubbed a hand over his cheek. It still felt numb, the recent slap lacking the usual sting. The street had returned to darkness, eroded only by starlight and the feeble flame of a nearby lantern. Something had changed, though. All the angles looked wrong. Erris's hand swung into view.

'Wait. Stop hitting me.' Thurin's mouth felt full of fur, his tongue too lazy to shape words properly. He decided that he was seeing the street from flat on his back, and that the spots of light swirling through his vision were actual stars. 'What happened to the monks?'

Erris turned Thurin's head for him. It was hard to see in the faint light but two bodies lay by the base of the wall. Erris produced a flame from his index finger. The Red Brother and the Grey were tied up with thin ropes, one of them struggling weakly, the other motionless. 'I jabbed them with the darts that hit me rather than you. Luckily they brought some cords with them.'

'Did I knock out the one strangling you?' Thurin didn't

remember the collision but he'd been moving fast and there seemed no way he could have missed.

'No, he was too quick for that. But you got him off my back and gave me the chance I needed. If he'd been less sure of his venoms and used his sword instead . . . it would have been a different story.'

Mali helped Thurin to sit up while Erris turned away to examine something.

'This is bad, right?' Thurin said. 'They were trying to kill us. And if we kill them – well, I don't want to kill anyone; plus, then we might have the nuns after us too, and they might drown Yaz and Quina for real.'

'Pretty bad.' Erris opened something in his hands with a click. 'If we let them go Eular will know far more than we want him to.' He put down the case he'd opened and pulled a tiny needle from his finger.

Mali scolded him.

'She's telling me to be more careful. This is a Grey Brother's mission kit. Full of venoms, poisons, drugs, and antidotes.' He picked out a vial and showed it to her. 'This?'

'What are you looking for?' Thurin hoped the answer was an antidote to make his muscles listen to his orders. Currently only his mouth and lungs seemed to be paying attention.

'Mali says that there might be a drug in here that erases recent memories and leaves the victim confused for several days. It's part of the standard set for Grey Brothers, apparently, but the herb is very rare because the ice is covering the marshes where it grows. So he might not have any.' He showed her another vial.

'You should let her look for herself,' Thurin said.

'I've already stuck myself on two hidden needles and have what's probably a toxic substance on my fingers. The whole kit's full of traps.' He showed her a black glass vial marked with two symbols. She shook her head. 'That's why I've not given you the antidote to the boneless venom. Mali knows the markings but says it might be poison anyway.' He held out a shiny steel vial. Mali nodded.

'And if that one's a trap too?' Thurin asked.

Erris shrugged. 'They did try to kill us.'

Thurin frowned. 'I feel fine. Just a bit . . . floppy.'

'Mali tells me they often use that toxin first. It's the fastest acting. But then you're easy to kill afterwards.' Erris drew a finger across his throat. 'If they were worried you might escape or they can't get close to you then they hit you with something deadly straight away.'

Erris moved to the two men and forced a few drops of liquid from the vial down each of their throats. The awake one tried to spit and to shout but evidently the dose of boneless that Erris had given them was considerably higher than that delivered to Thurin and the monk hadn't the strength to do more than whisper.

'And now?' Thurin lifted himself to his feet, surprising Mali.

'And now we go to Mali's house.' Erris untied the monks and restored the Grey Brother's kit to him, along with the darts that he'd thrown. 'These two shouldn't remember us, or make much sense for a day or two. With luck they'll wander off before they're found and not report in for some while.'

'Wait? Mali's house.' Thurin turned towards the girl, not using his limp muscles but instead moving himself with his ice-work. 'Didn't we just come from there?'

'Not the convent.' Erris gestured for Mali to lead the way. 'Apparently she has family in town. And if we're to infiltrate the Church rest house we're going to need to look more like city dwellers.'

*

Mali took Erris and Thurin on a confusing journey through streets that lay dark and lonely, interspersed with others aglow with street lanterns and the light from pillared entrances to walled compounds. They seemed to be climbing and the air, which had been thick with the smoke of many chimneys, became clearer as their route took them to the windward side of the city.

Mali came to a halt in front of a high wall in a wide, empty street flagged with paving stones. The starlit road lay empty and no buildings could be seen behind the walls, just the occasional tree rustling in the darkness.

'She says we have to climb over.' Erris pointed to the iron spikes topping the wall about a man's height above their heads.

'I thought her family lived here?' Thurin wondered if the residents weren't allowed out at night in this district. It would explain the lack of people. Maybe the very poorest were hidden away behind walls, crammed into even worse accommodation than the shanty town they'd passed through earlier.

Erris cupped his hands together for Thurin's foot, but Thurin – still wobbly from the Grey Brother's venom – simply floated himself to the top. Mali allowed Erris to lift her and Thurin pulled her up the remaining distance, using his mind again. Finally Erris executed a remarkable standing jump, caught the top of the wall and vaulted over, dropping rapidly from sight into a mass of vegetation.

Thurin looked suspiciously at the fall into darkness. The green stuff scared him when he couldn't see it properly. The space beyond the wall seemed full of trees and . . . smaller trees? All of it moving in the wind, whispering to itself, creaking like strange ice. 'Is it safe?'

Mali said something no more intelligible than the rustling of trees and gave him a light push which he resisted.

'She says "yes".' Erris's disembodied voice rose up from the seething mass below.

'How does she know what I asked?' Thurin stalled.

'She told me that the bond she formed with Yaz seems to be giving her some kind of intuition for your tongue. She's learning by listening.' Erris paused. 'So jump.'

Mention of Yaz bolstered Thurin's faltering determination and with a shudder he let himself drop slowly into the hidden greenery, clutching himself tight against its sharp, questing fingers and wet flutterings. 'This isn't . . . natural.'

Mali dropped beside him, presumably having hung from her remaining hand first.

'Come on.' Erris pushed Thurin forwards, one hand on his shoulder, steering him after the departing girl. Erris's eyes saw far more in the dark than Thurin's and guided him past several obstacles. Mali, it seemed, must have marjal blood as well as quantal and count shadow-work among her skills, or perhaps she just knew the terrain exceptionally well.

Thurin, feeling like the invalid of the group, stumbled on blind, staggering on watery legs and tripping at every other step. Despite earlier assurances that trees were non-sentient and not in the least malicious, it seemed that they took delight in slapping him repeatedly across the face with branchfuls of cold, wet leaves. He was still blinking and spitting out greenery from one particularly enthusiastic slap when they broke clear and he felt the crunch of small stones beneath his feet.

Ahead of them, across a wide space floored with gravel and studded with statuary, stood another great wall, this one pierced by many windows, light burning from some, others dark. A tiled roof slanted away from the top of the wall and many chimneys reached for the sky. It resembled earlier streets in the district where one house seamlessly abutted the next, though this seemed far grander, built from huge and impressively regular blocks of stone.

'Which one is yours?' Thurin hissed.

But Mali ignored him and Erris didn't translate. Thurin made to go closer but Mali pulled him back into the foliage. A silent moment passed, then several longer ones. In the distance he heard a faint crunch, crunch, crunch. He crouched beside Mali and Erris and watched as two armed guards passed, one with a lantern on a long pole slung over her shoulder. When the sound of their feet on the gravel had faded again Mali hurried over to the nearest window, ignoring what seemed to be the only door.

She reached for the sill, missed it with the hand she must still imagine she owned and bumped her stump painfully against the wall. Cursing, she said something to Erris and he lifted her up. A moment's fiddling with a knife and the lower half of the window frame lifted, carrying its flat, heavy panes of glass with it as it slid over the upper half. Mali slipped through and vanished into the dark room beyond. Erris slithered in after her and Thurin followed with far less grace.

Thurin blundered through the room beyond, knocking into what felt like heavy chairs covered in soft . . . stuff. Mali opened the far door a crack, allowing in enough light for Thurin to navigate around rather than through the obstacles. He discovered he was sweating: the place was as warm as the drying room, heat radiating from a fireplace where the faint embers of an earlier blaze still glowed.

Mali stuck her head out into the corridor beyond, looked both ways and then went out, beckoning the others to follow.

'Are we robbing the place?' Thurin hissed. The corridor was well lit by candles in alcoves and the floor was covered in soft, patterned rugs.

Mali led them around a right turn, a left turn, through a

small door, down stone stairs, and into a room that smelled like heaven must. A great fireplace lay black and empty but the heat was still considerable. Clearly cooking took place here, both on the metal spits in front of the fire and on the great iron stove. There were two clean worktables, a bench by the far wall, and metal hooks hanging from the ceiling from which depended a variety of objects for which Thurin had no names. Mali opened a door into a smaller adjoining room whose walls were lined with shelves, all piled with . . . things. Things that smelled as if they should be eaten immediately.

'What is it?' Thurin breathed.

'The servants' kitchen and their pantry,' Erris said.

'Servants?'

'The people who work for the great family who own the place.'

Thurin blinked. 'This is all one house?'

Erris nodded.

Mali meanwhile had gone into the pantry and was loading up one arm with items from the shelves. If her family were servants here it made sense she would know the place so well.

'And what's this?' Thurin reached up and took down a long string of linked cylinders from one of the hooks. They were dark, flecked with white and pink, and thick enough that he could just wrap his hand about them.

'Spiced sausage by the look of it.' Erris smiled.

'But what is it?'

'You eat it.'

Thurin raised the first to his mouth and looked at Erris to see if he was joking. He sniffed. The aroma made his mouth water. He took a bite. The stuff was firm, tougher than any of the fungi he'd sustained himself on his whole life.

'Oh . . . Gods in the Ice!' He spoke through a full mouth, chewing hard. 'This is even better than fish!'

Thurin was too preoccupied with the explosion of flavour in his mouth to notice that the door had opened until a tall, oldish man entered the room and began barking questions at them in green-lander gibberish. He wore simple black clothes that hung from a narrow body in sharp contrast to his pale skin. Two fierce eyes glared around a blade of a nose, and his white hair seemed to be standing up in shock or outrage.

Thurin raised an arm, intending to use his ice-work to immobilize the man, but Mali walked past him from the pantry behind and pulled his wrist down.

'Maliaya?' the old man gasped in amazement. He had more to say but then he spotted her stump and fell to his knees, reaching for her. 'Maliaya . . .'

And to Thurin's great surprise Mali threw herself into the man's embrace. Her grandfather?

After a moment of hugging her tight the old man broke gently away and stood up, composing himself with remarkable swiftness, blinking the brightness of tears from his eyes. He bowed to Mali and said something that sounded both neutral and formal.

'What's going on?' Thurin looked over at Erris.

'Mali didn't seem to want us to know, but apparently this is her family home. Our new friend appears to be one of the servants. It seems that Glosis is an important name in this city, which means that Maliaya Glosis is probably related to the emperor who rules all of it – and more beyond.'

CHAPTER 8

Yaz

Yaz and Quina emerged from the refectory, walking slowly as they attempted not to clutch their bellies. Their efforts at the dining table had been less heroic than that morning's. Neither had much room left and the understanding that this was not a one-off feast enabled them to exercise some restraint. Even so, Yaz would have held onto Quina for support if they hadn't been under close scrutiny from the crowd of novices exiting with them.

Sister Owl was waiting for them just outside.

'Your class is going to a Blade lesson. Your priorities should be Path and learning the language so I'll excuse you and give you private lessons in the scriptorium. But perhaps you would like to watch the start of the lesson first, so you have an understanding of what we do here?'

'Let's watch them fight!' Quina said immediately. She looked quickly at Yaz, staring furiously for her to agree and hissing, 'Learning languages sounds hard!'

Yaz was finding it quite easy, but she also wanted to see the novices fight, and so she nodded. 'We'd like that.'

'That's the scriptorium.' Sister Owl pointed to a small

building with an arched doorway and peaked roof. 'Meet me there when your curiosity is satisfied.'

The nun relayed the information to Wenna, who had followed them from the refectory. Yaz found Owl's words in green-tongue tantalizingly close to comprehensible. She wondered if Mali were experiencing the same thing with Thurin.

'Oh!' Giving a sudden guilty start, Yaz realized that, with all the marvels and excitement of the convent, she hadn't once thought how Thurin and Erris had spent the night. Had they been wandering the city streets all that time in search of Eular? Had they found him? Were they hurt?

'Yaz?' Sister Owl looked concerned.

'Sorry.' Yaz shook her head. 'I was just thinking of the others.'

Quina looked guilty. 'I should have gone with them instead of staying here to stuff myself. I could have helped!'

Sister Owl shrugged. 'None of us are particularly safe right now. And if you're to stand any chance then both of you have things to learn. Yaz in particular, but you too, Quina. Your friends are in good hands. Mali is a formidable talent. And neither the made man nor your . . . the other boy seem fragile.'

Yaz had to agree that Thurin and Erris had both survived many of the horrors of the Black Rock alone. Even if she were to set off after them she had no idea how to find them among the city's teeming thousands. 'We'll watch the fighting then come to you in the . . . scriptorium.'

Wenna led them to a great stone hall with a high peaked roof. It had been built right against the cliff edge, which, to Yaz's eye, used to the collapsing ice cliffs of a hot sea, seemed a great folly. They passed through tall double doors of wood studded with iron. Every door in the convent was wood, the chairs and tables too. Iron by contrast seemed more valued and rarer. After the Black Rock, where iron was everywhere and Quina's bead had been the only precious fragment of a tree for many thousands of miles, it still took some getting used to.

About half of the hall was an open space with a strange yellowish floor where the rest of the class were already gathered. Towards the back, tiered wooden seating stepped away, offering almost enough room for the whole convent to sit and watch. A corridor led through the tiers to the walled-off second half of the hall.

Eleven Grey Class novices had lined themselves up before a broad-shouldered nun in a red habit, all of them now wearing tunics more suited to fighting in. Wenna hurriedly led the way across to the group but Yaz and Quina only made it a yard or so before both stopped and knelt to feel the floor. On her first step Yaz had known something strange was going on. The floor was neither hard nor soft. It felt almost like . . . heavy snow. The stuff was yielding and warm and fell between her fingers like water, but she could see that it was like lifeless stardust, only in vastly greater quantities.

Yaz stood, letting the material pour from her hand, rubbing the remnants between finger and thumb.

'It's really tiny rocks!' Quina said.

'The same rock this building is made from,' Yaz said. 'And the same rock that it sits on.'

She and Quina became aware that they were the focus of attention. Some of the novices were struggling to hide their amusement. Others seemed worried, throwing nervous glances towards the nun.

Yaz went to join Wenna, who was explaining to the nun that Sister Owl had delayed them past the bell. 'Sister Owl said that the tribers can come to join her at the scriptorium after observing some of our training.'

With a start Yaz realized that the girl's words had stopped almost making sense and started actually meaning something. She said nothing, though, preferring to keep her new-found understanding to herself.

The nun – Mistress Blade, Wenna had called her – came across to look Yaz and Quina up and down. She stood a head taller than Yaz and had the palest eyes Yaz had seen in a green-lander. She looked old despite her apparent vigour, maybe fifty, and bore scars everywhere that lay exposed: face, hands, and wrists.

'Stand over there.' She pointed to a spot closer to the seating. Turning to the class, she made a fist of her right hand and smacked it into the palm of her left. 'The tribers want to see you fight. So pair up and show them how we do it at Sweet Mercy. Wenna, you can fight in your habit. Blade fist, full contact. Go.'

Within moments each novice had found a partner and stood facing them in a fighting stance. The hunska girl and the big redhead Yaz had shared her drowning with faced off against each other, both darting poisonous looks at her. Wenna faced another blonde novice who sported a livid bruise across one cheek. When Mistress Blade parted her hands the novices began to fight. All of them battled with swift and deadly efficiency, but their opposite number blocked as well as they attacked. The redhead compensated for her opponent's speed with strength and durability, being entirely on the defensive, as if encouraging the smaller girl to tire and slow, and allow a later retaliation. Yaz had seen the hunska among the Broken move and so she was less astounded by their speed. And she had seen Erris, and later Mali, fight, so she was less astounded by their skill – but even so, to see a dozen girls all so perfectly trained was remarkable. What amazed her was the sheer ferocity with which they fought. It seemed, for the short period between Mistress Blade parting her hands and bringing them back together in a resounding clap, that each novice genuinely intended the murder of the girl before her. And all of it without so much as a snarl or grimace, every one of them fighting with brutal perfection in the midst of the serenity that Sister Owl had trained them in at the top of Path Tower.

At the nun's clap the dozen novices parted, not even breathing heavily. Wenna had a narrow trickle of blood running from the corner of her mouth, another girl had one eye reddened and narrowed to a slit, but none of them made any attempt to tend to their hurts.

'Would you care to show us what they teach you on the ice?' Mistress Blade gestured to Yaz and Quina to select opponents.

Quina, who had understood nothing but the wave of the woman's hand, stepped forward nonetheless.

'Don't!' Yaz said.

'It's OK.' Quina grinned back. 'I'll take the slowest one.'

She walked up to the redhead who'd taunted them earlier, and readied herself the way Mali did.

'Not—' Yaz wanted to say 'not that one – she spars against a hunska all the time' but the moment had passed.

The bigger girl rolled her head to stretch her neck with an audible cracking, smiled a narrow smile, and raised her fists.

'Go easy on her, Kola,' Mistress Blade said. 'No broken bones.' She brought her hands together and at the signal Quina exploded into action. She moved in a blur, hammering out a dozen blows in no time at all.

Kola guarded her head and neck with two fists held close in, her arms absorbing the punches. Where the blows landed on her body she just seemed to soak them up. Quina didn't punch with the same focused power as the novices: she lost force with wide swings that announced each move ahead of time.

When Kola swept Quina's feet from under her it wasn't because Quina wasn't fast enough to avoid it: she just didn't see it coming because she was too tied up in pounding at her foe. Kola didn't take advantage, simply stood back and let Quina get up.

Quina's next attack lacked the breathtaking speed of the first. The long trek across the ice had built her endurance for the slow, endless slog. But when it came to the continued application of speed she tired quickly. This time she saw Kola's leg sweep coming, but too late, and ended up tumbling, but landing on her hands and knees rather than her back.

Quina's next mistake was to assume Kola would let her back up as she had the first time. The kick caught her midriff while she was still on all fours and sent her sprawling.

'Enough.' Mistress Blade stepped between them.

Quina stood, clutching her ribs and breathing heavily, still ready to fight but clearly not going to be victorious. She started to advance on Kola again.

'Enough.' Yaz took Quina by the shoulder. 'You did well. They train at this for years. Let them come to the ice if they want a real fight.'

Kola stretched her arms and raised an eyebrow at Yaz as if inviting her to try her hand. Mistress Blade repeated her earlier gesture, offering Yaz a choice of opponent.

'Take the red girl,' Quina wheezed. 'I softened her up for you.'

Instead Yaz walked slowly between the two facing lines of girls, passing Kola and her hunska partner, passing Wenna and her blonde opponent, and carrying on until she came to a halt before the other gerant girl, last in line. This novice, the biggest of them all, stood a good six and a half feet tall, more than a head taller than Yaz. Her powerful frame strained at the combat tunic she'd put on, muscles bulging. She had the raw-boned, heavy-browed features of all gerants, but an open smile, and calm brown eyes framed by short, slightly curly brown hair.

Yaz squared up against her. Somewhere down the line another novice snorted in scorn.

'Gently, Novice Hellma,' Mistress Blade cautioned. 'But not too gentle.' She brought her hands together for them to begin.

Immediately the gerant girl reached for Yaz, just as Yaz thought she might. Kao's instinct had always been to use his strength directly to dominate a foe. The gerants among the Broken had been similarly disposed to playing to their advantage.

Yaz grabbed Hellma's thick wrist. The past months' changes had robbed Yaz of much of her Ictha strength but enough remained to raise the gerant's brows in surprise and make her strain. She reached with her other arm and Yaz caught that one too, continuing to hold her off as Hellma sought to get a grip on her.

Hellma surged forwards and the other novices backed away as Yaz was driven backwards, her feet ploughing trails through the sand. In a sudden reversal Hellma drew Yaz in and, interposing a muscular thigh, flung her onto her back.

Yaz rolled away, heaving air back into bruised lungs, and got to her feet. She advanced on Hellma. This time the gerant threw punches, slower than the other girls' but still fast, no less direct, and with even more power behind them. Yaz managed to block one, turn away from another, but the third blow made her stagger. A fourth caught the side of her head.

A fifth slammed into her gut. Yaz swung back but Hellma knocked her arm aside and hit her again. Even with the rush of blood in her veins and anger building in her belly, the pain of the blow shocked her.

'Fall down!' Hellma smacked her forearm into Yaz's face and blood started to rush from her nose.

Yaz shook off the hurt and swung again, making contact and winning a grunt from Hellma. The gerant moved in with a sequence of precise punches and once more hauled Yaz across her hip to throw her on her back.

Mistress Blade clapped as Yaz rolled and clambered to her feet. 'Stop!'

Yaz wiped the back of her hand across her upper lip and flicked blood to the sand. 'No.' She advanced on Hellma, who looked helplessly over Yaz's shoulder to the nun.

'Finish it then. If that's what she wants.'

Hellma returned to her fighting stance, and waited. Yaz threw herself forward to grapple, but a big fist sent her reeling back. Hellma followed up, landing punch after punch. 'Fall down! Damn you, fall down and stay down.'

'It's only pain,' Yaz muttered through swelling lips. She shook blood and sweat from her hair, swinging a fist into Hellma's abdomen, the blow taking the gerant by surprise. Yaz landed a glancing blow to Hellma's jaw, and another more solid punch to her ribs. Hellma, losing her serenity, growled and fought back, pummelling Yaz with any number of blows.

'Fall the fuck down!' she snarled and sent Yaz staggering backwards with another heavy fist to the face.

'No.' Yaz shook the dizziness from her head and raised both fists. 'The Ictha die on their feet.'

Hellma frowned, her heavy brow furrowing. In the next moment a grin split her face, showing bloody teeth. She boomed out a laugh. 'The Ictha die on their feet! Ha! I like that!' And she came forward with her arms open. 'We'll call it a draw then, little ice-triber.'

And before Yaz knew it she was hugged then released. There was clapping from both sides and Quina was next to her, holding her up. 'What were you doing, you idiot? You could have got yourself killed! Oh, and you know their language now? How long were you going to keep that a secret? And what happened to "enough"? You stopped me—'

Quina would have kept on with her torrent of talking but as clapping and laughter died away one person's slow, solid clapping continued until all heads turned to the tiered rows of benches where a single observer now sat.

Once she was the focus of their attention, the woman stayed her gnarled hands just before they met in yet another clap and slowly spread them as she rose to her feet. She wore black robes not unlike those of the nuns but her steel-grey hair was uncovered and a large silver tree pendant hung from a chain around her neck.

A twinge of recognition ran through Yaz although Quina showed no reaction. The cold finger continued to run down Yaz's spine: she'd seen this woman before. And since she'd hardly been anywhere but the ice that meant—

'Mother Jeccis, we're honoured.' Mistress Blade made the sign of the tree, something Yaz had seen Mali and others do. 'To what do we owe the pleasure?'

'I heard there had been a miracle! So I came to see the evidence.'

'Jeccis!' Yaz hissed. That's where she knew her from: the Black Rock. There'd been two female priests, and neither could be found after the revolt. Jeccis and Krey. They must have escaped with Eular through the gate in the temple, breaking it behind them. Given the ease with which Jeccis spoke the language, this wasn't her first visit. Like Eular, she'd been a priest in two faiths at once.

'We should leave,' Yaz told Quina. 'That woman's from the Black Rock.'

Quina nodded. 'Can you walk?'

'Of course.' Yaz turned and stumbled. Quina moved quickly to support her. Yaz looked back at Mistress Blade, having difficulty focusing as one of her eyes was swelling badly. 'Thank you. We are going now.'

And together the two of them made their way to the double doors, watched by the amazed novices. Mother Jeccis didn't try to stop them. She watched them from her elevated seat, her dark eyes fixed on Yaz as she pulled the doors shut behind them.

'From the Black Rock?' Quina rounded on Yaz as the doors closed. 'What does she want? I'm not letting them drown us again! You have to promise, Yaz. Not that! You bring your fire and blow us both to pieces if that's the only way.'

Yaz nodded and started towards the scriptorium. All of her hurt now and fighting Hellma had begun to feel like a very stupid idea. 'I won't let them chain us again. Not for anything. I swear.' She leaned on Quina for support. 'If they try it we'll replace their convent with a big, smoking hole.'

And she meant it.

CHAPTER 9

The heavy door of the scriptorium led into a brightly lit chamber where several desks were scattered with things for which Yaz had no name. Later she would know them as parchment, quills, bottles of ink, blotters, trimming knives, brushes and paints for illumination, and myriad other tools of the trade by which thoughts that had been crystallized into words could be permanently bound into the world, copied, copied again, distributed beyond the reach of any fire, and stored on shelves amid a million other thoughts, all waiting for a questing hand and curious eye to set them free.

Nuns sat at two of the desks. One a tall, narrow woman with quill in hand, squinting at the text before her. The other, Sister Owl, gazing calmly at nothing, presumably deep in one of the trances she trained the novices in.

Sister Owl blinked slowly and turned her head towards the advancing ice-tribers.

'No new novice spends long at Sweet Mercy before finding herself on the rough end of a beating. It's one of the harsher lessons we teach here. The world will not go gentle on you and if you are to step back out into it wearing the red or the grey then you must learn to take and return its blows.' She paused and ran her gaze across Yaz. 'That said, I don't, however, recall ever seeing a novice so eager to learn as you, dear.'

'I had my own lesson to teach,' Yaz replied in green-tongue. 'I hope the novices and Mistress Path have learned something about those from the ice.'

'Remarkable!' Sister Owl eased herself from her chair and came across to study Yaz more closely, her already wide eyes becoming almost comically so. 'You've formed a thread-bond with Maliaya. It's the only explanation. There's an echo of her in you and of you in her. Nothing else could explain your mastery of our language.' She frowned. 'Unless you've known it all along – taught on the ice?'

Yaz shook her head. It still felt strange to have the un-familiar words slide off her tongue. She knew that she wasn't saying them quite the way the green-landers did, but the muscles she used to shape them were not used to applying the necessary edges.

'Perhaps you'll have the same aptitude for reading and writing.' Sister Owl waved them to stand either side of her at her desk. She indicated the parchment before her, the pale yellow surface covered in inked symbols.

'There was a priest watching us fight,' Yaz said. 'Mother Jeccis.'

Sister Owl curled her lip. 'Jeccis . . . I've met her before.'

'She comes from the ice. She was with Eular at the Black Rock in service to the Hidden God.'

Sister Owl gave one of her customary slow blinks, considering. 'Well, that is disturbing news. I wonder how many of our priesthood have been living double lives in this mountain of yours.'

'There was only one other,' Yaz said. 'Mother Krey.'

'At least we're not outnumbered then!' The nun held her chin in one wrinkled hand. 'It's a pity you've no proof to lay before the high priest. But the word of two ice-tribers will not go far against that of an archon and a priest. I assume that Eular sent her to check on your demise. She will cause trouble for you here but you're still safer at Sweet Mercy than anywhere else. The best we can do is continue as planned and to hope that your friends return from their mission with this Taproot of yours.' She returned her attention to the desk and directed a finger towards the parchment.

'It's like the Missing's script,' Quina said. 'From the walls!' She reached out to touch it but Sister Owl slapped her hand aside.

'We don't touch.' The nun took up a long, plumed quill and dipped it in the inkwell. With a deft hand she added another word to the parchment, her characters precise and well defined. 'Each symbol is a letter. Where they group together: that's a word. That word is "Ancestor".' She pointed to her addition, still glistening.

Yaz found it hard to concentrate knowing that Mother Jeccis was stalking the convent, seeking to do them harm. She stared at the collection of letters. They were less complex than the Missing's script but had a certain elegance to them. Nothing about the collection of lines screamed 'Ancestor' at her, but given time perhaps they would. The fringes of Mali's mind that still touched hers despite the distance between them would help her unlock the code. And perhaps if Mali were to become lost on the ice again she would fare better against the elements, armed with some of Yaz's instincts.

Sister Owl got out slates and chalks and took them to the back of the room to desks by a door that she said led to a room entirely full of writing, all of it kept in 'books'. Apparently parchment was too precious to practise on and so she set them to copying letters onto the slates. Yaz was relieved to discover that there were things these green-landers considered precious and that not everything was in such plenty here that it could be used without thought.

Quina enjoyed the work and Yaz did too. Neither of them had had the chance to draw before and to wipe away any mistakes then start again. Yaz would have enjoyed it more if she could see out of two eyes rather than one, and if her jaw weren't aching with the echoes of Hellma's punches.

'That girl hit hard,' she muttered, forming the curves of an 'a', the letter being frustratingly close to a circle, but apparently there was another letter that *was* a circle and so the small differences were important.

Even so, time passed more quickly than Yaz had imagined. She liked the smell of the scriptorium and the quiet, there being hardly a sound but the scratch of quills, and Quina's laboured breathing as she struggled to copy letters, tongue wedged between her teeth. Sister Owl moved between them with encouraging words, speaking to them in both languages and getting Quina to repeat her.

When the tolling of the novices' bell, Bray, shattered the silence, Yaz sat up from her work with a start, and immediately regretted it. She seemed to have pulled something in her neck on one of the occasions she was slammed onto her back.

'You're in luck,' Sister Owl said. 'They heat the bathwater on every five-day. Which is today! Every other day it's barely above freezing.'

'Bath?' Yaz repeated the unfamiliar word. Apparently the Ictha had no equivalent.

Sister Owl led them to the exit, waiting for the other two sisters now at work to weight their papers before she opened the door to the breeze. She pointed to a low hall with many small, high windows from which steam was venting as though a hot sea were hidden inside. 'The bathhouse. Your classmates will all be heading there from Blade training. If you hurry you'll beat the rush.'

Quina glanced at Yaz, shrugged, and made for the bath-house with some haste. Two older novices with wet hair emerged from the front door as Yaz watched. She looked back at the scriptorium, but Sister Owl waved her on, and with a sigh she hobbled after her friend.

Steps and a heavy door led into a steam-wreathed room where three more of the most senior novices were tying belt ropes, fastening shoe buckles, or combing their hair, all clearly in a hurry. The floor was wet and some of the flagstones were pierced with many holes to let water drain away.

Quina was already taking off her furs, and she hadn't many to take off. Yaz went to the door at the rear of the changing room and peered through at the long, rectangular pool with a narrow walkway all around. 'They swim here? But why?'

'Don't care! Can't you feel how warm it is?' Quina stepped out of her hide trousers then held them before her to shield her modesty as the older girls left, shooting glances and smirking.

'They swim naked?' Yaz asked, aghast.

'None of their clothes were wet,' Quina said, showing her teeth in a white grin. She looked painfully thin without her furs. Dropping her hides on the bench, she slipped past Yaz, hunska-quick, the black line of her hair where it reached down between her shoulder blades in stark contrast to the whiteness of her skin.

Yaz stripped hurriedly to her mole-fish skins, not wanting to be caught doing it when the others arrived. She was opening the pool-room door when she heard Quina's splash. She walked in, not sure of her footing on the wet stone, squinting to see Quina through the steam. She wasn't worried about her. All the ice tribes got their food from the hot seas, and all of them learned to swim early. Boats got overturned all the time, occasionally by whales and other large denizens of the deep, but most often when ice shelving from the cliffs sent great waves rolling from one shore to the other.

Quina surfaced on her back and let loose a long, sensuous moan.

'Get in here! It's . . . it's . . . mmmm.'

Yaz stayed where she was.

'They'll mock you,' Quina said without judgement.

Yaz felt her cheeks flush. She turned away, tearing off the mole-fish skins. They were too warm to wear in the southern heat anyway. She wouldn't need to be sewn back into them until she returned to the ice. Slowly, she backed towards the edge and started to lower herself into the water.

As soon as she felt the heat something melted inside her and she just let go, understanding Quina's sigh of pleasure in that instant. She submerged then surfaced, floating face down in the water like a dead thing. She'd never felt so deliciously, luxuriously warm. This, she thought, must be what babies feel in their mother's womb, and why they are so famously hard to eject.

'It's like we died and the gods took us,' Quina said.

Yaz managed a grunt.

'Glad you came?' Quina asked.

'I would have walked twice as far for this.' Yaz meant it too.

The Grey Class novices arrived with a succession of splashes and considerable laughter and chatter. They soon quietened and took to floating in the steaming water, letting the heat soak away the aches and pains of their fight training. Wenna surfaced close to Yaz, and a moment later, spouting water, so did Hellma, the gerant who had used Yaz as a punching bag.

The bigger girl winced as she studied Yaz's injured face. 'You were brave. Stupid, maybe. But brave. My friends call me Hell.'

'You should have told me you spoke our language.' Wenna sounded cross.

'I am sorry.' Yaz shaped the unfamiliar words. She didn't want to reveal the true reason for her sudden expertise. 'Mali has been teaching me but it was only recently that I started to get it.'

'And her?' Wenna looked towards a mist-shrouded blob that was probably Quina.

Yaz improvised. 'Quina is very fast at some things, slower in this one.'

'And maybe Maliaya is your special friend?' Hellma grinned.

Yaz frowned, confused. Did the girl know about their thread-bond?

Hellma's grin broadened. 'Never mind. Mali's a good friend to have. Her family are very rich, did you know? Not as rich as the Tacsis, of course.' Here she glanced at Wenna, who stared back, narrowing her eyes. 'But rich enough. What about you two? Are you princesses on the ice, living in ice castles? Or peasants living in ice huts?'

Yaz squinted at Hellma out of her good eye, confused by these words and concepts. Hellma laughed and changed the subject. 'You can take a hit, girl! None of this lot let me land one. I'm not really cut out for fighting.'

'No?' Yaz raised a brow and ran an eye over the few of Hellma's muscles visible above the water.

The gerant shrugged. 'I'm going to be a Holy Sister.'

'To pray and copy books?' Yaz couldn't see the attraction.

Hellma grinned. 'There'll be some praying, I guess. And I'm not so great with my letters. But there's more to the convent than that. It's a family. I want to work in the vineyard, grow grapes, make wine. Be with my sisters. Even Wenna, if she stays!' She laughed and splashed Wenna, who tried to scowl but couldn't quite manage it in the face of Hellma's good humour and splashed her in return.

Yaz lay back in the water. Something in Hellma's ambition reminded her of Jerrig, the Broken's vast harvester who had dedicated his days to tending a crop. 'I hope you get to grow grapes, Hell – whatever they are. It's better than being a killer.'

Emerging from the pool and braving the changing room naked tested Yaz's courage more than fighting Hellma had. But none of the novices paid her and Quina much attention, save for Wenna, who rose, picking up a pile of clothing from the bench beside her.

'Sister Owl sent these for you.' She pushed her burden into Yaz's wet arms.

Quina squealed with excitement and took the top half of the pile from Yaz. 'Nun clothes!'

Yaz put hers down on a clear piece of bench and tried to make sense of the strange items. Mali had told her they were made from the fur of a creature called a sheep, removed from the underlying hide and woven cunningly together to form flexible layers. Other items were made by weaving plant fibres together rather like the Ictha plaited their hair. That was technically interesting but not of great help when it came to working out what to do with individual items.

'Those go on first.' Hellma nodded to the bundle of thin

white cloth in Yaz's left hand. 'Small clothes. Don't worry. I'd never seen half this stuff when I got here. I was sold out of some no-name village. Hadn't even seen shoes. We just wrapped our feet in skins.'

With advice from Hellma, Yaz and Quina struggled into their various layers and laboured over lacing their shoes before finally pulling their novice habits around them. Quina finished last despite her swift fingers – a case of more haste and less speed being required. She straightened up, looked at Yaz, and burst into giggles.

'You look like one of them!'

'So do you!'

'Yes, but you *really* look like one of them!'

Yaz shook her head and glanced around. Only Hellma and Wenna remained with them. The rest of the class had streamed out, presumably bound for another class or perhaps yet more eating.

'Where now?' Yaz asked.

'We have a break in the novice cloister, and then Spirit class,' Wenna said. 'Sister Owl said she has other things to do so you two are free until tomorrow. Just don't be late to the dormitory after eighth bell.'

Yaz and Quina followed the other two out and went with them to the cloister.

'That priest – Mother Jeccis,' Yaz said. 'Does she visit the convent often?'

Wenna shook her head. 'I've never seen her before.'

'Priests come and go here,' Hellma added. 'They might want to consult the library or speak with specific nuns, or ask for the help of one of the sisterhoods.'

Wenna led the way under an archway leading to an enclosed square. Yaz glanced around at the convent buildings before following, half expecting to see Mother Jeccis watching her from some shadowed corner. She saw nothing though, just a few younger novices hurrying along and a chicken rushing wildly, wings a-flap, to get out of their way. Yaz turned back, a sigh escaping her, and went on through.

A tree grew at the centre of the cloister square and Quina had come to a halt, staring at it. Yaz also stumbled to a halt. 'It's so big.'

It wasn't big on the scale of the ice city, where the towers reached a mile into the sky. But those towers had exceeded her ability to comprehend them. The tree was big on a scale she could understand.

'It's not really,' Hellma said. 'It's just a young oak. A hundred years from now it'll be pretty much full grown. Then you won't be able to stretch your arms around it.'

Yaz watched the leaves fluttering in the wind. A countless horde of them, like fish in a shoal. Quina walked past her, one hand extended, reaching out to touch though she was still yards from the object of her fascination.

'And all these tables and chairs and doors . . . you make them all from trees?' Yaz couldn't see how it might be done.

'We do,' Hellma said without mockery.

Yaz left Hellma and went to join Quina, standing with her hands on the trunk of the great tree. Despite the constant motion above them, the dance of leaves, the swaying of branches, Yaz could feel no movement where her hands pressed against the rough bark before her.

'We did it.' Quina turned to her, eyes bright. 'We touched a tree. What would they say on the ice if we went back to them? They'd call us liars. Say we were mad, or full of devils from the black ice.'

'We did. And they would.' Yaz nodded. She tried to imagine Quell's reaction; she wanted him here to see this, to see her.

'It's not how I imagined it. None of it is, the trees or the people.' Quina shook her head. 'Not better or worse, just different.'

Yaz shrugged. She had never been able to paint any picture in her mind of what might await them. Not until Erris had shown her. She looked around at the cloister. A covered walkway ran the length of the square's perimeter, joined to the enclosing buildings. Most of the novices were sitting on benches under the shelter of the walkway's tiled roof.

'I never imagined that life could be so easy here.' She hadn't imagined that in consequence their main preoccupation would be making war and learning to kill. 'Or so dangerous.' It seemed that when the world stopped trying so hard to kill humanity, people themselves stepped up to fill the void. That saddened her in ways she had no words to express in either language.

When Yaz and Quina finally came away from the oak at the centre of the cloister square, the other novices were already leaving for their next lessons. The anticipated bell sounded as Yaz reached Wenna and Hellma.

'We're off to Spirit class.' Wenna said it with dread as if about to leave the tent naked on a polar night.

'Sister Mace isn't so bad.' Hellma shrugged.

'You can tell Hell's planning to be a Holy!' Wenna shook her head. 'We'll meet you at the refectory for the evening meal after seventh bell. Don't get into trouble.'

'We will be good,' Yaz promised. Green-tongue still felt awkward in her mouth. She translated for Quina, who laughed with genuine amusement, causing Wenna to turn and frown at them on her way out.

Finally they had the cloister to themselves. The day was dying and shadows had swallowed the square from side to side.

'So?' Quina asked.

Yaz eyed the growing darkness. The less she could see beneath the arches of the walkway the more she imagined that Mother Jeccis was standing there, watching them. 'We need to break into the Persus Hall,' Yaz said.

'Where?'

'The place where they sentenced us to death.'

'Hells no!' Quina shook her head. 'I meant: So, shall we sleep or swim before the third meal? They call it "dinner", do they?'

'Eular left my stardust on the floor there,' Yaz continued, ignoring Quina. 'And with a priest from the Black Rock sharing the convent with us, I really think I need a star to steer us by.'

CHAPTER 10

Thurin

'Her whole clan lives here, right?' Thurin hurried along at Erris's heels as they followed Mali and the elderly servant from the kitchen. He clutched a string of sausages in each hand and tried to hiss his question while chewing.

'Her immediate family. Seven people, I understand,' Erris answered. 'But most of them will be at the big house in the family estate. This is just the townhouse where they stay on visits to the capital.'

'Incredible.' They had already passed so many doors that Thurin could believe all of the Broken might live within the building and not feel crowded. The difference between Mali's family and those living in the shacks they'd seen earlier put Thurin in mind of the difference between the lives of the Black Rock's priests and those of the Broken, though even that separation seemed less marked than the one before him.

'Where are these clothes?' It felt as if they'd already walked a mile. Mali's idea to dress them like the locals was a good one. What you wore here seemed to convey all manner of information about your social status. Back in the Broken's caves it had all been about keeping warm and things had seemed much simpler. 'We need to hurry!' The servant's pace was proving infuriatingly slow. 'We've already wasted hours. Eular could be handing Taproot over as we speak.'

'We're taking an indirect path,' Erris said. 'Mali is keen not to encounter any of her family. She's told Johan here that is because it might endanger them.'

'But?' Thurin could hear the 'but' in Erris's voice.

'It may also be that we would be hard to explain.' He gave a wry smile. 'In any event, we can't go to the rest house until morning if we wish to be admitted as visitors rather than attacked as intruders. Eular has no particular reason for prioritizing Taproot over the meeting with the high priest. He's obviously mistrusted in some quarters of the Church so he won't want to endanger his relationship with his only superior. And even if he had suspicions he must be pretty sure we're dead. Either way, we're going to have to trust that he will put off any visit to the undercity until after his audience with the high priest. So we may as well do this right – get ourselves dressed like two lords – then get some sleep.'

The servant, Johan, brought them to a small room with a single narrow window. Another servants' room. On a table several piles of fabric were stacked in a haphazard fashion, along with a collection of small, bright steel devices for which Thurin had no name.

'Hides . . . mended . . . here,' Mali said.

Thurin blinked. 'Did you . . . did you just speak my language?'

Mali offered a quick grin. 'Yes.'

Johan opened a chest and started to take out clothes every bit as complex and colourful as those being worn on the grandest of the streets that Mali had led them through earlier.

'These belong to Mali's brothers,' Erris translated. 'They're here for minor repairs, or alterations for reasons of fashion, or just because they've been abandoned in favour of other, newer items. He says that if it will help Mali then we are free to take what we need.'

'Good.' Thurin reached out to take the garment that Johan was offering him. It looked needlessly complicated but he could at least see that it had arms.

Erris began to take off his boots and Mali turned away quickly, proving to be every bit as bashful as an Ictha when it came to naked flesh. Thurin shrugged off his jacket with a grin and let the furs fall to the ground. He remembered how shocked Yaz had been on her first visit to the drying cave when she realized that she would have to undress. He had supposed that Mali, closeted away in her convent with only the company of women, might be more curious about the subject of men, but she stood with her gaze resolutely fixed on the room's main entrance.

'How do I . . .?' Thurin paused halfway through the process of struggling into the item he'd been given. He had one arm through one tight sleeve but now lacked access to the space and angles required to thread the other arm through the other sleeve.

Mali twitched and half turned before recovering herself. Johan came to Thurin's aid, guiding him through the movements needed. By the time Thurin was sealed, with a series of small pegs that seemed to be called 'buttons', into the garment that Johan referred to as a 'shirt', Erris was nearly completely clothed, seemingly far more familiar with the thin, close-fitting items and the variety of complex fastenings necessary to keep them in place.

'Let me!' Mali finally turned and bent to help Thurin with the cords that secured his new footwear in place. 'I . . .' Once more she rediscovered her lack of a hand.

'It's all right.' Thurin tried to sound kind. 'I can do it.' He fumbled to make a knot. 'Almost.'

Johan returned from the chest with something new and inexplicable between his hands.

'What in the hells is that?' Thurin finished with his boot and straightened.

'I believe', Erris said, 'it's some kind of hat. A rather foolish-looking one, if I'm honest.'

'Expensive,' Mali said. 'Is all that matters.'

Erris pursed his lips and nodded. 'I guess she's right. The object of this exercise is to look rich. Money opens doors. Money turns away suspicion.' He reached out and set the hat upon his head.

Mali laughed and made a spinning motion with a raised finger.

'The other way?' Erris rolled his eyes and turned the hat through a half-circle. 'That's even worse!'

Mali made a flipping motion with her hand.

'Seriously?' Erris turned the hat upside down.

Mali nodded solemnly.

'You look like you have four rats fighting on your head.' Thurin boggled at the idea that the people of Verity thought such a thing might improve how they looked.

Erris frowned. 'I have only one compensation.'

'Which is?'

He nodded towards Johan, now lifting something else from the great coffer of discarded clothing. 'Yours is worse.'

They slept in an unoccupied servants' chamber. Thurin considered it by some margin to be the most luxurious room he'd ever slept in. The walls and floor were flatter and smoother than any within the Black Rock and nothing like the makeshift huts of the Broken: scavenged boards set up on raw rock beneath dripping ice. The bed proved soft and sported blankets of some kind of woven hair that were wonderfully warm. He pulled them over himself despite the fact that he could comfortably sleep naked in such heat. He just wanted to feel their weight and thickness.

For a while he lay back and watched the darkness, listening to Mali's breathing in the bed to his left and Erris's silence in the bed to the right. He thought of his people scraping their mean existence from the starlit ice, and of the multitudes here, warm and fed and free to wander in a way that neither the Broken beneath the ice nor the clans on top of it could ever imagine. He pushed off his covers and wondered about Yaz and Quina. Were they both dreaming now? And if not, what thoughts might be running through their minds?

Sleep refused to take him for the longest time. The darkness seemed to press on him like the black waters in which they had tried to drown him, and it felt as though he had to press it back or be engulfed. In the end, though, it was the memory of his exhaustion as he crawled from the sinkhole's ladder and lay beneath the all-encompassing blaze of the moon that pulled him down. He sank into a private oblivion and dreamed of nothing at all.

Dawn came fingering through the shutters and found the three of them dressing once more, Mali in her habit, Erris and Thurin in their unfamiliar finery.

'Wrong way round.' Mali spoke the ice-tongue with greater fluency than she had shown the night before, as if Yaz's mind had supplied her with more words while they slumbered.

Thurin sighed and started to wriggle his way back out of the shirt. He felt a pang of jealousy at the thought of Mali sharing Yaz's dreams. It seemed an unearned intimacy. He had trekked a thousand miles across the ice with her and Mali had joined them just days ago, plucked from a picture.

He laced his shoes, struggling to recreate the bows that Erris had effortlessly tied on his own. The things were a fraction too small and cramped his toes. They felt too thin to be of use. An invitation to losing toes. But this wasn't the ice, he reminded himself. Here nothing seemed to freeze and everything baked when the moonlight came.

'How do I look?' He stood up and spread his arms.

'Handsome,' Mali said.

Thurin felt a heat rise in his cheeks although the girl was just a child. 'I meant will I pass as one of you?'

'As long as you don't open your mouth,' Erris said.

Johan returned to escort them from the house. They followed him along lantern-lit corridors, passing servants bustling this way and that, carrying silver trays, linens, coal in buckets, all bound on separate and complex tasks. Thurin tried not to stare.

Even in the areas of the house not frequented by the family to whom all this effort was dedicated there were marvels everywhere. The green-landers, at least in this great city, seemed to have time to inject artistry into all corners of their lives. Plaster mouldings hidden in ceiling corners where few eyes would ever roam were fashioned in swirls and patterns that fascinated the eye. Metalwork around fireplaces showed curling iron leaves; even a poker was twisted and ended in a fanciful knob that looked like it might open into some new marvel.

'Quickly.' Mali waved them through a door into the dazzle of the day while Johan watched them from among the storeroom's shelves, arms folded, eyes stern, as if charging both Thurin and Erris to protect this errant shoot of the Glosis clan.

Thurin stumbled out into the warmth and light of the day, squinting against the brightness. Mali hurried them across the gravel and into the greenery. By day the colours were shockingly vivid, the motion and complexity of the bushes both daunted and mesmerized Thurin. All around him the thick trunks of trees rose, branching above his head into innumerable parts, each supporting a green weight of leaves.

As they advanced towards the unseen outer wall Thurin discovered that green wasn't the only colour on display. 'What are these?' He trailed a hand cautiously over a long and tapered object, growing from a green stem but a brilliant red. It looked almost like one of the fruiting bodies of the fungi that the Broken farmed, though their colours were muted compared to these.

'Flower.' Mali waved him on urgently. 'Opens under the moon.'

'Bioengineered.' Erris passed him. 'Evolution and artificial satellites keep to different chronologies.'

Thurin wondered if he were learning green-tongue as swiftly as Mali was learning ice-tongue, because clearly Erris wasn't talking his language but he had seemed to recognize a word or two. He moved on, seeing more of the closed flowers in various sizes and colours. Reaching the wall, he vowed to return one night and see them bloom in the blaze of the focus moon.

With Erris's help all of them managed to get over the wall without Thurin having to exert his ice-work. The part of his mind that drew on the source of that power still felt a little raw from the night's exertions, but sleep had helped. If he had his way he would keep from using the talent for a while. Likely he would not have his way. By contrast, the part of his mind that drew on the source of his fire skills felt overfull and ached not from use but from neglect. It often seemed to Thurin that

103

the two talents dwelt in separate halves of his brain, constantly engaged in a low-level war for control. Not unlike the Broken and the Tainted had been for the generations when they fought for sole ownership of the ice caves.

Verity opened before them, the sun burning huge and red, seeming to consume half the sky and nearly free of the rooftops. Shadows slanted towards them, painting the wide street in stripes.

By day the city amazed Thurin more than ever. The night had focused his attention on one overwhelming thing at a time. Daylight opened up distant views and crowded a thousand questions into every glance. So much so that instead of seeking answers Thurin kept his gaze on the stone-flagged road and followed Mali more closely than ever.

'That's better,' Erris said. 'Men of our standing wouldn't walk around the city staring at everything like they were seeing it for the first time. The rich are aloof. They don't spare any attention for the lesser orders. But neither, I suspect, do they become fascinated with the ground in front of them. Try walking around like you own the place. Or we could get spotted.'

'You think there'll be more of those monks?' Thurin asked.

'Possibly. Mali says there aren't many of them in the city at any one time and that even an archon can't just tell them to drop what they're doing and take his orders. But depending on how much sway Eular holds, there may be more, yes. And even if you do a much better job of not looking like a peasant stuffed into a jacket that cost more than your village, the Grey Brothers are masters of disguise – which means they'll be pretty good at seeing past it too. Let me take the lead.'

Thurin's anger surged, bringing with it his old resentment of this perfect, ancient, and ageless man that Yaz had somehow fished out of an echoingly empty ruin. He stopped in the street and turned on Erris. 'You think you're so much less likely to be spotted?'

'Well.' The older man smiled, not seeming to take offence. 'I was thinking that not speaking the language recommended you for the back lines. But, as it happens, I can also do this . . .' He stretched out a hand before him and, as Thurin watched, the skin tone began to lighten, slowly but noticeably, shading away from its customary deep brown. 'In addition I can reposition my jaw, cheekbones, and even flex my skull if necessary. Though that will take a little longer.'

Thurin tried to keep the grin from his face. 'All right. You win. You can lead the way into danger.'

CHAPTER 11

The Church rest house was not a house. It was far larger than the mansion in which Mali's small family rattled around. Thurin positioned it somewhere between a palace and a city district. Like the whole city, it had its own surrounding wall, and within that perimeter a varied collection of buildings.

Gaining admittance proved remarkably easy, dressed as they were and in the company of a novice in her habit. Thurin was not required to speak and Erris too might have passed without opening his mouth, though he did volunteer a few unintelligible words after Mali had said her piece to the Church guards at the gate.

Even at this early hour the compound was crowded. More of the Church guard stalked the compound within, clad in flamboyant armour and ceremonial plumes. Once again, Thurin had to wrest his eyes from innumerable intricacies of decoration that suggested these people had too much time on their hands. Despite his efforts, he still found himself staring as an elderly priest shambled past in robes that bulged to such a degree that it seemed several shorter people might be hiding beneath them.

'Thurin!' Erris hissed.

'What's wrong with him?' Thurin hissed back.

'He's just fat.'

'Fat?' Thurin didn't understand the word.

Erris – who currently looked a lot less like Erris than he had when they left Mali's house – raised an eyebrow. 'It's what happens when you eat a lot more than you need for a long time.'

'Ah . . .' Thurin wasn't sure whether he was joking. But a Church guard leaning in the shade of a tall building was eyeing him curiously through the Y-shaped slot of his overly ornate helm so Thurin decided to let the subject drop and move on.

Mali led the way. They circled a hall that served as a residence for visiting Holy Brothers. Twice. She muttered something to Erris.

'Where's this archon's residence?' Thurin hissed.

'She doesn't know. But the important thing is to keep walking as if you have a goal in mind. If you look lost it draws attention. And suspicion.'

Mali chose a new direction and they walked across a wide, tree-lined square with a towering statue at the centre. Thurin risked a glance as they passed. The statue was of a man, or a woman, smooth and devoid of features. It stood in sharp contrast to the detailed ornamentation to be found every-where else – even on the guttering of buildings where stone animals every bit as strange as the horse waited with open mouths to vomit rainwater away from the walls.

'The Ancestor,' Mali muttered. 'Don't stare.'

Thurin quickened his pace, keen to put space between himself and this Ancestor. The Broken and the ice clans had no statues of their gods, but, like the priests of the Black Rock with their Hidden God, Arges, it seemed the green-landers liked to fashion their deity in stone. He hoped that the Ancestor wasn't also a malevolent spirit haunting his temple, but going on experience he wasn't about to take it for granted.

Mali paused to ask a question of two black-robed monks engaged in a discussion over what looked to Thurin like a square of strange white cloth covered in black squiggles. One of them peered down at her from beneath bushy grey eyebrows and waved dismissively towards the far corner.

'Archon Eular should be this way.' Mali set off towards a tree-lined alley that led out of the square between two tall buildings.

Before she reached it, a solidly built woman stepped into her path. Like many within the compound she wore a black robe, but her hair was neither covered like a nun's nor shaved like a monk's, and a silver amulet in the shape of a tree hung around her neck. She asked Mali a sharp question.

Erris leaned towards Thurin and muttered, 'One of Eular's friends. From the Black Rock.'

Mali stammered an answer and the woman barked another question. Mali had both hands, or rather one hand and her stump, under her folded arms, hugging herself tight as if cold, and the priest peered suspiciously at her more than once, as if trying to see the hidden injury.

The woman seemed on the point of making another demand when Erris interrupted, perhaps concerned that she would order Mali to unfold her arms. The priest turned her gaze on him and Thurin noticed that she had one brown eye and one a pale blue, neither of them the least bit friendly. The mismatched pair glanced his way from beneath a heavy brow before returning to Erris. Her face was a convincing argument for gerant blood, raw-boned and brutal, but Thurin overtopped her.

Whatever Erris said seemed to unsettle the priest. He'd spoken with a calm authority and now brushed at some imagined dirt on the rich fabric of his sleeve before walking away without seeking permission. Mali followed, and Thurin, forcing his mouth into a smile, hurried after them.

'That', said Erris as they passed between the first of the trees, 'was Mother Krey, seemingly a priest of both the Hidden God and this Ancestor Mali's people keep. She was part of our reception committee when we arrived at the Black Rock.'

'Wasn't there another one who escaped at the end?' Thurin asked.

'Mother Jeccis. An older woman. We should keep an eye out for her too.'

Thurin shivered. He didn't want any reminders of his time in the Black Rock or of his fight to find his own way into it while the wind tried to kill him. Luck had saved them this time. Erris had changed his face and Thurin hadn't met any of the priests save the regulator whose long and corrupt life had ended in the mountain.

'Do we have to worry about her following us?' Thurin asked.

'Yes.' Mali quickened her pace.

Thurin glanced back to see Krey standing where they'd left her, still staring after them. With a mental effort he exerted his ice-work to stop the legs of a large man heading past the priest. A small shove as the man toppled proved sufficient to angle his fall into Mother Krey, bringing her to the ground and immediately occasioning half a dozen other people to crowd around offering help.

'Quickly! Let's move!' Thurin hurried past Mali.

The gates of the four archons' residences all faced onto a wide square sporting an elaborate fountain at its centre. Mali

109

brought them to gaze at the stone confection where water spouted from the mouths of surprised-looking fish. The rest house, as well as being a place for clerical travellers to stay when visiting the capital, appeared to be a place where elderly priests, scribes too ancient to push a quill, and other Church dignitaries now crumbled by age came to fritter away their twilight years. Old men and women shuffled here and there around the great square as if they had no particular destination in mind, now and then sparing glances for Thurin and the others, laden with that particular disapproval that the elderly often reserve for those still impertinently holding onto youth.

Each residence had an outer wall, presumably to ensure the archons' privacy lest some minor cleric wanted to drop by unannounced – though these walls looked sufficient to stop small armies unless they came equipped with lengthy ladders.

'That one.' She nodded towards the easterly gates. It wouldn't have mattered which gate she had indicated: they were all tall works of wrought iron, curling and twisting to several times the height of a man and each guarded by four armoured guards, plumes waving in the breeze.

'We'll just do what we did at your house last night,' Thurin suggested.

The other two nodded and Mali led off between Eular's residence and its neighbour to the left. They followed the wall where possible, keeping to its shadow. The rest house compound was more crowded than the pre-dawn streets of the aristocracy and offered fewer chances to overcome a wall unseen. They were heading towards structures that Mali indicated as belonging to one or other faction within the Church: scribes' hall, abbots' manse, and, closest, the personal guard barracks. The wind brought an animal smell from the barracks that reminded Thurin of Eular's horse but there were none of the beasts apparent, just a low trough containing dirty water from which they might drink.

Thurin kept glancing round, sure that at any moment Mother Krey would rediscover them or an alarm bell would ring out as it had at the convent to herald Eular's arrival. He looked up at the wall looming over them. 'We should hurry!'

'Here?' Mali asked.

'Not here.' Erris shook his head. 'Too many eyes on us.'

There didn't seem to be any better alternatives though.

'We need a distraction . . .' Thurin tried to imagine something.

'You could start a fire?' Erris suggested, nodding to the smoking chimneys of the abbots' manse.

'No!' Mali looked shocked.

Thurin shrugged. He could understand. These were her people even if some of them were infiltrators. 'Maybe I could bring down part of a building?'

Erris frowned. 'They're not made of ice, you know . . .'

'Watch!' Thurin grinned, glad for once to know something that Erris didn't. He furrowed his brow and a thin snake of water slithered out of the horse trough. He kept it on the ground, flowing across the flagstones, following the joins so as to be less noticeable. It took effort, as much as lifting hundreds of times the weight. He focused all of his brain on the complex task of keeping different parts of the snake moving in different directions as it wound its way across to the abbots' manse. The tail end left the horse trough with the water level several inches lower while the head end was still only halfway to the manse.

Mali and Erris purposefully avoided watching his progress to avoid drawing the attention of passing clerics to the travelling water, though he could tell that both very much wanted to look.

The snake hurried up the side of the building at a point where it looked likely that rainwater would descend. On reaching the sloping tiles it made a more direct line towards the nearest chimney, spiralled around it and yard by yard vanished into the smoking hole.

'You're going to block it?' Erris hissed.

'No.' The idea hadn't occurred to Thurin but he supposed it might also work, filling a room below with smoke and eventually bringing any abbots within coughing their way into the open with streaming eyes. 'This.'

Now he reached out, closed his fist, and drew it rapidly in towards his chest. The action helped his mind focus. The water he'd formed into a ball inside the chimney near the top now jerked towards him, some spraying out into the sky. He pulled harder, grunting with effort, and slowly at first, almost imperceptibly, the chimney leaned towards him then with a loud retort broke free. The heavy cylinder fell ponderously onto the tiled roof, rolled to the gutter with a great clattering and fell in a shower of broken tiles. The crash as it hit the ground and shattered into a thousand pieces was very satisfying.

Every head turned towards the crash. Most of the half-dozen people in sight began to move towards the spot where the chimney had landed – as if collectively they might assemble the shards and repair the damage.

'Quick! Do it now!' Erris said.

A sharp pain blossomed behind Thurin's eyes as he lifted himself swiftly to the top of the wall. Erris practically threw Mali at him and he barely caught her with his ice-work. Both of them began to fall down the far side as Thurin took physical hold of the girl and cushioned their impact on the flagstones beneath.

There were perhaps ten yards between the wall and the side of the mansion it surrounded. All bare and exposed. Without warning, two creatures came tearing around the corner with deadly speed, their claws scrabbling at the stone floor to make the turn. It took Thurin a moment to understand what they were. The Broken brought down tales of dogs with them from the surface but Thurin had never laid eyes on the creatures until his brief encounter with an eidolon in the ice city above Haydies. These were not like the sled dogs that the eidolon had torn apart for their flesh. They were perhaps as large but instead of long silver-white fur they had sleek black hides, and their heads seemed bigger, blunter, more full of teeth.

The silence of their rush was both terrifying and mesmerizing. Up above him Thurin heard Erris hit the far side of the wall, fail to catch hold of the top and fall back outside with a muffled curse. Mali snapped into her fighting stance, but what she could do against two such masses of frothing ferocity Thurin couldn't imagine. Still without so much as a howl both dogs launched themselves into the air in a last great bound that would end with them hammering into Mali and Thurin, each missile a sleek mass of muscle and teeth.

CHAPTER 12

The dog aimed at Thurin's throat had foam-flecked jowls, rows of gleaming white teeth, and a wild, maniacal look in its eye. Not since the hoola's attack on the ice had Thurin felt so like prey. Terror threatened to paralyse him. And whatever gruesome end awaited him would surely also be visited upon Mali.

At the last moment Thurin's mind unlocked. He seized hold of both hounds with his ice-work and launched them over the wall, making some attempt at a soft landing. The pair of them sailed over Erris as he reached the top of the wall on his second attempt. A moment later he was over and dropped to land at Mali's side.

'Flying dogs?' Erris turned towards Thurin with a questioning look.

Thurin shrugged. 'A fallen chimney won't keep them distracted for long.'

'Neither will dogs,' Mali said.

'She's right.' Erris crossed to the building and took hold of the shutters over one of its many windows. 'We need to do this quickly.'

114

Thurin glanced left and right. Dozens of windows studded the wall, both at ground level and on the first storey. The plan which in Thurin's mind had wavered back and forth several times between 'crazy' and 'it might just work' had returned firmly to crazy. 'It's a big house and a small box. Plus, if he's still here he'll probably have it on him.'

'I should get a better sense of where it is when we're closer to it.' Erris pulled slowly until the shutter's hinges surrendered to his strength. Faint screams reached them from the far side of the wall.

'Me too,' Thurin muttered. 'When I see it I'll know exactly where it is.'

Erris reached for the window, which, like those of the richest houses, comprised dozens of small diamonds of glass leaded together within a rectangular wooden frame. Mali knocked his arm aside and moved in close, holding her knife. 'Put the shutter back on. Stealth! No one must know.'

While a slightly shamefaced Erris pushed the shutter's metal fittings back into the stonework, Mali worked dexterously on the window with her thin blade. Thurin watched for more hounds, nervous and wondering if the green-landers used still more fearsome animals to guard their homes. Hoola perhaps? He was on the point of asking about hoola when Mali stepped back and the whole window swung miraculously out. Mali leaned in, checked the room beyond then scrambled through unaided.

'Come on!' She beckoned with her stump.

Thurin clambered after her, followed by Erris, who closed the shutter, returning the room to a gloom broken only by what light found its way through the slats. Next he fully closed the window, locking it with the catch that Mali had somehow defeated. The archon's house wasn't dissimilar to

115

the grandeur of Mali's family home but the walls to either side were lined with shelving packed with . . . something . . . that looked nothing like the glittering treasures the Glosis had displayed at every opportunity.

'Books,' said Erris mysteriously and crossed quickly to the door.

Thurin followed, marvelling at the softness underfoot. The entire floor had been covered in some kind of thick, patterned fabric. He wondered how those raised in such luxury, shielded from all the hardships of the world, would cope should they ever find themselves in the kinds of trouble that had characterized his own life of late.

Joining Erris by the door, Thurin could hear a faint but unearthly wailing. 'What is it?'

Erris held a finger to his lips as Mali set her ear to the door to listen. They gave her several moments of silence.

'It's not the type of sound that I expected to hear anywhere above ground,' Erris muttered. 'That's technology at work. Something from a much earlier age. My time maybe. Or even before.' He tried the door handle. 'Locked.'

'Don't break it.' Mali knelt and brought her eye level with the keyhole.

Thurin had expected her to produce some kind of tool from the inner pockets of her habit and then start poking at the hidden mechanism within the lock. Instead she stared at it intensely for long enough that Thurin was about to interrupt with a question when she suddenly reached forward as if plucking something from the air and the lock surrendered with a soft click.

They moved cautiously through the dimly lit mansion. It had a deserted air about it, as if it hadn't been used for a long time. Clearly Eular, lacking eyes, had no need for the place to sparkle or for the many lamps and candles to be lit, so the servants had kept the illumination to the minimum required for them not to trip over things in the dark.

Erris led them in the direction of the strange wailing. Thurin reached out with his ice-sense, trying to feel for anyone nearby as he had when avoiding the guards within the Black Rock. The mansion was largely empty. Only once did he have to pull Erris back to allow someone to go by without seeing them. He caught a glimpse of the person as they passed the end of the corridor, a young woman carrying a silver tray. The scent of food in the covered dishes reached his nostrils and it smelled even better than the pantry at Mali's home. His stomach rumbled.

'Two people ahead on the left,' Thurin warned as they reached another corridor. The wailing was louder now. 'They're not moving. Just standing there.'

'Guarding something, maybe.' Mali advanced to the corner and knelt in the shadows by the edge. Cautiously she peered into the more brightly lit corridor and then withdrew. 'Two men. Armed. Standing before a door.'

'Maybe Eular's in there?' Thurin said.

Erris pursed his lips. 'I'm getting the sense that Taproot's box definitely is. In fact it's probably the thing making that awful racket.'

'Why would he do that?' Thurin had to admit that the sound grated at his ears. It wouldn't take long to become very irritating.

'To stop Eular taking the box everywhere he goes. To make Eular put it under guard somewhere out of earshot.' Erris started towards the corner, balling his fists.

'Wait.' Mali caught his arm.

'She's right,' Thurin whispered. 'She's right,' he repeated more loudly, realizing that the guards standing closer to the wailing box wouldn't be able to hear him. 'How quickly will you be able to silence them? Especially without killing them? If either of them has hunska blood the chances are they can raise the alarm before you get to them.'

'You think you can knock their heads together from here?' Erris asked.

Thurin frowned. His earlier efforts had already strained the part of his mind that provided the muscle behind his ice-work, and to crash the two men together in a way that would render them unconscious rather than just hurt or dead would require a finer touch and more experience than he possessed. 'Maybe?'

Mali puffed air through her lips and shook her head as if the two men towering over her were fractious children. 'Stealth! Not violence.' She pushed between them and returned to the corner, peering around once more.

Thurin and Erris exchanged glances. It was true that both their methods would have left a trail that could not be erased. Mali still clearly intended to leave without anyone ever knowing they had been there at all.

She stared down the corridor, employing the same intensity with which she had studied the lock earlier. As if the two men were puzzles that she could undo. It took longer this time. Long enough for Thurin to consider putting his fingers in his ears to block out the box's increasingly annoying siren. This time, when she reached out to pull an invisible thread, Mali used her missing hand and Thurin had to imagine the ghost of her fingers plucking at the air. There was no click, just an exclamation from one of the unseen guards and a swift exchange, followed by the sounds of running feet.

Mali moved back, straightened, and massaged her temples.

'What happened?' Thurin asked.

'He had to go,' she said, hiding a grin.

'Go?'

'To the privy.' Mali bit her lip and turned back to the corner. 'Now for the other one.'

It took less time for the second guard to suddenly decide that he urgently needed to be elsewhere. He ran off after his comrade and Mali stepped out into the now-vacant corridor, beckoning Thurin and Erris to follow.

'We'll have to work fast,' Mali said, and then proceeded to spend an inordinately long time staring at the lock to the door that had been under guard. Eventually the mechanism surrendered to her threadcraft but not before Thurin became convinced the men must be only heartbeats from returning.

The room beyond had no windows and lay dark. Erris took up one of the lamps from the corridor and the light showed a room where everything was shrouded beneath white sheets. Finding the box, however, was no problem: the siren gave its location away. They dug out an iron coffer from beneath a pile of rugs and cushions that had been used to deaden the noise.

'They'll hear!' Thurin shouted.

'What?' Erris cupped a hand to his ear.

'They'll hear!'

Mali ignored them both and knelt to apply her threadcraft to the third lock of the day.

Thurin expected it to take longer, given that the coffer was clearly designed to be secure, but somehow Mali had it open in less than half the time she'd taken to open the door. And there, lighting the interior with its own glow, was Yaz's box of ghosts. A world of people, worlds perhaps, all held within a white cube that could almost be encompassed in two hands.

Erris snatched it up, flipped it open, and shouted into it, 'Reduce volume!'

Immediately the siren's call shrank from howl to complaint, a level closer to what had emerged when the coffer was closed and covered up. A moment later Taproot sprang into being above the mouth of the seemingly empty box.

'That took long enough!' Taproot stared around at the three of them. 'Where's Yaz?'

'Not here,' Erris said. 'And we can't be for long either. We need to leave the box. If Eular finds it gone he'll know we're not dead and everything will get much more difficult. Not that it wasn't difficult to start with!'

'And how do you propose I leave the box, young man?' Taproot arched a brow.

Erris produced between finger and thumb the gleaming needle that Taproot had first given to Yaz deep in the undercity of Vesta. It had been sufficient to carry a reduced version of Taproot to Haydies where they'd rescued this fuller copy of the man.

'I can't fit into that!' Taproot waved the needle away dismissively. 'That was the whole point of this box.'

'We've got company coming.' Thurin could sense someone approaching, right at the outer reaches of his water-sense.

'The point is' – Erris jabbed the needle towards Taproot's ghostly midriff – 'that we have no time to argue. We need whatever part of you is required to defend the ark against Seus. We need it in this needle. And we need it now!'

Taproot slumped, defeated. 'That's a lot of information. It won't leave much room for much of me.'

'You'll just have to leave your charm and personality in the box for Seus to question,' Erris said, lacking – in Thurin's opinion – some measure of sympathy for the man's fate. 'Quickly!'

Thurin put a hand on Mali's shoulder and leaned down so she could hear him above the siren. 'Someone's coming towards the corner where we were. Can you make them go away?'

'I can try.' She hurried to the door.

Erris glanced after her then returned his attention to Taproot. 'So?'

'I'm doing it as we speak. I think you'd be better served if you took the box though and just let—'

'We can't have Eular knowing we've got what we need. This way we might have days without Eular or Seus on our trail,' Erris insisted. 'To stand a chance of getting the ark open Yaz is not only going to have to handle four full ship-hearts – stars larger than any she's held before – she's also going to have to find them somewhere. She can't do that with those two trying to kill her.'

Taproot let out a dramatic sigh. 'It's done. The needle holds what you'll need. Now—'

Erris snapped the box shut and returned it to the coffer. 'Increase the volume back to what it was.' He closed the coffer and started to gather the rugs to cover it again. 'Mali, I need you to lock it again!'

Mali returned from the doorway. Thurin could sense that whoever had been approaching had come to a halt. What Mali had done Thurin couldn't tell. The person might suddenly have become fascinated by their own hands, or now be busy getting an imagined stone out of their shoe, or even fast asleep on their feet. Neither could he tell whether the person could see the door to the box-room from where they stood. It was entirely possible that they could.

Mali placed her hand over the lock and it clicked. 'It's easier the second time.'

'Good to know.' Erris piled the last of the coverings over the coffer. 'Do the same to the door on the way out.' He turned to Thurin, holding out the needle. 'Keep this safe.'

'Why me?' Thurin hesitated to touch the thing.

'Because it's holding the best hope for humanity now,' Erris said, pressing his lips together.

Still Thurin didn't reach for it.

'And you're closer to these people than I am, even if you don't speak their language.' Erris sighed. 'Also, you can fly. You've the best chance of getting away.'

At last Thurin took the needle. It hardly weighed anything. It was difficult to believe how much it carried. He pushed it through the lapel of his jacket where the material was thickest.

With the box wailing behind them, the three reached the doorway and, after peering out, Mali waved them on. Moments later they were finding a new path through the mansion, evading the returning guard stalled by Mali at the last corner, who seemed obsessed with scraping something from his sleeve.

'We just need a window and we're out clean,' Erris murmured.

Thurin wondered if Eular was even in the building. Perhaps he had already gone to his audience with the high priest. It pleased Thurin to have stolen from under the old man's nose – to be on top of the game for once. According to Yaz, Eular was more than just old. He'd been using the Missing's magic to skip through the years, sleeping away decades, stepping from the ice to the green lands, propping up several identities using the power of his thread-work. He'd been playing the Broken and the ice tribes for fools for generations. But not this time.

'In here.' Mali pushed against a door from the long corridor they'd been following. It opened onto a room strewn with shrouded furniture and lit by two large, shuttered windows.

They clambered from the window back into daylight and Thurin found himself disorientated, unsure whether the wall across from him was the one they'd scaled to get in. Choosing the best route by which to leave the compound unobserved was going to be a tricky decision. 'They'll have the dogs by now? And figured out where they came from?'

'Maybe.' Erris frowned. 'Chaos can be quite chaotic.'

'We came in over there.' Mali pointed.

Thurin rapidly stretched his water-sense out, hunting for trouble. 'Nobody close by on the far side. And . . . people coming this way around that corner.' He pointed towards the front of the house.

With the options sharply narrowed their decision proved easy. They hurried to the wall directly before them and Thurin lifted both himself and Mali swiftly over, gritting his teeth against the strain that made his skull ache.

Erris proved better at getting over this time and they all dropped to the far side together, Erris hitting the ground hard enough to crack the flagstone beneath his feet. He straightened to find himself face to face with two ancient nuns, both as wrinkled as Sister Owl and with wild tangles of white hair escaping their wimples. Thurin had somehow missed sensing them in his haste.

Erris gave them both a polite bow and went to join Thurin, who had landed more gently with Mali behind the pair. Fortunately, the old women seemed to have fallen into the confusion which sometimes drowns the elderly in their final years. They simply smiled and nodded before moving on again with uncertain steps.

Mali led the way back through the grounds. In a short space of time they'd left the quiet isolation of the archons' houses behind them and were once more rubbing elbows with all manner of travelling clergy in the main thoroughfare of the compound. The mood seemed more energetic than earlier, with more glances cast their way, but whether that was down to the escaped dogs or to it just being later in the day was unclear.

'I can't believe we managed that!' Thurin shook his head. 'I mean, what are the odds?'

'Well, let's not fall at the last hurdle,' Erris muttered, nodding ahead to where five armoured Church guards were advancing down the street, their ceremonial plumes waving above the crowding clerics. Five plumes, four white bundles of feathers and one longer red bundle.

Thurin kept his eyes on the ground as he followed Mali, until he remembered Erris's words about looking suspicious. He raised his gaze in time to meet the eyes of the senior, red-plumed guard. The man passed on without comment, seemingly bound on some urgent mission.

The main gates loomed ahead, standing open to the city beyond.

When Mother Krey stepped into Mali's path it was as if she had emerged from one of Eular's magical doors – though the truth was probably just a trick of the crowd as it thickened towards the gates. She held a staff that she'd not been carrying before, a black length of wood that she lowered to block the novice's way.

Thurin couldn't understand the woman's question but she asked it in a mild enough voice. He was sure she was speaking to Mali but her mismatched eyes settled on his, bright beneath her heavy brow.

Erris answered in Mali's place, his tone the same mix of slightly bored arrogance and command he had summoned before. Again, it worked the same charm, as if possession of a great house and fine clothing lifted one above suspicion. Mother Krey inclined her head and gestured for them to pass. Thurin felt her eyes on him every step of the way. He straightened his back and walked with a purposeful stride, determined to play his role.

'Enjoy the city,' Mother Krey said to his back.

'I will, thank you.' Thurin answered without turning his head.

A beat passed before both Mali and Erris looked at him in horror. Another beat passed before Thurin realized what he'd done. She'd spoken the ice-tongue and he'd answered in it.

'Is it too late to run?'

But Erris and Mali were already facing the priest. Mali reached forward as if she was plucking invisible hairs from the air in front of her. The Black Rock priests were all quantals, though, and schooled by Eular in such arts. As Thurin turned he saw a scornful smile on Mother Krey's lips. Stretching his ice-work out towards her, he seized her, unleashing enough power to hurl her over the nearest roof. But instead she merely rocked back on her heels. Whatever control was preventing Mali from pulling Krey's threads was also keeping her flesh beyond the reach of Thurin's mind. She showed her teeth as if to ask if that was all they had.

Erris balled his fists and stepped towards the woman but Thurin caught his shoulder. Quell's story of the priest Valak summoning his power beneath the Black Rock had left a deep impression. 'She's like Yaz. She can blast you to pieces.'

'She's nothing like Yaz,' Erris snarled. But even so he hesitated.

'Run?' Thurin suggested.

'Run!' Erris turned for the gate.

Mali was already running.

Mother Krey's grin of anticipation faded as Thurin also turned to flee. He didn't understand what she shouted but it seemed a fair bet that it was, 'Stop them!'

CHAPTER 13

Yaz

Getting into Persus Hall proved easy. The place where Yaz and her companions had stood trial two days earlier was deserted. Only when reaching for the handle of the main door and seeing the lock just below did Yaz consider that she might need a key. However, the convent didn't appear to see the need to use its locks. The door swung noiselessly open on oiled hinges.

Quina followed Yaz into the gloomy interior. 'I don't like it here.'

Yaz wasn't keen on the place either. Sitting in grand chairs surrounded by lore written in books didn't in her opinion make murder any less savage than that intended by the Tainted when they came howling at you. And having to stand there and listen to others debate your fate was a peculiar form of torture, whether you understood the language or not.

The great courtroom echoed with their footsteps. Yaz remembered that Eular had stood up from the judge's chair and produced the stardust taken from her pocket when she had been captured. He had held out the glowing handful as if it were evidence of some sin, then killed its light, speaking the words of some prayer to make the nuns believe it was the power of the Ancestor at work rather than his own. The grey dust had sifted lifeless from his fingers and fallen to the floor.

'It should be somewhere around here . . .' Yaz went to her knees before the great wooden stand behind which the judges had sat.

'Maybe he took it away.' Quina came to a halt beside her.

'It's nothing to him. He must have taken whatever stars he needed before he fled the Black Rock. And after the trial he thought we were all going to die the next day on his orders, so why bother with scraps?'

She ran her hands over the stone-flagged floor, trying to listen for the song of the tiny stars. Eular had put them into the deepest sleep – the kind that rock and stone know – but they were still alive, still stars, and their song still trembled beneath the silence.

'What are—' Quina bit her words off as Yaz raised a hand to shush her.

Yaz drew in a long, slow breath and tried to find the calm centre of herself that Sister Owl had been telling them about in Path class. She released the breath even more slowly and as the air left her lungs a faint glow began to show along the edges of several flagstones. Another breath in then out and the stardust had returned to wakefulness. Yaz ran her palm across the joints where the dust had gathered in the cracks between the flagstones. The dust rose in a thin and glittering stream to gather beneath her hand.

When she turned her palm up she held a small, glowing ball full of muted ocean blues, ice green, and sky white.

'Can we go now?' Quina glanced around.

'We can go.'

*

They went to the dormitory afterwards, finding the hall for Grey Class empty. Yaz sat on her bed contemplating the handful of stardust she'd recovered. She'd built stars before. It was just a matter of concentration . . . Quina watched her for a bit then took to striding around the room from bed to bed, not touching the floor.

'Bored!'

'What?' Yaz muttered.

'Bored! You've been looking at dust for hours.'

'Hours?' Yaz looked up, surprised.

'Well, a long time anyway.' Quina bounced down to sit on the bed, nearly causing Yaz to spill her handful. 'You better not let any of the others see you with that stuff.'

'No,' Yaz agreed, her eyes returning to the glow.

Time passed before Yaz was again aware of Quina speaking. 'That's the bell for the third meal. Dinner they call it. I'm going. You should come too.'

'Uh.' Yaz frowned, still listening to the star song.

'The others will be coming back with me. So hide the dust away.'

'Hmmm.' Yaz glanced up.

'I'm serious.' Quina walked away. She paused at the door. 'I can't believe you're missing out on food. They'll have more bacon!'

That reached Yaz: her mouth started to water. 'Soon. I'll come along soon.'

Yaz blinked and missed dinner. When Quina came back with the other girls Yaz was still sitting cross-legged on her bed, focused on the dust in her hand, still sorting the grains, finding pairs whose song fitted together in the closest harmonies. Joining the dust in little clusters where ten became six became two became one. Stars, almost too small to see, joined each other as drops of water will when their surfaces touch.

Seeing the light within her hands the other novices began to crowd round asking questions. Yaz looked up, disorientated, seeking Quina. 'Where were you?'

'I told you!' Quina shook her head. 'Meal number three!' She pressed both hands to her belly. 'Number *three*!' She fell onto her bed, lost from sight among the novices circling Yaz. 'You should have put the stars away when you heard us coming. You can work on them tomorrow.' She yawned mightily.

Yaz, suddenly guilty, put her hand under her pillow and pulled it out again free of even a speck of stardust. It was too late. Her audience remained.

'What is that stuff?' Hellma repeated, a frown furrowing her broad brow.

'Didn't the archon take that from you?' Wenna demanded.

'I hid the dust,' Yaz called out to Quina in ice-tongue. 'Now how do I get the novices to stop talking about it?'

'I'll distract them,' Quina called back. 'But you have to translate for me.'

'All right.'

'Everything I say. Promise?'

'Promise,' Yaz said, intending to keep her word despite the fact that Quina wouldn't know whether she did or not.

Quina stood on her bed and clapped her hands over the novices' babble. 'Listen to me, green girls! I'm going to tell you about . . .' She paused. 'You should be translating this, Yaz.'

Yaz repeated Quina in green-tongue.

'Boys!'

Yaz felt her cheeks burning but at the same time fought a desire to laugh. 'What do you know about—'

'Just translate, you.' Quina folded her arms. 'The men of the north aren't that different from your green-land men.'

Yaz translated.

'Bigger and stronger,' Quina said. 'But then we have a winter night that lasts a month and we stay in our tents all that time. So obviously our men need a lot of stamina.'

'Quina!'

'Just tell them.'

Yaz translated.

What followed left Yaz mortified and stuttering while the novices abandoned any pretence at going to bed and sat with eyes wide and jaws dropped. Very little of the vividly graphic information matched with what Yaz's mother had told her about the mechanics of conception. Yaz wanted to protest certain points but was too busy fishing through Mali's vocabulary for suitable words. Also, Quina imperiously waved aside any attempt at questioning her wisdom. Mali didn't know many of the right words and so Yaz didn't either when it came to green-tongue. At times she had to resort to using the names of vegetables or household objects in place of Quina's original, but it was clear that the novices were getting the gist of it.

Hellma shook her head. 'That doesn't seem possible . . .'

'Ssssh!' said another girl, eager to hear more.

'Standing up?' Wenna had both hands knotted in the ends of her blonde hair, tugging nervously.

Yaz continued to translate as best she could. At least none of the novices seemed the least bit interested in her handful of glowing dust any more.

Finally, having grown louder and more demonstrative, Quina gave one more energetically mimed explanation then fell backwards into her bed, arms spread.

'And that's it . . .' Yaz concluded, apologetically.

A stunned silence followed, and then a slow retreat as the novices made their way to their own beds, debating in furious whispers.

Yaz edged across to Quina. 'Was . . . was any of that true?' She tried not to sound horrified.

Quina snorted.

'Well?'

Quina started to wriggle out of her habit. 'Maybe. I've seen how the sled dogs do it.'

'But *you* haven't . . .'

'Nope.' Quina tossed her small clothes to the floor and crawled under her covers.

Yaz felt a little relieved. 'Why did you say all that then?'

'I'm tired of not speaking the language.' Quina shrugged. 'I still can't. But at least now they're listening to what I say. Plus you needed a distraction. No need to thank me.' She yawned mightily. 'And I've done the abbess a favour.'

'You have?'

'Sure. All these girls here. The abbess wants them to stay and be nuns. After what I told them I can't see any of them wanting to leave to find a man.'

CHAPTER 14

Yaz woke to the sound of novices' chatter as they dressed for the first class. Many of them were still discussing the lesson that Quina had delivered the previous evening. Some were beginning to doubt that there was as much howling involved as Quina had insisted.

Yaz tried to rise and found herself aching more fiercely from the beating Hellma had given her than she had at any point since it was handed out, and her left eye didn't want to open. With a groan she started to struggle up.

'Don't,' Quina yawned from the neighbouring bed. 'They've got another lesson on punching each other until they fall over. We can sleep in.'

'Knives today!' Wenna mimed stabbing as she walked past the end of Yaz's bed.

'Stay in bed,' Hellma advised, looming over Wenna.

'We're doing blade-path after the lesson,' another girl said.

Hellma groaned. 'You should come and see that, Yaz. It's fun to watch. Lots of falling. No fun to try. Blade Hall, after the bell, through the arena and under the stands.'

Yaz nodded and then translated for Quina, who clapped enthusiastically.

'We'll come along if Sister Owl lets us.' Yaz yawned. She lay where she was and watched the novices filing out. The next thing she knew was that Quina was shaking her awake.

'You went back to sleep. This place is making you soft.' Quina frowned. 'Also, your face is a mess. You should have dodged more.' She swayed swiftly from side to side by way of a demonstration.

Yaz lifted up on her elbows, yawning hugely. 'I'm tired. I was up most of the night.'

'Doing?' Quina raised a suspicious eyebrow.

A blue-green star the size of a thumbnail floated up between Yaz and Quina from beneath the covers. 'Doing that.'

Quina pursed her lips. 'It's a start. But didn't Taproot say we were going to need full-sized stars to open the ark? Whatever full-sized means. Four of them?'

The idea of that made Yaz's head hurt. She focused on something more comprehensible. 'We missed breakfast!'

Quina looked crestfallen. 'There's still two more meals . . .'

Yaz nodded. This plenty would take some getting used to. 'We should find Sister Owl. She'll probably want to give us more lessons.'

Quina made a sulky face. 'I'm never going to learn their words. It's easy for you. You've got that Mali floating around in your brain.' She paused. 'You sure you can't just put a hand on each side of my head and squeeze until I know all that stuff too?'

Yaz grinned, thinking of Mali and her sharp dark eyes. For one moment it seemed as if she could actually see the girl right there in front of her, like a waking dream. And in the next something grabbed Yaz with implacable strength, hauling her away, away from her bed, from the room, from the convent, from her very skin itself. Just for a heartbeat all she could see was light.

'Blue.' The word left her lips and she gasped in a breath as if she'd been drowning in the Glasswater once again.

'Yaz? Yaz!' Quina's face was very close to hers, her voice too loud.

'Yes?' Yaz blinked. She felt dizzy, as if she were spinning, though the room remained still. She pushed Quina back.

'What happened?' Quina asked, looking worried.

'Happened?'

'You were just sitting there, like you turned to stone. I couldn't move you. It was like you were frozen only not cold. Not even—'

'Not even what?' Yaz was alarmed now.

'I couldn't touch you.'

'That just sounds silly. Anyway, it was just a moment. I saw something. A blue light.'

'It wasn't just a moment. It felt like ages. A lot longer than I could hold my breath, for sure. And it was like there was something I couldn't see covering your skin so my fingers slid off.' Quina sounded as if she were in earnest, but Yaz had heard her lie extensively and with confidence only the night before.

'I'll ask Sister Owl about it. You think we should go and see if she's at the scriptorium?'

Quina frowned. Despite her intelligence and her frustration at not understanding the language, she seemed in no hurry to learn. In the distance the novices' bell, Bray, tolled the end of one period and the start of another. 'Let's go see this blade-path thing that Hellma was talking about!'

'Huh?' Yaz was still wrestling with the idea that she'd slept her way through the whole of the novices' first lessons.

'Come on! I want to see them fall!' Quina had Yaz's hand

now and was dragging her out of bed with surprising strength.

Yaz struggled into her clothes, taking twice as long to get her habit on as a consequence of trying to do it too fast. At last she was hobbling down the dormitory steps in pursuit of an impatient Quina, who appeared to have forgotten about Yaz's bruises.

Not even the remarkable phenomenon of molten snow falling from the sky slowed Quina down. Yaz opened the double doors to Blade Hall to find Quina waiting for her on the sand, bouncing around since her enthusiasm rarely allowed her to be still.

'I prefer snow.' Yaz wiped both hands through her wet hair and shook the water off them.

'Come on!' Quina turned and raced off down the dark tunnel that led beneath the tiered seating.

Yaz followed, blind until a door opened up ahead. It had closed again by the time she reached it but she found the handle by touch.

Quina had stopped just beyond the door. They were in a large square room that was lit from on high. What made it unusual was that it was much taller than it was wide. The effect was to make it a wide shaft running from ground level to the rafters of the hall's peaked roof. Looking up gave Yaz a strange chill and for a moment the light seemed tinged with blue. She shook off the feeling.

A great net had been suspended just above head height to cover the whole area with just a small gap near the wall with the door they'd entered by. Above it a coiling confusion filled the remaining space. It took Yaz a while to make sense of it.

A great length of twisted metal, a rod as thick as Yaz's arm, had been coiled into the gap between the roof and the net, making many twists and turns. Dozens of cables supported the structure, anchored to the wall or the rafters. None of it looked at all stable. It swayed gently to and fro as Yaz watched. And way above Yaz, close to the rafters, was a small platform where two or three novices could be seen dangling their bare legs over the drop. Another one joined them through a door that opened onto the platform. It looked like Hellma. She peered over, waved, and shouted, 'Hallooo!'

Quina waved and shouted, 'Are you going to fall now?'

By way of an answer another girl, Wenna, stepped out from the platform onto the metal rod, the top of which Yaz now saw reached to just by where the girls were sitting. Yaz assumed the rod must be hollow – a pipe Mali would call it – otherwise the weight would be too much to support.

'Gods!' Quina sounded in awe as the pipe started swaying. Clearly it was delicately balanced and even Wenna's weight had set it going.

The girl swayed with the pipe, her arms extended to either side, feet curled on the metal. If she fell it was a long way down. The thing had been arranged to make hitting lower sections of the pipe on the way unlikely, but it didn't look impossible.

Wenna found her centre and advanced slowly. Where the pipe dipped sharply Yaz was sure the girl's bare feet would slip, but somehow she managed not to. She advanced a few yards and a whole curve of the structure moved unexpectedly. The pipe was jointed and counterbalanced, allowing it to flex like a snake as the weighting changed.

'She'll fall!' Yaz gasped, certain. The novices on the platform whistled and called. But Wenna didn't fall. She waved her arms, twisted her body, and steadied herself before moving on down the pipe towards a place where it made three great coils that looked wholly impossible to negotiate. Again, Yaz shivered as the earlier chill revisited her. The light shaded towards blue once more and something seemed to tug at her. 'No.' She gathered her focus and watched Wenna.

'You all right?' Quina looked over. Yaz waved the question off.

Another girl came out to join the waiting novices, further crowding the small platform. Hellma, still standing, called out at Wenna, 'Hurry up and fall off. You know you're going to and there're girls waiting here!'

Wenna hissed back some sharp retort, but somehow, as if Hellma's taunt had been a push, she began to sway once more – slowly at first but unable to compensate. She started to shift her feet, then pin-wheeled her arms, and finally, with a despairing curse, she dropped like a stone.

Dust burst from the net as Wenna hammered into it. She bounced a good two yards and landed on her front near the edge. A quick slithering motion had her dropping neatly over the edge to land beside Quina. Clearly she'd fallen before. Many times.

Yaz had lots of questions. She asked the biggest first. 'Why?'

'Hellma,' Wenna muttered darkly. 'Just wait until her turn comes. She never gets more than four steps.'

'No, I didn't mean why did you fall. I meant . . . *why*?'

'Oh, right.' Wenna made for the door. 'It's a game, mostly. Sister Owl says it helps walk the Path – but that's only for quantals and even they don't really see how it helps. And Mistress Blade says it's good for balance. And Mistress Shade says we should get used to falling. And Mistress Spirit says it builds character. So there's that too.' The door closed behind her.

Hellma hammered into the net. Yaz hadn't even seen her step off the platform. She clambered out rather less elegantly than Wenna had and landed heavily.

'Heh. I normally get further than that. Still, at least it was all over before Wenna got back to the platform.'

'What's that?' Quina asked, pointing to a strange device high on the wall. A metal disc with something hanging down beneath it.

'That counts how long you take,' Hellma answered, guessing the question. 'We don't use it because none of us have ever got to the end. But once you can make it to the end then the competition is to see who can do it fastest.' She walked over to the door. 'Want to try?'

Yaz truly did not but she translated for Quina, who, showing unexpected common sense, answered, 'Why?'

Whatever unlikely answer Hellma had for Quina it was not one that Yaz got to hear. That tugging sensation she had felt a number of times since waking now returned with a vengeance. One fierce yank pulled her from her body. For a disorienting moment Yaz felt as if she were a point of consciousness in some vast blackness, a lone star in some ancient heaven where even the red embers of the galaxy had burned into ash. The next breath ushered in even more strangeness along with a lungful of curiously stale air. She didn't seem to be herself any more. Her wrist ached and two huge figures loomed to either side of her, tall as gerants but of slimmer build. All this was secondary to the source of the light. A blue light, and at its centre a blue star larger and stranger than any Yaz had ever seen.

A distant voice wavers through her mind: *Time is the fire in which we burn, but time itself is burning here and this is what it looks like.*

Yaz finds her eyes fascinated by the light. She can't look away. She can't worry why her body is not her own, or where she is, or when, or why. She's gone, and forever has come to play.

CHAPTER 15

Thurin

Thurin ran for the gates, feeling sure at each new stride that a searing blast of Mother Krey's power would slice through him. He'd seen Yaz call on the Path and shatter rock. He'd seen bodies torn apart by the blinding energies Yaz had unleashed and still sincerely wished that he had not.

Erris could doubtless run far faster than either Thurin or Mali but even if he were minded to abandon them he couldn't have gained that much ground. The gates were little more than thirty yards ahead but the way was blocked by a crowd of Church travellers, mostly headed out, but at a glacial pace.

Erris barged through as fast as he could without breaking bones, and Thurin bent his mind to the task, hauling elderly clerics aside left and right.

The expected destruction had not yet arrived by the time the three of them reached the line of Church guards forging their own way forward against the flow. Thurin guessed that Mother Krey would rather they were taken into custody by the guards than leave her having to explain a street strewn with corpses, not to mention having to explain her own perhaps hitherto unknown powers.

Not unreasonably the six armoured guards ahead of Thurin seemed to feel that they could overpower two men and a one-handed girl without having to draw swords on a packed thoroughfare. They were rapidly disabused of that notion. Erris casually tossed the largest guard over his shoulder into the cleared space behind him. Thurin shoved the three closing on him and sent them sprawling to the ground, taking down several clerics on the way. The single guard who made to grab Mali found himself evaded and at the same time tripped.

Erris led the way through the gate after felling the guard captain with a punch to the head. Shouts went up and the crowd, becoming aware of the altercation, began to thin.

'They're getting . . .' Mali said a word in green-tongue.

'Things called crossbows,' Erris explained, shoving another man out of the way. 'They're weapons that throw small spears over great distances. Accurate and dangerous!' He turned into the street that ran along the rest house's perimeter wall and began to run. 'They'll have the city guard after us soon. We need somewhere to hide.'

Thurin turned and pushed the legs of several pursuing Church guards out from under them. He wasn't used to running and already his lungs were labouring with the effort of keeping up with Erris and Mali. There didn't seem to be any safe place to stop. There were people everywhere, pausing in their business to stand and stare as the three of them ran past. A novice and two nobles pelting through the streets must be an unusual sight. The shouts behind them were distant but multiplying as others took up the cry.

Erris looked back and saw Thurin struggling. He veered off the street into a narrower way that led between tall houses. People watched them from the windows and the doorsteps. Mali called out something unintelligible to Erris and took another corner. Up ahead two small horses were tied by a water trough outside a building with an open doorway above which hung a brightly painted board. Mali led them in, slowing to a walk as she reached the entrance.

The space inside was dim and crowded with chairs and tables, most of the chairs unoccupied, most of the tables bare. It smelled strongly of several things, only one of which Thurin could identify: the basic reek of humanity. Several old men with mugs of some foaming liquid looked up in surprise as Mali passed quickly by them. Their eyes widened further as Erris and Thurin followed in their finery, Thurin still panting and sweating.

'Out the back.' Mali led them on and the stink increased to the point where Thurin's eyes began to water. She pushed through a weathered door and they were in daylight again, in a small courtyard that was more like a well, with three-storey buildings rising on all sides, reducing the sky to an irregular rectangle of blue. Ropes crisscrossed the space above their heads, hung with clothes; a small tree, dead and leafless, stood in a pot in the widest of the four corners. Thurin could see no other doors, just a scattering of shuttered windows higher up.

'We're trapped,' Erris said.

'If we get out,' Mali countered, pointing skywards, 'they won't know which direction we took.'

'Let's rest first.' Erris squatted down as if he might need time to recover from their run.

Thurin squatted too, not wanting to subject the fine fabric of his trousers to the grimy flagstones. He tried to breathe less deeply, letting his heart slow a little from its frantic beat. Mali frowned and walked a circuit of the tiny courtyard,

141

looking up at the walls as if there might be a route she could climb with one hand.

'At least nobody followed us out,' Erris said. 'The more money you have the more eccentric you're allowed to be. That's how it was in my day, anyway.'

'What's that noise?' Thurin cocked his head. As his breath calmed he began to notice an annoying high whine, skittering across the upper ranges of his hearing.

Mali, finishing her circuit, blinked at him then looked away as if the question were beneath her interest. Thurin looked at his arms and chest, wondering in alarm if it might be one of the tiny creatures Yaz had talked of – insects, she'd called them. Some of them were too small to see and some of them could wound you, though Thurin wasn't sure of the mechanism. Surely a bite from so small a creature would go unnoticed . . .

He cocked his head to one side, then to the other, and the high-pitched whine got louder. He patted his hand where he thought the noise was loudest and whipped it away in shock, not bitten but tickled. 'The needle!'

Erris stood as Thurin rose to his feet.

'It's vibrating!' Thurin pulled the needle free from his collar.

'Yaz used it to show a direction.' Erris plucked a thread from his jacket. 'Hang it on this.'

'No need.' Thurin had the needle on his palm, fighting the urge to close his hand against the tickling sensation. The thing jittered around then stopped. He turned his hand, keeping it horizontal, and the needle jittered some more until it pointed in the direction it had before.

'Someone's coming,' Mali said. The sound of voices and hard boots on wooden boards reached them through the courtyard's single door.

'You help Mali.' Erris went to the door. 'I'll hold them then join you up top.' He set both hands to the door just before it shuddered under the impact of someone's shoulder. 'Better hurry!'

Rather than tax his ice-work Thurin opted for a strategy of assisted climbing, letting Mali cling to his back. Where the wall failed to offer a window ledge or shutter top to help him Thurin employed his magic to support them both. But he'd clambered around Vesta's undercity enough times to do a reasonable job of climbing, even with a passenger who seemed to be trying to throttle him.

Close to the eaves of the tiled roof Thurin looked down in time to see a yard of steel erupt from the door that Erris was holding shut. The sword's blade emerged just above shoulder height and Erris snapped his head to one side, avoiding the thrust save for a graze to his left ear. He stepped back and booted the door with enough force to tear it from its hinges and flatten the guards behind it.

With remarkable agility Erris ran across the small space, leapt, lodged one foot where a loose brick had fallen out, and launched himself back across to catch a windowsill. In three more leaps he caught the edge of the roof just about the same time that Thurin lifted himself and Mali onto it.

Erris smashed one fist through the tiles in search of something sufficiently well anchored to support his weight, and with his other arm swept a mass of tiles down towards the doorway where guards were beginning to emerge after picking themselves off the floor outside the privy.

Mali released her death grip on Thurin and he scrambled to the roof ridge where, out of sight of those below, he felt safe to look around. The cityscape looked very different from the rooftops. Sloping planes of terracotta and slate replaced the narrow, crowded streets. Chimneys punctuated the view, a great profusion of them, spewing smoke into the wind. He could see Verity's grand buildings rising above the sea of rooftops, their spires reaching for the sky, and – although the size of the city amazed him – Thurin could even see beyond the outer walls to the green expanse of forest and field. Somewhere the green must give way to the frozen wastes, but the distance overcame his vision before that point. He sucked in a breath, amazed to find himself in a place where the eye could stretch so far and see no hint of the ice that had held him all his life.

'Quick!' Mali joined him.

'Where do we go?' Erris beside her.

Thurin patted his jacket. For a heart-stopping moment he had no memory of doing anything with the needle and imagined that he might even have let it drop, forgotten and discarded by newly busy fingers. But then he found it, shoved back through the material over his collarbone.

He held the needle's blunt end lightly between finger and thumb, angling it until the tickling buzz stilled. 'That way.' Somewhat redundantly he pointed, echoing the needle's directions.

'We should stick to the rooftops,' Erris said.

'Hmmm.' Thurin awkwardly scrambled down the far side towards the sharp edge where the tiles stopped and empty air began. The fact that his ice-work could support him had not removed his fear of heights, and somehow the city made each drop look longer and more fatal than any had out on the ice where the whiteness had seldom seemed particularly far beneath him.

He beckoned to Mali. 'I'll try to get us acr—'

Erris sprinted down the slope and leapt out across the gap. While the streets around them were relatively narrow

144

it was still not a jump that Thurin would ever bet on making. Especially not with high stakes.

Erris's take-off floundered, his weight and strength combined to smash tiles and splinter wood, reducing the thrust imparted to his leap. Had he landed just a couple of feet lower he would have hit the wall beneath the eaves of the opposite roof. Instead he hit the slope, shoulder first, and vanished into the space beneath through a hole of his own making fringed by splintered rafters and shattered tiles.

'Well . . .' Thurin stood gingerly, hoping that there weren't yet any guards in the street below, and that if there were they didn't have these crossbows that Erris had mentioned. 'Well, we can't do much worse than that.' He extended a hand to Mali. 'Let's go?'

CHAPTER 16

The rooftop escape succeeded in some measure, though due to speed rather than stealth. Thurin and his friends were able to plot a course across the city that those tracking through the streets were hard pressed to follow. The needle kept to its line and a string of damaged roofs and tile-scattered streets would in due course lead anyone wishing to find them along the same path.

'Well?' Erris cocked his head. He was crouched with Mali in the shelter of three chimneys that emerged together from the latest of many roofs to host them.

'It's reversed. We must have passed what it was pointing to.' Thurin lifted the needle to show the others.

'Between this roof and that one?' Erris gestured to the one they'd just leapt from.

'Must be down in the street . . .' Mali made no attempt to peer over.

'Under them, more likely,' Erris said. 'Taproot's guiding us to the undercity.'

Thurin shook his head. 'We're not ready for that. We don't have Yaz. And she hasn't got the stars we need yet.'

'What we need right now is an escape.'

Thurin couldn't argue with that, and if Verity's undercity was anything like the one the Broken used to scavenge then it would be an ideal place to lose a pursuit. He leaned forward so he could see into the street, supported by the invisible cushion of his ice-work. 'It looks like all the other streets.' A handful of citizens were craning their necks to look back up at him, alerted by the crash of Erris's arrival on the roof, surprise written on their faces.

'We need to get into the cellars.' Erris edged forward on his backside. 'Best do it quickly before the guards get here.'

Whether by accident or design Erris's slow forward shuffle turned into a fast forward slip and he fell in a shower of loosened tiles before Thurin could react.

'Is he—'

'He's fine.' Thurin reached for Mali's hand. Erris had landed in a crouch, shattering the flagstone beneath his feet and shedding debris as he stood.

Thurin steeled himself against the fear of the drop and the mental effort of arresting their fall, then stepped off the edge, pulling Mali with him. They landed among the bewildered locals a few heartbeats later. Erris had already pushed his way through the large double doors of the building opposite them – whether they had been locked or not was unclear.

Mali shouted something to the growing crowd with as much authority as a young girl could manage, then followed Erris in. Thurin looked around apologetically for a moment longer and hurried after her.

The doors, which Erris had left ajar, were truly huge, big enough for a cart and horses with room to spare. The space beyond proved both cavernous and cluttered. Some kind of storage place, stacked up to the rafters in some places, bare in others, an array of sacks, crates, and barrels offering few clues to Thurin as to their contents. The place smelled of must and dust and fainter more tantalizing things.

'Look for a trapdoor!' Erris called.

Thurin and Mali both ignored him. The novice set her shoulder to the doors and began to shove them closed on the curious faces outside. Thurin turned his attention to the needle still in his hand. Erris had once mentioned a saying his people had about a needle in a haystack being hard to find. Thurin had a notion that having a needle among all these stacks might make what they wanted *easier* to find.

While Mali struggled one-handed to place a locking bar across the doors Thurin let the needle jitter between his finger and thumb as he walked slowly among the piles of goods.

'Somewhere over there.' He pointed. 'Under those sacks, maybe.'

Erris shot him a look then set to work, hefting aside sacks that looked to weigh more than a man.

Mali found a broom and positioned herself behind Erris's efforts, sweeping aside the dust and loose grain.

'There's something here.' She brushed with more focus to reveal the outline of a large block set among the smaller flagstones that covered the floor.

Thurin knelt and dug the dirt out of a depression near the centre that might once have held an iron ring. 'Can you shift it?'

Erris sized the thing up. 'It'll be tough to get leverage. It really needs an anchor, a rope, and some sort of hoist.'

A blow set the main doors shuddering. A man's voice called out in a commanding tone.

'We'll need something quicker than that . . .' Thurin offered. 'Maybe you could punch through it?'

Erris looked at his fist and then doubtfully at the slab of rock before them, more than a yard on each side. 'Can't you do some . . .' He waved his fingers. '. . . water magic?'

'On what?' Thurin looked around.

'Well, there's barrels of . . . something.'

Thurin could sense that some of the nearby barrels contained mostly water but what he would do with it he couldn't imagine.

The doors shuddered again and a sword blade slid gleaming between them to lift the locking bar.

Thurin started towards the entrance. 'We can't just stand here argu—'

A detonation took his words away as Mali knelt swiftly beside the slab and brought her fist down on it, sparking with power. The stone shattered and fell in pieces into the black throat it had covered. Mali's hand retained enough light to illuminate the upper tract, brick-lined and pale with nitre at the lower reaches. 'Down?'

Thurin glanced at the opening doors where guards were crowding through, their weapons silhouetted against the day. 'Down.'

He reached for Mali's hand, but then thought better of it and reached for her with his mind instead. His ice-work found nothing to hold on to; with the Path-power still echoing in her Mali was a blank to him, his talent skittering off her like fingers trying to clutch melting ice.

'Hurry!' Erris spun and hefted a sack, tossing it towards the first three guards through the doors.

Mali offered her handless arm to Thurin and he took a firm grip before stepping into the hole. Gravity seized him but he tempered his fall, pulling Mali with him and knotting

149

his other hand in her habit so as not to lose her to the drop. Out of sight now the sack hit its target and men went down with clattering and groans.

Mali threw the last of her energies ahead of their descent to reveal a shockingly deep shaft and finally a distant bottom to it. The sounds of conflict faded above them.

'Will Erris be all right?' Mali craned her head to see. The shaft was too wide to brace against both sides in the way Thurin might try, but it could be spanned with the horizontal length of his body. Hopefully Erris could work something out because the distance was far greater than any jump he'd made to date.

'I'm more worried about us if we're still in his way when he drops!' Thurin let them fall faster and then cushioned the last ten yards, landing with a jolt in cold, ankle-deep water. He pulled Mali to the side.

'I can't hear . . .' But then they both could, a rushing, jolting succession of sounds that seemed to indicate a dangerously fast and poorly controlled descent.

Erris landed face down, cushioned only by knees and elbows. The impact sounded like the bone-crushing, fatal kind, and Thurin's insides twisted at the thought of the damage done. Contrary to expectations though, and without a groan, Erris rolled aside, just as a heavy sack hammered into the spot he'd occupied, showering all of them with water and grain in equal measure.

'Ouch.' Erris lay on his back in the black water, illuminated by the last glimmers of Mali's power.

Thurin rubbed his temples. Not since his escape from the Pit of the Missing had he strained his ice-work so much. 'Ouch.'

Mali looked from her palm, where faint streamers of power still crawled, to her stump, bound with stained cloth.

She looked from Thurin to Erris and said nothing, but her message was clear enough. Time to get on with it.

'So . . . which way?' Thurin stared blindly into the darkness. 'And perhaps we could have a little light?'

'How?' Mali asked. The Path seemed to be an all-or-nothing kind of thing, delivering power in big, dangerous lumps, good for knocking down walls, less good for chasing shadows away.

'Erris can make that flame that doesn't burn anything.' As Thurin spoke Erris clicked his fingers and a flame flickered into being in the middle of his palm, revealing that he had yet to stand after his fall, and was sitting in the water.

'All fires burn something.' Mali frowned, leaning in to stare at the tiny fire. 'Mistress Shade teaches this.'

'She's not wrong,' Erris conceded. 'This' – he raised his palm – 'burns me. So I would rather not light our way in this manner for long.'

'Well, there's not exactly much else to burn down here.' Thurin looked from one wall to the opposite. They'd fallen into a circular, brick-lined tunnel barely high enough for them to stand upright at the middle.

'You'd be surprised what will burn if you put enough effort into it.' Erris scooped up a handful of water and then stood slowly, dripping. 'Anything up to iron.'

Thurin shook his head. 'You can't burn metal.'

'Ah.' Erris curled the hand holding the water into a fist, spilling remarkably little of it. 'There are different kinds of burning. Chemical and nuclear.' A flame sprung up above his closed fist, brighter and fiercer than the one in his palm, which he now extinguished. 'Here I'm breaking water into its components then recombining them in a flame. But the energy is coming from me first – our ancestors could burn water far more efficiently. The hydrogen at least. Fusion, they called it. It's how the stars burn!'

'You're burning water!' Thurin clung to the fragment of what Erris said that he had understood. He stared hard, straining his water-sense to understand what was happening. Somehow Erris was breaking the water apart and then burning the pieces. 'You can't burn water!'

'I kind of am . . .' And Erris led off, splashing along the tunnel.

Thurin hurried after him. 'We're trying to find a way out now, right?'

'We are. I don't know if Krey is going to come down after us, but whether or not she comes herself it's certainly not going to be very healthy for us down here once Seus is alerted to our presence. Or for Yaz up there once Eular knows we didn't drown. So getting out is our priority. It's not as if there's much we can do in the undercity without Yaz anyway. We need to find the ark, of course, but we can't open it without her and the stars.'

The flooded area ended after a hundred yards or so, the water leaking away into some underground stream that Thurin could sense weaving through fractures in the bedrock. He willed the water from his clothes and even his boots were almost dry by the time they reached the first forking of the way.

'Left or right?'

'Try the needle,' Mali suggested, brushing grain kernels from her hair.

'We should have done that back where we came down.' Erris pulled off a boot and tipped out dirty water.

Thurin did as suggested. It pointed resolutely at the join where the two routes came together.

'Maybe these tunnels were made more recently than Taproot's memories of the place,' Erris suggested.

'He knew the way in,' Mali said.

Erris shrugged. 'There are other ways he might have for knowing how to get in. Stuff still leaks out of the undercities. Stuff that can be detected and triangulated . . .'

'We don't even know if he's pointing us at the ark, an exit, or something entirely different that he wants us involved with.' Thurin peered into both tunnels. 'Let's go left.'

It didn't take long before the forgotten sewers of earlier incarnations of the city, tangled one generation through another in some vast unsolvable knot, led into the deeper and more durable undercity. An undercity that in its turn had once been nothing more than a footnote to the great city of the Missing which reached for the heavens from this spot.

Footnote or not, Verity's undercity dwarfed the more recent encrustation now occupying the ground above it, the modern city that the emperor called his capital, and whose inhabitants generally considered it to be the greatest city to be found anywhere along the length of the Corridor.

'We're still going down, I notice.' Thurin's job for the past few hours had been to reach out with his water-sense for potential danger and also for any seeps from which Erris could take more fuel.

'Sometimes further in is the only way out.' Erris shrugged and raised his fist to illuminate a side chamber.

'Why is it so empty?' Mali asked.

'I guess our ancestors took everything they could millennia ago when the four tribes first came here.' Thurin ran his fingers along a furrow in the wall where it looked as if some ancient vein had been chipped out. 'Maybe others came back over the centuries, more desperate, hunting for things considered worthless in richer, more enlightened times. But eventually either the whole undercity gets mined out or it just gets too deep and dangerous to be worth the rewards. My own people spent generations at it . . .' He paused, struck by the thought that they must still be scavenging in Vesta beneath the stone beneath the ice. It took a moment of mental adjustment each time he remembered that although his life had changed utterly and completely over the last half a year, the lives of the friends and extended family he grew up with must even now be grinding along in the same rut, ruled by the same needs and wants as they had been for so long.

'I think we're lost.' Mali strode around the perimeter of the chamber they'd entered, eyeing each of the four exits in turn.

'We're not lost. Erris never forgets anything. He can walk us back to where we started any time he wants.' Thurin put his back to one of the walls and slid down until he was sitting on the stone floor. He wasn't convinced he could get up again. The day had been . . . taxing. 'Erris also never gets tired.'

Erris inclined his head. 'Not physically. But I do need to sleep. I think if I didn't then I'd be certain that I was just a copy of myself. A toy that Vesta made to amuse herself.' He kicked a loose stone across the floor.

'I thought you didn't sleep.' Thurin was unused to hearing Erris be anything but confident. 'You just lie there at night, not moving, eyes open . . .'

'I don't need to close my eyes to dream.' Erris shrugged. 'We should get some rest. If we don't find another way out of here tomorrow then maybe we can climb back up to that warehouse. They're not going to watch it forever.'

'I suppose so.' Thurin eyed the ground. It wasn't any harder than the ice. The room was warm. He'd slept in worse places. 'Just a few hours.'

'I'll take first watch,' Mali said.

'Nothing to watch.' Erris extinguished his flame.

'First listen.'

Erris made some reply but Thurin had already sunk beneath the words into the pit of his exhaustion.

A time that might have been a night passed, broken by strange dreams. When Erris finally ignited a new flame and stood to go Thurin felt sore in every limb but more whole between his ears. The stone floor had punished his body but sleep had soothed the ache that seemed to have moved in to stay after his efforts beneath the surface of the Glasswater.

Erris led them through more dusty halls, through more galleries, and twice through natural caves that the Missing seemed to have incorporated into their design. The place was deserted but more so than the two other undercities Thurin had experienced. This one held few signs of any activity that might postdate its original occupation. None of the Broken's ropes and ladders. None of Haydies's destruction. Just dust and silence. It might be that it had nothing to offer, or it might be that this quarter of the undercity was deserted for its own good reason.

'We've not seen any of the Missing's script,' Thurin noted.

'No.'

'Maybe the city mind has nothing left to hide so it doesn't bother keeping anyone out,' Thurin guessed. It was the only significant difference from the undercity he'd explored many times before back beneath the ice. Thurin knew that a sober comparison would conclude that the undercities of Vesta and Verity were very similar despite the thousands of miles that stood between them. To his eye, though, they seemed somehow to be two very different things. Perhaps it was just seeing the place by the flicker of a flame rather than the steady glow of stars. This was a different kind of emptiness.

155

Maybe the coming and going of the Broken somehow injected a hint of life into Vesta's echoing voids that was absent here. The silence seemed to shiver with a need to speak, as if it had been kept too long, stretched beyond its limit, wanting only the slightest excuse to break and unleash a thousand years of screaming.

'Thurin?'

Thurin jumped and barely resisted crying out.

'Yes?' He sounded terse even to himself as he turned towards Mali.

'Stairs.' She pointed. 'Going up.'

The return to the sewer tunnels was a relief. They felt less haunted. They hadn't been walking long before Mali stopped again.

'There's a light.' She pointed to a pinprick of brightness that might have been a mote of glowing dust ten yards off, or a blazing fire in the far distance.

'Daylight?' Thurin didn't expect an answer.

'Let's find out.' Erris set off towards it. They'd been walking down a long tunnel, circular in cross-section, and brick-lined. It stretched ahead of them towards the light.

There'd been no question about whether they would investigate. The light might have been an avatar sent by Seus to tear them into shreds, or just a lone star resting in a niche. But something about a light in an utterly dark place exerts its own draw, and this one proved irresistible. The light had a blueness to it that fascinated Thurin's eye, a changing blueness, and, rather than considering the danger, his mind was filled with the question of whether it was a deep and dark blue, or the bright blue of a newborn's eye, or of a cloudless Corridor sky.

'There's someone ahead.' Erris's voice came deep and slow.

Thurin tried to see past him. It seemed there might be

more than one someone but the light made it hard to see and even harder to concentrate. He squinted. At least two someones were standing further ahead, facing the light. In truth, rather than standing, it looked more as if they were walking but had simply stopped mid-stride as if frozen in place.

'I don't like this.' Mali's voice came from behind Thurin and seemed shriller than normal, its pitch elevated by fear perhaps.

'Should we . . . call to them? Watch them?' Thurin paused and tried to blink the blueness from his mind. He reached for Taproot's needle and a voice seemed to shiver up from it, vibrating through his fingertips: *Time is the fire in which we burn, but time itself is burning here and this is what it looks like*. The light came from a star. He was sure of it. Different from the stars Yaz had mastered before, but still a star, and its strangeness wrapped him.

'Something's wrong here.' Mali's voice sounded too high even for her. 'Something's wrong with time.'

CHAPTER 17

Yaz

In the stories of Zin and Mokka that the Ictha have kept through an untold number of winters it wasn't the presence of the gods that most fascinated Yaz. It was the way that Zin and Mokka somehow seemed to live outside time, undiminished by the years. Zin fathered the great tribes and Mokka bore them. And yet, on his last day, Zin came to his Ictha sons and his Ictha daughters, finding that they alone of all his children still remembered him. Generations had passed. But then again, Zin was a man who once spent fifty years trying to capture the grace of a leaping narfin in a single kettan. Fifty years whittling on the tooth of a leviathan, paring from it a weight of ivory greater than a man. Fifty years reducing that tooth from something taller than himself to something that would fit upon his palm, and ultimately to a speck too small to see. Half a century after which he stood and blew the last dust of his efforts from his hand and went to stand upon the cliffs of ice and watch the sea, waiting once again to see a narfin break from the waves.

Mokka's patience was even greater, though she would never spend her time in so foolish a pursuit as trying to imprison in static ivory that which lives only in the fluidity of a moment.

Time's shackles had meant little to Zin or to Mokka, and yet Yaz had seldom been able to forget that her years were numbered, that childhood would release her to a brief majority before age reached up to claim her.

Now, however . . . now was forever . . . a perfect crystal blue held her, and by holding her in its flawless prison . . . set her free.

'Yaz.'

It was the first word in an age. Maybe the first word ever. 'Yaz!'

The repetition faded, like ripples on a sea, lost among a meaningless myriad and forgotten.

'Yaz. You need to look away. The light is dangerous.'

Yaz didn't understand the words. The light was everywhere and everything. Looking away made no sense.

'My eyes. Focus on my eyes.'

Yaz knew the voice. An old woman's voice. She spoke the ice-tongue well but without any inflection that might mark her as Ictha or Quinx or Axit or . . . Yaz remembered that there had been a time before the blue took her.

'My eyes.'

She saw the eyes – no face, just two dark eyes, almost lost in the dazzle of the light.

'Yaz!'

Yaz squinted, trying to meet the woman's dark gaze.

'Yaz!'

There was a room beyond the woman. A room with a single narrow window. Daylight, then a starlit night, then daylight and a flash of red as the sun sailed across the thin span of sky on offer.

'Yaz.' The woman's eyes held her.

Two hands clasped Yaz's, two ancient hands, bones and skin, but warm even so. Sister Owl, her over-wide eyes focused on Yaz.

'Why . . . why am I in bed?' Yaz sat up.

As she did so a novice, who'd been dozing in a chair near the door, leapt to her feet with a startled cry and ran out of the room yelling for Sister Sun.

Sister Owl blinked and drew in a deep, gasping breath as if she had emerged from beneath still waters after some long immersion. She glanced towards the door now slowly swinging shut in the novice's wake, then returned her gaze to Yaz. 'You've been . . . incapacitated.'

Yaz pulled her hands from the nun's grasp and rose from the bed. 'I feel fine.'

Sister Owl remained in her chair on the opposite side. 'It wasn't an illness or an injury. It was—'

'I remember a blue light.' Yaz rubbed at her eyes, trying to remove the dazzle, or the memory of it. 'Mali! It was something to do with Mali. I was seeing through her. I was in her!'

Sister Owl nodded. 'When two people are thread-bound one can call the other into their mind. One can surrender their body to the other's control. Cases of swapping have even been documented.'

'But I didn't do anything . . .' Yaz trailed off, remembering the strange sensation before the light filled her mind. She'd been pulled from her own body.

'Both of you need to learn control. Early on one can be drawn to the other in moments of panic or distress.'

Yaz looked up at the narrow window and frowned at the slice of evening sky. 'Well, something went wrong with it. I didn't share Mali's mind or control her body or even share it. Maybe for just a moment but then there was this . . .'

'Blue light,' Sister Owl said.

'Yes.' Yaz tried to remember anything else that had happened but the light was all her memory would show her. 'Mali's in trouble. I'm sure of it. That means Erris and Thurin are too. I need to find them!' She turned for the door.

Sister Owl raised a hand. 'Novice Mali is very likely in trouble. But whatever else her danger might be it is not immediate. If anything it's the exact opposite.'

'How long have I . . .' Yaz looked down and realized that her novice's habit had been replaced with a nightgown. However long she'd spent staring through Mali's eyes at that star – somehow now she was sure it was a star – it was long enough for the nuns to carry her here and change her. The sky had grown dark too. Hours at least.

'Eighteen days.' Weariness filled the old woman's voice.

'Eighteen . . . *days*?' Yaz shook her head. 'That can't be right!'

'It isn't.' A tall, pale-skinned nun entered the room, bowing her head to avoid the doorframe. The returning novice followed on her heels. 'The correct figure is three weeks. Sister Owl joined your immobile state for several days while attempting to free you. Neither of you had a measurable heartbeat.'

'Sister Sun.' Owl inclined her head. 'My apologies for any distress caused. Few healers have to deal with such strange patients as Yaz and me.'

'But what happened to me?' Yaz wanted to know. 'Is Mali in danger? Where is she? Why did you leave me so long? Why—'

'It's dangerous to leap without looking.' Owl gave a tired smile. 'Without my preparation and reading we might both have been stuck for much longer than the three days we apparently shared. As to Novice Mali's fate – I believe that she is probably among the safest people on Abeth right now, and will be for thousands of years to come unless we rescue her. But believe me when I say there's no rush.'

'But what happened?' Yaz cast about for any sign of her clothes.

'I believe that Mali has encountered an artefact of the Missing known as a time-star. It has been suggested that they result from accidents where a shipheart overloads. All that the records say is that time itself slows, or speeds, as you approach them. The victim doesn't notice but seen from further away they appear to slow to the point where their movement becomes imperceptible. If they were to turn around they might witness the world rushing through the years, and before they were able to run back out of the star's area of effect the world they knew would have passed into a new age.'

'We have to help her! Erris and Thurin will be with her too!'

'We do.' Sister Owl nodded. 'But before that we have to help you and Quina. Both of you have more immediate problems. Speaking of which . . .' She turned to the tall nun. 'Have the past three days seen any developments I should be made aware of, Sun?'

Yaz drew her knees up, not listening to the nuns' whispering. Three weeks? A memory of the blue light haunted her mind, so seductive that even now her thoughts wanted to return to it and become lost again in a timeless moment. 'Quina! I need to see Quina!'

Yaz looked up and found the room dark save for the light of a single candle. Quina, who had been dozing in a chair beside the bed, leapt to her feet. 'What! What is it?' Then seeing Yaz she caught her in a fierce hug, hunska-fast. 'You're back again!'

'I . . . I am back . . .' Yaz blinked and detached herself from Quina's embrace. 'Owl was here a moment ago.'

'You froze up again,' Quina said. 'Sister Owl said it might happen a few times. Echoes, she called them. But not for weeks, just hours or minutes, and then moments and then nothing.'

'Well, that's . . . deeply worrying.' Yaz looked at Quina. She seemed different in the candle's light. Her hair was longer, her face was less bony, and she had a deep bruise across the whole of her left cheekbone.

Quina frowned a moment and worked her mouth as if trying to spit something out. 'Not . . . worry.' Two words of green-tongue.

'You're learning!' Yaz grinned, then frowned. 'What happened to your face though?'

Quina's hand moved to her bruise. 'I'm learning to fight too! Hell did this but I got her back a dozen times!' She echoed Yaz's frown. 'Not that she noticed. That girl's like a wall.'

Yaz shuffled off the bed and stood up. She felt a little stiff but not three-weeks-without-moving stiff. Her body still ached from the beating Hellma had given her. She pressed her stomach with both hands. 'I'm not even hungry.'

'Well, we did stuff ourselves.' Quina grinned. 'Weeks ago!'

'Let's get out of here.' Yaz started for the door.

'In your nightgown?' Quina nodded to the darkest corner where Yaz could swear she'd already looked. Her habit hung there, shoes beneath.

'What did I miss?' Yaz began to dress, still unfamiliar with the undergarments and various ties.

'Eular knows we're alive. Both his witches are in the convent to keep watch. And Abbess Claw has been fighting some big battle over it all. But while you were out of it the inquisitor couldn't do much.'

'Inquisitor?'

'Inquisitors and watchers work for the Church, hunting for anyone who needs punishing.' Quina shuddered. 'They came for us the day you froze up. But really they're only interested in you. They've not done much, just asked questions. Wenna said there'd be worse coming once you woke up. But you can't drown someone who isn't breathing. The nuns only managed to move you out of the blade-path chamber because Sister Owl worked some magic. You were standing there for a week though, creeping us all out. You must have watched me fall a hundred times!'

'You tried the blade-path?' Yaz was amazed.

'Sure. Wenna dared me. It's easy.'

'Easy?' It had looked impossible.

'Easy to fall off, I mean. Getting far along it takes years of practice. One of the girls can get halfway . . . Most novices become nuns without ever having reached the end even once.'

'Has Eular been here?' Yaz's blood had run cold at the mention of drowning, but the idea that Eular might have poked and prodded at her while she was frozen in time gave her a chill that was somehow worse.

'Not that I know of. Just Krey and Jeccis. They're bad enough. They're not the only ones to come here because of us though. There's also the inquisitor, his watchers, and some people they call Academics. It's been busy. Things will get much busier now you're awake. Like I said, they don't really care about me. It's you Krey and Jeccis want. We should probably leave. I don't think it's going to go well for us here.'

Yaz pursed her lips and tied the rope that secured her habit around her waist. 'We'll have to think about what to do. We need to save Thurin and Mali and Erris. We could run tonight if we have to, while they think I'm still frozen.'

She went to the door, opened it a crack, and peered out into the corridor beyond.

'Got to be quiet out there,' Quina hissed. 'Nuns everywhere.' She joined Yaz at the door, closing it again in case anyone waiting in the darkness outside might hear them talking. 'Getting out of the convent unobserved is going to prove difficult. I sneaked out last week to the caves to check on Theus. He's gone, by the way—'

'Gone?'

'You need me to explain "gone"? He only looks like a dog, you know? He's not going to sit in one spot for a month just because you tell him to. Not that a dog would do that either. I mean, unless their butt got frozen to the ice. Which does happen . . . Anyway, like I was saying, one of the Grey Sisters followed me. She's Sister Moon – really nice, you'd like her – and the stars are still where you left them with Theus, but, well, now all the nuns know about them too.'

Yaz bit down on any hot reply. Quina hadn't known how long she would be incapacitated, and Theus might have had the key to unlocking her from the time-star. 'It can't be helped. I should bring those stars here though. We may need them.' Thinking about the Watcher's eyes that she'd left with Theus made her remember the star she'd made using some of the dust recovered from the courtroom. She patted her habit pockets. 'Where's my star?'

'Sister Owl took it.'

Yaz shrugged, though the loss did pain her – making the star from its components had been an intimate process and she'd felt a bond with it. 'Let's go get the big ones!'

CHAPTER 18

Yaz led the way out into the corridor before realizing that she didn't actually know where she was, and that although she and Quina had arrived at the convent together, Quina now had weeks' more experience of the place than she did.

'I want to go to the dormitory first,' she whispered, pushing Quina ahead of her to guide the way.

Quina nodded. 'Then we leave.'

Quina made for the lighter end of the corridor where a lantern burned with its flame turned so low as to be barely a flicker. Doors like the one they'd come out through lined both sides of the passage, with a larger door at the end. Quina moved quietly and quickly, not stopping until she reached the final doors. They emerged into a blustery night, red stars scattering a clear sky, a dozen lights burning in various convent windows. For the first time Yaz noticed that one star alone among the host above was white, twinkling brighter than the others. She stood staring for a moment.

'That's the Hope.' Quina understood her surprise and spoke more loudly now so as to be heard above the wind. 'It can't be seen in the north or the south.'

Yaz shook her head. They even had different stars in the Corridor. She turned to see where she'd been sleeping. The building behind them was a short, low extension from the great Dome of the Ancestor.

'They had you in a nun's cell.'

'Let's go.' Yaz was glad to be out in the freshness of what seemed to her a mild enough breeze, but she felt watched, as if the night held not one but several pairs of eyes trained in her direction.

The convent seemed deserted. Yaz wasn't sure of the hour and neither was Quina, who'd been allowed to sleep in the nun's cell following Yaz's awakening that day. Quina kept yawning as they approached the dormitory building. They hurried up the steps and pushed in through the main doors into the hallway.

Quina closed it behind them, shutting off the starlight they'd navigated by. 'Chances are a Grey Sister was watching us. Sister Moon or one of the others. I don't think there are many here but they're out at night and they don't miss much.'

'I'll just sneak in and get what I need.' Yaz felt her way to the Grey Class dormitory doors and eased it open. The faint light leaking from the hooded lantern by Wenna's bed showed both rows of beds, their occupants little more than suggestions in shadow.

One of the girls rolled over as Yaz passed, muttering something incoherent. She made her way to the head of her bed. The mattress and covers might have been shaken or even laundered while she was frozen in time, but fortunately this didn't matter. Yaz went to the wall and moved her hand over the joints between the large stone blocks. Here and there small plugs of dirt fell away and the remainder of her stardust flowed out like snow crystals streaming across the ice. She closed her fist around the small mass, willing it to silence. For a moment she stood where she was, distributing the dust between her inner and outer pockets. Fortunately, for nuns who swore a vow of poverty, the sisters of Sweet Mercy still set a lot of store in pockets despite not being supposed to own much of anything to keep in them.

Satisfied, Yaz went quietly back towards the door. As she passed Wenna's bed a hand shot out and knotted in her habit. A blonde head emerged from beneath the covers. 'Hssst.' The hand yanked to indicate Yaz should bend over.

'Wenna?' Yaz knelt beside the bed, keeping her voice low.

'You need to get out of here.' Wenna skipped any small talk. 'My family know things. They're going to execute you and this time the archon will get his way about the axe. So unless losing your head doesn't bother you then you've got to escape. Tonight! I told Quina something like this would happen soon but she wouldn't leave without you. The Inquisition are here. You've got to go. Go. Run. Don't look back. Don't get caught. No matter what.' Wenna caught Yaz's wrist and gripped it tight before releasing her. 'Good luck.'

Yaz didn't know what to say so she left in silence. She'd not really felt that she knew Wenna well and the girl's concern touched her. She supposed that you didn't have to know someone well in order to be concerned that they don't die a horrible death.

Out in the lobby Quina rose swiftly from the stairs as Yaz left the dormitory. She led the way to the main doors then paused rather than open them. Yaz couldn't see her friend's face, just a patch of thicker darkness where she stood.

'What?'

'Maybe we should find a better way of leaving,' Quina whispered. 'I've been going to their Shade lessons. They take this stuff very seriously. We're not going to get out of here unless we're clever. And it's not just the Grey Sisters – they might possibly let us go – there're watchers from the Inquisition . . .'

'Wenna mentioned them. She said you should have left weeks ago.'

'It's not me they're after—'

'They'll kill you just the same. The nuns threw you into the Glasswater. Don't forget that!'

'We could go out one of the windows at the back,' Quina suggested.

'Not sure that'd work.' The windows were small and high up, and even if Yaz could fit through one it seemed impossible that they'd manage it without waking the whole dormitory.

'The windows on the top floor are bigger.'

'Maybe we could—' The outside doors just in front of them opened, admitting a flood of lantern light and a blustery wind, sharp with ice.

'Just the novices we were looking for.' The voice of an old woman.

Yaz squinted against the glow, shielding her eyes with a spread hand. Two figures stood on the steps, cloaks flapping around them, more behind them. She blinked and focused. Two priests: Mother Jeccis and a larger, younger woman who might be Krey, the Black Rock priest that Yaz hadn't seen during her time there.

Mother Jeccis half turned to wave forward one of the people behind her. 'Inquisitor Melcom, if you would have your watchers take these two into custody on behalf of the archon.'

Something dropped from above them all, a core of blackness trailing darkness behind it like a cloud of smoke. A person-sized something. It landed beside the steps without a sound. The inquisitor's lantern made little impact on the shroud of night but within heartbeats the darkness thinned to reveal a narrow woman, her young face scarred and weather-beaten. She studied the world with curiously opalescent eyes and wore a habit not unlike Yaz's but grey and cut to allow more freedom of movement.

'Sister Moon!' Quina sounded relieved, though why the addition of a trained murderer to the forces blocking their way should please her Yaz was unsure.

'This is Sweet Mercy.' Sister Moon spoke in a soft, conversational tone. 'The Inquisition and the priesthood are here by Abbess Claw's invitation. No official investigation has been sanctioned.'

'Abbess Claw knows very well—'

Sister Moon silenced the younger priest with a raised hand. 'Mother Jeccis, I'm sure you understand Church law. You may request that these two novices be taken into custody if you have a charge to level at them. And I will of course be happy to apprehend them for you. After that their fate would be in the hands of the abbess. Or – should there be an objection of sufficient weight – an ecclesiastical court.'

Mother Krey reached into her robes and brought out a tightly rolled scroll. 'This' – she brandished the document at Sister Moon as if it were a weapon – 'is Archon Eular's demand that his original call for beheading be carried out since the convent's traditional execution methods have proved to be flawed. It bears his seal and I have been deputized to witness the decapitations on the archon's behalf. Though I understand that you've failed to apprehend two of the criminals who escaped the water.'

'I'll consider that a request that Novices Yaz and Quina be placed under convent arrest,' Sister Moon said. 'And I have been authorized to agree to that request.' She beckoned to Yaz. 'You come with me. You too, Novice Quina.'

'I don't think so.' The inquisitor, a large bald man with remarkably deep-set eyes, stepped forward to intervene; the three watchers stood at his shoulders, hands settling on the hilts of hitherto unseen swords. 'I've been burning corruption out of the Church for twenty years. I'm not having my authority questioned by some nun so new to her habit it hasn't had its first wash yet.'

Mistress Shade simply appeared at the inquisitor's side, close enough to be intimate. There was no shroud of darkness to leak away as there had been with Sister Moon, no swift descent from on high. She had not been there, and then she was. Blonde hair uncovered, pale skin reddened by starlight. The inquisitor dwarfed her but she seemed so unconcerned by him that her lack of worry somehow became its own threat. '*I* question your authority, Melcom Lexus.'

The inquisitor shrank back as if finding himself too near a fire. 'This path is . . . unwise . . . sister.'

'Paths are not my business, brother. The Path is Sister Owl's concern. My business is the business of endings. And I do not mind how I get there.'

Without another glance at the man, Mistress Shade gestured for Yaz and Quina to precede her, then brought up the rear as Sister Moon led the way.

'Have a care, mistress,' Krey muttered as they left.

Sister Moon took them to the one place in the convent where the natural rock of the plateau formed a mound. A low cave mouth opened in the outcrop, leading onto the set of steps that Sister Owl had taken them down after their official drowning in the Glasswater. Yaz followed the assassin down the steps into darkness.

'We can't see anything, you know?' Quina called out from

behind Yaz. 'Seems like half the novices have shadow-work – they can see in the dark,' she added in a lower voice.

'Wait.' Sister Moon's footsteps faded ahead of them. A sharp scraping rang out and then a moment later light blossomed as she lifted a lantern. 'Come on.'

The nun waited for them at the door of Shade class where Mistress Shade educated novices in the arts of poison, the manipulation of shadow, and how to kill with wire or dart.

'I'm going to have to put you in the recluse again, I'm afraid.' Mistress Shade took over the lead, walking past the door to the classroom and on along a rocky tunnel. 'We can't be seen to be being too soft on you. There will be some sort of trial.'

Quina turned on her heel and made to run.

'*Not* like last time, I hasten to add.' Mistress Shade did not break stride. 'Archon Eular has left the capital and the high priest plans to oversee the proceedings. She's a fair woman.' She took several silent strides. 'Fairish.'

'I'm not letting them drown me again!' Quina hissed at Yaz in ice-tongue.

'I don't think anyone's demanding that,' Yaz replied. 'They want to cut our heads off. Much quicker. But' – she raised her voice over Quina's complaint – 'I don't plan to let them, whatever this high priest of theirs might say.' Whatever she might say to calm Quina's fears though, Yaz was worried. Both Krey and Jeccis had Path magics to pit against her own, and even Sister Owl might be compelled to work against her if the high priest ruled in Eular's favour. On top of that it was the nature of her power to be spent in an extravagant burst that could not be swiftly repeated. That wouldn't protect her against a convent full of knives and swords and envenomed darts. The truth was that both she and Quina were at the mercy of the green-landers' Church and its internal battles.

They walked some distance along an increasingly narrow tunnel, passing three doorways. Mistress Shade went left where the tunnel forked and halted twenty yards further on, indicating the gate in the bars that sealed off a small cave. Yaz sighed and walked in. Quina hesitated.

Yaz took hold of a bar in each hand. 'It's not these that are keeping us here, Quina. We're no less trapped on my side than on yours. At least this way there's still a chance for the abbess to argue our case.'

Quina entered with a snarl. 'I love the green lands. But why, when people get so much, do they suddenly start killing each other at the drop of a hood?'

Yaz settled down with her back to the rear wall. Quina's question was one she had no answer for. At least no answer that didn't make her sad.

CHAPTER 19

They spent two days in the recluse. The nuns fed them well, and Sister Owl came down to teach them. The lessons staved off boredom. Quina was set to copying letters on a slate. She enjoyed the idea and practice of writing, and Sister Owl praised the swiftness with which she learned, saying that it was easiest to acquire such skills at an early age. While Quina scratched out her symbols, Owl and Yaz talked about stars.

'Sister Moon told me of her discovery in the undercaves.'

'She followed Quina' Yaz said, failing to keep the accusation from her voice, 'in secret.'

'She's a Sister of Discretion. It's in her nature to pry. We can't know which secrets are a danger to the Church until we know what they are.'

Yaz made a disgruntled sound.

'The stars at that entrance to the undercaves are much larger than the one I found on you when you were frozen. I removed it out of concern that it might be the source of your malady.' The old woman frowned and her face, already a mass of wrinkles, furrowed further. 'I must say that those stars had an . . . unsettling effect on me. I felt unready to pick one up. So I didn't. But I understand that a shipheart is considerably bigger.' She held up her hands to frame an imagined sphere the size of a child's head then shuddered. 'If the malaise that emanates from a full-sized one increases as much between your larger stars and a shipheart as it does between your small star and the larger ones . . . then I can't understand how anyone could tolerate to even be near a shipheart.'

Yaz pursed her lips. 'It's not going to be easy.' In truth she was far from sure she could do it. 'But none of us are going to have a chance to know the answer unless we can find one.' She hesitated, and then decided to share a secret. After all, if Eular got his way and the Church killed her, the task would have to fall to Sister Owl or Mali or some other who might yet be found. Defeating Seus was everyone's fight, but it was more immediately the green-landers' battle. It was their green Corridor that Seus would close when he gained control of the ark, and with it the moon itself. She didn't know how quickly the ice would flow over these lands without the moon's nightly blast of heat. Sister Owl would certainly not live to see the last tree succumb. But perhaps Mali would if she lived to be as old as her teacher. 'I made the small star from hundreds of tiny ones. I've broken and remade a star the size of the ones in that tunnel mouth. The stars that I left there were the eyes of a monster that Eular made. The Watcher. The ones I have left I kept on purpose because they seem very similar to each other, as if they could once have been part of the same large star. I might be able to make a shipheart out of them.'

Sister Owl looked at Yaz for a long silent moment, a dark, appraising regard. 'Remarkable, child. Remarkable. I've not heard of such a thing. More importantly, I've not read of it, and these old eyes of mine have spent more years following the line of quill across page than most of my sisters have lived. You must have a truly rare skill.' Again she frowned, as if the rarity were more troubling than comforting.

They spent the rest of their time discussing the Path and the stars. Yaz contributed her personal experience, while Sister Owl shared the wisdom and observations of what seemed like a thousand scholars across many centuries. For the first time Yaz began to see what writing offered. The potential to make words and thoughts immortal. The potential for ideas to be pitted against each other and for some few to rise victorious from the fray, but for the others to survive on dusty shelves, waiting against the moment that they might once again find favour, or that the problem to which they were the key might rise to prominence and draw them from obscurity. The green-landers, at least the ones within this empire she'd wandered into, worshipped their ancestors, and Yaz wondered if this might be because the written word gave those long-dead ancestors such a strong voice and presence among them. The Ictha had their stories, of course, but they might change from telling to telling, from generation to generation. And their number dwindled in comparison to the books she had seen in the convent's library, each of which could hold many tales. Perhaps the Ictha had their gods because their ancestors' voices were buried beneath the years, whereas the green-landers merely had to stretch out an arm to take hold of the voice of some long-dead father's father's father, still strong and clear and perfectly preserved amid the marks left by the scratch of an inky feather.

Not much of what Sister Owl had to say made sense to Yaz, even when she let it rattle around in her skull after the nun left them to sleep. But some of it did. Some pieces of the wisdom and lore she scattered before Yaz turned out to be the keys for mental locks, each opening onto a treasure of new ideas and possibilities. To turn any of it into something useful would, however, take time.

And while time held three of her friends captive it had escaped her completely.

'It's time.' Sister Moon came hurriedly to the bars, startling Yaz from her thoughts. 'They're coming.'

Moments later Yaz heard the distant sound of boots on stone.

'Are they going to kill us?' Quina gripped the bars. The high priest had arrived early on the previous day and the interested parties had apparently been locked in debate until late in the night.

'I don't know. But they will if you don't submit to the court's justice. All of us here have to obey it as if the Ancestor had spoken directly.' The woman looked sad but stern. 'We're sworn to the Ancestor and to the Church of the Ancestor. It's the foundation of our belief. Just as the Rock of Faith is the foundation of our convent.'

Yaz resisted pointing out that the Rock of Faith was so full of holes that not long ago she had been lost among them and had worried she might never find her way out. 'We're ready,' she lied. Any words of false comfort she might have had for Quina went unspoken as the approaching escort arrived, lanterns held high. They packed the narrow tunnel: the bald inquisitor, at least three of his watchers, and behind them several Church guards. Mistress Blade accompanied the inquisitor at the front of the group, wearing her deep red habit and a sword at her hip. To hear Quina talk, the woman could defeat all of them even if they came at her together. She'd made quite an impression on Quina over the weeks that Yaz had been trapped by the time-star.

The walk to Persus Hall was both too long and too short. Yaz's unwilling feet ate the distance piece by piece. The inquisitor's watchers had brought with them iron yokes identical to the ones that had been used in the first attempt to drown the ice-tribers. Sister Moon, either out of sympathy, or concern that Yaz might bring the ceiling down on all of them, had refused to allow their use.

'The yoke is for those accused of high crimes. Yaz and Quina have already been accused, sentenced, and executed. The high priest is here simply to investigate Archon Eular's claim that their survival was not a miracle.'

'They're still accused of the original attack!' The inquisitor had bristled.

'They were found guilty of that attack and thrown into the Glasswater,' Moon had countered. 'No law of our Church requires that executed criminals remain yoked after sentence has been carried out.'

The inquisitor pointed at Yaz. 'They clearly haven't been executed!'

'That', Moon said, 'is what the high priest is here to decide. Do you presume to prejudge her, Inquisitor Melcom?'

Sister Moon got her way. Yaz was glad. She wasn't sure what she would have done if they'd tried to close a yoke about her neck and wrists again.

This was Yaz's third visit to the great courtroom. The first time had been confusing and terrifying, with Eular in the highest chair and the whole convent packed in to watch these strangers receive their dues. The second time it had been echoingly empty and she had recovered the stardust that

Eular had scattered. This time the audience was smaller, adults only. On the left side of the hall stood a handful of nuns, including Sisters Sun and Moon, and the mistresses of Path, Blade, Shade, and Spirit. This last woman Quina said went by the name Sister Mace when not using her teaching title. On the right side Inquisitor Melcom joined Mother Krey, who stood with more of his watchers and a small troop of Church guards. Also with them were three people in long robes, a man in green, a woman in violet, and another in blue, all startling shades that reminded Yaz of the coloured panes in Sister Owl's windows up in Path Tower.

'Academics,' Quina hissed. 'Mages from the city.'

Abbess Claw sat in one of the four smaller chairs several steps down from the high priest's chair, which had been occupied by Eular during the first trial. Mother Jeccis sat in another, at the opposite end to the abbess. The high priest looked tiny in the great, carved throne, whose back rose high above her, terminating in swirled turrets. The wood was almost black, and her robes were similarly dark, making it seem almost as if her face and hands floated there without a body to support them. She was a thin, bird-like woman with bright blue eyes, old but by no means as ancient as Sister Owl.

Yaz watched the high priest as Abbess Claw introduced all the important parties and invited Mother Jeccis to state Archon Eular's grievance. Mother Jeccis stood to address the court, though her words were intended for the woman behind her. As far as Yaz understood it, in the absence of the Church's four archons it was only High Priest Kerra's opinion that mattered here.

'On the eighteenth three-day in the seventh year of the reign of our glorious emperor, Edissat, second of his name, Archon Eular and—'

'Let us assume that I am familiar with the details of their trial, good mother.' The high priest's voice was almost comically high, like the chirping of a bird. 'What is the substance of your complaint?'

'These two criminals' – Mother Jeccis indicated Yaz and Quina with a gnarled finger – 'and the two that escaped the convent. Yaz of the Ictha, Quina Hellansdaughter, Lestal Erris Crow, and Thurin—'

'Would it be fair to say', chirped the high priest, causing Jeccis's face to darken, 'that the substance of your complaint is that the survival of these four after being thrown yoked into the Glasswater was *not* a miracle as Abbess Claw maintains?'

'It would, high priest,' Jeccis said through clenched teeth.

'And, Abbess Claw, now that we are convened within a holy court of justice: do you still believe that this event was indeed a miracle of the Ancestor?'

Abbess Claw remained seated. 'I believe all miracles are the work of the Ancestor, high priest.'

'This was the doing of a marjal water-worker!' Jeccis snapped. 'Half your novices can work similar tricks.'

'Well . . .' Claw inclined her head. 'I doubt that many of them could work such an impressive feat in any element, but' – she raised a hand to ward off Jeccis's interruption – 'the real question here is: what *is* a miracle? Are we saying that the Ancestor cannot work miracles through their children? Is it only a miracle if the magic arises without apparent source?'

'Yes!' snapped Jeccis.

The high priest pursed her withered lips. 'It would seem to degrade the currency of miracles if we were to title every impressive deed of marjal or quantal magic an instance of divine intervention.' She looked over at the Academics with a slight smile. 'Are our secular friends from the Academy to be officially known as miracle-workers?'

'That would seem unwise, high priest.' Abbess Claw nodded slowly as if persuaded.

Yaz gripped the wooden rail before her, glad that Quina's mastery of green-tongue wasn't yet sufficient to follow the discussion. She had hoped that Abbess Claw would come armed with clever defences and argue the high priest around to her way of thinking. Instead she seemed to be letting Eular's second in command walk all over her.

'So the survival of these two criminals—'

'Novices,' Claw protested.

'The survival of these two novices', Jeccis continued, 'is just the work of a talented *criminal*, now escaped, motivated by his own desire to survive and owing nothing to divine intervention.'

'It's a possibility,' Abbess Claw admitted. Yaz's blood ran cold. Beside her Quina seemed to be understanding the conversation's direction of flow, tensing to fight.

A note of triumph entered Mother Jeccis's voice. 'I move that they both be executed immediately in a manner that this time leaves no doubt that they are both dead.'

The high priest rubbed at her chin. 'Abbess Claw? Do you have anything to add?'

'Well. I should mention the second miracle.' The abbess set both hands to the crozier resting across her legs.

'What second miracle?' Jeccis sneered. 'Did the Ancestor conveniently descend to perform a miracle for these ice-tribers just before they were collected from their cell?'

'Descend, Mother Jeccis?' Abbess Claw raised an eyebrow. 'The Ancestor is always among us. And even a priest needs a little faith. The Ancestor has performed countless documented miracles over the last five centuries. Our Church

181

libraries are full of such accounts. Some of them quite lengthy.'

Jeccis folded her arms. 'And what, pray tell, was the nature of this miracle?'

'Surely you remember the arrival of Inquisitor Melcom at the convent?'

'Hardly miraculous. Where there is dissent the Inquisition comes to adjudicate.'

'Inquisitor Melcom arrived convinced of the novices' guilt and ready to pass sentence. And within moments of his arrival, Yaz, who was watching the girls on the blade-path, was removed from time itself. She became impervious to all harm, physical or magical. Saved by the Ancestor. None of us have ever witnessed such a thing, not even Sister Owl, who has seen five emperors on the throne. And no mention of such enchantment is made in our library. It was a miracle, not worked by Yaz but worked from outside, from another source, the divine source. A miracle.'

Mother Jeccis snorted. 'If it was a miracle then what was its purpose? What did it achieve? She just stood there like an imbecile statue, and now she still stands in court accused of her crime. The other girl too. No magics were worked on her, miraculous or otherwise. No, abbess, you're going to have to try harder than that.'

'Two important things were changed. One is that, shortly before Yaz was returned to us, the high priest showed an interest in the case, and said she would adjudicate when both the accused were fit to stand trial. And the other is that a second miracle was provided for the high priest to consider.'

Yaz drew a deep breath into her starving lungs. The abbess had deftly circled around Jeccis until the old woman tied herself up with her own words. But none of it would matter if the high priest didn't want to be convinced.

The high priest's eyes, disconcertingly blue even at this distance, were fixed on Yaz. For a long time she was silent. She glanced once at Quina. 'The blade-path, you say?'

'Yes, high priest. I believe the other novices were showing it to Yaz and Quina for the first time.'

'I would like to go there.' The high priest stood, robes falling and flowing around her diminutive form. 'If a miracle was performed there, I wish to stand in the place. Maybe it will clear my mind. And I can hardly stand in the mud beneath the fathoms of the Glasswater.'

And so it was that the high priest, accompanied by Yaz, Quina, the abbess, both priests, the inquisitor, four of the convent's five mistresses, and three mages, left Persus Hall and shuffled across the convent, bowed against the ice-laden wind, to Blade Hall, nestled on the very edge of the Rock of Faith, perched above a great cliff at whose distant base trees rustled.

The mage in the violet robe, a lean woman with long grey hair, walked closest to Yaz and seemed to study her with particular intensity, her pale blue eyes not leaving Yaz for the whole of the excursion.

The inquisitor had complained about leaving the watchers and guards but the high priest said she had utter faith in the ability of Mistresses Path, Blade, and Shade to handle any two novices in the history of all convents everywhere. And went on to point out that while the blade-path chamber was exceptionally tall, there wasn't a vast amount of floor space. Yaz bit her lip thoughtfully at this. The high priest knew about the blade-path. Abbess Claw must have known that she was familiar with the game.

They followed Abbess Claw through the hall's great doors, across the sand of the training area and along the tunnel to the blade-path chamber. The abbess brought a lantern in from the corridor and lit several around the chamber as the others shuffled in.

Yaz stared up through the net at the snaking, multi-jointed pipe above, supported by dozens of cables but still able to swing and lurch as a novice's weight moved along it. The start was lost in shadow. On the previous and first occasion she'd visited the room there had been lanterns up on the platform where the novices began their attempt.

'The miracle happened here.' Abbess Claw indicated the spot where Yaz had been frozen.

'Hardly a miracle,' Inquisitor Melcom sneered. 'A dose of the right toxin will have the same effect within moments. A rigid paralysis. Isn't that one of the first venoms a Grey Sister is taught to brew?'

'It is,' Mistress Shade said. 'But if I were to jab you with this pin' – she lifted her hand and Yaz caught a gleam from something between the nun's finger and thumb – 'I could then cut your throat and you'd die. Though you'd probably remain standing for some time.'

'Yaz was outside of time,' Sister Owl supplied. 'Impervious to harm. The building could have fallen on her and she would not have noticed or been injured.'

The high priest came to stand in the spot where Yaz had made her connection with Mali and seen the time-star. Amid the crowd of nuns, priests, and Academics, she was by far the shortest and seemed almost a child beside the tallest of the mages. She looked around briefly at the faces turned her way then raised her eyes to the twists and turns of the blade-path.

'It's been a long time.' The high priest sounded wistful.

'You were very good at it, Kerra, if I recall.' Sister Owl came to stand with the high priest, gazing upwards.

'I fell a thousand times before I completed it. I didn't hold the convent record – that was Jomma Jotsis, if I recall correctly.'

'Jomma Jotsis . . . whatever became of that girl?' Sister Owl asked.

'Married a Scithrowl lord and ran off to live east of the mountains. Always was a wild one.'

Jeccis made a sour face and looked as if she wanted to interrupt, but Abbess Claw elbowed past her to join Owl and the high priest. 'I never made it to the end. Do you remember your ti—'

'One hundred and fifty-nine counts.' The high priest answered before the question was finished. 'Jomma managed one hundred and fifty-seven. I hated her for that for years. She held the record among the current novices the whole time I was here.'

Abbess Claw lowered her gaze, rubbing her neck. 'It's one hundred and twenty at the moment. A novice in Holy Class. Should make a fine Grey Sister.'

'Of course,' said the high priest, looking back at those gathered around her, 'the all-time record holder is with us right now. Sister Owl secured that particular honour. Happened years before my time, but I wish I had been here to see it. How anyone could finish the course in a count of twenty-six makes no sense. You would have had to do it at a flat sprint . . .'

'I was going pretty fast.' The ancient nun allowed herself a small smile.

Inquisitor Melcom made a cough that was not really a cough. 'And even that was not a miracle.'

The high priest nodded to herself. 'Melcom makes a good point. I really shouldn't be reminiscing. Two girls' lives are in the balance here. You don't feel this time business was a miracle, Mother Jeccis?'

'I do not.'

'She was outside time!' Owl said.

'It was unusual, yes.' Mother Jeccis glanced at Yaz with narrowed eyes. 'But the unusual or rare are not miracles.'

'So what does have to happen for you to concede a miracle has occurred?' Abbess Claw asked. 'Must the Ancestor appear personally and say so? How many more inexplicable things must occur? One more? Ten more? A thousand more? Would you like Yaz to walk on water for you? What would tip the balance? Perhaps you want her to walk the blade-path from end to end on her first try?'

Mother Jeccis's scowl, which had been deepening with each of Abbess Claw's challenges, now changed as a cruel smile tugged at the corners of her mouth. She turned to look at the high priest.

'I do.'

'What?'

'I do want her to walk the whole blade-path on her first try.'

Abbess Claw looked aghast. 'And that would be a miracle, would it?'

'If she did it while blindfolded.' The smile showed teeth now.

'Nobody could do it blindfolded!' Claw snapped.

'If I may?' The grey-haired mage in violet approached the high priest.

'Academic Yelna?' the high priest looked surprised. 'You have something to add?'

Yelna inclined her head and shot a pale glance at Yaz. 'Only to say that there are many types of magic that the accused might employ to give the appearance of a miracle without actually requiring the Ancestor's hand to reach out to help them. Perhaps a dose of groton would be appropriate?' She bowed her head and backed away.

Mother Jeccis seized on the idea. 'Of course she should

186

have to take groton. It's the only sure way to guarantee she can't use magics to help her.' The priest turned to Inquisitor Melcom. 'You carry groton, don't you?'

The inquisitor nodded. 'Can't have quantal or marjal suspects trying to fool us.'

'But groton makes you dizzy,' Mistress Shade interjected.

'It really would be a miracle then, wouldn't it?' Mother Jeccis sneered.

The high priest thinned her lips, looking up at Mother Jeccis. 'It would certainly be a miracle. The only question is: Are we abusing our faith in the Ancestor, ignoring what has already been done and demanding more as if the Ancestor serves us rather than we the Ancestor?'

'Three is a holy number, high priest,' Mother Krey said from behind her.

'Did not St Kerber call upon the Ancestor three times at the gates of Goloroth before the fire smote them?' Inquisitor Melcom intoned.

The high priest looked grim. 'Archon Eular was very clear when he came to see me that he had worries some or all of the criminals he had sentenced might survive through trickery. He had worries that not everyone in a position of authority at Sweet Mercy respected his decision. How will Church law continue to be respected if those condemned to death evade punishment through cleverness or luck?'

'To be fair,' the abbess said, 'they were condemned to being thrown into—'

'Legal technicalities are all well and good if there are miracles involved, Claw, but at my elevation I have to think about how these things look to those outside this convent. How the people and the emperor see it. How the clergy from the Marn to the mountains see it. I require that both the spirit and the letter of the law be met.'

187

'But Eular was lying!' Yaz burst out. 'He doesn't even believe in the Ancestor! He's been a priest of the Black Rock for centuries—'

'Enough!' Despite her high voice and low stature the high priest could inject command into her words. 'He is an archon of the Church. You are a wanderer from the ice. Found guilty in this convent of robbery and murder. Abbess Claw says a miracle saved you from drowning. One more will save you from falling and will clear your name for good. You may take this challenge in place of your friends since the abbess seems to think that the hand of the Ancestor is on your shoulder.' She set her jaw. 'I have spoken.'

Mother Jeccis nodded, then added, 'Either there will be a miracle, or the girl deserves to die. So we should take the net away – it serves no purpose either way.'

CHAPTER 20

'How in the hells am I supposed to do this?' Yaz hissed at the abbess.

She'd been taken to the far corner of the blade-path chamber, allegedly for spiritual counsel. Abbess Claw was grim-faced. 'Pray.'

'That's it?' Yaz hadn't expected actual spiritual counsel.

'I'd hoped that the high priest would be persuaded by the fact you had been shielded from the Inquisition. I'd hoped that in this place, reminded of her past glories and her years as a novice, she would see the Ancestor's hand in this matter, or show mercy, or both.'

'Hoped . . .' Yaz muttered bitterly. She remembered that Claw had also failed to save her from Eular's punishment. They had had to find their own way out of that.

'All I can suggest is that you play to your strengths.'

'My strengths?'

'And pray for a miracle.'

'Another miracle,' Sister Owl said. 'We've already had two.'

Yaz's temper control had deserted her. She waved a hand

at the twisted metal suspended in the many fathoms of open air above them. 'How am I not going to fall off?'

The only answer was the return of Mistress Blade with a hooked pole to take down the net.

Inquisitor Melcom followed the nun over. 'The groton.' He held a small black pot between finger and thumb. 'For the prisoner,' he added unnecessarily. He removed the lid and dipped his index finger into the grey paste within.

'I can do it myself.' Yaz curled her lip at the thought of the man feeding her.

Melcom put the pot back into a pocket of his robe and reached towards her. 'It's given. Not taken.'

Yaz resisted the urge to bite off the finger thrust at her face and instead closed her mouth firmly. The moment of choice had rushed at her with unexpected speed and now hovered just before her face on a man's fingertip. If she took their poison then the Path would be beyond her. The chance to exit the world in a sudden blaze, and to take Quina with her, would have passed. When she fell from the blade-path, and was killed by the fall, Quina would be abandoned to whatever cruel justice the Church dictated. Taking the poison was only briefly extending their lives and setting them up for greater suffering. She defocused her eyes, seeing past the finger, seeing the line of the Path, a blazing crack through reality, close enough to seize in both hands. She started to reach.

'Don't do it, Yaz.' Sister Owl's eyes swam with tears. 'I can feel what you're doing. I can stop you too. It would be dangerous for both of us. But this room is full of my sisters. I can't allow the destruction you're thinking of.'

'What else can I do?' Yaz could feel the cold fire of the Path tingling just beyond her fingertips.

'Have faith. It doesn't have to be my faith. Have faith in yourself. You've done the impossible before.'

'But I don't know how to do *this*!' Yaz glanced up at the coiling pipe above her. 'A few months ago I'd never even climbed anything. This . . . thing . . . it takes years of practice. You want me to do it poisoned and blindfold!'

Sister Owl's withered hands closed around Yaz's. 'Sometimes all we can do is try. And you're not wholly without resources . . . are you?'

Yaz knew she was trapped. She bared her teeth at the inquisitor. 'Do it.'

Melcom smeared the greasy toxin inside her lips. She could feel the tremble in his finger. He knew how close to destruction he'd been. He stood back to watch as she closed her mouth and licked it off. It tasted fishy. If it was made from a fish it would be the first she'd eaten since arriving in the green lands – a miracle in and of itself in the eyes of her people.

'How fast does it work?' The inside of her mouth already felt tingly.

Melcom seemed more relaxed now. 'It works faster on a dart but this form is easier to store and cheaper to make. It will take full effect by the time you've climbed to the platform.'

'I'd better go now then. You wouldn't want me losing my balance on the stairs,' Yaz growled.

Mistress Blade and Mistress Shade accompanied Yaz as she made for the door. Mother Jeccis followed.

'You've got a plan, right?' Quina asked as they passed her.

Yaz offered a brave smile.

The staircase up to the platform where the blade-path began was a long, narrow square spiral, and the shifting of shadows across the wall as the small group climbed was disorienting. Twice Yaz stumbled.

191

'If you can't climb stairs walking the pipe will be interesting,' Mother Jeccis commented.

'It's the groton,' Mistress Shade said. 'All I can suggest is to take your time and wait for moments of *clarity*.'

'No helping her!' Jeccis snapped.

'The high priest said that she should be blindfolded and poisoned. Not that she be given no advice,' Mistress Shade replied.

Yaz hadn't missed the stress on the word 'clarity'. It was one of the trances that Sister Owl taught the novices in Path Tower, but Yaz hadn't even had a whole lesson on the subject and it was something novices took months, maybe years to master.

There was barely room on the small platform for the four of them. The drop to the distant floor yawned before them and a vertigo reached up for Yaz, seeking to haul her down. She'd climbed endless cables in the undercity, descending shafts deeper than the one before her, but the groton was distorting her vision, making it seem an impossibly long fall, filling her with rootless terror, sapping the strength from her legs.

Far below her the lanterns of the high priest and the others seemed as distant as stars in the heavens.

'I have to blindfold you now.' Regret coloured Mistress Shade's voice as she reached into her habit and brought out a thick band of black material.

Yaz focused on the opposite wall where the great dial and pendulum hung, ready to count the times of the rare novices who could complete the course. Her stomach was in rebellion. The Ictha lived solely off the fruit of the sea. Many of the creatures they hauled from beneath the waves or trapped under the ice shelf at the borders of the Hot Sea had fashioned themselves to be unpalatable. The Ictha in turn had grown to resist their toxins. If the choice was to starve or be poisoned then the Ictha chose the latter and learned to live with it. Even so, whatever resistance had been bred into her, the groton was still having an effect. She felt unsteady and nausea churned her stomach. She could hardly defocus her eyes to see the Path which now lay far beyond her reach, an almost invisible thread at the very limits of her perception.

'The girls put resin on their feet to stop them slipping.' Mistress Blade pushed something sticky into Yaz's hand as Mistress Shade bound her eyes.

'You're not to—'

'Complete the blade-path on her first try, blindfolded and poisoned,' Mistress Blade spoke over Jeccis. 'That's what the high priest said. She can have the same as any other novice. Or are we to grease the pipe, cut off one of her feet, and throw spears at her too?'

Yaz hurriedly rubbed the resin on the sole of one foot, then the other. Standing blindfold on one leg she began to pitch forward, saved from the fall only by the quick hands of one of the mistresses. It did not bode well.

'Are you ready, Yaz?' Mistress Path asked.

'No.'

'The test begins,' Mother Jeccis called out. 'No further aid can be given!'

Yaz began by standing as still as she could. She felt herself swaying, but less now that the distractions of sight had been taken from her. She thought of the lanterns below her, distant as city lights from the main hall's window slits.

She thrust her hands into her habit. The sleeping stardust lined several of the garment's many pockets. 'Wake up.' She muttered the words. 'Wake up.'

They'd said that the groton put the powers of a quantal or a marjal beyond use. Certainly Yaz's connection to the Path had been weakened. But on the long journey from the north Theus had said one thing that rang true among his many lies. Theus had said she shared his blood. He'd said that the old saying – *The Ictha are a different breed* – was true. Even the Ictha's oldest tales of Zin and Mokka agreed. They had been here before the four tribes crossed the black sea and beached on Abeth's shores. The Ictha were the Missing. An outcast clan, self-exiled, mixed and mingled with those who came after, but like all the old bloods the Missing's blood showed strongly in some. And it showed in her.

'*Wake up.*'

And the stardust woke. She saw its glow with her mind's eye. This power was a gift of the Missing's blood. Groton, it seemed, had little impact on it. Still . . . what could be achieved with a handful of dust?

'Get going, girl!' Jeccis said. 'The drop's waiting.'

Yaz ground her teeth and pushed hard, tearing the seams in her pockets. She brought her hands out and knelt to feel for the start of the pipe. She found it open, presumably so that any moisture that entered by the many joints could escape again. Ominously, it moved even beneath the pressure of her hands.

She stood slowly and raised her voice. 'I call upon all my ancestors. Grant me the miracle of your power.'

As she spoke she willed away the glow of the stardust and sent a small stream of it down her leg, across the outside of her foot and into the pipe. In her mind's eye she could see it through the metal, snaking away along the twisted length, drawing in the blade-path without the need for eyes. Eular would appreciate the trick.

'Grant me a miracle.' She sent the bulk of the dust up across her ribs, out along her arms, and into the palms of her hands, almost all the journey beneath her habit. She made fists around the small lumps of stardust.

She placed one foot on the blade-path. With the sight of the drop hidden from her all sense of vertigo had gone. She imagined that the floor lay mere inches below. Behind her the two nuns were praying quietly. Yaz stretched her arms out wide, found her balance, and stepped forward, placing her other foot on the pipe. Immediately she began to wobble. She didn't fight it. Instead she reached out with her mind and held the two masses of stardust where they were. Exactly where they were.

In the undercity she had borne nearly her entire weight by willing a single star to rise and clinging to it with both hands. The stardust couldn't give her anything like that amount of lift, but it didn't have to. At the extremity of her reach all it needed to do was provide enough force to correct her wobbles.

Yaz took another step. Whether the dust could correct her balance when the pipe swung beneath her, she couldn't say, but here and now, with a slow, steady step, seeing the pipe before her as a thin, glowing line, almost like the Path itself . . . she could do it.

Another step. More. She was walking the blade-path blind-fold. Behind her, silence reigned as the nuns left their mouths open and forgot to pray.

CHAPTER 21

A day had passed since the blade-path miracle and the high priest's declaration that Yaz was blessed by the Ancestor. The novices of Grey Class had welcomed her back to the dormitory with considerable enthusiasm. The girls who had come closest to finishing the test themselves seemed most impressed with the miracle. Hellma, having never got more than a few steps along the pipe, had no real appreciation of the difficulty involved with the latter sections. She thought it more miraculous that Yaz still wore the bruises that she'd been given in their fight weeks ago in her first Blade lesson.

Quina rode the excitement with the other novices, chatting away at great speed in a mix of ice-tongue and broken green-tongue. She'd become very popular in the dormitory, despite, or perhaps because of, the fact neither she nor the girls she spoke to understood more than half of what the other said.

According to Sister Owl, being blessed erased all sins and crimes – at least in the Church's eyes – and gave the recipient a fresh slate on which to begin anew. Yaz didn't know enough about the Ancestor to have an opinion, but she wasn't prepared to forgive herself so easily. Eular's charges against her might have been entirely false, but he had been correct about her in the past when he called her an agent of change. That change, whether beneficial or not in the long run, had caused many deaths both beneath the ice and within the Black Rock. She had taken some of those lives herself when she unleashed the power of the Path during the battle with the Tainted in the ruins of Vesta. A blessing didn't wash that blood away any more than water did.

An awkward breakfast followed during which Yaz felt more of a stranger than she had on the day they arrived. Somehow the blessing and the stolen weeks put a barrier between her and the other novices, though Quina, who had benefited from the blessing in a similar way, seemed perfectly at home. She had even managed to make friends with the pair who had mocked her drowning, the dark-haired hunksa, Niome, and the red-haired gerant, Kola.

Yaz watched Quina from time to time and tried to imagine her as she had been less than half a year before, walking the ice with her family and clan, seeing nothing but frozen waste from one day to the next, never knowing warmth, never eating anything save fish, sometimes hot from the sea, but most often frozen. She imagined Quina ahead of her in the regulator's queue, knowing herself broken and clutching her stolen bead of wood as a talisman against her inevitable fall.

If nothing else Yaz had done that one good thing. She had brought Quina out of that hole in the ice full of darkness and insanity and delivered her into the plenty of the Corridor. Both of them had seen a world wholly beyond their imagining. Several worlds, in fact, if you counted the Broken and the Tainted, the Black Rock and Haydies.

Quina chose that moment to break from her laughter over

some small matter with Wenna and glance at Yaz. Her dark eyes filled with some new emotion.

'Are you all right, Yaz?'

'What? Yes. Of course.' Yaz became uncomfortably aware that she was blinking away tears.

'We'll get the others back,' Quina said, not caring if the rest of the novices were hearing. 'Sister Owl says they're safe. We have time.'

Yaz nodded and looked down at her food, trying to get a grip on herself. Time had been fickle of late. Just as the ice had revealed itself to hide great and unexpected secrets, time too had proved less reliable than she had always believed it was. On the other hand, Quina was correct. They had time – something they'd not had for an age. Ever since she had dropped into the Pit of the Missing, Yaz had been, as Erris would say, on a clock. She'd had to save Zeen before the Tainted ruined him. She'd had to escape Eular before he used thread-work to change her mind. Even on the endless trek towards the Corridor their dwindling supplies had urged them on: no day could be wasted, no rest taken.

'What's our next lesson?' Yaz looked around the refectory at the four long benches, at the novices bent over their food. This was their life, day after day: lessons, progress, learning, tests, challenges. Their hunger had been taken care of, freeing their bodies and minds to be directed to other ends. It was her life now, unchained from the all-consuming task of simply not dying.

'Shade,' Quina said through a full mouth.

Yaz had thought they were only attending Path lessons but Quina's enthusiasm persuaded her not to question the idea and she went to the Shade lesson without complaint. The girls filed into the room where Sister Owl and the abbess had talked to Yaz and her friends after they escaped drowning. Yaz sat there as Mistress Shade spoke about some plant of the green lands from which poison might be brewed. She tried to pay attention but her mind wandered towards the blue light that held Mali and Erris and Thurin. Weeks of her life would pass for each moment of theirs. She might be grey and old when Thurin finally thought to turn around and walk out of there, unchanged from the young man he'd been when he entered the time-star's aura.

'Are you still with us, Yaz?'

Yaz blinked and found that a complicated mass of green had been laid on the desk before her, stems and leaves and gleaming white berries. 'I . . .'

She looked around, startled, to find the other novices had stripped the berries from the plants they'd been given and were doing something fiddly with the black seeds and pale flesh. Scattered laughter went round the room, quickly silenced by Mistress Shade's narrow stare.

'You think this funny, Novice Gully?' The nun turned on a mousey-haired girl who sat behind her.

'N-no!' Her voice held genuine fear.

Mistress Shade flicked the girl's ear, making her wince. 'You're welcome to lie, but at least do it well. I've taught you to be more convincing than *that*.' The nun returned her attention to Yaz before looking around the class. 'There's a lesson here. Laugh for us, Yaz.'

'What?'

'Don't tell me that your remarkably swift acquisition of our tongue has suddenly failed? Laugh! You've just had half a dozen examples. They were laughing at you. Laugh back.' She clapped her hands together. 'Laugh!'

'Uh . . .' Yaz glanced about, embarrassed. She tried to laugh. Even to her ears it sounded so wrong as to be comical.

Across the room Hellma burst out with a laugh of her own before clamping both her huge hands over her mouth.

Mistress Shade lifted a finger for silence. 'That *was* funny,' she acknowledged. 'But also difficult. To fake amusement convincingly is a skill that many are unable to master even after considerable practice. Laughter is more honest than tears. Never mock someone for their laugh – even Hellma who laughs like a horse – because that's as true a thing as the nose on your face. Tears can be faked. And even when true they are often for ourselves, imagining the tragedy visited upon us, rather than for the victim of the situation. Laughter, however, is unfiltered – both the when of it and the how. It's as true as a sneeze or the little death, emotion is escaping us under pressure.' She moved between the desks. 'In Shade we train killers and to do that we spend more time on people than on knives' – she produced one of the latter from nowhere and stabbed it into the desk before Quina – 'or poisons.' She flicked at the leaves in front of Yaz. 'These are often our tools, but it is more important to understand the material to which we apply our tools. The most dangerous person in the room is not the swiftest blade or the deadliest poisoner, it is always the one who understands everyone else best. And understanding everyone else begins with understanding yourself – which is why the lessons I teach here really begin with Sister Owl in Path class. The clarity, patience, and serenity trances are excellent keys to the self. You learn about others by watching – but everything you see is seen through the lens of yourself.' She set a finger to the centre of her forehead. 'Here is where we first learn what we need to understand others.'

The following lesson was with the one mistress Yaz had yet to meet, Mistress Academia, and it was taught in Academia Tower. This was not, Quina assured her, to be confused with the Academy in the nearby city where the Academics who had been present at their second trial had come from. The mages called themselves Academics but their study was that of the marjal magics they dedicated themselves to, not of the histories and natural sciences that the novices were taught in Sweet Mercy's Academia lessons.

Yaz followed the novices up the spiral staircase with a measure of trepidation. She'd been less intimidated by the magics of Sister Owl and Mistress Shade because she had magics of her own and had been told several times that she'd been given a large helping of such talent. The nuns' battle skills were of course impressive, but Yaz found it hard to set much store by a person's ability to kill others. Murder and war were, in her opinion, a kind of sickness that took over men's minds when they had too much plenty and too much leisure. As if the species were unable to be content, and when the wind and the ice ceased to torture them they had to find ways in which to torture each other or even themselves.

Mistress Academia, however, had powers that evoked both admiration and awe in Yaz. She had command over the written word, in execution and interpretation, constituting a wide window into a vast legacy of learning and history. To the Ictha it would seem as if a miraculous, unsuspected, and hidden world had been opened to them. Even to Yaz, whose mind had already been broadened with knowledge from sharing in both Erris's and Mali's minds, it was far more of a miracle than her completion of the blade-path – a task that had seen her impossibly close to falling on half a dozen separate occasions. So close, in fact, that Yaz could almost believe the invisible hand of the Ancestor really *had* been there that day, holding her to the blade-path.

Yaz shuffled into the back of the classroom. Mysterious charts adorned the walls and, behind the mistress's desk, wooden shelving extended to the ceiling with tight-wrapped scrolls poking out of numerous nooks. The nun herself was a woman of uncertain years, her smooth skin at odds with the stray strand of silver hair that escaped her headdress. She had a solid build, much like the Ictha, and looked more suited to the ice than Yaz did herself, her changes since the pit having melted the weight from her bones.

Mistress Academia tapped her desk with a long nail, seemingly allowed to grow specifically for this purpose whilst all the others remained short. Her grey eyes found Yaz in the silence that followed, appraising her for a moment.

'We were talking about the first Durnish invasion,' the nun said, looking around the class. 'A time when this nation stumbled over its pride and fell into a war from which it could not tear free no matter how much it bled.'

Yaz sat and listened with rapt attention to details of battles at sea and on beaches, a war fought between a people she knew very little about and a people she knew nothing about. It struck her that the numbers of men and women hewing at each other in these battles exceeded all the peoples of the three northern ice tribes, from newest babe to greyest head. And that each of the populations – that of the empire and of this land of Durn across the Marn Sea – likely held more souls than all the tribes of the ice, both north and south. Moreover, the empire and Durn were just two of many nations queued along the Corridor, encircling the world and doubtless barely aware of their more distant neighbours, sharing nothing but the light of the moon that sustained them all.

The lesson ended, time was spent in the cloister, food was eaten, and Yaz found herself readying herself for bed once again.

She changed into the nightdress that had been provided

for her and sat back, watching Quina mock-fighting with Hellma as Wenna and Gully offered advice. It amazed Yaz that, having walked thousands of miles from her own family, Quina seemed to have found a replacement here in the green lands. Yaz eased her still-bruised body beneath the covers of her bed and closed her eyes. On the ice she would be an adult, expected to contribute a full share of labour, ready to have her own tent, ready to marry, to have children of her own. Here they still called her a child and showed her that she had a nearly endless amount yet to learn before they considered her fit to face the world on her own.

She fell into her dreams thinking of that tent, shuddering on the ice, and of the warmth within it, snuggled amid the sleeping hides. In her dreams strong arms wrapped her and drew her deeper among the covers. Familiar arms, trusted, caring, representing a home and a safety she had yet to find. But whether they belonged to Quell, to Erris, to Thurin, or to some other still waiting among the years to come, she couldn't say.

On the following day Sister Owl came to excuse Yaz from Blade class, and while Quina went off with the others the nun took Yaz to recover the Watcher's eyes. Or, more accurately, Sister Owl went as far as the top of the Seren Way and then sent Yaz to retrieve the stars.

'I haven't been down this path since I turned eighty. Getting old might be the Ancestor's way of telling us it's time to join them, but it's quite an inconvenience when the Ancestor keeps calling but never actually comes to collect you. In short, Yaz, pray you never have to get as ancient as I am.'

Yaz followed the narrow trail as it snaked back and forth across the width of its near-vertical descent. Far below her a green carpet of forest reached out towards the farmlands between the Rock of Faith and the city of Verity. Yaz longed to go down and investigate. The only greenery she'd properly laid hands on so far was the plant from which she had been supposed to make poison in yesterday's Shade class. She resisted, though, and kept her eyes on the rocky slopes. It took a bit of investigation before she rediscovered the crack from which they'd emerged to escape the caves, but she found it before too long. The stars drew her to it.

Rather than squeeze into the dark fissure, Yaz called on the Watcher's eyes and brought them floating towards her, lighting up the tunnel in blues and greens. Their proximity, which drove most people away, soothed her in a manner she found hard to explain and suddenly made her realize she'd missed their presence. Like fire, too much would undo her just as it undid others, but stars of this size brought a sensation more equivalent to the warmth of the hearth. She let them move around her on the slow spirals they liked to take.

'Theus?' She spoke his name then called out loudly, 'Theus!'

No reply. She'd thought it unlikely that he'd returned but considered it worth trying. Maybe he'd worked out a way to chase his 'better' half through the ark into whatever *beyond* the Missing had taken themselves to. Maybe he no longer needed her to wield the stars required to open the door for him. Theus had never had any interest in any of them other than in service to his own needs. His desertion did not surprise her.

'Theus!' Her voice rattled off into the darkness. With a shake of her head she turned away and began the trek back to where Sister Owl was waiting for her on the plateau's edge. The stars' song reverberated at the edge of her hearing, and their presence opened the Path to her. Usually it required an effort to see past the world to the Path and to the thread-scape that overlaid everything that was not the Path. With the stars close by it now almost required an effort *not* to see that alternative, deeper reality. Yaz made the effort. Seeing the more boring path at her feet was more important right now than seeing the other Path in all its glory. She didn't want to trip on a rock and tumble down the steepness of the slope. That would be a poor end to her ambition.

By the time she rejoined the nun Yaz could feel the climb in the backs of her thighs. 'I got them,' she announced unnecessarily.

'I can see!' Sister Owl stepped back as though Yaz were a fire too hot to be close to. 'We should get these somewhere safely out of sight, and out of reach.' Owl led the way back, setting a pace that was both frustratingly slow and at the same time clearly difficult for her to maintain.

Sister Owl took Yaz to Path Tower and led her up the spiral staircase that gave access only to the classroom at the top.

'There are hidden rooms in the tower.' The nun stopped about halfway up the stairs.

Yaz, unused to buildings of any sort, had not really considered the matter but, now that she did, it seemed odd that the width of the tower seemed to accommodate only a narrow staircase from the room at the bottom to the room at the top.

'Picture the Path, set a hand to my shoulder, and follow me. Only me. Take no diversions.' The nun waited silently for the grip of Yaz's fingers.

Yaz took hold.

'Those stars of yours may be unsettling', Sister Owl said, 'but they're having an astonishing impact on my powers. There are drugs the Red Sisters can take to increase their strength for a while. This seems to be a similar thing, but aimed at quantal powers. I'd read about it of course but . . .' She coughed. 'In any event, let us proceed.'

Three steps should have smacked Yaz's nose into the stonework. Instead she found after five steps that she stood with Owl inside a curved room without doors, on whose walls, floor, and ceiling a vast array of sigils had been inlaid in silver. They looked similar to the Missing's script. A little less complex perhaps, but potent and hinting at shapes beyond the surface on which they were written.

Yaz stacked the stars one upon another in a small pyramid on the floor. 'So, they'll be safe here?'

Sister Owl smiled. 'Most novices' primary concern on their first visit is how they got here.'

'Ah.' Yaz smiled back. 'I've walked through walls before.'

Sister Owl shook her head in slow amusement. 'Despite having a hundred years to my rear, I still find you ice-tribers manage to surprise me. And yes, they will be safe here. They seem to have been secure enough in the mouth of a tunnel for a month – but it's safer here. And there's no better place to experiment with them. These sigils will channel away any power that is accidentally released, even if it would have levelled the tower were it uncontained.'

Yaz nodded. 'You know I can't stay long. My friends—'

'Are safe,' Sister Owl insisted.

'I can't trust that. Not when I know who it is that wishes to harm them. Eular might not have my strength when it comes to the stars but he is strong, and he's spent lifetimes studying them. He knows secrets, techniques . . . I can't trust that he doesn't have a means of getting to the others inside the time-star's bubble. And what would happen if he just had someone throw a spear at one of them?'

'I don't . . .' Sister Owl frowned as if she'd never considered such a thing.

'And Seus sits behind Eular with much more power at his disposal. Maybe his war against you has been fought in secret thus far, trying to wrest the Church and the emperor away from the people by stealth, but that's likely because it wasn't so important to him as it might be now. This empire is strong. You have armies, and mages, and the sisters and brothers in grey and red. But you've never met his hunters. They're not things of your world, they're older and worse, and I don't know if your emperor or his empire could stand against them.'

'You'd be surprised by the things this empire has withstood, child.' Sister Owl seemed to stand straighter and taller, and the threadscape boiled behind her with connections to a thousand memories. 'But it does seem that your talents are the key here, if your Taproot is to be believed. And faith drives me to believe him. An old romantic like me can't ignore salvation offered by a being that carries such a name. The tree of the Ancestor connects us to the most distant past by a single root, questing deep into the vanished years. The taproot. Sister Cloud would have approved of a Taproot coming from the lost days to save us. And maybe she even saw it in that pool of hers. Maybe that's why she died with a smile on her face.'

'I still need to rescue my friends.'

'What you need is a plan, or failing that . . . a weapon. You need to join these stars into a single star, the equal to a shipheart. Once that's done, if you can control it, then you should be very hard to stop.' Sister Owl held out the small yellow star that Yaz had made from the stardust in Persus Hall. 'This showed me your promise, and those' – she indicated the glowing pyramid of eyes – 'confirmed it. It seems that the bigger the star the more it opens the Path to those with power. With a shipheart in your hands you should be equal to most foes and ready to at least try to tackle the task of unlocking a time-star.'

CHAPTER 22

Days slid by and, within the confines of the convent, beneath the high priest's blessing, Yaz felt as close to safe as she had for a long time. Yes, Jeccis, Krey, and Eular were out there somewhere, wishing ill upon her, and yes, Seus could potentially send a minion against her even in the heart of Sweet Mercy, but still, she no longer felt that tingle of danger across the back of her neck.

The need to rescue Thurin, Erris, and Mali was a constant pressure, but since Sister Owl assured her that the main danger for her friends was simply that Yaz would grow old and die before finding a way to save them, the pressure was not crushing.

If her life at the convent seemed less dangerous, it was not without challenge. Yaz showed no aptitude for the fighting taught in Blade classes. Other than in strength and endurance she found herself outmatched in all the necessary qualities. Academia lessons were fascinating but difficult. Away from history, the focus on numbers and manipulating them made her head ache. In Shade she proved to have little aptitude for stealth or for mixing ingredients.

'It's simple,' Wenna admonished her. 'It's just like cookery!'

'On the ice we eat fish. Raw.'

'That's it?' Hellma looked horrified.

'That's it.' Yaz pursed her lips. 'Well, some of the southern tribes have dogs, and they'll eat them when they die.'

'Ug—'

'Raw,' Yaz added, before Wenna could claim that was cooking.

But as difficult as Yaz found many of her lessons at the convent, none of them came close to the mind-bending task of joining the Watcher's eyes together into one great star. It was a puzzle in more dimensions than her eyes could fathom. Part of Yaz had begun to suspect that they couldn't be assembled one piece at a time as she had managed with the stardust when making her small star. The bigger the stars got the more they resisted each other. If she joined five of the six then the resultant star would fight the inclusion of the sixth with a force that made all earlier barriers seem like wind-driven ripples compared to the boat-drowning wave a collapsing ice cliff drove before it.

In sessions working with Sister Owl in the secret sigil-lined room, Yaz edged towards a solution a hundred times, only to find the understanding upon which she was building her efforts to be flawed. Sister Owl brought in books from the convent library and even sent to the main Church library in Verity. Big, fat, leather-bound books: dusty and ancient, flimsy collections of pages loosely stitched together, tomes sporting iron locks, scrolls looking so fresh that the ink might still be wet. She brought in battered little volumes in the languages of Durn and Scithrowl, translating for Yaz as she read aloud. Several of the books even used a different alphabet and read back to front. In desperation, she arrived one day with her arms full of bundled sticks scored with a thousand char-lines, spelling out the secrets of a land that had once been nothing but jungles and now lay beneath the ice. Another time she took from her habit what might have been a veil but was instead a small curtain of string, each sporting many knots of different types at different positions – another language conveying more mysteries.

Some of Owl's secondhand wisdom was of considerable help. Some just confused. One iron-locked book hindered, steering them down the wrong path for several days. It would, Yaz thought, have been better if the key had been lost.

The green-landers surprised Yaz by counting their years. They counted them both inside the reign of any given emperor, and from the foundation of the empire itself. So they were in the seventh year of the current emperor and the 412th of the empire. Even more surprisingly, they even named individual days, albeit with staggering lack of imagination. One-day through to seven-day, then repeat. And on every seven-day there were no lessons.

On seven-day most of the novices went into Verity visiting family or exploring, the younger ones under the watchful eyes of nuns. Since the city was the place where her friends had disappeared, the place where they had stepped out of time and taken themselves beyond mundanities like the passage of days, named or otherwise, Yaz was keen to follow.

Sister Owl had other ideas. 'Here we can protect you. What Sister Moon and the other Greys do goes unseen but it means you can sleep at night without care. There are other safeguards too: threads I've pulled from the background to use as alarms that will let me and others know when strangers cross them.'

'I'm a grown woman,' Yaz protested. 'I've crossed the ice. Battled horrors underneath it—'

'And', said Owl, 'the city is as different from the ice as the bottom of the sea is. You have no idea how to defend yourself there. It's unlike anything you've seen.'

Yaz curled her lip, about to say she wasn't afraid, even though the old woman's words were seeding doubt in her mind.

'Plus', Owl added, 'it isn't just you who is at risk. Quina won't stay here if you don't. And should you come to harm your friends aren't going to be leaving that time-star's influence any day in the next thousand years. You serve them best by staying here and working on making your shipheart.'

Yaz reluctantly had to agree. When Wenna, Hellma, Gully, and even Kola and Niome, who Yaz had forced to share the horrors of drowning, asked both the ice-tribers to go with them into town, Yaz had to refuse.

'Oh, come on, Yaz!' Quina begged. 'Wenna's father lives in a house bigger than the whole convent and made of gold. She's said we can visit.'

'It's dangerous for us out there.' Yaz repeated Sister Owl's wisdom through gritted teeth. 'And we have others depending on us.'

'Depending on you, you mean,' Quina said.

'And I need you, Quina. I can't fight like you. I'll need someone to watch my back when I'm ready to go and help the others. You can't do that if Mother Jeccis gets her hands on you in some Verity street.'

Quina pulled a face and nodded grudgingly. 'But we can see them off. To the edge of the pillars at least.'

Yaz thought it was better if they didn't but said yes anyway. And so they set off with the group of chatting novices. Yaz found herself bracketed by Hellma and Kola, dwarfed by both the gerants and reminded of Kao. She missed the boy at odd times and it made her heart ache in a way she had always assumed to be a figure of speech but turned out not to be. Kao's death always led to Maya's. Yaz steered her thoughts firmly away from Maya and tried to smile along with the girls' enthusiasm.

They wound a path through the great forest of pillars, the girls' voices echoing from ancient stone. The presence of Kola and Niome in the group brought home to Yaz how much things had changed since her arrival, which really didn't seem that long ago. She supposed she had Quina's indefatigable need to gossip to thank for that. Well, Quina and the blessing.

At the edge of the pillars, where a single column strayed out from the hundreds behind to stand isolated on the plateau, Yaz came to a halt.

'We'll say goodbye here.' She narrowed her eyes at Quina.

'Come with us!' Gully wheedled. 'Wenna won't take me to her mansion without you two!'

'It'll be fine,' Niome said. 'We'll protect—'

A sharp cry cut her off and, looking past the novices, Yaz saw out on the open rock a single figure racing towards them. At first she thought it was a nun, but the runner wore a robe rather than a habit, and there was something frantic about the way they sprinted, careless of any pothole that might catch and break an ankle.

'Get back!' A cry rang out across the rock.

'It's a man . . .' A nervousness edged Wenna's voice.

'A boy.' Hellma seemed less worried.

Something about the stranger rang a warning in the back of Yaz's memory. Quina stepped closer to her, close enough that their shoulders met.

The cry repeated. 'Get back!' It hadn't come from the young man racing towards them. The pillars confused the ear with their echoes. It came from a nun in a red habit who had broken from cover behind the novices and now passed them at speed on a line to intercept the intruder.

'Sister Wool will stop him,' Gully said.

'That she will.' Wenna's confidence returned.

The robed man, understanding that he'd been seen, began to howl with unchecked rage as he ran.

'Tainted,' Quina breathed in the ice-tongue and gripped Yaz's wrist.

'Not here?' Yaz's mind didn't believe it but the knot in her stomach said her body did.

The Red Sister came to a halt in the man's path some ten yards ahead of him, and barked out an order for him to stop. He didn't break stride, just raised his arms as if to barge her aside. He held his hands in claws. Sister Wool merely swayed aside and left her leg in his path. The man went down hard, sprawling onto the limestone. Sister Wool was on him with hunska speed, pinning him to the stone.

'Don't touch him—'

But Yaz was too slow. It had all happened already. The man thrashed and bucked, screaming all the while. Wool's look of calm confidence fractured, not from her captive's efforts, which she looked well able to contain even fuelled by the strength of madness as they were, but as if some horror had materialized before her eyes. Yaz knew it for what it was. The demon inside the young man was trying to force its way into the nun.

With a cry the man broke free and scrambled to his feet, bleeding from a scalp wound and torn across his hands and face where he'd slid across the rough stone. Wool fell back in confusion. Only thirty yards remained between the novices and the madman. He started sprinting towards them once more.

Wenna Tacsis moved forward and crouched in her favourite fighting stance from Blade Class.

'Hey!' Hellma hurried after her. 'Me too!'

Niome and Kola exchanged glances and followed.

'No!' Yaz found her voice. 'Run!'

But the four girls stood their ground. Quina broke the paralysis fear had wrapped her in and moved with Gully to go to join the others. Yaz caught hold of her. 'They're fighters.'

The madman came on, blood-painted, robes torn and flapping, unleashing terrifying shrieks despite his obvious need for breath.

The novices braced for impact but the man went down again, tumbling, almost reaching their feet. Yaz thought that he'd at last tripped but caught the flash of steel from a throwing star embedded in the back of his knee. Sister Wool was back on her feet and had another of the stars ready to throw.

'Don't touch him! Don't touch him!' Yaz shouted. Running forward, she barged Hellma aside as she headed for the man.

The stranger looked up, a savage grin across his bloody face, and began to crawl rapidly towards them, dragging his injured leg. Yaz backed away, pulling Wenna with her. 'Keep away from him – he's sick!'

The boy – Yaz could tell he was a boy now, even through the blood – fixed crazed eyes on her. He shuddered strangely and stopped crawling. His mouth fell open and with a black tongue he said, in a calm voice wholly at odds with his appearance, 'They've got me.'

'What?' Yaz continued to stumble backwards. Wenna offered no resistance now, and the other novices were retreating too, horrified.

'They've got me!' A wildness infected his voice. 'They've

got me!' Shouted with a strange broken mirth. 'They've got me!' A furious scream. 'Th—'

Sister Wool's foot cracked into the back of his head and he collapsed, boneless, slumping down onto the stone. '*I got you.*'

For a long moment they all stood and stared at the limp form before them. Yaz was the first to speak. 'Get Sister Owl. There's something very wrong here.'

CHAPTER 23

Sister Owl arrived as the boy, who looked about Quina's age and had Yaz's height, began to stir. Sister Wool had used loops of cord to bind the captive's feet and wrists, using the end of her blade to lift a limb where necessary, and at no point touching him.

'You novices go on with your day.' Owl waved Wenna and the others away. 'Not you two – the blessed girls – I need you here.'

Reluctantly, Hellma and Wenna trailed after Gully, who seemed keen to leave, and Kola and Niome. Quina, who had lost all inclination to visit Verity, remained without protest.

'Should we take him to the convent?' Sister Wool asked. She considered the prone form before her. 'He looks like a proxim.'

'A what?' Yaz asked.

'A proxim, a student at the Academy,' Sister Owl explained. 'Those who manage to complete the classes there become Academics, Academy Men.'

'Mages,' Quina said.

'Mages of a lesser magic.' Owl nodded. 'They study the

marjal skills. But their talents can be very diverse and quite formidable. The question is why is this one on the Rock of Faith behaving as if he ate brainwort?'

'Maybe he ate brainwort,' Quina said, looking momentarily hopeful.

'Were his lips blue?' Sister Owl asked.

Quina shrugged. Yaz closed her eyes, trying to remember. Wool shook her head. 'No.'

'He's tainted.' As Yaz spoke, the boy rolled over, eyes wild in a bloody face. He grinned wolfishly, exposing teeth broken when his face had hit the stone. 'A devil's in him. A piece that the Missing cast off.'

The proxim began to test his bonds, snarling all the while, watching Yaz as if he were a dog and she a choice slice of lungfish.

'He is possessed. That much is certain.' Sister Owl's eyes held a defocused, glassy look as she examined the threads. 'The spirit inside him is powerful, but broken. A curious mix of anger, malice . . . even humour.' She extended a wizened hand towards the boy as he writhed helplessly, trying to get at her now. Bony fingers plucked at the air. 'It feels both extremely new and, at the same time, old beyond words . . .'

'A new fragment of something ancient?' Yaz asked.

'Perhaps.' Owl's brows rose in surprise and she turned her witch-sight towards Yaz as if seeing her anew. 'You may well be right.' Her gaze lingered, and then returned to the boy, who had started roaring in rage, bloody froth around his lips. 'There's not much awareness in there yet. It's too new to know who or what it is – perhaps it will never progress far along that path. Certainly it will take time.'

'But he was saying things,' Yaz protested. 'He must have some wits about him.'

Owl frowned, as if she found that hard to believe. 'What was he saying?'

'They're getting me . . .' Yaz said.

'They've got me,' Quina corrected. 'In the ice-tongue.'

Yaz's eyes widened. She hadn't noticed the language. 'Would they study that at the Academy?' she asked.

'It sounds unlikely.' Owl cocked her head, studying the proxim. 'The boy is in there too, pushed to the back of his own mind.'

'I've seen this before,' Yaz said. 'Can you help him?'

Owl's frown deepened. 'I really don't know. It would be incredibly difficult to untangle the two of them thread by thread. It could take months. And if they're entwining together again while I worked . . . It's certainly not something I've tried before.'

'So,' Yaz said. 'We take him back to Path Tower and keep him in the secret room.' She saw that the nuns were staring at her. 'What?'

Owl and Wool exchanged glances. 'Church law says those possessed by devils must be put to death by—'

'Drowning!' Quina burst out. 'We come somewhere where all the ice is melted and what do you people do? Use it to kill!' She pushed Yaz's shoulder. 'You do it. Like you did for Kao and Zeen.'

'That was dangerous . . .' Yaz remembered hammering the star onto Zeen's chest, terrified that the force of the blow or the trauma of separation would kill him. It hadn't, but it had shattered her star into small pieces.

'It was fast!' Quina gestured to the snarling boy. 'The longer this takes the more the story spreads the more chance that the abbess is going to have to throw him . . . where we went.'

Yaz looked at Sister Owl. 'So that's the choice. I hit him

with my kill-or-cure solution. Or he gets dragged into the convent and murdered?'

'He seemed ready enough to murder you,' Sister Wool countered. 'The evil in him tried to take me over when I fought him. I felt it crawling across my mind.' She shuddered.

'Church law may be a blunt instrument and sometimes overly harsh,' Sister Owl said. 'But the devil's too dangerous to be soft with. If the boy dies the devil dies with him.'

'Gone forever?' Yaz remembered the devils she'd burned away with starlight back in the Tainted's black caves. She hadn't properly appreciated what they were back then. Even now, Theus was still only a fraction of a man, but it had become a large enough fraction that she could see his humanity, albeit shrouded in ego, greed, selfishness, cruelty, vanity, and anger. 'Both of them dead and gone?'

'The books say that devils who are trapped in a dying host are taken to the border between life and death – that's the Path. To die you don't follow the Path as we do when we take power from it – you cross it width-wise. The devils can linger there for as long as their diminishing power lasts, but eventually they must either cross over and be lost forever, or they must find a host on that border who is brought back through the skill of healers, and ride them back into the world of the living.'

'I'll need a star, one of the Watcher's eyes.'

'Best if you run. If I go back into the convent I'll be bound by law to report this.' Sister Owl waved her away. 'Can you get through the wall by yourself?'

Yaz was already running. 'Pretty sure.'

'Be very sure.' The old woman's voice grew faint behind her. 'You don't want to end up in the wrong—' Distance swallowed the words.

Yaz pounded across the open space in front of the convent

buildings, drawing a few curious gazes. She passed the steps of the abbess's house and followed the curve of the great Dome of the Ancestor before threading narrow paths through a scattering of smaller structures. Path Tower loomed suddenly before her and she ran under one of its four walkways, crashing through the door at the end and into the portrait hall. Moments later she was halfway up the spiral staircase looking for the spot where Sister Owl had led her into the hidden room at least a dozen times before. She would just have reached out for the stars to locate them, but the room's sigils deadened their song and put them beyond her sight.

By defocusing her vision Yaz could study the threads. Not only the fundamental threads that spelled out the permanence of stone and the air's ever-changing ways, but those that spoke of a history of coming and going. Thread trails crisscrossed back and forth through the wall, speaking of a thousand transitions, perhaps some made by novices who became nuns, lived to a grand old age and had been in their graves for many years now.

Yaz laid her forehead against the stone, trying to feel the flow of the Path. It was there. Much weaker than it had been in the deep places of Vesta's undercity where Erris had taught her to walk through walls, but there nonetheless.

She focused on the Path and let it take her.

The journey through the wall was usually a short one, but on this occasion Yaz saw the room as a glowing shape, translucent, and delineated by its sigiled walls, sitting a distance from her amid a sparse but snow-laden forest. The room twinkled at her like a light in a far-off window.

Yaz remembered this place, this strange space between here and there, an interconnectedness that her mind patterned as this frozen forest. She had been here before. Taproot had brought her and had waited for her in his hut, with a light at the window. She glanced up at the white sky that somehow managed to leave the trees thick with shadow. She'd worried that the dark stain of Seus's hand might already be encroaching overhead but the whiteness, while bleak, remained unsullied.

Only as Yaz began to run did the sky start to darken and the temperature begin to plummet. The thin branches reaching into her path shattered as she crashed through them, already frozen to the core. The cold seared her lungs and burned across her skin. The room wasn't more than a hundred yards away now and the trees ahead stood stark against the sigils' glow. The ground hurt her feet, fallen needles doing little to blunt its iron-hard ridges. A tree exploded without warning, the frozen sap expanding within its trunk until the wood could no longer contain it and surrendered suddenly to the mounting pressure. Shards of icy wood peppered her side. Seus's black hand covered so much of the sky that Yaz could see nothing save the glow ahead and the trees silhouetted by it.

Thirty yards, twenty. The cold had got into Yaz's muscles, stiffening every limb. Her lungs no longer took what she needed from the wickedness of the air. She stumbled and fell mere yards from the room, almost close enough to reach out and touch the sigils floating before her. Both knees smashed down onto soil that a hammer couldn't crack and if she could have she would have howled in pain.

I know you now. I see you now.

The voice came from everywhere and ran through her with dreadful intimacy.

I know you. I see you.

Yaz didn't want to touch the ground. Her skin would

freeze to it and tear away. The flesh of her fingers would die. But she couldn't walk. The strength simply wasn't in her. Instead she advanced a few paces on her knees, then fell forward, catching herself on her elbows and forearms. Her vision was darkening beyond the enfolding night, placing black spots before the sigil-glow – black spots that multi-plied and grew and would soon meet, obliterating her sight.

Between the distant explosions of trees Yaz could hear her limbs creaking, the part-frozen muscles protesting against being flexed. An unintelligible grunt escaped her icy lips: all that escaped of her rejection of Seus's will. The remnants of 'You – won't – kill – me.' A brightness passed through her, body and mind. She was through the wall. She found herself on her hands and knees, with all the sigils shining as if they had just absorbed some great overflow of power. The fingers spread before her on the sigiled floor were uninjured, her muscles failed her and she pitched to the ground, rolling onto her back. No part of her was frozen. The room was warm, her body too. But when she released her breath in a long groan it frosted the air.

I don't want to kill you. The voice shivered through the sigils, almost inaudible. *You're my key.*

Yaz clambered to her feet, shaking from the memory of the cold that had filled her mind. She limped over to the barrel-lidded casket that Owl kept various treasures in. The lock was a heavy chunk of iron but Owl always left the key in it. Yaz opened it up and took the topmost of the glowing stars. It fitted comfortably in her palm, too big to close her fingers around.

She turned slowly towards the wall through which she'd just come, finding that she had little appetite for a second journey. Taproot had said that Seus guarded the ways through the Hayes gates. She hadn't imagined that he could also police the spaces between two sides of particular walls in Path Tower. The reach and focus of his influence suddenly terrified her. Had Seus been watching her every move, playing her as some piece in a game far beyond her understanding?

Yaz steeled herself for the return journey. Time was of the essence and a boy's life depended on her. But had Seus let her go or had she escaped him? Would he be waiting for a second attempt, or would he let her pass unmolested after his show of strength?

It wasn't as if there were many choices. She could wait and hope that Sister Owl could save her – thrusting the nun into the teeth of danger instead of herself. Or she could brave a second passage. In any other room she might consider blasting a physical exit through the wall, but the sigils here were designed exactly to prevent such an occurrence.

Yaz steeled herself, found the threads of previous comings and goings, and followed them back towards the wall. She wouldn't put Owl into danger on her behalf. She looked past the world, past the wall, and stepped forward, already shivering . . .

. . . A moment later she stumbled onto the stairs, still clutching her star.

'I got it.' Yaz arrived breathless at the edge of the pillar forest, guided by the proxim's raging. She spotted Wool, Quina, and Owl standing around their prone captive, all of them tiny at the base of the weathered pillar.

'Good!' Quina injected the word into the relative quiet as the boy filled his lungs for more howling. 'Maybe you can shut him up!'

'I need him on his back,' Yaz told them.

Wool levered the boy over using her scabbarded sword, pinning his bound hands beneath him. She anchored him there by thrusting it behind his spine and in front of an elbow, preventing him from flipping back over.

'This isn't subtle,' Yaz said. 'It's not a delicate unbinding of threads. I just make the star blaze, force the demon into his core, then hit him on the breastbone very hard. I've only done it twice . . .'

Sister Owl raised an eyebrow. 'It sounds dangerous. But he doesn't have many choices. Be careful – the demon's a strong one.'

'You've met others?'

Owl suppressed a shudder. 'I've lived a long life. I've visited the cliffs in Scithrowl where the black ice is exposed at ground level. I've heard the devils whisper. Felt their malice. I've been across the sea to Durn. There are trees there, sick-woods, that endure the meltwater from the black ice. The moon comes and black streams flow. There are forests in Durn where no one should wander.

'The Durnish shamans cut themselves staves from the darkest of those trees. And the Durns make their barges from the timber of sickwoods that grow on the grey margins. We've fought three wars with the Durns in my lifetime. So yes, child, I've met demons and devils before. This one' – she gestured towards the struggling proxim – 'is as strong as any I've encountered before. Maybe worse. Be thankful it's new to its skin. And to his.'

Yaz approached the boy carefully. One of his eyes had turned black and, as he looked her way, the power of rage and malice behind the stare hit her like a blow.

'Who are you?' Yaz asked.

'Who? Hoo! Hoo! Hoo!' The boy snarled and gabbled. 'Keto! Toke! Kote!'

Yaz raised her star with a sigh, letting the light blaze from it. Immediately Quina and Wool stepped back. Owl kept her ground and stood on the hilt of Wool's abandoned sword to prevent the boy from rolling.

'Keot! Keot! Keot!' the boy snarled, kicking both legs to try and drive himself back from the star.

Yaz gathered her strength. She felt no pleasure in destroying the demon. Maybe once when she had thought them beings of pure evil she had been happy to burn them away with the purity of starlight. But now she knew them for what they were – broken parts of real people, cut away in a quest for perfection – she pitied them. Yes, what had been cut away was the worst of what lay in those long-vanished individuals. But even so, she knew she had anger in her, selfishness, cowardice, and a host of other ills. And while she might not relish those parts of her personality – while she might seek to redirect and redesign them – to cut them loose and abandon them to infinity seemed harsh.

'Get further back!' Yaz called to Quina and Wool. 'The demon will try to jump to you.'

She set the star burning with an intensity that hurt her eyes even though she held it above her head. Three deliberate paces brought her to the boy's side. She could feel the demon inside him retreating to his core while questing for her weakness, for any flaw that might offer a way into her mind.

Yaz swung the star as she fell to one knee beside the proxim. In the moment she struck she saw his face change, an awareness showing as if the demon had released its hold. The star hammered down onto his sternum, releasing its pent-up energies in a great flash that threw Yaz back onto the stone.

'Yaz?'

Yaz felt herself floating. She could see nothing but the green-blue light of the star, shining at her from every direction.

'Yaz?' That irritating voice again. And someone shaking her.

She opened her eyes to a cold sky with a clot of blackness looming in the midst of it. For a moment she struggled, thinking Seus had found her again.

'It's me! Quina.'

The blackness resolved into her friend.

Yaz hauled on Quina to pull herself up into what turned out to be a sitting position. 'Did I get rid of it? The demon? Is it gone?'

Quina nodded.

'Good.'

'But . . .' Quina's voice came out thick with emotion. 'I think the boy's gone too.'

Yaz pushed Quina aside. 'Don't be stupid. He can't be gone—' She stopped, seeing Sister Owl and Sister Wool kneeling beside the proxim.

'It wasn't your fault.' Sister Owl let Wool help her up, knees creaking. 'The demon was too strong to go without taking the lad with it.'

Quina helped Yaz to her feet. The star lay a few yards off, glowing dimly. 'I killed him.'

'The demon killed him.' Sister Owl hobbled across. 'Keot killed him rather than let go.'

Yaz curled her lip. 'And now the demon's waiting on death's borders, waiting for a ride back into the world?'

The nun nodded.

'He could come back anywhere?'

'No, they can't travel. Not far anyway. He would have to be here, or near here.'

'How far can they—' Yaz realized she was just prolonging the conversation so she wouldn't have to look at the boy she'd just killed. A hot tear rolled down her cheek.

'Go back to the convent, dear.' Sister Owl set a hand to Yaz's arm and steered her in the right direction.

Yaz tried to turn back. 'What will happen to him?'

'Sister Wool and I will take care of the proxim. We'll say the prayers and lay him before the Ancestor. Then word will be sent to the Academy. Quina, take your friend back to the dormitory.'

With Quina tugging on her hand, Yaz allowed herself to be led through the multitude of pillars once more. She didn't see any of them, just the image of the boy in his torn cloak, face bloody, and of his eyes in the moment just before she struck.

'What did he mean?' Quina asked.

'What?' Yaz blinked and looked at her.

'What did he mean? The demon. He was shouting, "They've got me." Who has? It doesn't make sense. Why?'

'He was raving. None of it made sense.' But even as she said it Yaz realized that when saying 'They've got me' had been the only time he *wasn't* raving. The only clear thing he'd said. 'Maybe it was the proxim saying it.'

'Was there more than one demon though?' Quina insisted.

'No . . .' Yaz was pretty sure she would have sensed if there had been more than one. More than just Keot.

'So.' Quina tugged Yaz to the side to avoid her walking into a pillar. 'So if it was the demon saying it . . . who are *they?*'

'I don't know.' Yaz didn't keep the anger from her voice. The boy's dead face filled her mind and she wasn't interested in Quina's silly mysteries. She pulled her hand free from her friend's.

They walked ten paces in silence. Then another ten.

'The mages had him. The Academics. The demon escaped them in the body of one of their students!' Quina exclaimed.

'I don't care.'

'And he came here – from the city – right here – and told you, "They've got me."' Quina stopped in her tracks. 'How many demons do you know?' she called at Yaz's back.

Yaz came to a halt and turned around, frowning.

'Theus,' Quina said. 'The Academics have got Theus. That was part of him in the boy.'

Suddenly Seus sparing her life after all Eular's efforts to kill her made sense. Seus had called her his key – how did he know that now and not before? 'They're getting Theus to talk!' A cold knot formed in Yaz's stomach. 'They're breaking out his secrets. And he knows what Taproot told us. He knows how to open the ark. He knows. And now Seus thinks I'm his key . . .'

CHAPTER 24

'We have a tradition of each year sending our best novices to contest their skills against those of the Academy's most talented proxims. We have four classes so there are four visits a year. The next would be by Holy Class in ten days.'

'That's too long. We need to get Theus out of there now,' Yaz said.

Sister Owl pursed her lips. She was sitting on the large chest where she kept the treasures she shared with novices in her classroom. Yaz and Quina remained standing, too tense to sit in one of the too-small novice chairs.

'The Academy is attached to the emperor's palace and filled with marjals trained to various levels of competency. Many of the masters there are deadly practitioners of the elemental arts; others specialize in shadow-work or in rarer skills. The Church has very little authority within the Academy and certainly our abbess has none. If Seus has corrupted some of their number then it would be about the most dangerous place you could go.'

'But Quina and I are blessed,' Yaz said. 'Surely the

Academics wouldn't attack us if we made a legitimate visit?'

'Why should we go at all?' Quina asked. 'Theus never did anything for us that wasn't for himself. And from what you say he's already told Seus Taproot's big secret. Seus knows how to open the ark now, and he knows you're his best bet to do it.'

Yaz was tempted to agree. Perhaps Theus and the Academics deserved each other. She didn't like the idea that the iron dog, Zox, who bore Theus's essence, should be rewarded for his loyal service by being left to the mages to dissect. Though now that she thought about it, was any of the dog's service really loyalty? Originally, he had been moved to unfold from his cube at Vesta's urging, the city mind still holding some concern for Erris's wellbeing. And later his actions had been dictated by Theus.

'Well?' Quina prompted.

'Theus knows more than that one secret. He shares with Seus and the other city minds knowledge dating back to the time before the Missing left. His people made the stars from . . . from whatever they're made from. He understands the gates. He knows things we don't even know we don't know. He's valuable to us. How far have I got putting the Watcher's eyes together? It's been days on days and I haven't managed to make two into one, let alone six of them simultaneously. Theus has knowledge that isn't in Sister Owl's books. He's older than all the empire's libraries. If we let the Academics break him down we'll never know what we lost and whether it would have saved us.'

Quina looked at her feet. 'I don't like him.'

'You don't have to come.'

'Of course I'm coming, you idiot.'

Yaz grinned, then looked at Sister Owl, still sitting on the chest lid, dangling her legs as if she were ten rather than ten times ten. 'We have to go now. We can't wait for Holy Class to go for their competition.'

'How else will you get invited in?' the nun asked. 'If you go in without an invitation, they can do what they like to you and call it justice. We've no idea how many of them are under Seus's thrall, just a spy here and there, or Atoan himself and all the masters of the school? It seems impossible that it could be so many . . . but it is true that we've suspected the Academy of seeking unhealthy influence over the emperor and his brother for some years now.'

Yaz thought of the young proxim running at her over the rock. At first she had thought he was a nun. At a distance she'd mistaken his robes for a habit. There wasn't a vast difference close up either. 'How does the Academy find its proxims?'

Sister Owl allowed herself a thin smile. 'Children are brought to the great hall for testing. Some by their parents, some by other means. A few present themselves.'

Yaz looked down at her habit. 'I think I've been a novice long enough. I want to join the Academy. You should too, Quina.'

'We're neither of us marjal. They tested me at the Black Rock.'

'You don't need to be marjal to be tested – you only need to be a marjal to be accepted.'

'And you think you're just going to see Theus wherever they test new blood off the streets?' Quina asked. 'Then fight a way out of there?'

'I think it's a good start. And once we're over the doorstep then all sorts of things could happen. In fact, I intend to make them happen.'

Sister Owl got off her perch carefully and walked,

somewhat stiffly, towards the stairs. 'I will accompany you. As novices you would be chaperoned. And unless you *are* accepted by the Academy and renounce the convent then you'll remain novices. Besides, I have a few old friends in the mages' ranks. It's about time I caught up with some of them – before the Ancestor sees fit to gather me up.'

Yaz and Quina waited outside Path Tower while Sister Owl collected things she thought she might need from her secret room. Yaz had warned the old nun about her encounter with Seus between one side of the stonework and the other. Owl had widened her eyes in surprise and frowned. 'I've been opposing him for decades – though it wasn't until you arrived that I learned his true nature. If he could reach in and take me then I'm sure he would have done so already. I fear I erred in sending you for the star alone. Your path through the wall was perhaps less safe than the one I tread.' And so saying, she had vanished through the stones.

'What's keeping her?' Yaz muttered again. 'I should go back up.'

'What, and get yourself lost in the walls again?' Quina peered at the distant columns that divided the convent from the rest of the plateau. 'Speaking of Seus: we should speak about Seus.'

Yaz frowned at her friend. 'We should?'

'Have you ever thought about what he's offering all these people who work for him? I mean, they're not idiots, are they? Eular and the priests. These mages?'

'He offered Eular a warm mountain and the labours of the clans and the Broken. Plus the promise of the green lands. Eular was going to take this city with an army of people like you and me. The people he had in his harnesses at the Black Rock outnumbered the Red Sisters, Grey Sisters, and Mystic Sisters at this convent, and probably the mages at the Academy too.'

Quina looked around her. 'This place can't last. Owl says the ice is closing from both sides. The Corridor gets narrower every year. Mistress Academia taught us about it. In two centuries you'll probably be able to shout from the northern ice and be heard on the southern. And that's only if the moon doesn't fall out of the sky. They say it's dropping slowly, and if it does fall then the ice will close over this rock in our lifetime.'

Yaz's frown deepened. 'What are you trying to say? We should join with Seus? He wants to make the moon fall! And he's been trying to kill us ever since the pit.'

'And instead we're risking everything to rescue Theus of the Tainted, who has already given away our biggest secret and who tortured and murdered the Broken for generations. I'm not saying one's better than the other. I'm just wondering whether it's as clear-cut as we seem to be saying.'

'I'm trying to help more people than just us,' Yaz said. 'That's the difference. That's why I'm going to save Theus and why I'm not siding with Seus.'

'Where does it end, though? With your friends? With your clan? With the tribes of the north? With this nation? The whole Corridor? You can't save the world . . .'

'No,' Yaz said quietly. 'But maybe it's better to try and to fail, than to succeed in saving only myself.'

Quina just stared into the distance, making no reply. Yaz looked at her own hands, pondering. She supposed that Quina had had much more time to think about their options. She'd had all those weeks while Yaz lay paralysed in time. Quina had always had a quick mind, keen to explore every possibility.

Quina broke the silence. 'I'm saying I want to understand why they choose him. Don't you?'

'Because they want power. Because they're scared of being on the losing side. Because if the moon's going to fall anyway then they'd rather be the ones to bring it down and to have a promise of a life on the other side of it. A good life,' Yaz said.

'And why is that such a bad thing?' Quina asked. 'I've been learning their history, these green-landers. They spend all their time trying to kill each other. It's war all the time, on both borders. Every nation is a clan, a huge one, and when the ice takes their land to the north and south they try to replace it by pushing their frontiers wider, out to the east and west. These nuns are killers. The Red Sisters have slaughtered thousands on the battlefield, and the Grey Sisters have murdered just as many behind the lines. You can fight the cold and hunger out on the ice, or each other here and die warm. I just want to know why we shouldn't be on the winning side? We stopped Eular bringing war to the green lands, but we didn't know that war was here already: war is how they live in this place. They make the Axit look like peacemakers.'

Yaz had to snort at that. It was true, all of it. Everything except that they should consider Seus as a possible ally. 'I see what you're doing, Quina. You want me to give you an easy answer. I know you know what we're doing is the right thing. But it's a hard thing and it's difficult to argue yourself into a hard path when easier ones are there for the taking.' She spread her hands. 'I can't do it. You'll have to listen to that annoying voice inside – the one that makes you do the right thing rather than the wrong one.'

Quina pressed her lips together and gave a reluctant smile. 'I suppose so.' She paused, and then opened her mouth to say more, but the door behind them creaked open and Sister

Owl emerged, bundled against the elements and carrying a satchel that she thrust at Yaz to carry.

'Come on!' The nun shuffled between them. 'Can't stand around gossiping all day.'

The convent, in addition to chickens, and pigs – which Yaz had yet to see – owned three mules, which Yaz discovered were similar to horses but smaller. Two were young, sturdy beasts used to haul a cart down the Vinery Stair, loaded with full barrels of red wine on the outward journey and empty on the way back up.

The third mule was an elderly creature with a white tufted beard and one milky eye, reminding Yaz curiously of Pome's right-hand man, the gerant Bexen. It seemed to have a similar disposition to the gerant as well, trying to bite Yaz whenever she turned her back on it. But with Sister Owl, who rode on its back, the mule – known as Old Lady, and presumably just as Lady in her youth – was always well behaved.

Quina and Yaz walked behind as Sister Owl rode on the mule. The old nun had taken a Holy Sister's black habit to wear over the blue habit of a Mystic Sister, as added protection from the elements for her old bones. She led them down from the plateau on a path that wound its way from the heights at a much gentler incline than the Seren Way. Quina explained that the ordered green rows stretching out from this side of the Rock of Faith and sheltered by two of its prominences were a plant called a vine on which grew the fruit from which wine was made by a complex process.

'Can't they just eat the fruit?' Yaz asked, perplexed.

'You can. I've tried one . . . they're delicious.' Quina smacked her lips. 'But this thing they do . . . this *cookery* . . . it's supposed to make it even better.'

Yaz sniffed the air, filtering past the animal's pungency to pick out a confusing host of other scents. She was eager to reach the base of the plateau and find herself truly in the green world for the first time since her arrival.

The wind, which for the Corridor had been strong up at the convent, remained lively down at the bottom. To judge by the bundled heap of cloaks and furs that was Sister Owl, the green-landers considered this cold.

The vegetation, which Yaz lacked the vocabulary to break down into pieces, seethed and flapped in the wind as if any stronger gust would begin to tear it apart.

'It does that when the ice wind blows,' Quina explained as if she wandered regularly among the fields. 'The leaves fold up. Everything hides itself away. And when the sun comes and the air is still it all jumps up again. You're not seeing it at its best.'

Yaz resisted asking when Quina had seen it without her. Whether at its best or not the place fascinated both her mind and eye. Her gaze found it difficult to settle on any one thing. The complexity and variety threatened to overwhelm her. Short green, long green, waving green . . . gradually Mali's knowledge began to filter to the fore of her mind and Yaz started to understand field from hedge from tree from grass. She touched the hedges, trailing her fingers through the tightly folded foliage, letting the twigs scratch at her and the barely frozen frost melt on her skin.

They walked along the road to Verity, with Yaz and Quina sharing in the growing sense of astonishment that Thurin must already have experienced. Taking in the strangeness, the numbers, the variety. A crowd had gathered in front of the vast gates to the city, all pressing forward to get through. It seemed no smaller than all of the ice clans gathered together at the Pit of the Missing, and yet it was presumably a tiny fraction of those within.

It was a relief to escape the crush and pass within the city walls. The interior remained crowded but at least there was room to draw breath. All around them were buildings, many both grander and taller than anything the convent had to offer save the dome. Towering structures packed the main streets, growing larger and still more grand as Sister Owl led the novices steadily closer to the emperor's palace.

Yaz could still see glimpses of the emperor's home over the rooftops but it looked more like a building intended to be held against a sea of enemies than a palace: a stone fortress that might have been built back in the days that Mistress Academia taught about when the empire was a collection of warring states and Verity a town built on the ruins of older empires, huddled around the oldest ruin of all, the ark.

Having the old nun ride before them did have the welcome effect of forging a path through the crowds. The citizens of Verity seemed to show a good deal of respect to nuns, and even novices, which might be a sign of piety or just of common sense, as it was apparently no secret what sort of training the novices of Sweet Mercy received. Yaz also suspected that Sister Owl was pulling a few threads as she went, convincing those ahead of her that they wanted to turn away to the left or the right to let her pass.

'There are so many people!' Quina exclaimed for perhaps the fourth time.

'You should see it on a day when the ice wind's not howling,' Sister Owl said. 'Most folks are huddled in their homes today, seven-day or not.'

Quina and Yaz exchanged glances but neither mentioned that breezes don't howl and that the deeper puddles were just crusted over with ice, not even frozen full thickness.

As they left the city gates further behind them the crush

of humanity continued to ease and Yaz found that she could walk a straight path even without Sister Owl forging the way. The streets were broad and cobbled, with grand establishments to either side, towering to three and four storeys, restaurants below, guest rooms above. Mali's vocabulary crept into Yaz's mind, providing names for the services on offer: blacksmiths, wheelwrights, leatherworkers, saddlemakers, tack shops. But most common were the hostelries crowding the side roads, and packed with people, to judge by glimpses through shutter slats and through doors opened hastily to admit new customers before slamming closed against the wind. Later the high street gave over to establishments dedicated to decorating the rich: tailors and jewellers, silversmiths and goldsmiths.

Even huddled in their coats and cloaks, the inhabitants of Verity were a riot of colour to Yaz. The convent had offered more colours than she'd seen in her life, but here the convent's predominant limestone shades and the blacks and greys of most of the habits seemed drab by comparison.

She noticed, in the sheltered fronts of some of the establishments, that the citizens would lower their hoods revealing the fascinating array of arrangements they applied to their hair. Yaz had always considered the primary function of hair to be in helping to keep her head warm. The Ictha knew that it did its job best when left to its own devices. At her only gathering she had seen that the Axit tribe braided their hair, but only for the celebrations. And those who had lost children that day cut their braids, leaving their scalps bare. But here in Verity it seemed that the cutting and shaping of hair must be a national pastime, judging from all the curls and ribbons and braids and waves and ringlets. Yaz tried to imagine having the time and inclination to cut or braid her own black mane. For the first time she wondered if Erris considered her a savage. His people must have been as far above the citizens of Verity in these matters as the greenlanders were above the ice tribes. What would Erris think if she had her hair shaped like a city dweller? What would Thurin think? Quell would laugh at her – she was sure – or at least he would want to.

Sister Owl clip-clopped ahead of them and eventually they passed through an area of the grandest houses yet and came to the emperor's palace – or, more accurately, fortress.

'That's the Academy there.' The nun pointed to a collection of buildings clustered around the north wall, currently in its shadow.

'There's a star here. A powerful one.' Yaz could feel it, hear the edges of its song, much deeper than that of the Watcher's eyes.

Sister Owl allowed herself a small smile and shook her head. 'There's no hiding anything from you, novice. The Academy has the only intact shipheart I know of.' She paused. 'Well, the time-star your friends discovered in the undercity is a shipheart too and it's not been broken into pieces, but it's definitely broken in some sense. The shipheart is the Academy's greatest treasure, the prize of the grandmaster, the mage Atoan.'

They advanced in silence, accompanied by the clack of the mule's hooves on the cobbles. The only boundary around the place seemed to be the open space between the Academy buildings and the nearest of the grand houses. No guards were obvious either. Yaz wondered if the mages relied on magical defences instead.

They reached a long low structure with many windows and shrouded in an unpleasant, complex reek. A legion of chimneys ran along the ridge of the roof.

'It smells like Shade class,' Quina muttered. 'Only worse.'

'They practise many forms of alchemy here.' Sister Owl sounded as if she disapproved. She led them towards the central courtyard and away from the stink of the alchemists' laboratory.

In many ways the Academy was very similar to the convent: a variety of buildings, some whose purpose Yaz could guess and others that puzzled her. Most faced onto a great paved courtyard that ran to the outer wall of the palace, where a building larger than Blade Hall but of similar design had been built in a manner that suggested it might have grown out of the palace wall rather than simply being sited close to it.

'That's Proxim Hall,' Sister Owl said. She pointed at a smaller hall on the far side of the courtyard. 'Applicants are tested over there.'

As they reached the middle of the courtyard, unchallenged by any guards or officials, a group of twenty or so boys and girls emerged from a nearby building, all of them in the same kind of robes the proxim had worn. They carried scroll tubes and walked quickly towards another building, sparing a few glances for Yaz and Quina.

A man walked out from the pillared entrance to another building, a warrior of some sort, wearing a shirt of fine metal links and carrying a spear across his shoulder. He wore a robe of vibrant green with thin gold stripes running from shoulder to hem, and on one arm held a great round shield displaying a black tree against a red and rising sun. He gave Sister Owl a solemn nod and strode past.

'One of the emperor's guards,' Sister Owl said. 'They patrol around the palace and provide security in the Academy. So any violence in this place would rapidly pit you against the emperor himself.'

A faint pulse ran through Yaz from the soles of her feet

to the top of her head, or so it seemed, but neither Owl nor Quina reacted. The mule didn't so much as twitch an ear.

'I can feel the void star.'

Sister Owl gave her a blank look.

'The void star, the heart of the city. It's what the city mind lives in.'

Sister Owl blinked. 'How far beneath us is it?'

'I don't know,' Yaz said. 'If it's the same as in Vesta . . . then miles.'

'Miles.' Sister Owl frowned as if struggling with the concept.

'I couldn't feel Vesta's void star from the upper levels. But maybe I'm . . .'

'Becoming more powerful.' Sister Owl finished the thought for her.

Sister Owl dismounted with Quina's help and looked about her. She huffed and, nodding to herself, set off towards the largest hall, the one abutting the emperor's walls. She led the mule behind her.

'I thought they tested the applicants over there?' Yaz pointed to the smaller hall across the courtyard.

'I'm an old and forgetful woman,' Owl said. 'And what we want is probably in this direction.'

They approached the towering doors of Academy Hall, coming under the close scrutiny of two palace guards stationed at the steps.

'They're not going to just let us walk out of here with Theus,' Quina hissed.

Yaz silently agreed. Especially if they needed to take Zox too. The iron dog would attract attention in the streets. Compared to the emptiness of the ice, the Broken's caves and the priests' halls in the Black Rock had seemed crowded.

Compared to those places the convent seemed packed. But in Verity the crush of humanity reached entirely new heights. The idea of passing unseen or being able to hide had to be abandoned. Yaz realized now why in Shade lessons the arts of stealth and disguise were taught so seriously. In the green lands such things were vital in situations like this.

'I expect . . .' But Yaz didn't have to manufacture some encouragement she didn't really believe in. A guardsman stepped towards them.

'Sister. Can I help you?'

Sister Owl nodded and peered up at him. 'Indeed you can, young man.' She handed him the reins and left him holding the mule as she hobbled past. 'Yaz, Quina, I'd appreciate a little help on the stairs.'

Yaz knew this to be Owl's own brand of the deceptions taught in Shade. Owl climbed forty-five steps to her classroom several times a day. But appearing more helpless than she was made whatever manipulations of the threads she was undertaking more effective. The second guard, a solid woman with streaks of iron in her black hair, merely glanced at them then looked away as if she'd seen nothing.

Yaz and Quina helped Owl to the great doors, and to a smaller, more human-sized door set in the left one. An iron hatch opened before anyone even thought to knock, and a dark eye looked out at them, the second hidden behind a velvet patch. A twitch of recognition crossed Owl's face, maybe a hint of distaste.

'Yes?'

'We've come to see someone about something.' Sister Owl's fingers twitched as she manipulated the threads, tugging here and there. Yaz could see some of what the nun was doing but the subtlety and swiftness of it was beyond her.

'That's considerably less specific than might be expected,

sister.' The man's voice remained completely level but Yaz couldn't help thinking he was mocking the old woman.

'You're wearing the mendant sigil, aren't you, Ballo?' Owl lowered her hands.

'I am.'

'I've brought these novices to be tested for the Academy. They're interested in changing direction. I would like Mage Atoan to interview them personally.'

The man behind the door considered this new information. 'The testing hall is across the courtyard, sister. And the grandmaster is currently otherwise engaged. I can pass on your request and I'm sure a response will arrive at the convent in due course. You're from Sweet Mercy?'

Sister Owl pressed her lips into a thin line, gathering herself. 'I am Mistress Path from the Convent of Sweet Mercy and I expect the courtesy of a swift response from Atoan.'

Ballo lifted his patch to reveal an eye that contrasted sharply with the dark one through which he had previously regarded them. The mismatch put Yaz in mind of Mother Krey of the Black Rock, but in this case the second eye was unlike any other Yaz had seen, having a golden hue and a curious gemlike quality such that it seemed almost to glow of its own accord.

'Hmmm.' He made a quick study of the nun, then of Yaz and Quina. 'I'm sure the grandmaster will be interested in meeting you.' He lowered his patch again. 'But the fact remains that he is otherwise engaged. I will pass your request along with alacrity. Good day to you, Mistress Path.' And with that he slid the iron cover smartly back across the viewing slot.

Sister Owl showed her teeth and harrumphed. 'Many of the higher orders wear sigils – like those on the walls of the hidden room – and some offer physical protection. A sigil-robe, whilst fabulously costly, can deflect all but the most powerful blasts of Path energy. Our friend on the other side of the door was wearing the mendant sigil, which protects against quantal thread manipulation or marjal empathy. In other words, you have to change their minds the old-fashioned way.' She looked back at the hall to which they'd been directed. 'It would be unwise to pass this doorway without invitation. So it seems we must present you at the testing tables in Proxim Hall.'

Yaz continued to stare at the door before them. She stepped forward and laid her right hand against it. 'I know what's occupying this Atoan. He's torturing Theus. Breaking Zox apart.'

'Maybe so.' Sister Owl turned. 'But this city, this empire, is bound by laws. The strength of the convent, the Church, and all the institutions is given to us within those boundaries and if we cease to honour them then we damage ourselves as much as we might damage any perceived enemy. I see no other option.'

Yaz said nothing, only closed her eyes and moved closer to the door. So close in fact that her forehead bumped softly against the wood. She could hear the two songs. The song of the shipheart, faint at this remove – the weakest of the two – but closest. And the song of the void star, miles down but filtering up nonetheless, so slow and deep that she caught only snatches of it as it reverberated through the longest bones in her body. Both songs told her that they issued from examples of the same thing, something no different from the smallest grain of her stardust, just on vastly different scales.

She focused on the shipheart. In her mind's eye she could see it burning, through the door, through the walls and pillars and passages of the hall beyond. She saw the shapes of sigils around the star, tiny in the distance. Many sigils – not so thickly clustered as those on the walls of Path Tower's hidden room but still plentiful, their distribution spelling out the shape of the room.

Although the internal structure of the building did little to stop the star's light reaching her mind, it interacted enough for her to form a dim impression of the place. The hall was not one great open space but divided into floors and rooms and corridors. The star lay towards the middle on the ground floor.

'Yaz?' Quina repeated her name.

'Huh?' Yaz kept her eyes closed.

'Thank the gods – I thought the time-star had you again and you'd be standing on these steps for a week! What are you up to?'

Yaz shook her head slightly.

'What are you doing?' Quina persisted.

'Getting their attention,' Yaz muttered. She reached out to the shipheart and it responded, changing the tone of its song and the quality of its light. 'Here . . .'

The shipheart offered some resistance and the sigils seemed to get in her way, like layers of netting blocking the invisible hand she reached out with. Yaz gritted her teeth, extending her reach to find a grip on the star and refusing to relinquish it or to accept anything other than obedience. Working with stars at a distance was like trying to carve a kettan at arm's reach. She could achieve only the simplest of tasks, and the easiest of those for Yaz had always been movement. She pulled the shipheart closer. In her mind's eye she saw the walls and doors as ghosts of themselves, layered over each other. She struggled for focus, attempting to steer the star.

'Yaz?' Sister Owl this time. 'What are you doing?'

'Give . . .' Yaz's mouth curled into a snarl of concentration. '. . . me . . . a moment.'

She pulled harder, twisted, turned. The star emerged from

the sigil-lined room. Immediately she felt the shipheart more strongly, its song ringing out louder, as if the sigils had shielded it.

'What's that noise?' As Quina spoke Yaz caught the first muffled cry of alarm through the door on which her forehead rested.

'Just one . . . more . . . moment.' She heard a crash. More screams from within. And then a scream from Quina and a grunt of strained surprise from Sister Owl. The mule gave out a raucous bray and ran off with a clatter of hooves.

'There.' Yaz pulled her head back as something hit the far side of the door with a dull thud that rattled the iron cover of the viewing hatch.

She turned to see that Quina's speed had taken her ten yards back and that Sister Owl had retreated a quarter of that distance to the bottom of the steps.

'What have you done?' The nun looked pained, as if standing too close to a fire.

'I brought the shipheart to me.' Yaz could feel the star's power burning across her skin. It was the most discomfort a star had caused her since she'd first met Erris close to the void star in Vesta. But how close she had been to that, she'd never really known. The star's song reverberated through her, buzzing in the cracks between her thoughts, its refrains echoing in the back of her mind. The Path blazed before her, daring her to touch it, to plunge her hands into the river of its power. She pulled on the shipheart again and the doors creaked, moving outwards by some tiny fraction. Beyond the doors she could hear sounds of distant commotion.

'And what now?' Owl asked.

'Now I think Atoan will want to talk to us.'

CHAPTER 25

A disturbance to the left of the doors dragged Yaz's attention from the shipheart even though it was separated from her by just three inches of timber.

It wasn't a noise so much as a feeling. With her senses laid wide open by the shipheart's proximity she could see that around one particular spot on the wall the threads were boiling through the air like steam above a bubbling pot.

As she watched, a stone arm emerged from the middle of one of the great blocks of sandstone that made the wall. The rocky limb moved as if it were alive, with the stone flexing around it like a layer of mud. A moment later a shoulder pushed through and the stone flowed back from the reaching hand to reveal flesh-and-blood fingers.

By degrees, as if freeing himself from a thick and clinging pudding, a man emerged. The last remnants of his stone cladding flowed back into the wall, and the surface flattened so that no sign of his passage remained. He stood there, a tall man of middling years, a line of grey running either side of his head and into the thick black hair that had been shorn to within two inches of his skull. His robe was a rainbow's dream, a joyous riot of colour that made a marked contrast with his expression, which mixed sourness with surprise, anger, and a degree of apprehension. He narrowed dark eyes at Yaz, identifying her as the likely cause of the chaos.

'Explain.' Grandmaster Atoan did not raise his voice but the restraint required not to do so trembled through that single word. He glanced at Quina, dismissed her and settled his gaze on Sister Owl.

'I'm not sure I can.' The old woman's voice also showed signs of strain, though for a different reason. 'Your shipheart appears to have moved.'

Atoan waved an arm at the doors and, after various scraping and thudding noises, they began to swing open. Yaz stepped back to avoid being hit.

The shipheart hung in the air at chest height, a star so large that if Yaz were to try to encompass it in both hands her fingertips would be a couple of inches shy of meeting. It was a blaze of golden light, almost the white of the Hope star that sat in the crimson heavens. Like all stars it seemed more of a flat hole into another place than a sphere. Yaz imagined that she might reach an arm through it and perhaps find herself immersed in the Path up to the shoulder.

The light was so bright, the sight so mesmerizing, that for a long moment Yaz didn't even register the iron cage around the star or the long chains trailing back from it into the great foyer beyond.

Atoan squinted against the glare. 'How is she doing that?' he asked Sister Owl.

'Which bit?' The nun seemed rather overawed by the shipheart, despite the many years to her rear.

'All of it . . .'

'Well, this is why I thought you'd be interested in assessing her,' Sister Owl said. She raised her voice. 'Yaz, could you do something about the brightness?'

Yaz reached out towards the star and made a twisting gesture. Normally she required no hand waving to command a star but this one seemed to treat commands as requests and to require that they be underlined.

The shipheart's blaze fell to a glow that no longer hurt the eyes. It seemed now to be a sphere of perfect whiteness across which veins of gold slowly waxed and waned.

From somewhere back in the entrance foyer Yaz caught a startled gasp and a hissed: 'It does that?'

The star's aura faded too, though it remained powerful, allowing some of the mages Yaz could now see in the foyer to edge forwards.

The grandmaster advanced on Sister Owl but stopped some yards shy of her position. 'Return the shipheart to my vault!' he called out, aiming his orders not at Yaz but at the Academics.

Several of the mages took up the far ends of the chains. Yaz recognized a mage in a violet robe as the woman Yelna, who had been present at her second trial, representing the Academy along with two others. She had been the one who had helpfully suggested Yaz be given the poison groton to ensure her impossible task be that bit more impossible.

Holding the four chains, eight mages began to tow the star back into the Academy, and Yaz immediately understood two truths. Firstly, that none of them could command the stars like she could, and secondly, that none of them could get much closer to the shipheart than at the end of a five-yard tether. The grandmaster had come through his own wall not to impress them with his prowess, but because his doors were blocked by the shipheart.

*

As the golden star retreated down the long passage leading into the heart of the hall, Grandmaster Atoan advanced up the steps to join Sister Owl, his eyes on Yaz all the while. 'You needn't have knocked for admission quite so loudly, sister. But you are correct. I am very interested in making the acquaintance of this novice.' He glanced towards Quina. 'These novices.' And returned his gaze to Yaz. 'Allow me to extend you an invitation to lunch. It should be served quite soon now.'

Much to Sister Owl's evident surprise they found themselves being led into Academy Hall by the grandmaster himself, down a long corridor lined with doors where objects lay as if dropped during the race to get away from the shipheart's advance: a plate of small pastries, a scarf, a curious triangle of green stone. Atoan stepped over these without comment. Further on, a door hung off its hinges, splinters of the wood from around its lock scattered on the tiled floor. This must have been where the star had forced an exit. In the room beyond, a hole had been broken through the wall. The chamber was strewn with broken plaster and snapped pieces of timber. Yaz could sense the shipheart in the space beyond, once more within the sigils' dampening aura. She resisted apologizing for the damage and disruption. For all she knew, Atoan could be in Seus's service, and she'd had far too few Shade classes to be able to say a convincing sorry to such a man.

The hall proved bigger than Yaz had imagined, which meant in turn that the palace that dwarfed it must be still more vast than it had first appeared. The corridor continued on and came at last to a large chamber cutting up through all four layers of the hall to a many-windowed dome in the main roof. Galleries surrounded the perimeter at every level and a handful of nervous Academics or Academy staff stood watching from on high as if worried that the shipheart might be on the move again.

Atoan crossed the chamber and unlocked one of the doors that faced onto it. He beckoned them in. 'My office.' He stood aside whilst Owl and the two novices went through, then waved to someone they couldn't see. 'A meal for four. Quick, quick!'

The grandmaster's office was luxurious. A thick, intricately patterned rug covered the floor. The desk behind which Atoan seated himself was polished to a high shine and the wood, a deep red in colour, had been carved with all manner of geometric beading, with inlays of other woods to decorate the top.

A fire burned in the hearth, making the room almost unbearably hot, and all the wall space was taken up by grand shelves on which even grander books were packed shoulder to shoulder, interspersed with the occasional curio.

'Sit, sit!' Atoan indicated upholstered chairs in front of the fire, and as he did so three of the chairs turned to face the desk. 'Well, you know me – Atoan – and I recognize the esteemed Sister Owl of course. Whom else do I have the honour of meeting?'

Sister Owl opened a hand towards each of them in turn. 'Novice Quina. Novice Yaz.'

'You have remarkable powers of control over my shipheart.' Atoan cut to the chase. 'I am of course fascinated to talk to you about how you learned to do these things. But I imagine you already knew I would be. It was a clever way of getting my attention. But why did you want my attention?' He leaned back in his chair, his vibrant robe flowing around him.

Under the grandmaster's scrutiny Yaz realized that she didn't have it in her to lie or to play a part even though those things were tools for survival here in the green world just as survival on the ice could depend on the detailed stitching of a hide or the best method for walking into a headwind. Rather than lie badly and be thought a fool, she decided to speak as plainly as the mage had, and to rely on her strengths.

'You have a companion of ours trapped here.'

Sister Owl shot Yaz a wide-eyed look.

'Trapped?' Atoan cocked his head to one side, his expression puzzled. He steepled his fingers before his lips. 'That seems unlikely. We don't hold people here against their will. In fact, it's more difficult getting in than out, as you've experienced. What's your companion's name? What does this person look like? How old are they? Perhaps I've seen them.'

Yaz found herself wrong-footed by this unexpected response. Was Atoan using lies on her now despite the fact she'd opted for honesty? 'He's called Theus.' She watched the mage's face for any sign of recognition.

'We have a Thebus, but she's a girl and has been with us two years . . .'

Yaz glanced at Sister Owl who offered her a neutral look as if to say, 'You dug the hole – you get yourself out of it.'

'You'd know Theus if you'd seen him.' Yaz decided to stick relentlessly to the truth. 'He's . . . well, he's a . . .'

'An iron dog,' Quina pitched in, a heavy accent to her green-tongue. 'With half a god in it.' She nodded, warming to her subject. 'The bad half.'

'Remarkable!' Atoan raised both eyebrows, though Yaz couldn't decide whether his surprise was genuine, or perhaps he'd identified them as from the ice tribes now and was treating their claims with the gentle scepticism grandfathers reserve for the tales of little ones. 'Well. I know of no iron dogs within the Academy – but I can certainly send

252

word and find out if one of our alumni has one hidden in their laboratory.' He glanced at Sister Owl as if he wanted to mouth the words 'iron dog?' but thought better of it.

A knock at the door broke the uncomfortable silence and, before Atoan had a chance to respond, the door opened. Yelna, the mage in violet robes, strode in, followed by a woman in a white tunic holding a tray with four plates on it, and then a man in a black tunic who Yaz immediately recognized as the doorkeeper, Ballo, by virtue of the purple velvet patch over his left eye.

'I hear these girls wish to enter the Academy,' Yelna said, smiling as if she expected Yaz not to remember her from the trial.

'They appear to have done so, my dear.' Atoan gestured and a table moved from the wall to position itself before Sister Owl and the novices. The woman with the plates began to lay out the meal.

'Ballo says they wish to be tested for proxims. That's what they told him before . . .'

Actually it had been Sister Owl who had said that but Yaz kept her mouth closed.

'Well.' Atoan nodded to the server as she placed his meal before him. 'That is good news. It would be very useful to have someone with Yaz's talents here.' He looked at the steaming plate in front of him, then glanced mean-ingfully at the mage in violet. The server and Ballo both took the hint and retreated, but Yelna held her ground. Atoan sighed. 'This is my wife, Yelna. Would you care to join us, dear?'

Yelna gave a crooked smile and came further into the room. Atoan's magical furniture shifted and a chair slid out for her to sit beside Sister Owl.

'How is he doing that?' Quina muttered in the ice-tongue.

Yelna, who clearly had keen ears, leaned around to look at Quina. 'Wondering about the chairs?' Without waiting for confirmation she pressed on. 'My husband is a master of rock-work, the rarest of the marjal elemental skills. Perhaps the talent lies hidden in one of you as well.'

'But they're made of wood . . .' Yaz said, glancing down for confirmation.

'Held together with iron nails. A skilled rock-worker can manipulate metals too, though not as strongly.' Yelna stood up and turned her chair over, untroubled by its considerable weight. 'And these are made especially so Atoan can show off.' She tapped a metal plate secured to the bottom of the seat.

'Yes, thank you, dear.' Atoan looked a little nonplussed at having his secrets exposed.

Yaz nodded, thinking it rather clever. She supposed she could manage something similar with the suitable positioning of small stars. Though stars were harder to come by than iron.

Atoan waited for Yelna to sit and then gestured to the table. 'Eat. Please. I'm going to. I'm famished. Pushing through walls always leaves me hungry.'

Yaz realized that the meal – some sort of stew in a china bowl – smelled delicious. For several minutes she ate steadily, though not with the same focused dedication she'd shown at the convent refectory tables when she'd had her first taste of green-land plenty. She listened to Atoan as he gave an informal but practised account of the Academy's history and studies. It would, she thought, be handy to be able to pass through a wall in the manner he'd shown them. Seus might haunt the hidden paths the quantals could tread, but surely not even he could interfere with a rock-worker's passage.

As Atoan described the process of induction and where

new proxims of Yaz's age would be housed, Sister Owl interrupted.

'Even if either of the novices decides that they wish to leave the convent they will still need to accompany me back to Sweet Mercy this evening to formalize the process with Abbess Claw. The timescale for their return to the Academy would be a matter for future debate.' Sister Owl had mentioned this to Yaz and Quina earlier, both because it was true – though more flexible than she was implying – but also because it ensured that they would not have to remain beneath the same roof as Seus's agent or agents.

Atoan frowned. 'It's very important that I gain an understanding of your methods for moving the shipheart before you go. And I'm sure you would like a chance to exercise your talents in earnest. As far as I know, Sister Owl, Sweet Mercy Convent does not own a shipheart . . .'

'No,' Owl agreed grudgingly.

'Nor, indeed, any star of any size?' Atoan persisted.

'I'm sure we could lay our hands on some if the need arose.' The nun pushed back her bowl and folded her arms.

'Owning a shipheart and laying a hand on it are two very different things.' Atoan smiled.

Yelna, who had not been eating, rose from her seat. 'I'm sure Yaz will want to stay with us. Life here is so much more comfortable than up on that draughty rock. And hasn't the Church already made two attempts on her life?'

Yaz narrowed her eyes at the woman, who had suggested that she be poisoned during that second attempt. 'Quina and I are from the ice. Draughts don't worry us. And if we were prepared to obey Sweet Mercy's laws to such an extent that we let ourselves be thrown into a hole to drown . . . then we will certainly follow the abbess's instruction regarding how we depart, *if* we depart.'

Atoan, seeming to take alarm at that 'if', held out a placatory hand and shot his wife a hard stare. 'I'll arrange a tour immediately following the testing. And no need to worry about issues of timing. This is the Academy – we work wonders here!'

'You can stop the sun crossing the sky?' Sister Owl raised a doubting brow.

'Actually . . .' Atoan rose behind his desk. 'We really can. Come with me. You'll like this!'

CHAPTER 26

Mali

The star's blueness fascinated Mali even as she puzzled over the situation. A star of such enormous size, left untended in a disused section of sewer tunnel? Its colour was unlike any star she'd seen – she'd seen blue stars before, but this one . . . something about the blueness suggested that it was rushing towards her at impossible speeds, while all the time standing still. And a song seemed to reverberate through her. Yaz had talked of the stars singing, but Mali had never truly heard their music until now. In her distraction she nearly stepped on the corpse of a rat but managed to avoid putting her foot on it at the last moment. She scolded herself and tried for the clarity trance as she carried on. Mistress Shade would be ashamed of her, walking blind into what felt so much like a trap.

The blue light worked its way into her mind and drove her clarity away. Even so, her questions stubbornly remained: why were Thurin and Erris slowing in front of her? And why was the tunnel ahead starting to crowd with motionless figures? She hadn't seen any at first, but with each yard that she advanced more coalesced out of the light, always turned away from her, pointing towards the star, none of them yet in reach.

Mali turned and looked behind her. Something zipped across the tunnel back along the way they'd come. A rat? But surely no rat could move at even a quarter of that speed. Other somethings zipped across further back, even faster, just flickers of motion.

Confused, she called to the others and, receiving no answer, was about to go after them when her eyes found the rat corpse she'd passed. It was being torn apart by something, several small somethings, all moving too swiftly to see properly. With a cry she rushed towards it, and as she did so the small somethings slowed to the point at which she could make them out. Just rats eating their own, scattering before her. By the time she reached the littered remains all the rats had gone – the last one scurrying away quickly but no faster than Mali would expect.

'What's going on?' She looked back towards the light, squinting. Neither Thurin nor Erris had turned, though both seemed to be pretty much where she'd left them, as if frozen in mid-step. She glimpsed something moving slowly along the edge of the tunnel, heading in the direction of the star. One of the fleeing rats. But instead of amazing her with its speed it seemed to be slowing as she watched it.

In need of another corpse to experiment with, Mali drew one of the throwing stars she'd been issued with when she left the convent. She'd never been one of the most accurate of throwers, and the likelihood of her getting a rat would usually be pretty low . . . but with one this slow? She threw.

The bladed disc whirred from her hand but then stunned her by rapidly losing speed, as if the air were as thick as honey. She watched it chase the rat. It soon became obvious it would be yards shy of its target. Somehow, she'd misjudged the speeds involved. She watched bemused as the star crawled forwards, failing to drop to the ground, its rotations resolving from a silver blur into something visible. She wondered if hunskas saw the world like this. At last it hit the floor where the rat had been, making a peculiarly deep sound.

'It's about time,' Mali muttered to herself.

Realization widened her eyes. 'It really *is* about time!'

She understood it, and the knowledge both horrified and astonished her. Every yard closer to the blue star slowed time drastically. So when she looked back, away from the star, she saw the tunnel rats as blurs, because compared to them her time was crawling by.

How much time had passed for the outside world? Hours? Days? If she ran back she might find a week had passed. If she ran deeper in to tell the others and break them free of the star's fascination maybe months would pass before they escaped. Or years, or lifetimes! She had no way of judging.

She needed to stop this now. Right now. Or Yaz and Quina might be old women before she saw them again. Or long dead. Especially as their situation had not been one that suggested longevity was an option.

Mali considered the Path. She had touched it recently but something about the proximity of such a large star had opened it up to her again. She could walk the Path, gather power to herself, and launch it at the star in an effort to destroy it or at least stop it doing what it was doing. But how many people were trapped ahead of her? Something about the drastic slowing of their time was stopping the light from revealing those closest to the star. But she knew, from the way that they kept appearing as she had moved in closer, that the tunnel ahead must be packed with the star's oldest victims, all of them thinking that much less than an hour had passed, some of them having been there since the star first came to rest in this spot. If she blasted the star her power would cut through untold numbers of innocents on its way.

A violent solution seemed to be out of the question. Instead, Mali looked to the threadscape. The star's light showed it to her with unequalled clarity. The threads had never been so precise and comprehensible before, though their complexity was still overwhelming. Mali sought out her own connection to the star. Whatever it was doing to her would be reflected in the threadscape. Or rather, reality was just her eyes' inter-pretation of the threadscape. Every interaction began here, in the fundamental truth of the Path.

Mali found the threads that linked her to the star. She gathered them in a bundle, using the fingers of her missing hand to pluck each one from the host then grasping them in her flesh-and-blood hand.

Sister Owl would know what to do, no doubt. A fully fledged Mystic Sister would be trained in the subtle arts of thread-weaving. But Mali was just a novice, not even halfway through her education. And who in the Church knew about the stars anyway? Mali gritted her teeth and gathered her strength. 'Release me!' she shouted, and at the same time yanked savagely to pull free the threads that bound her to the star.

Mali found herself beneath the redness of the sun on a rare, almost windless day. Before her rose the Dome of the Ancestor, the huge structure dwarfing her, its limestone blocks taking colour from the light. The song of Holy Sisters came faintly from the many narrow windows piercing the dome's walls in a band just above head height.

'Thank the Ancestor!' Mali let out a sigh of relief and turned, looking for Erris and Thurin. Instead she found a young novice, considerably shorter than her, racing past, probably late for Spirit class.

'Blessings, sister!' The girl swerved around her.

Mali grinned. She'd never been mistaken for a nun before. A frown replaced the grin as she realized she didn't recognize the novice. She knew every girl in the convent by sight. She could name most of them without needing to ponder.

'Mistress Path.' That was who she needed. Sister Owl would understand what had happened, how Mali had been transported from the city to the convent, and where the others were.

Mali turned until she sighted Path Tower. At least that was where she'd left it. She set off towards the spire, aching in every limb, as if she'd not just yanked on the bundled threads but on each of her muscles as well.

As she walked it seemed that somehow, impossibly, she was walking the Path too. It was nonsense of course. A hallucination. Some echo of the time-star's magics. She shuffled across the Rock of Faith, and yet, somehow, she also strode the Path. Not as she did on those rare occasions when she edged along it for a few steps, gathering power and hoping that when she fell off back into the world she would be able to own it. This was different. She strode the Path confidently, full of a power so vast she couldn't comprehend it, a power that filled her, overflowed her, and streamed around her, as though the Path were a river and she was a fish swimming through.

Mali pushed the curious hallucination from her mind and focused on the world of stone and wind and flesh.

A couple of nuns emerged from the laundry. Another vanished into the scriptorium, but none of them looked her way. Mali found her vision too blurry to make out at this distance which nuns they were.

The tower waited patiently as she hobbled towards it, amazed at her own exhaustion. She pushed open one of the four doors and entered the portrait room at the base. A senior novice was studying one of the paintings. She turned when Mali entered.

'Sister Pan. Ancestor's blessings.'

Mali didn't recognize the novice and, as she closed the distance between them, she realized that despite being very clearly a young woman rather than a girl, the novice was scarcely taller than she was.

'Pan?' It struck her that this novice, a novice she didn't even know, had guessed the name she was planning to adopt when she became a nun. She hadn't even told Sister Owl yet. There hadn't been a good moment. The girl must have heard tales of how Mali defended herself with the ice-triber's frying pan out on the ice . . .

Shaking away her annoyance, Mali focused on her mission. 'I'm looking for Mistress Path.' Her voice came out in a reedy croak as if she'd overused it.

The novice's eyes widened, then she frowned in concentration. 'This is one of those mind games you get us to play, isn't it? Should I be looking for myself too?'

'What are you—' Mali bit off the question in irritation. She narrowed her eyes at the novice and enunciated in a tone that dared her to mess with her further, 'Where is Sister Owl?'

'I know this one!' The novice grinned and pointed behind Mali.

Mali turned, and saw what she'd expected to see. An empty room. 'I haven't got time for this. You'll give me a straight answer or I swear the abbess will—'

The novice ran past her, obviously nervous. 'She's here! She's here!' And set her hand to a portrait on the wall, close to the door Mali had entered by.

Mali followed her. 'It's her!' She blinked away sudden tears. Sister Owl's large eyes regarded her out of a gently smiling face. A young face. In the space above her head two disembodied eyes watched the world with a dark all-encompassing gaze. And bordering it all, a darkness filled with wings and feathers. 'But they don't paint you till you're dead . . .' She laid her hand against the picture. 'Oh . . . Ancestor's blood . . . I'm *old*.' She brought her hand closer to her face. It was bones clad in wrinkles. Even the darkness of her skin seemed sprinkled with dusty grey. 'I'm old.'

'Are . . . are you all right, Mistress Path?' the girl asked uncertainly. 'Should I fetch Sister Rose?'

Mali wiped away tears. She wasn't sure if they were for Sister Owl or for herself.

'Mistress Path?' the girl repeated, concern filling her voice. 'Maybe you need to sit down? I'll run and get a chair.' And she was gone, clattering away up the stairs at a speed Mali couldn't hope to match.

Looking at Sister Owl's portrait, Mali was suddenly full of fear and felt more alone than she had ever been in her life. 'Help me, sister. I'm lost and I don't know what to do.'

As she said it the door nearby opened and a novice stood there framed in the light.

'Yaz! Oh, Yaz! Thank all the gods!' Mali spoke her blasphemy in the northern ice-tongue, reaching for her friend. The girl stepped back smartly, her face stiffening as if struck.

'Mistress Path?' She studied Mali's eyes. 'How do you know that language? How do you know that name?'

'It's me, Yaz. It's Mali.' Mali reached for her again. It was Yaz. Her eyes might be old but they weren't *that* bad. The girl had the same wide-shouldered frame, the same copper skin, the same broad cheekbones. An ice-triber. An Ictha.

'I am Zole.' The girl replied, keeping to the green-tongue. The moment of doubt that had cracked her armour had passed. Her control now returned, she held her face in a mask that seemed neither surprised nor frightened.

'I . . .' Mali faltered and lowered her arm. The girl was the spitting image of Yaz, but she wasn't Yaz. Her eyes were black, so black you could hardly tell iris from pupil. How had she not seen that from the start? She wasn't Yaz. Mali could see that this girl held herself much tighter than Yaz did, so free of emotion that if you took a cursory glance at the threadscape you might think she wasn't there at all.

The other girl was back, chair in hands. She positioned it and tried to get Mali to sit in it. 'Sister Pan, please. Help me, Zole. She should sit down.'

Zole made no move. 'Sister Pan is a warrior, Suleri. She sits when and where she wishes to.'

Zole's faith strengthened Mali at the core. The girl might not be Yaz but they shared more than looks. The time-star had done this. Somehow Mali had been thrown decades into her own future. It felt like a century, judging by how frail she was. 'Come with me . . . Zole. You, Sul . . .'

'Suleri, sister.' The girl looked hurt. Perhaps Mali had been her teacher for years.

'Yes, dear. I'm old and sometimes my mind slips. Run along now.'

The novice glanced at Zole as if for confirmation then hurried for the nearest exit.

Mali turned and made for the stairs. She found them a labour but Zole offered no help, and she discovered that if she took them much more slowly than she wanted to she could make a reasonable job of ascending. In the gloom of the spiral steps it was hard for Mali to block out the mirror

264

world where she walked the Path, with glory blazing up, white hot, in every place she set her feet.

A third of the way up Mali stopped for a rest. She studied Zole again in the half-light. 'You're a calm one, novice.'

'I am.'

'Ictha?' Mali asked in the ice-tongue of the far north.

Zole watched back, her eyes like black stones. 'I do not speak of the ice.'

Mali pursed her lips and nodded. 'Not Kac-Kantor then. In my limited experience it's hard to shut them up.' She resumed her climb.

Sister Owl had shown Mali the way into the first of what were reputed to be three hidden rooms within the tower. Rooms that could only be accessed by walking through the wall. Now, in place of solid walls, Mali just saw the open archways leading into each of the sigil-lined rooms. She chose the third, furthest up the tower, a place she had never been before.

'Follow me, Zole. Closely.' And she stepped through.

The sigils coating the walls of the third room were more complex than in the other two, and there was a barrel-lidded casket on the floor. She recognized it as Sister Owl's and guessed that she had inherited it. Mali turned and found Zole standing behind her, arms folded. In the sigils' glow the novice's eyes glimmered with unsuspected emotion.

'Do you know me, Zole?'

The novice nodded.

'I mean: Do you *really* know me?'

She nodded again, lips in a bloodless line.

'How?'

Zole shook her head. A tight, quick negative.

It came to Mali in a moment of epiphany, a moment of strange blue light, and the memory of the smile in Sister Owl's painting. The same smile that Owl had offered her at least once a day for years. Mainly when she thought Mali wasn't looking.

'Yaz. It was Yaz, wasn't it?' She paused. 'I was foretold.'

And more surprising than any answer, positive or negative, Zole – who even on this brief acquaintance gave the impression that she was carved from ice – burst into tears.

CHAPTER 27

Yaz

'If you'll follow me.' Atoan led Sister Owl and her two charges from his office.

'I'll meet you up there.' Atoan's wife hurried away in a swirl of violet robes.

Yaz worried that the woman might be going to alert whoever had Theus imprisoned, but short of tackling the grandmaster's wife to the ground and beating a confession out of her she didn't seem to have any options. She watched Yelna stride out of sight around a corner and hoped that if the woman was planning to move Theus then she might make a mistake in her haste. Theus had, after all, managed to get word all the way to the convent while the mages had all the time they needed to deal with him.

Atoan led them to a set of spiral stairs. 'These will take us to the top floor of Academy Hall. There's quite a view from up there.'

Sister Owl laboured up the stairs on creaking knees, muttering that she was sure there were interesting things to see on the ground floor.

'Interesting indeed!' White teeth showed in Atoan's smile.

'But none so uniquely suited to our needs, or indeed to the subject in hand.'

A corridor led to what Yaz guessed was the front right corner of the hall. It seemed little frequented, and held a dusty, neglected air. Atoan struggled briefly with the heavy door at the end. It gave way with a groan and a squeal of hinges, opening onto a peculiar chamber. A large room, square from what Yaz could see but almost filled with another, circular, room nearly as large and into which several doors gave access.

'We don't use this area much, but in times of need it can be extremely useful.' Atoan took the nearest door into the inner room and guided his guests into a wedge-shaped division which narrowed to a point at what must be the centre of the circular inner room. Light streamed in through a slim window in the slanted ceiling, a single pane of glass keeping the weather at bay. The pane was larger than any Yaz had yet seen and no doubt manufactured through the mages' artifices. Unlike the rest of Academy Hall, this room lay bare, containing only an ornate high-backed chair and a plain stool.

'Interesting architecture,' Sister Owl muttered.

'Functional,' Atoan said. He pointed at the wall to their left and a foot-long spike of stone emerged, casting its shadow below it. Atoan twisted his hand and number runes appeared in an arc below the spike. 'A sun-dial,' he explained. 'It helps keep track of time. See how the shadow is touching the one-rune? In three hours it will touch the four-rune and you will have plenty of time to make it back to the Rock of Faith before dark.'

Yaz exchanged a quick glance with Quina. Seeing the sun was enough to know the time of day. This business with shadows and numbers was clever but pointless. She said nothing and just nodded.

Atoan beckoned them towards the pointed end of the room.

'There's a star here . . .' Yaz could hear its song – a peculiar combination, powerful but muted. Even though she couldn't see the star she knew it sat just beyond the pointed end of the room and that its light was a red unlike any she had seen before. 'It's moving . . .' She had been going to say that it was rushing away from her. It felt as if it were. But also it was still where it had been. The contradiction left her dizzy.

'Now.' Atoan gestured to the chair. 'I propose to start with Quina. I'll need to ask her a series of questions aimed at uncovering any marjal potential she may have.' He peered back into the chamber beyond. 'Where's that wife of m—' But Yelna opened the door, breathless, before he could finish. A swirl of wind accompanied her through the doorway, lifting dust. 'This could take hours,' Atoan apologized. 'Yelna, if you could take Yaz and Sister Owl to see the elemental library in the meantime?'

'Of course.' Yelna gave a conspiratorial smile and came across to join them.

Yaz thought Sister Owl would protest that she was too old to trek all over Academy Hall, but the mention of books seemed to invigorate her.

Yaz followed the nun and joined Yelna outside the wedge-shaped room, still wondering about the hidden star. Sister Owl had made no mention of it. Yelna shut the door behind them and gestured to the corridor. 'This way, please.'

They managed six paces across the room before the door behind them opened.

'If I could have Yaz in now, please.' Atoan stood in the doorway.

Yaz blinked. 'I thought it was a long series of questions . . .'

'Never-ending!' Quina squeezed past Atoan, covering a yawn.

'But you've only just . . .'

'I know! The shadow never moved. The sun just froze in place.' Quina yawned again. 'Was the library good?'

'Time runs faster the further into the room we go,' Atoan explained. 'I'll be able to test Yaz and spend as long as our discussion about the stars requires, and we'll still be finished before you can take more than a few steps.'

'But that's . . .' Sister Owl blinked in astonishment.

'Very useful,' Atoan said. 'Yes, it is! I told you I could stop the sun.'

Yaz went to join the mage in the doorway. 'There's a time-star at the far end of the room. A red one that makes time speed up as you approach it.'

'Remarkable! You seem to know a lot about it already.' Atoan beckoned her forward. 'We have to go in together, otherwise one of us will get very bored waiting for the other.'

They advanced in step to the two chairs, Atoan aiming for the grand one, leaving Yaz the stool. She felt the red light of the time-star tingling on her skin despite there being a stone wall in between them.

'If your friend were watching us from the doorway she would see us accelerating towards these chairs and then jittering around at high speed as hours passed for us in heartbeats for her.'

Yaz took her place. Less than a year ago she had never known there were such things as chairs, so it hardly mattered to her which she sat in. The stool would be price-less among the northern tribes. A single bead of wood had been the prize of the Kac-Kantor. What would the Ictha think of her now? She wanted Quell to see the green lands. She missed him.

'I'm going to ask a series of questions. There are no right answers, so just reply with your first thought.' Atoan started his questioning. 'When is fire most like water?'

Yaz thought that Thurin would know but having no idea, herself she simply said, 'When it flows.'

Atoan continued, his list of questions rapidly beginning to seem endless. Yaz answered each in turn, sparing little thought for them. Her replies became more careless and after twenty or so simply spilled from the tip of her tongue. It seemed that somehow the mage's questions grew from her answers, both guiding and chasing her through a maze she couldn't see. Even the cadence and rhythm of the questions seemed to serve a purpose, slowly creating some kind of trance state not dissimilar to those Sister Owl taught the novices in Path class.

Most of the questions concerned the elements; some of them wandered into the subjects of light and dark, others concerned friends, loyalties, emotions, and the like.

Yaz's voice grew tired and she wondered what the mage would think if she told him that in the Black Rock his endless questions were replaced with four stars, each brought close to the test subject in turn. Still, she supposed that while his method was lengthy he was manufacturing the time it took, and in that he too was relying on the magics of the Missing or on the generation of the four tribes that first beached their ships on Abeth. Not magic, 'technology', she corrected herself. Erris would call it technology. No more magical than the metalwork toys that clacked around, driven by a coiled spring. But both were magic to her.

'Yaz?'

Yaz realized that Atoan had stopped asking questions and

that her throat was very dry. 'Is it over?' She felt different but wasn't quite sure in what manner.

The grandmaster nodded.

'And?'

'And your friend has a lively brain. She's everything we look for in a proxim – except she hasn't a drop of marjal blood in her veins. While you, Yaz, are a conundrum. You're unusual in ways that I've not seen before, but I don't think you're marjal. You're very likely a quantal, and the nuns will know all about that. But I think you're something else too. Something new, and I don't know what.'

Yaz had an idea what. The mage had sensed that she shared blood with the Missing. Somehow Atoan's web of questions helped him to see how people interacted with the world. Yaz thought that the same or deeper insights might be gained from a close study of the threadscape, but maybe his methods were better for a quick result.

'So you won't want me in the Academy then?' Yaz had never seriously intended to join the mages in their institute but it did intrigue her, and the idea of being in the heart of the city in a place of investigation and exploration did appeal. The convent had an enormous amount to teach, but at the same time they seemed more concerned with what they already knew than with discovering new truths.

'I thought you came to find your friend? This mysterious Theus?' Atoan countered.

'Why spend all this time testing us then?'

Atoan smiled. 'Talent is rare. We're always looking for new recruits. And with you it was important for me to know the possible origins for your skill in manipulating my ship-heart. Though it seems I've not been completely successful on that front.'

Yaz frowned. Something had changed, but she couldn't

put her finger on it. 'We should get back to the others. Did you even start a search for Theus?'

Atoan stood. 'I didn't. Which was remiss of me. But I will now. And outside this chamber very little time has been lost. We still have plenty of time to discuss—'

'Wait!' Yaz suddenly realized what the difference was before and after Atoan's questioning. 'Where's the star?'

'What?' Atoan looked puzzled.

'The star!' Yaz repeated. 'The time-star! It's gone.'

'Gone? Atoan turned towards the room's apex. 'But that's impossible . . .'

Yaz stared too. Beyond the stonework she sensed nothing. No redness, no paradoxical static retreat, no star. The time-star's aura had been a strange one, powerful but heavily muted so that she hadn't sensed it until close enough to be in the fringes of its effect. It wasn't that close now. 'There's nothing there.'

Atoan released his grip on the carved turrets decorating his chair's back and strode towards the door. 'We'll soon know. If it's not there then—' He stopped. The shadow cast by the stone spike had swung through a fair portion of its arc and no longer painted the same line that it had.

Yaz ran to the door, half expecting to find herself locked in. She hauled it open and came to a dead halt in the doorway. A crumpled figure in a habit lay face down amid a wide pool of blood. Yaz had no words.

'What's going on?' Atoan stopped at her shoulder.

'Quina?' But what had, in one shocked moment, looked like black hair was a headdress. Yaz fell to her knees, reaching for the body, gathering the woman to her. 'Sister Owl . . .' Blood had poured from a single wound between Owl's shoulder blades, soaking the outer habit and making the black material glisten.

273

'How – how could this have happened?' Atoan strode past Yaz into the room, looking left and right. The surprise in his voice convinced Yaz that he was as shocked as she was.

Yaz hadn't held a dead person before. Maya had been taken by the eidolon. Kao had been swept away in the flood. Yaz had been hauled from the Broken's caves before the aftermath of their battle with the Tainted had to be dealt with. Even the proxim boy had been taken swiftly away by others. His death rolled through the numbness of her mind, an isolated thought from the darkness. She would have to tell Atoan about him. The boy would have friends who needed to know and grieve, a family . . . She looked down and found her hands bloody, as if in accusation of her crime, with Owl the punishment. The old woman weighed nothing in her arms. The years had eroded her, leaving nothing but a shining will bound around old bones and hung with wrinkles.

'Where's Quina?' Suddenly Quina's whereabouts pushed aside all other thought. Yaz set Owl down and clambered to her feet again. 'Where's Quina?'

'Making her escape, I don't doubt.' The air around Atoan seemed to darken with power; the walls themselves began to groan as he threw open the door to the corridor and roared, 'Murder! Kidnap! Find the novice!'

'What?' Yaz stood, astonished. 'Quina didn't do this!'

'I suppose she didn't kidnap my wife either?' Atoan rounded on Yaz, dark eyes blazing.

'Yelna!' Yaz understood in the moment she spoke the woman's name. 'She took Quina! Quick, what are her powers? Tell me!'

Atoan barked a disbelieving laugh. 'Yelna's the victim here!' He paused and somewhere a bell began to toll. Running feet could be heard in the corridor, coming nearer. 'Yelna's the victim! And Mistress Path, of course.'

Yaz opened her mouth to protest Quina's innocence and found the words caught in her throat. Hadn't Eular seemed to be on her side right up until the moment that he wasn't? He'd played her, pretended to be just a wise old man. He'd been kind to her – seen past her flaws to her potential. Then betrayed her just as she escaped the ice caves. She hadn't seen that blow coming. She would never have thought it would be him behind the horrors of the pit. Not if you'd given her a thousand years to think it over. But Quina, she'd actually been talking about throwing her lot in with Seus. She'd been saying it just before they left the Rock of Faith. Yaz looked down at Sister Owl's body. No. She was losing her mind. There was a chasm between having doubts and stabbing an old woman in the back. A yawning chasm. One that Quina would never cross.

Two proxims arrived, senior ones, two young men. 'Grandmaster!'

'My wife has been abducted and Sister Owl has been murdered. I want Yelna found *now*!'

A younger proxim arrived as Atoan finished, her long blonde hair in disarray, panting. 'But . . . I saw Mage Yelna not long ago. I helped her carry the injured novice down the stairs.'

Atoan's face went stiff, his brows rose, and a new intensity entered his stare as if he were trying to compel a different truth from the girl before him.

'She must have had an accomplice,' Yaz said, feeling guilty for doubting Quina if only for a moment. 'Someone to move the time-star while we talked. There would have been hardly any time to do it, and it would need fine co-ordination . . . How could they have—'

'Ballo.' Atoan made as if to spit an unpleasant taste from his mouth. 'Yelna's brother has far-sight, he can see into places where he's been before without going back there. He could have worked the chain to raise the star to the roof as we sat down to talk.'

'So where are they? They could be in the undercity by now!' Yaz started towards the doorway, though she hadn't any idea where she was going. She was alone now, and the crushing weight of realization fell on her. Quina was gone, Thurin, Erris, and Mali were gone. Owl was dead. And blessed or not, how would the nuns react if she went back there with the news that she'd got their oldest and most revered sister killed?

'Find my wife!' Atoan roared. 'She's to be arrested and brought before a full council! Spread the word!'

'And her powers?' Yaz repeated her earlier question in a defeated voice.

'Air-work,' Atoan answered, looking down at his hands. 'She controls the winds. She can also command lightning if there is a storm, and smaller lightnings even if there is no storm – even indoors. She probably stunned your friends with a shock of that sort.' He shook his head. 'She's always been ambitious, but I never thought she would deal with the powers of the underdark.'

'You know about Seus then?'

Atoan nodded. 'The Academy has known about the old gods for centuries. Some of our number have traded with their minions, but it was long ago decided to outlaw the practice. The servants of the Missing have no love for our kind. Ultimately any gift they give is aimed at our destruction. They lead us by our pride and when we've given them sufficient length of it they hang us by it.'

For a man just betrayed by his wife the mage seemed

remarkably calm, but perhaps it hadn't been as big a surprise to him as it might. Yaz's very brief exposure to their relationship had left her with the impression that it was a guarded one, lacking the easy familiarity of her parents.

Atoan continued: 'Why would she take your friend though?'

Yaz knew the answer to that one. By holding Quina, Seus's minions would seek to pressure her into opening the ark for them. That couldn't be allowed to happen. But Quina could be anywhere. And if Yaz refused to cooperate, what would happen then? She looked down at her hands, still crimson with Sister Owl's blood, and found her answer there.

CHAPTER 28

'I'm going to need your shipheart.' Yaz started towards the door again, then stopped. 'And your time-star.'

'What?' Atoan seemed so taken aback by the enormity of the demand that he couldn't frame an answer.

Yaz reached out to her utmost extent, first with her mind to sense the faint, muted aura of the time-star, and then with her hand to coax the thing into motion. It was hard to move: in the grip of her thoughts it felt slippery and heavy. Someone had raised the star from its original position and she guessed it must now lie on the hall's roof, perhaps on the edge of a shaft that would return it to the centre of the circular room.

With a violent motion Yaz cast the unseen star from the roof towards the great square at the heart of the Academy complex. She imagined it would be safe enough there for a short while, and of no particular danger to students or staff.

'Come on.' Yaz walked past the proxims and down the corridor without pausing to see if any of them were following her. 'A mistress of the convent is lying dead on your floor, Grandmaster Atoan. I think the nuns of Sweet Mercy would look poorly on any mage who wasn't prepared to loan their resources to the effort of bringing her killer to justice and freeing the novice who's been taken.'

Yaz wiped her hands on her habit as she descended the stairs, trying not to think of Sister Owl abandoned in the room above. The Ancestor had her now. Yaz was sure of it. The Gods in the Sky and the Gods in the Sea held no sway in these green lands. The Ancestor had taken Owl and her body was of no more use to her. It would go into the soil and play its part in the cycle that sustained life. A cycle that the ice had broken everywhere else.

'Andrei, Alicia, get that search started, damn you! Tell Master Crane I want him to organize it. Find Yelna, and Ballo too. And have Mistress Teehan read the runes. I want to know if anyone else is in on this.' Atoan barked more orders at his proxims then hurried to catch up with Yaz. 'What are you going to do?'

'Find my friend,' Yaz said. 'Everything's connected. You know that. I just need to find the right thread.'

Academy Hall was in uproar by the time Yaz approached the shipheart's vault. Mages, proxims, and staff were hurrying in all directions, many sparking with magic of one sort or another, others calling out Ballo and Yelna's names along with those of new suspects accused of involvement. It seemed that fractures had run through the mages' community for many years and that Yaz's arrival had broken them wide. She thought of Eular sitting by his unfrozen pool. 'You're an agent of change, Yaz.' He hadn't been the friend she'd thought he was, but he hadn't lied. The pool had frozen the instant she disturbed it. All that change needs is somewhere to start. She was sick of it. She wanted some day to arrive in a place that didn't even notice her, let alone collapse as a consequence of her addition.

Yaz approached the vault – still littered with debris from the broken wall – through the outer chamber. She could feel the star's power pressing on her, despite the buffering effect of the sigils lining the room. Behind her, Atoan's footsteps faltered.

Rather than bother with the locked iron-bound door, Yaz called the star to her through the hole it had previously put in the wall. Its golden light flooded out ahead of it and Atoan fell back with a soft curse. The iron cage around the star knocked loose a few more chunks of plaster as it passed through the hole. The four attached chains began to rattle their way through the gap in the shipheart's wake. As the star closed the distance between them to a yard and then a foot and then mere inches its power began to burn across Yaz's skin, a brightness too sharp to be borne for long, a pricking that pierced skin and flesh, seeking bone. Whispering started at the back of her mind. Uninvited thoughts bubbled up. Dark and unworthy thoughts. Had Quina only feigned incapacity to continue the charade of friendship in case Yaz found her? Had she been in league with Yelna and Seus for weeks now? Maybe even out on the ice. Perhaps Quina had been corrupted on one of their journeys through the haze-gates. Seus could have led her astray, luring her into his frozen forest and tempting her with the promise of power. Quina knew where her best interests lay. She had always been too clever for her own good.

'Novice?'

Yaz gathered her thoughts with a shudder. She found that she'd been staring into the whiteness of the star, her mind lost in memories of ice.

'Yaz?' Atoan called again.

'I'm fine,' she lied. 'I'm working on it.'

In the shipheart's light everything became clear as diamond

ice. The river that flows through all things widened to a thundering cataract, and the threadscape that foamed around it somehow shook off its customary confusion and opened itself to her gaze. What had been incomprehensible before now screamed its meaning at her. She had wanted to find the thread that joined her to Quina, but couldn't pick out such a fine connection amid the myriad filaments of the threadscape. But now, with the shipheart lighting her mind on fire, Yaz immediately saw the link she needed. It wasn't a gossamer thread but a cable comprising a thousand interwoven strands. There were threads of association, threads of friendship, connections that led back to the moment of their meeting and to every moment since, threads that wound through abstract angles into the futures that waited their turn. She saw, out in the corridor beyond Atoan, the path that Quina had taken entering the hall, and another leading out again.

Yaz reached for Quina's bundle of threads and took hold. She pushed the star away from her, gasping in sudden relief. 'I can find her now.' The threadscape had faded somewhat but Yaz retained her hold on Quina. 'I'm taking the shipheart with me. You should clear your people out of the way.'

'That belongs to me! And you can't take it out into the city! You'd cause chaos. The citizens will panic.'

'They should.' Yaz advanced, bringing the star behind her, keeping it a couple of yards distant. 'If they knew what was coming they would. Seus has been reaching into your Academy. He's reached into your family. Soon he'll reach up into your city. You should want me to fight him. And to do that I need your stars.'

Atoan retreated before her, looking conflicted, his vibrant robes shimmering in the shipheart's light. Others coming up behind Yaz, or in the corridor ahead, both saw and sensed the star's presence and swiftly changed direction, no more willing to approach than if the passage were full of flames.

Yaz advanced, keeping to a steady pace despite her desire to run. The chains trailed noisily along the corridor behind her.

Atoan decided to look as if he were leading the charge rather than retreating before a novice. He strode ahead, calling for everyone to clear the way. And as they reached the great doors he unbarred them with a wave of his left hand before opening them wide with a wave of the right. Yaz suspected that, like the furniture in his room, the doors had iron plates to facilitate the grandmaster's manipulations.

Yaz emerged from Academy Hall with the stares of a dozen mages burning on the back of her neck. She knew it was Atoan's sanction that protected her. The shipheart wouldn't ward off a firestorm, flying rock, razored shadow or whatever other magical violence they cared to wreak upon her.

Once outside, she sent the shipheart flying overhead at a distance where its aura wouldn't trouble anyone on the ground. The chains and cage were becoming an annoyance and a hazard to navigation. Yaz reached out to the star, focusing on the heat sigil, the first sigil she had ever seen. She printed it on the white surface, and within moments the iron cage had begun to glow red. She felt the first pulse of heat reach her despite the twenty yards between her and the star.

'What are you—'

The spatter of molten metal on stone cut Atoan short, followed by the noise of falling chains and then the crash of the cage. Arka had been right. Everything melts if you get it hot enough.

Yaz went to examine the red time-star, which also lay in

a mess of chains. Curiously the flagstones around it were scattered with rust and broken ceramic.

'The star was held in a china cage. Delicate but impervious to time. Any iron that gets too close rusts away.' Atoan watched her with distant eyes, perhaps considering his wife's betrayal.

Yaz picked up a length of chain and threw it underarm at the star. The chain seemed to accelerate towards the star, and the section that made contact exploded into a shower of rust. The star itself remained unmoved.

She walked towards the time-star, and turned back just a yard from it to see that the world around her had ground to a halt: Atoan now a statue, her wider audience holding its breath, a bird in flight frozen in place, wings aching for the next beat. She had stepped outside time. She could grow old before the bird's wings stirred. She wasn't trapped, though. This was the opposite of the blue star that held Mali and the others. If they were to turn they would see the world racing, and perhaps it would grow old before they could cover the distance to escape their star. Mali's bird would not wait for her return before it flapped its wings. Mali's bird would lay dozens of eggs, die, and countless feathered generations would hatch then pass away before she could leave her time-star's influence.

Yaz tried to move the time-star but the thing paid no more attention to her than a rock would. She bit down and strained. Nothing. Not the slightest motion. She crouched and made to reach for it but stopped with her fingers still a foot from the blazing red surface. She remembered the chains becoming rust and jerked her hands back. Her reaching hands would have been ageing more swiftly than the rest of her. Weeks could have passed by for them in the time she had perceived. If she touched the star her hands would wither and die, millennia passing for them in the time it took her to blink with eyes nearly a yard more distant from the star.

'But I moved it before . . .'

Yaz understood. She walked away until the frozen bird began to beat its wings once and fluttered away, indicating she had joined the time stream that carried everyone else. Now, with effort, she could move the star. Had she moved it while within its aura, from the outside it would have been travelling faster than the swiftest hawk. Apparently the time-star broke the laws of time but not of motion. Yaz had been trying to move it at vast speeds. From outside she could move it at more modest velocities.

Yaz used her mind to wrest the time-star from the flag-stones and lofted it to join the shipheart. Both stars were identical in size, but whatever had broken to create the time-star from a working shipheart had left it difficult to control, as if it were melting ice always slipping through Yaz's fingers, shooting away if squeezed too hard.

Yaz became aware that across the Academy compound many of those who should have been in pursuit of Yelna and her allies were instead staring at her and at the stars above her in slack-jawed wonder. Despite the sun having only recently passed its zenith the stars still drew the eye. She sent them higher. It was hard. They were a burden on her mind and she would rather have tried supporting a grown man on each shoulder than both the shiphearts together. Combined they were much more than twice as difficult to handle as either one was separately. Even so, she kept them up on high, ground her teeth together and focused once more on the thread that bound her to Quina. Slowly at first and then with a steadier stride she began to follow it.

Atoan walked beside her. 'Yelna has hours on us. If she rode off out of the city we'll need plenty of resources to catch up.' He spared an uneasy glance for the stars above them. 'Can you ride?'

'She won't have left the city,' Yaz said. 'She might be under it, though.' It was a guess, but if they wanted to use Quina to force cooperation regarding the ark it would be better to keep her close in case verbal threats weren't sufficient.

'So where is she then?' Atoan asked.

'You tell me.' Yaz spoke through gritted teeth. 'I can follow where they went. Or at least where Quina went. I don't know where they ended up. Can't your mages tell you?'

'I'm sure they're working on it. But Yelna knows us. She knows how to throw us off her scent. And Ballo, her brother, will be watching us. If we get too close they'll move. This is going to be tricky.'

Yaz came to the Academy's perimeter. The thread led back into the city, away from the emperor's palace, though according to the nuns the ark should lie directly below the palace.

'Shouldn't you stay here to organize them?' Part of Yaz wanted the grandmaster with her, employing his magics against the mages who'd taken Quina. Another part worried where his loyalties lay. Face to face with his wife he might turn to her side, or at least prevent Yaz from taking whatever action was needed to save her friend if it meant injuring Yelna.

Atoan shook his head. 'Organizing mages is akin to herding cats. Master Crane will do as good a job of it as I would. I sent word to let him know what I expect. If my colleagues want to remain at the Academy they'll follow orders. Best to let them get on with it. Besides, you have my stars. Also, what would Abbess Claw say if she discovered I'd let one of her novices go from the Academy directly into danger all by herself?'

Yaz shrugged. It would be useful to have the mage watching over her, as long as she could trust him. While she was focused on following the thread she would be vulnerable to attack. In fact she was vulnerable to attack whatever she was doing. The ice offered a clear view of approaching danger in all directions. Here in this crowded city an attacker would be invisible until the last moment. If Yelna's brother was watching them right now, the opportunities for ambush were limitless. Even so, what were her choices? Not going after Quina wasn't an option.

Yaz walked swiftly, feeding Quina's thread through her hand, hardly seeing the grand buildings looming ahead, mansions of the city's richest families jostling to be close to the emperor.

When the sharp cry rang out behind her Yaz turned too slowly to save Atoan. He hit the ground before she could catch him. The arrow jutting from the back of his shoulder had to have been loosed from the window or rooftop of one of the Academy buildings.

'Run!' he gasped through gritted teeth. A jerk of his uninjured arm tore a hail of broken stone from the plaza's paving slabs and sent them blindly towards the Academy, peppering the walls and shutters. 'Run!'

CHAPTER 29

Yaz ran, expecting an arrow to sprout between her shoulder blades at any moment. A detonation sounded behind her and the surfaces of the flagstones all around her shattered into dust, billowing into the air. She knew it to be Atoan's work. The stone dust would hide her from archers, at least until the breeze stripped it away.

Yaz ran, heart pounding, dragging the stars with her on high. The dust made her cough and choke but she carried on, cursing when she saw the first blue shreds of sky above her. She veered to the left and sent her stars right, hoping to confuse the aim of anyone seeking to bring her down. Perhaps this minion knew Seus needed her alive, perhaps not, but either way an arrow through the thigh wouldn't lessen her usefulness.

The cloud thinned around her and the first thing Yaz saw was a figure watching on in bemusement. A figure in a habit.

'Gully?' Yaz raced towards the mousey-haired girl.

Somewhat belatedly, the novice dropped into a fighting stance. Gully had never been one of Mistress Blade's most prized pupils and right now her astonishment had turned to fear.

'It's me! Yaz!' Yaz realized that her habit was no longer black but grey and trailing dust like smoke. She grabbed the girl's arm and hauled her onwards. 'Run!'

Gully, to her credit, began to run. 'Where?'

'Away!'

'Wenna lives there!' Gully pointed at the walls looming to their left.

'How do we get in?'

'The gate's around the corner.'

The wall didn't turn for fifty yards and Ballo no doubt had his eyes on them now, directing however many of Seus's agents he had with him towards their location. Yaz wanted to be on the other side of that wall immediately.

'I'll boost you over.' She came to a sudden halt, skidding on her heels.

'Boost me?' Gully took longer to stop and looked up at the wall doubtfully. 'I won't make it standing on your shoulders.' Then she saw the stars overhead. 'What in the hells are—'

'Quickly!' Yaz crouched and brought the heels of her hands together to form a step. 'You're going to have to catch the ledge.'

Gully gave a worried shrug and ran back towards Yaz. Her foot hit Yaz's hands and Yaz lifted, with her thighs and with her arms. With a grunt of effort Yaz raised her arms to full stretch above her head. Gully was slightly built and had at least had some gymnastic skill drilled into her in Blade Hall: at the apex of Yaz's lift she leapt for the overhanging ledge at the top of the wall, catching it with her fingers. A swing and a twist and she had a leg over it.

Yaz knew she had no chance of climbing after her. She

glanced back at the Academy buildings. The dust still hung around at waist level, hiding Atoan. It hadn't been a fatal shot. Perhaps he'd been lucky. Or perhaps his wife had ordered the bowman to just wing him. Yaz didn't know how far an arrow could travel or if the archer was still watching from one of the distant windows, but she felt distinctly vulnerable standing at the base of the wall. Bracing herself, she called the shipheart down at speed and seized it with both hands. Grinding her teeth against the discomfort, she made it rise. Back in the undercity beneath the Broken's caves, Yaz had slowed her fall by clinging to a smaller star. The shipheart lifted her smoothly over the wall and she lowered herself into the greenery on the other side.

Gully, who had dropped down close by, staggered away from the shipheart's aura with a cry of distress. Yaz sent the star away, calling the time-star to join it and keeping both among the foliage of the trees lining the wall so that neither would act as a beacon to guide her enemies to her.

'We should find Wenna,' Gully said in a faint voice, still shivering from her brush with the star. She stumbled through the neatly trimmed bushes and onto a gravel path leading towards a mansion that, had Yaz not already seen the palace, she would have taken to be the emperor's home.

The area between the gardens and the mansion was paved and sported not one but two fountains along with several nude statues which, had Yaz had more time to consider them, would have brought the blood rushing to her cheeks. The Tacsis family guard, however, proved to be alert and efficient. The detonation not far from their walls and subsequent dust cloud had clearly sparked their concern and now four guards with short swords in hand came running across the plaza while three more exited from the main doors, two with spears and one winding a crossbow.

Yaz hauled on the time-star, ripping it from the foliage and bringing it close behind her. She grabbed Gully's arm and hauled her back into the star's aura. The girl, still further from the star than Yaz, turned her head slowly, astonishment in her face, and said in a deep, drawn-out voice, 'What have you done to them?'

Yaz stepped towards Gully so that their time would be passing at the same rate. The guards remained frozen in the act of running. 'I've done nothing to them. I've used Atoan's time-star to speed us both up.'

'Atoan?' Gully's eyes widened. 'The grandmaster?' She scanned the bushes as if expecting the mage to walk out brushing twigs from his hair.

'Yes.' Yaz opted not to explain further. Instead she studied the guards, noting the direction in which each of them was running. 'We're going to try to get inside. If they catch us, don't fight, but it'll be quicker if we can just get past them. Get ready – see where you'll need to run. You go first. They'll start moving as soon as you advance.'

Gully gave her a nervous look.

'It'll be fine. Go!' Yaz gave the girl a light shove.

As Gully sprinted forward she slowed. Yaz took a step after the girl, then another smaller step. Now both Gully and the guards were moving, but slowly as if wading through thick mud. Yaz watched while Gully, using the advantage of a pre-planned route, twisted past the contingent of four guards and raced towards the three just reaching the bottom of the steps from the main doors. The novice threw herself into a tumbling roll that took the feet from the centremost of the trio and came up behind him, running for the doors.

Yaz took this as her cue and charged forwards too, her sudden acceleration from a standing start startling the closest guards. She barged one woman to the floor, sidestepped another, and then felled a second from the group by the steps who had turned to give chase to Gully.

Yaz made it through the doors just a heartbeat ahead of the pursuing pack, but it was enough of a lead for Gully to slam the doors in their faces and swing the locking bar into place.

The foyer's magnificence – an expanse of patterned and polished marble stretched before her towards two sweeping staircases that climbed left and right to a gallery with a pillared balustrade – distracted Yaz for a moment. A surprised serving boy in livery almost as vivid as Atoan's robes of many colours stood slack-jawed, watching them. What Yaz had taken to be an intimidating second wave of guards turned out to be polished suits of armour standing sentinel around the perimeter of the room.

'Wenna!' Yaz's plans for finding the other novices didn't extend much beyond the front door. 'Wenna!' Shouting Wenna's name constituted most of what remained.

'Keep moving!' Gully suggested, and sprinted towards the double doors at the back of the foyer.

'Wenna!' Yaz gave chase. The guards outside had begun to beat on the outer doors.

The far doors opened onto a long, broad corridor lined with niches and pedestals displaying an array of glittering wonders. Yaz paid them scant attention as she tried to keep up with the fleet-footed Gully. 'Wenna!'

In the end Wenna found them. As they reached the far end of the corridor, only to come face to face with a massively built guardsman emerging from some chamber beyond, a voice called out from one of the doorways they'd run past.

'Gully? What in the—'

Wenna emerged into the corridor, still wearing her habit and with Hellma and Kola looming at her shoulders.

'Who's that with—' She paused and waved at the guardsman, who stood taller even than Hellma, to go away. 'It's fine. She's a friend.'

'It's Yaz!' Niome, Kola's small hunska friend, squeezed out past Hellma.

'Why's she all grey?' Hellma muttered.

Guards appeared at the opposite end of the corridor, running through the doors, blades in hand.

'What in the hells have you done?' Wenna asked. She shook her head and walked towards the advancing guards, hands raised. 'It's all right. They're friends!'

'I told you I wouldn't get in without you,' Gully said to Yaz, somehow managing to look pleased about the whole situation.

Wenna turned back. 'Well? What's going on?'

Yaz opened her mouth to speak but found she had too much to say, too many words on her tongue, all crowding to get out at once.

Gully spread her hands and spoke into the pause. 'I was going back to the convent. Sister Oats told me to meet her at the Tacsis gates so she could escort us all home. Yaz came running up all covered in dust and said I had to get her to you because . . . because of something.'

'Quina's been taken and mages are trying to capture me too.' Yaz managed to speak by avoiding talking about Owl. Those had been the words that she couldn't force out.

'This is about that proxim up on the Rock.' Wenna looked at Gully and then at Yaz with narrowed eyes. 'Have the mages all gone mad?'

'Some of them have.' It was easier than the truth. 'Look, I know where Quina is. Or at least, I can find her. But there's a mage, Ballo, who can watch me wherever I go and I need—'

'You need Sister Owl. She can sort this out,' Wenna said.

'Did you leave her back on the Rock?' Hellma asked.

Yaz pressed her lips together in a tight line to stop them from twitching, to keep the grief at bay. Owl's death *hurt*. And Yaz had only known her for a handful of days. These novices had spent years under her care.

'Where's Sister Owl?' Wenna asked. 'You were with—'

'She's dead.' The words took her by surprise.

Wenna took a step back and raised a hand to her cheek as though Yaz had slapped her. Her eyes, bright with tears, found Yaz's. 'Take that back.'

'That's . . . not funny,' Hellma rumbled, confusion clouding her face.

'A mage killed her in Academy Hall.' Yaz looked down at her dust-coated hands. The powdered stone had stuck to Owl's blood. 'Yelna, Atoan's wife, stabbed her in the back.'

'No . . .' Gully's thin whisper broke a growing silence.

'Not Owl.' Hellma tried to say it with conviction. As if belief and head shaking would return the woman's life.

'In the back?' Niome muttered, as though the detail was somehow important.

'They've got Quina.' Yaz choked on her friend's name. Saying it again felt as if somehow it brought with it the full burden of their shared struggle, from the depths of the pit to the Corridor, and the weight of affection that had built along that journey. The idea that she had doubted Quina twisted like a knife in Yaz's guts. There had been a moment, standing over Owl's corpse, when Yaz had wondered if Quina's hand had planted that knife in the old woman's back. 'They've got Quina.'

'Quina?' Wenna seemed to register the name for the first time. 'The mages took her?'

'Yes. I'm going to follow them. But they're watching me and they've got archers—'

'Ballo? He can see into places he's been before, yes?' Wenna asked.

'How did you know that?'

'My family know everyone important. And it pays to know about mages. Especially if they're your neighbours and you have secrets.'

'Has he been here?' Yaz's heart sank. Of course he'd been here. She hadn't been in the Corridor long but long enough to know that the rich and powerful here occupied themselves by throwing parties.

'Yes, but only into the gardens, the feast hall, the ballroom, and the guest chambers. It doesn't pay to let a man with such talents wander. That's what my mother says. Speaking of my mother – let's go. It's hard to get my parents' attention but after your entrance . . .'

Wenna hastened down the corridor. The foyer doors opened a moment later at the far end and two tall blond men, both richly dressed, strode through. 'And then there're my brothers! Run!' Looking worried, Wenna turned on a heel and began sprinting for the opposite doors through which the huge guard had exited.

'Come back here, little nuns!' one of the men boomed, his voice full of laughter.

Wenna clearly didn't trust the tone and Yaz gave chase with the others. They burst through the doors at the end into a large, high-ceilinged chamber hung with magnificently decorated shields. Six doors offered new exits. Wenna chose one and a race ensued, through seemingly endless chambers and corridors, passing scandalized maids, knocking over at least one aged retainer and a stand bearing something that shattered with an expensive crunch in their wake. They paused, panting, in a shadowed corner where an ancient suit of armour stood in relative neglect, scarred by past blows and pitted with age.

'My great-grandfather wore this against the Durns,' Wenna said. 'Drowned in it in the shallows just a few yards off Pegga Beach.' She undid two buckles and reached into the breastplate. 'My secret stash . . .' She brought out two long knives and handed them to Hellma and Niome. Reaching in again, she brought out more knives and a handful of gleaming, many-pointed throwing stars. Within moments she'd armed all of them except Yaz. Even Gully had a short blade, though it looked more suited to the dining table than for murder.

Yaz raised both brows and coughed meaningfully.

'You've not been trained,' Wenna said. 'You'd be more dangerous to us and yourself than any enemy. We'll keep you safe.'

With that, Wenna led off again. Yaz didn't argue about being armed. She'd owned a knife once and even used it to save her life, but compared to the others she was like an infant in such matters. The mansion stretched on before them but Wenna moved with purpose and several turns later she brought them to a halt in a darkened room lit only by what little daylight leaked through the shuttered windows.

'We're going to use the escape tunnels,' Wenna said, going to one of the cushioned benches and wresting an oddly shaped iron hook from beneath it. 'We'll leave the house and come up somewhere that Ballo won't be looking for Yaz.'

'Escape tunnels?' Yaz struggled with the concept.

Wenna went to the fireplace and inserted the hook into a small ash-filled slot beside the hearthstone. 'Kola, keep the door closed. Hellma, help me lift this. Gully, don't touch anything.'

Within moments Wenna and Hellma had lifted out a hefty section of stone to reveal a dark shaft with iron rungs embedded in the wall.

'We'll need a light,' Niome said, casting about for anything useful.

'I know the way by touch.' Wenna slipped into the shaft. 'Stay close. Don't get lost.'

Hellma squeezed in after Wenna, looking far from happy. Gully inserted herself next before Niome. Kola released the door. Nobody had tried to force an entrance. She gestured to the hole with a broad hand. 'After you.'

'I'd best go last,' Yaz said. 'I'm bringing the light.'

No reaction showed on Kola's wide, bland face other than the slight elevation of one red eyebrow. She followed Niome into the darkness. Yaz meanwhile went to the closest of the shuttered windows and set her forehead to the slats. She reached out with her mind, finding first the more distant shipheart, the undamaged one, and then the faint signature of the time-star, its redness filling her mind and setting it racing. She drew both to her, the time-star coming more slowly and requiring most effort.

As the shipheart approached, Yaz opened the wooden frame holding the leaded diamonds of glass that kept out what the people of the Corridor considered to be wind. The stars would of course draw attention to the room, but smashing an entrance seemed a poor way to repay Wenna's kindness, no matter how many windows her family owned. She opened the shutter at the last moment and allowed the two stars in.

The shaft was wider than Yaz had feared and descended steeply. The light of the two following stars combined into a red-gold radiance that sent her shadow reaching down the ladder beneath her. Kola was waiting for her at the base of the shaft but retreated with an oath as the shipheart came closer.

'Go on,' Yaz said. 'I'll be the rearguard.'

The tunnel was round in cross-section, large and dry, and lined with tightly fitting blocks of stone. Even in retreat, the Tacsis family wouldn't need to get their finery dirty or have to bow their heads. Yaz followed the others, now shadowy figures quite far ahead of her, though at times it wasn't clear if they were leading her or fleeing from her pursuit. She imagined she must present an intimidating aspect, backlit by two large stars.

The tunnel forked several times: a remarkable effort had gone into ensuring the family's safety. From what she'd heard in Academia class, Yaz imagined it to have been a worthwhile investment. Living next door to the emperor, whilst desirable in terms of influence and presence, was also historically a hazardous occupation, and the ability to flee a ruler's mercurial temper was a prerequisite for any dynasty aiming for longevity as well as riches.

'Keep those things back there!' Wenna had come to a halt at the end of the tunnel. A shaft led upwards, iron rungs serving as a ladder. 'Where did you even get them?'

Yaz stopped the stars following her and advanced to rejoin the novices. 'I took them from Academy Hall. Atoan let me. Not all the mages have turned.'

'Turned to what?' Hellma frowned.

Yaz pressed a hand to her forehead. She hadn't got time to explain everything. Or even any of it. Or rather, thanks to the time-star, she had, but the emotional strain was too much to be borne. 'There's a secret war for the ark. An enemy beneath the city wants to open—'

'Enemy?' Wenna asked. 'Whose enemy?'

Yaz drew a breath. 'Life's enemy. He's called Seus and he wants to bring down the moon.'

That took away their questions for a moment, and then another longer moment. 'Quina.' Hellma focused on a problem she could grapple with. 'How do we get her back? You said you can follow where she's been?'

'I can.' Yaz tried to find the thread that would lead her to her friend. This far from the shipheart it was faint but she managed to pluck it from the seething gossamer mass before her.

'But if we follow their path then Ballo will find us,' Wenna said. 'He's lost you so he'll keep an eye on the route they used to take Quina away.'

'You can't just find where Quina is?' Gully asked. 'You have to track her?'

'We need a Quina compass . . .' Hellma muttered.

Yaz defocused her gaze and considered the thread in her hand. 'It's a thread that joins us.' Mistress Academia had told the class a legend that she said the tribes had brought with them across the black sea. A hero entering a labyrinth to confront a beast had spooled out string behind him so he could find his way back out.

'Can't you . . . pull it tight?' Hellma frowned.

Yaz said nothing, deep in thought, but raised the thread to her eyes between finger and thumb, and began to back towards the shipheart. As the star's golden glare brightened, the thread thickened from finer than a hair to something more like the cord bound around Yaz's habit, and she saw that yes, perhaps she might just pull on it. Hand over hand Yaz drew in the slack, pulsing her will along the thread until she sensed resistance, a tension that told her the cord had been drawn into a taut, straight line, arrowing through all obstacles, aimed at Quina like one of the green-landers' compasses pointing north. 'I've done it.' To the others she must look like a dark slash across the shipheart's awful brilliance. 'I can find her without following.'

Still they didn't move.

'Let's go!'

And as if released from paralysis all five novices ahead of her made for the ladder.

CHAPTER 30

'This way? You're sure?' Wenna looked around, sniffing.

'Yes.' Yaz could smell it too. The stink of humanity. Like the caverns of the Broken but somehow worse. Among the mansions of the Sis, even given the competition for space close to the palace, there was still plenty of room to breathe. Here in the slums the crowding buildings were brick rather than stone, tall but teetering, half the windows unshuttered with just dirty rags to fight the wind. Sewage ran down the centre of the street, or rather it crept, the reek of it eye-watering.

Narrow faces, pale and sunken, watched the novices from open doorways and yawning windows. Shattered roofing slates littered the road. Even the buildings looked ill, the brickwork stained like old men's skins, cancered, pitted by the weather and neglect.

'Nobody would ask too many questions if you came down here carrying a body,' Hellma muttered. She looked worried, hunched over as if to minimize her size.

'Are we at least getting close?' Niome asked. 'Can you tell that?'

'Not without the shipheart.' Yaz wasn't going to bring it down and cause panic in the slums. She'd sent both stars very high until they were mere twinkles against the clouds. It was even more difficult to sustain them at a distance but she'd made the effort hoping they might escape notice or even if spotted at least not clearly mark her position. She didn't have to keep them directly overhead, but for some reason as they went higher it became more difficult to support them from anywhere but exactly beneath them.

Following the straight line to Quina that her thread now prescribed was impossible amid the convolution of alleyways that the slums presented, but they were making progress. Yaz's boots were thick with mud. If matters weren't so pressing she would have given in to her fascination and bent down to touch the stuff. She wanted to squeeze it through her fingers. The closest thing she'd seen to it was the blubber that Ictha cut from the rare whales that they managed to land. The Corridor world still had so many mysteries and wonders to present to her but here she was between a murder and a kidnapping, stalking through the city with blood on her hands, expecting to meet a spear at every turn.

'Watch out!'

The action was over by the time the words were out. Niome tripped Wenna and brought her to the ground. An arrow shattered on the wall behind them. Hellma, Kola, and Gully stepped into doorways.

'Yaz!' Niome hissed furiously as she dragged Wenna into the cover of the corner.

Yaz found that she alone was left standing in the open. She hurried to join Niome and Wenna.

'Ancestor!' Wenna spat mud from her mouth and sat up, brushing ineffectually at her filthy habit. Less than an hour earlier she'd been surrounded by gold, silver, and polished marble. 'Ouch!' She wiped a hand on a still-clean part of her outer habit and set it to her shoulder. It came away bloody. 'The bastard scratched me!'

'It would have hit your throat.' Niome shuddered.

'What are we going to do?' Hellma called from her doorway back down the street.

'Advance!' Niome said. 'I think I got him. But there might be more.'

'Got him?' Yaz asked.

'Throwing star.' Niome opened her hand to show another of the bladed metal discs resting on her palm.

'Really?' Yaz hadn't seen her throw it. She guessed even Quina would be hard pressed to act so swiftly, throwing a weapon in return while barging a friend out of an arrow's path.

Wenna stood, holding her neck since her sudden sideways journey had sprained it. She curled her lip in a snarl, eyes bright with anger. 'Come on then.'

And to Yaz's amazement Niome slipped out into the open, quickly followed by all the other novices.

Ahead, a sizeable brick of a building stood amid several ruined tenements, looking as if it were next on the waiting list to collapse. It sported several large and vacant windows on the upper floor.

'Slaughterhouse,' Hellma muttered. Though whether that was the building's former function or a prediction Yaz didn't know.

'How are we getting in?' Kola eyed the closer end where double doors wide enough for ten to enter side by side stood closed with planks nailed across them to keep it that way.

'Feeling strong?' Wenna asked.

'Not that strong!' Hellma spoke over Kola, who was saying much the same thing.

Further discussion ended as a voice rang in their ears, seeming as if the speaker were among them though there was nobody to see. 'Throw anything else and your friend dies.'

Figures began to appear around the corner of the building's far end. Quina came first, hands secured behind her, head held back by her hair, and a blade pressed to her throat. Yelna held both the knife and the hair. She watched the novices over Quina's shoulder through narrowed eyes. Beside Yelna came Ballo, hunched within robes whose indigo was only a few shades different from Yelna's violet and, like hers, spattered with bloodstains. The blood on his robes looked so fresh it might still be warm. He regarded the girls from a lopsided face, his amber eye much bigger and brighter than the other, so large that the bones of his skull had distorted to accommodate it.

'Don't meet his gaze,' Wenna hissed to the others.

Ballo's hunch made him shorter than his sister and he peered up at them from beneath his outsized brow. Behind him a third mage stepped into view, this one in pale red robes, the material so thin that every breath of the wind rippled them around his lean form. Taller than the other two, his hair and eyes and beard were all black, his skin copper like Yaz's but somehow he gave the impression of being full of a great light even though no whisper of it escaped to warn the eye.

'I admit, I wasn't expecting you to find us.' Yelna kept her voice low and even but somehow it found every ear; a trick of her wind-work, Yaz imagined. 'But this changes nothing. You know what Seus wants from you, Yaz. And you can see the first instalment on the price you'll pay if you're stupid enough to defy him.'

Yaz took a step forward without meaning to and, although Yelna didn't seem to move, a bright drop of blood rolled down Quina's neck beneath the mage's blade. Niome half raised her hand, another bladed projectile glittering in her grip, but she made no move to throw it.

'I know this one's fast but if she tries to escape she'll cut her own throat.' Yelna nodded towards her brother. 'Yaz will follow Ballo. The other novices will return to the convent. Once you've done what Seus requires of you then you and your friend can go back to living on the ice or whatever it is that you want to do.'

Yaz bowed her head. 'Go.'

'What?' Wenna sounded disbelieving. 'You're not going to do what they say, are you?'

'You said they were going to bring the moon down, Yaz!' Hellma's brow had rucked up into a remarkably furrowed frown.

'Go!' Yaz raised her voice. 'It's the only way.'

'We can't let her,' Niome said. 'Not if she's using you to do that.' She gave Quina an agonized look. 'Sorry . . . but it's the whole Corridor . . .'

The dark-haired mage snarled and bright flames lit along his fingers, pooling in his palms as he raised them, giving out more light than regular flame. 'She's saving your lives, little novices. Better run.'

'Don't!' Yaz didn't have to pretend to sound terrified on the novices' behalf, but this had been what she was hoping for. An excuse to bring the shipheart down without the mages turning their powers on her friends. 'Don't hurt them. I'll drive them away!'

The star dropped from on high, a white-gold meteor descending to Abeth. The mages, still yards from the star, showed the strain of withstanding its aura. Yelna grimaced and two more rivulets of blood appeared beneath her blade, the fire-mage's flames flickered blue then green, weakening in his hands. The light of the star reflected in Ballo's huge eye and he stumbled back with a curse. Wenna and the others had to run before the star even reached Yaz. Betrayal mixed with horror in their expressions. Gully fled back the way they'd come, screaming. The other four lasted moments longer then broke and ran too.

Yaz had the star now and set both hands to it, turning them to silhouettes against the brightness as the shipheart burned her flesh and tortured her mind. The threadscape opened to her as it always did when the shipheart came close, allowing her access that maybe even Sister Owl had never achieved in all her decades of study and practice. It was as if reality's skin had been torn off, revealing the complexity of muscle and fat, artery and vein that drove the world's actions. Sister Owl had said that every marjal skill, all their magics, were just instinctive manipulations of certain kinds of thread, one set for the fire-workers, another for ice-work, even Ballo's eye was just drawing on threads that connected it to places he'd visited in the past.

The quantal's power came in two flavours. One was the brutal hammer of the Path, power limited only by what any given person's body could channel without breaking apart. The other, subtle manipulation of the threads from which existence is woven. In theory this direct pulling of threads could duplicate any marjal skill, but in practice no quantal had the talent to match a marjal in whatever particular sphere their blood had gifted them ability.

Yaz, however, had the shipheart boosting her as it slowly tore her apart. The Grey Sisters had drugs that would make you stronger or immune to poison or swifter of mind. Each came with its own price. The shipheart was Yaz's drug and it made her better at everything her blood gave her. The blood of the Missing. She reached out slowly, seeking focus.

'Send the shipheart back up.' Yelna spoke through gritted teeth. 'You'll be bringing both stars, but keep them away from us.'

Yaz found what she was looking for amid the vast array of threads. The shipheart's light brought one bundle into focus. Threads joining her to the future of the blade in Yelna's hand. Threads running back into the past, speaking of the blade's forging, of the beating hammer, the quenching, the smelting of ores, the iron-rich rocks hewn from the ground . . . Yaz seized them all and yanked them in the unsubtle brute-force way that Grandmaster Atoan did without ever seeing them. She wanted only to duplicate his power, to mimic his talent for moving metal.

'No!' Yelna cried out in amazement as the knife pulled her hand away from Quina's throat. The exclamation of surprise ended when Quina, who had somehow freed her arms, elbowed the woman in the face. In a fraction of a heartbeat Quina had slipped out of Yelna's grasp and floored Ballo with a commendably executed kick to the left kidney.

The fire-mage raised both burning hands and as he did so the flames around them vanished into a heat haze, reappearing around the shipheart. Yaz released the star with a cry of pain, throwing herself back from the ball of fire that engulfed it. She rolled across the broken flagstones, hugging her burned palms beneath her armpits. Something bright burst between Yelna and Quina with a crack. Fast as the hunska girl might be, lightning was faster. Quina fell to the ground twitching, with small arcs of lightning crawling across her habit.

Yaz snarled, putting all her pain, anger, and shock into that one guttural noise. She kept her hands where they were and reached with her mind for the shipheart, ordering it into the midst of the mages. To her great surprise the star ignored her. She could feel its presence but the mage's fire somehow walled the shipheart from her will. She didn't think it was the fire itself but the working of his marjal will – the storm in the threadscape all around the star. She could tell it was taking all his effort and doubted he could maintain it for long, but for now the shipheart wasn't listening to her. Clearly Seus had taught his allies something even the grandmaster didn't know.

Quina lay on her side, stunned, not far from the knife that Yaz had jerked from Yelna's grasp. The mage had seen the weapon and, ignoring her brother groaning on the ground, was bending to retrieve it. Yaz stood and started to run at her, blistered hands clawed and reaching.

Yaz fully expected to meet a bolt of lightning but either Yelna had exhausted her supply or was simply too scared of Seus to risk killing her. Instead a blast of wind struck her, strong enough to pick up loose bricks from the crumbling slaughterhouse. Someone went down behind Yaz with a cry, rolled away by the gale that instead of dying down was somehow strengthening.

Yaz's habit flapped out behind her, cracking like a whip, but she'd lived a life in the jaws of the wind since before she knew how to walk. Instinct brought her centre of gravity down until she was leaning so far forward that a sudden cessation of the gale would see her pitching face first onto the flagstones with too little time to block her fall.

Rocking forward, Yaz sought footing with her left boot while her right leg bore the whole thrust. She advanced, a few inches at a time, into the throat of a hurricane, curving her body as the Ictha do to prevent themselves being lifted by a gale.

The windblast died and Yaz fell. She managed to not smash her nose on the stone and glanced up to see a look of disbelief on Yelna's face. Quina was stirring. The knife that Yelna had been reaching for was gone, taken by the wind. Ballo had stayed on all fours while the fire-mage continued to engulf the shipheart in flames, his face pale with effort and beaded with sweat.

Groaning came from behind Yaz and a glance showed her that Hellma and Kola lay entangled against a post, surrounded by wind-blasted detritus. They'd come back as soon as the mage's fire had deadened the star's aura.

Yelna was moving again. She'd found another, smaller, knife on her person and had reached Quina. Yaz pushed herself up but the mage already had a hand knotted in Quina's black hair, the other moving the blade beneath her chin.

Something small and silver hissed past Yaz's ear as she made to rise and thunked into the back of Yelna's knife hand with a meaty sound. The woman screamed and fell, clutching the hand with the throwing star embedded in it. Wenna came out of nowhere to flatten Ballo just as he found his feet.

The fire-mage released the shipheart, turning his attention to the nearest novices, who happened to be Wenna and Quina. The fire hidden behind his eyes flared and a furnace glare replaced both orbs. The white flames of rage licked across his hands as he raised them. Yelna might have planned for Quina to be a hostage but to look at him the mage was past caring. The blaze in his hands intensified and he drew them back, the fierce light of his stare focused on the two girls. Yaz went cold inside. They were going to burn. There wasn't time. For anything. Quina was going to die.

In the next moment the fire-mage was falling. Flames billowed briefly around him and snuffed out as he hit the ground. His sudden collapse revealed Gully standing behind him, somewhat self-consciously, a bloodstained brick clutched in both hands.

CHAPTER 31

Mali

Although she knew that she stood in the grip of a star that was letting the world rush past her while she stood mired in time, Mali was also somehow exploring a distant future in which she stood in Sister Owl's place as Sweet Mercy's Mistress Path.

Mali knew that what she saw around her could not be real. Her own body, no longer thirteen but surely at least a hundred, must also be a lie spun by the time-star amid a web of falsehoods. And yet it felt so true.

She reached her hand out to the ice-tribe girl standing with her in the sigil-wrapped room. 'Zole . . .'

The girl almost blocked Mali, a fighter's move, but she mastered herself and at Mali's tentative pat she sucked in a breath as if drawing all emotion back into her core. Within heartbeats her face returned to its impassive self, focused and ready, with only the faintly glistening trail of tears to testify to that moment of . . . of what? Weakness? Mali wasn't sure. She knew next to nothing about this Zole who stood before her but it seemed, even on the basis of their brief acquaintance, that being Zole might well be a very difficult job.

'I am still imperfect, sister.' Zole bowed her head. 'More time with the shipheart will allow me to continue my advance. There remain weaknesses to purge.'

Mali pulled her hand back, shocked. 'You're cutting yourself? Throwing pieces away?'

Zole met her gaze without a flicker of emotion. 'A weapon must be honed. A stick does not become a spear without carving off that which prevents its sharpness being felt.'

Mali struggled for words. A blue light was starting to crowd the edge of her vision and she felt herself being drawn back to her time. 'But why? What about you? What about—'

'Some things require sacrifice, Mistress Path.' She reached out and held Mali's wrist just above her missing hand. A new intensity entered her eyes. 'You understand this. You know that there are many kinds of sacrifice. You know that some prices should never be paid – unless they are paid willingly by those who are themselves the currency.'

Blue light had filled the room, reducing Zole to a shadow.

'Wait—' Mali fought to stay there, with Zole in Path Tower in some unknown future.

'You *understand* this,' Zole repeated. Her grip on Mali's wrist weakened, or faded.

'She told you to say this. Didn't she? Yaz told you? Who is she to you?'

Zole's words reached her faintly through an ocean of blue light. 'She is coming for you.'

CHAPTER 32

Yaz

'Watch them both. They're still dangerous!' Wenna took charge of her prisoners. The novices had tied Yelna and Ballo's hands behind their backs using lengths trimmed from the cord-belts that bound their habits. Yaz hoped they'd done a better job than Yelna had at securing Quina's wrists behind her.

Hellma and Kola had brushed themselves down after being rolled across the square by Yelna's hurricane. Both had scrapes and grazes. Something had cut Kola above the left eye and blood made its way down her face in a persistent trickle. She didn't seem to notice it.

Wenna pushed Yelna towards the far end of the slaughter-house. 'She can still shock us with lightnings, and he can still play tricks on your eyes. So, if they start something – stab them.'

'We should tie him too.' Gully was still standing over the fallen fire-mage, apparently under the impression that being whacked around the back of the head with a brick was something you got up from and walked off after a brief rest face down in your own blood pool. Hellma and Yaz exchanged glances.

'Yes . . .' Hellma put a broad arm around Gully's shoulders and steered her after Wenna. 'I think he'll be out for a while yet.'

Yaz imagined the mage would be 'out' for the rest of his life. The man had been moments from incinerating people she cared about: she had no tears to shed for him.

Niome pushed Ballo ahead of her, taking no account of his awkward, shuffling gait. Mistress Path had been killed and the novices were not inclined to mercy, sweet or otherwise.

The doors at the far end of the great hall were in better condition and stood ajar. Kola pulled them wide and then stood there, staring.

'What is it?' Wenna shoved Yelna forwards so she could join Kola and see.

The slaughterhouse had been gutted and even the flag-stones had gone, torn up to leave a rough earth floor, still dark with old blood. What drew the eye lay at the centre: a shifting, dream-like miasma, a glowing fog in which disturbing shapes formed in one moment only to dissipate in the next. And in the centre of this strange, tendrilled mist, a dark something hung on meat hooks that were in turn attached by chains to the rafters high above.

'Zox!' Quina started forward and nobody was fast enough to stop her.

The iron dog hung by his forelegs, stretched out as he had been when Theus had used him to walk on two legs rather than four.

Quina stopped herself before she got within five yards of the dog, still presumably containing Theus. Faint outer tendrils of the mist wound about her and she faltered, pressing the heel of one palm to her forehead as though confused or in pain or both.

'Quina!' Niome, following, reached her and started to pull her away.

'What *is* that thing?' Wenna asked, frowning.

'It's . . . complicated.' Yaz went to help Niome. She noticed as she did so that a body lay at the foot of a half-rotted ladder leading up to a section of treacherous-looking walkway that afforded access to two of the eight windows on the left side of the building. A bow and a spill of arrows lay close by. Niome's first kill, brought down when she flung her throwing star earlier. A remarkable feat.

Hellma knotted a hand in Ballo's robes and dragged him towards Yaz as she returned with the shivering Quina. 'What have you done to her?'

'Me?' Ballo managed a sneer. 'Nothing. The spell works on its own now. She's just caught the edge of a nightmare. Any further in and it would have killed her. There's nothing you can do here.'

'I'll be all right.' Quina's voice was faint and a tremor ran through it – the opposite of her normal confidence, which bordered on the brash. She looked as if she'd seen her whole clan slaughtered in front of her.

'Nothing we can do?' Yaz turned to consider Ballo, avoiding his gaze since even the edges of it were disconcerting. 'But you can. You'll undo it for us.'

'Or what?' Yelna found her tongue and her old arrogance returned with it. 'You'll murder us like you murdered Kareem and poor Renard over there?'

Yaz resisted pointing out that Renard had been trying to stick arrows through children. She turned from Ballo to meet Yelna's gaze. *Or what?* It was a valid question. How far would she go to get what she wanted? The convent had

313

taught her about the existence of things that she had never wanted to know existed. Torture. The business of inflicting pain for punishment or to secure compliance. It seemed to Yaz that, like the Ictha's dilemma over the Pit of the Missing, it was a question where a reasonable-sounding case could be assembled in favour of a monstrous act. In the scales where many were weighed against few, the toppling of children into an icy hole, and the cutting or burning of a helpless prisoner in search of much-needed information, could both be seen as unpleasant necessities of real life. Yaz had decided, however, that the scales themselves were a crime. Lives couldn't be measured out in parts, wrongs couldn't be ordered and accepted, they were to be fought.

'You should undo your magic, Ballo,' Yaz told the mage. 'Seus wants to kill us all. You're helping him simply to avoid being first in the queue. But you're still in the queue, what-ever you do for him.'

Yaz thought she saw a moment of doubt in the little man's eye but his defiant smirk returned. Perhaps the need to refuse to admit he'd been wrong was more important to him than becoming right. Some men gave the impression that if given the choice between admitting fault or death, they would save you the bother of carrying out the sentence and cut their own throats.

'When the ice comes, Seus will make us kings and queens of the undercity. There's no stopping it. The Corridor has been closing all our lives. All our history. Give him what he wants and maybe you too can have a throne.'

'I say we stick a knife in him and twist until he does what we want him to.' Niome drew her blade.

'Just twist his arm. He'll break or it will.' Wenna motioned to Kola. 'Or do it to this one.' She shook Yelna. 'She was the one that killed Mistress Path. Right, Quina?'

Quina gasped as if Niome's knife had been stuck into her and given a savage turn. 'She's dead?' The words came out broken. Faster than thought, her hand cracked out to slap Yelna across the face. 'Why? You didn't have to kill her!'

Quina's handprint stood out across Yelna's cheek and up across the side of her head, white outlined in crimson. Blood oozed from the corner of her mouth. Even so, she managed a crooked smile.

'You children don't properly understand what you're dealing with. That old woman tried to thwart our master, and she died. She died easy. What do you think is going to happen to you?'

Ballo spoke up, his tone more conciliatory. 'The city under our feet is a hundred times the size of the one crusted over the surface. Compared to Seus's domain, Verity is like the hovels where the frost clans live on the margins.'

Yaz knew that wasn't true. She'd seen the endless empty chambers of the Missing's undercities before. But somehow that seemed less important than the vision Ballo's words summoned before her. Interlocking halls, pillared and vaulted, glittered in gold and silver, making even Wenna's home seem tawdry.

'Seus promises only death and pain for those who oppose him. But for the chosen few . . .' Ballo's words painted an image of chains and blood and gleaming instruments of torture, only for that image to be replaced by elegant thrones before a banquet table heaped with a diversity of fruits and meats. Yaz couldn't even name most of the feast and realized these things couldn't have come from her own imagination. She shook her head violently and the pictures vanished, replaced by a seething disturbance in the threadscape, the workings of Ballo's magic unveiled.

315

'Enough!' Yaz reached for Ballo and threw him to the floor. 'We're not torturing anyone and these two aren't getting away with what they did. I want them both taken to Sweet Mercy. We can't risk giving them to the Academy. I don't know who's in charge there now.'

Yelna raised both brows. 'Atoan is!'

'One of your friends put an arrow through Atoan,' Yaz said. 'And if he dies that will be another crime for you to answer for.' She looked across to the other novices. 'Quina will stay with me. Wenna, you're in charge of getting these two to Sister Oats and then back to the convent. Use them as hostages in case you run into the people they've got hunting me.'

Wenna shook her head. 'We should all go!'

'We came here for Quina,' Hellma said. 'We're not going to leave her here. You should both come back with us. Whatever that . . . thing . . . is' – she waved a hand at Zox hanging in the clot of slowly swirling nightmare – 'it'll be here when you come back. Or it won't. I'm not sure which is better.'

'We went through a lot with Theus,' Quina said, staring at the iron dog, her brow furrowed as if remembering the spell's touch.

'I thought you said it was called Zox,' Wenna said.

'It's . . .' Quina began.

'. . . complicated,' Yaz finished.

'Anyway,' Hellma said, 'we're staying.'

Yaz looked the bigger girl up and down, forcing herself to remember how young she was. 'That means a lot. Sister.' She clasped Hellma's thick upper arm. 'But this is the war you've been training for most of your life. This is how you serve the Ancestor. And in war we do the hard things. We play our part, even when that means we can't be there to fight beside our friends. Sister Owl has been murdered and Abbess Claw has to be told. The murderers have to be brought to Church justice.' Yaz's glance flickered to Yelna, who had assisted at her own convent trial and done her best to see Yaz die. Perhaps the woman would have a chance to taste some of the nuns' harsh punishments if they weren't reserved just for novices. 'Getting these two back is a dangerous mission and one that needs all of you to be sure it succeeds. But I have to stay here and sort this out. And I need Quina. She knows Theus and is wise to his tricks.'

'I thought he was a friend.' Hellma frowned at the iron dog as if wondering how some kind of strange statue could be anything except an object.

'It's compl—' Quina began.

'A tricksy friend,' Yaz said.

With some grumbling, the novices took their leave, hugs were exchanged, Hellma's particularly bone-crushing. She pressed the hilt of her knife into Quina's hand, ignoring any protest. 'I'll pick up another one outside. Just don't cut yourself. Your knife-work's terrible.'

Wenna and Niome had their blades in hand, ready at the prisoners' backs with the promise of stabbing should any magics be attempted. With a final 'Ancestor's blessings' they walked away.

'We should have let them stay.' Quina stood at the corner of the building, watching the others retreat across the uneven flagstones. Gully paused by the fire-mage's body and started to say something, but Kola tugged her on.

'Maybe.' Yaz turned back towards the doors. The image of the dead proxim flashed before her eyes. 'But Theus is our problem. A poison we brought from the ice to the

Corridor. We should be the ones to deal with him. And, besides, I don't want to see any more of our friends die.'

'No.' Quina fell in behind her. 'We don't.' On that they could agree.

CHAPTER 33

Yaz positioned the shipheart and the time-star just inside the slaughterhouse entrance and closed the double doors, lifting the locking bar into place. She had no intention of bringing them near Theus, especially in his weakened state. Lesser stars had come close to destroying him when he was far better able to resist them.

'Tell me again.' Yaz watched the nightmares' slow rotations around Zox. Sometimes it just looked like mist swirled across a hot sea, but then she would glimpse something so disturbing she had to clench her jaw against the possibility it might truly have been whatever horror her imagination furnished to fill out the shape. Occasionally colours flushed through the mist, a pulse of red running to the extremes of every tendril, surprising her by how close they'd reached towards her, or a sick green blush spreading slowly from one side to the other.

'It was like a nightmare I used to have before they dropped me in the pit,' Quina said. 'I don't remember it now.'

That last part sounded like a lie. Yaz considered the threadscape and how the spell seemed to constantly draw in threads from her and from Quina, like drops of ink in water spiralling down through a hole.

'It's clearly trying to break Theus down. They got at least one secret out of him but they obviously want them all. He's one of the Missing and knowledge is the mages' business. Even if they weren't in Seus's thrall they'd be doing this.'

'I bet he told them about you straight away,' Quina said. 'To save himself. He doesn't care about the moon or us. He just wants to follow his people.'

'He wants to follow himself. He wants to be whole again.' Yaz could understand that at least. And if this was the worst of Prometheus, unchecked by noble instincts, then little wonder his methods were murderous. In the Corridor his excesses hardly stood out against man's own long history of bloodshed. 'The spell is focused on him. He's the centre of the gyre. I could walk in and undo it.'

'Or be undone.' Quina shook her head. 'You don't know what it's like.'

'You won't tell me,' Yaz countered.

Quina looked at her feet. 'I only had a flash. But you were in it. And your eyes . . . they were awful, and I could tell you hated me.'

Yaz didn't want to touch the miasma surrounding Theus. Every part of her objected. She would rather someone from the Church or the Academy came to unravel Ballo's wrong-doing. But time was not on her side. Theus didn't look as though he would endure much longer. Plus, Yelna and Ballo had maintained a remarkably brave face in spite of their defeat. As if they believed help was on its way. Possibly they had a misplaced faith in the power of their master and allies. Or, more likely, other rogue mages were on their way to the slaughterhouse even now, accompanied by some of Seus's horrors. Yaz had glimpsed several of Seus's creations through

Taproot's windows onto the ice. She had no desire to meet any of them in the flesh.

'It's very quiet out there.' Quina glanced at the doors, then up at the yawning windows.

Yaz listened. On the way in, the streets and alleys had been noisy. The slums were dirty and stank but they were anything but deserted. But now? No sounds of children playing. No babies crying. No traders shouting.

Had all that stopped when Yelna loosed her gale upon them? Or . . .

'Let's get this over with quickly and get out of here.' Yaz reached towards the outer layers of the nightmare knotted around Theus, then withdrew her hand. 'If I get stuck in here, find your way to the convent and get help.'

'Don't—' But, quick as she was, Quina couldn't move fast enough to stop Yaz's fingers touching the spell.

A tendril of mist wrapped about Yaz's arm, darkening as it wound tight. And in the next moment the slaughterhouse was gone, replaced by unrelenting blackness.

The dark revolves around her but it is not until three points of brightness resolve that she can explain how she knows it to be spinning.

Yaz wonders if they are a trio of stars, spaced evenly about her, but she understands now that they are three figures, each in its own pool of light for which no source can be seen. They revolve around her, coming closer, and slowing as they do, until there is no motion, just three men standing a little beyond arm's reach, observing her in silence.

Their names return to her with the belated recognition of faces that it should have been impossible to forget. Quell, Thurin, Erris.

'You were always going to leave.' Quell is unchanged from

the day she stood at the edge of the pit – burdened with his question she had stepped into the fall. 'Something in you wouldn't let you stay. If your blood hadn't broken you, you would still be broken.' He had asked her to share his tent, share his life, bear his children. It should have been all she ever wanted. He is a good man, handsome, caring, solid, dependable, every inch the Ictha. 'Something in your mind is broken, Yaz. You don't know how to be happy. You don't know how to be satisfied. All of it was never going to be enough for you.' There's a sadness in him. A pain that she put there. 'You would have left anyway.'

Yaz looks down, only for a moment, but somehow it is Thurin who faces her when she looks back up. He's so many things that Quell is not. Lean rather than broad. His features narrow and sharp. Closed rather than open, dark eyes haunted. Dangerous rather than dependable. He wasn't made to live on the ice. Yet he came there, for her, drawn from the darkness of his caves into the blind whiteness. For her.

'I gave up my world to follow you.' He says exactly what's on her mind. He doesn't need to say the rest. It's written on his face. He knows it was a poor exchange. The disappointment, the slow realization has been dawning on him for months. He chased a dream and when the wind stripped that dream away Yaz was all it left.

'I'm sor—'

But it's Erris who stands before her and he doesn't need her apologies. He is neither hurt nor disappointed, only mildly amused.

'You're less than an infant to me,' he says. 'You thought Mistress Path was old? I was more than ten times her age before they laid the first stone of the convent in which she lived out her life. You think the Missing are another breed? It's not blood that makes us strangers but the passing of years. I've grown so distant from your kind that I stand closer to Taproot, closer to Seus, than to creatures of flesh and blood.' He shakes his head, pushing a slow smile from his face. 'Romance was on your mind? You thought there might be . . . fire . . . between us? You embarrass yourself, child.'

'I made a mistake,' Thurin says.

'You are a mistake, Yaz.' Quell frowns.

'A disappointment.' Thurin studies his hands.

'A foolish girl.' Erris's dark gaze rests on her without emotion.

Yaz isn't surprised, for these are merely truths that she has carried with her across uncharted miles of ice. But they are truths she keeps locked tight and on the rare occasions they have escaped in the past it has been one at a time, and though they have rocked her to her core she has managed to wrestle them back into the black vault where thought and memory do not go. Now all three sit together on shoulders that lack the strength to carry them.

She finds that she is on her knees and that a well of sorrow has opened in her chest. Heartache enough in which to drown.

Her hands are on the floor and tears patter to the ground between them.

They stain the stonework.

And the stain spreads. It moves. And even in the depths of her despair some small part of her is curious and her eyes track the stain as it reaches her fingers, blackening them.

'Dear gods.' The voice that speaks within her mind is cruel, uncaring, familiar. '*This* is your nightmare? Three doe-eyed boys being mean? Hells, you should see mine. There's some *serious* shit going down there! I mean baby siblings dying at my hands, beloved dogs being broken and burned, lifelong ambition shattering a heartbeat before victory. Classic stuff. And here you are mooning over Mr Boring, Mr Moody, and Robot Boy? If I had a stomach I'd puke here and now.'

'W-what?' Yaz is blinking away tears, heaving her breath into an aching chest. Somehow she's all snot and weeping, as if she'd been at this for hours.

'You can't really think these three nobodies define you? I've been around the block, tribesgirl. You think your three best chances at happiness lie with the first three males you meet who look to be the right sort of age and have all four limbs and their own teeth?'

Yaz had been going to say that Mother Mazai says the gods put our life-matches before us because the ice is too big to wander hunting them. But that sounds a bit silly here in the Corridor where you can't take four paces without meeting a new person. So instead she asks another question.

'Who – Who are you?'

'Me? It's yourself you should be asking that question to. This isn't who you are. The spell's got under your skin. Shake it off or you're useless to me.'

'Th-Theus?' Yaz remembered now. There had been a spell.

'What's left of me, yes. Thankfully I got most of the ego and that comes in handy for irksome empaths like your bug-eyed friend who thinks he's some kind of wizard.' Theus barked a laugh.

'Ballo's not my fri-'

Theus cut her off. 'Now, once again, who are you?'

'Yaz of th—'

'Forget the Ictha. That's no more who you are than the last pair of gloves you took off.'

'Yaz.'

'Yes. You, Yaz, singular. An island like everyone else. A fortress. Now open your eyes.'

'They are op—'

'JUST DO IT!'

Yaz blinked and she stood before Zox, who hung motionless amid the fraying spell, even now dispersing like the mist of a breath.

A red glow flickered in the depths of the iron dog's black eyes. It turned its blunt head with a slight squealing of metal on metal. 'You didn't save me a mage?'

'A mage?' Yaz found herself unsteady on her feet. Erris, Thurin, and Quell's scolding voices still echoed at the back of her head, but she supposed they were just her own voices, owned by the same kind of demons that the Missing shed before they left. The same kind of demons that filled the iron shell before her. 'Why a mage?'

'Because I'm bored of this stupid service unit,' Theus snarled. 'I want to wear flesh again. Stand upright. Scratch my arse. Or at least someone else's.'

Yaz pressed a hand to her forehead, trying to squeeze out the headache that had taken root. 'Can you get down?'

'If I could do you think I'd still be hanging here, you stupid—'

Theus swung violently to one side as the leftmost of the chains suspending him went loose and began to clatter down from on high with a noise like iron rain.

'I'll get the other one!' Quina sprinted across the slaughterhouse to some sort of ratcheted wheel on the opposite wall. Within moments Zox hit the floor, with a dull thud, only to be covered in yards of descending chain.

Theus groaned and flexed his metal limbs. 'Did you bring it?'

'Bring what?' Yaz asked.

'The piece of me I sent to get you.'

'Someone died because of that,' Yaz snarled.

'People die all the time. Did you bring it?'

Quina joined them. 'It called itself Keot.'

'I don't give a fuck what it called itself. Did you—'

'The boy died. The demon went with him.' Yaz realized there would be no contrition here, no apology, no guilt. If Prometheus had owned the capacity for such things then it had gone with his flesh into whatever paradise the Missing had abandoned the world in favour of.

Hells!' Theus smashed at the ground with Zox's forelegs, gouging the earth. 'Of all the stupid . . . How could you let that happen?'

'I told you we should have left him to the mages,' Quina said. 'What use is he?'

Yaz drew a deep breath and tried to suck all her anger and accusations back inside her. Serenity. Sister Owl had spent more time teaching that than anything else. Followed by clarity. Yaz needed both. 'We saved Theus because he's going to help us open the ark.'

Theus attempted something that looked like a shrug. Metal grated. 'I'll need it open when I finally get back that piece you let go. And if I wait around too long I suppose you'll get old and die on me.' His nostril slots opened and he sniffed sharply. 'Do you have the four shiphearts yet?'

'No.'

Theus raised Zox's head and turned his solemn gaze on her. 'Three?'

'I've "borrowed" one from the Academy.'

Theus slumped. 'Just put those hooks back and haul me up again. You're worse than my nightmares.'

'And I took a second one but it's broken.'

'A time-star?' Theus looked up again.

'Yes. Can you fix it?'

'No.'

'Well, we need to go and rescue the others now.' Yaz started towards the doors, though she didn't actually know how to get into the undercity. Quina joined her.

'Need to?' Theus didn't follow them.

Yaz tried to think of a reason that might motivate Theus. 'They have Taproot.'

'So? All we need to get into the ark is you and four shiphearts.'

'And the only reason I want to open the ark is so Taproot can get in there and defend it from Seus who is going to work out a way in otherwise, with or without shiphearts. And now *you've* told him I might be able to open it he's trying to get hold of me rather than just kill me!'

'You say that as if it's not an improvement.' Theus sat Zox down like one of the Quinx sled-dogs. 'You want him to kill you?'

'He'll kill me afterwards.'

'Cup half empty.' Theus looked between Yaz and Quina. 'I want the ark open. I don't care who goes in or who comes out. As long as I get to ascend. I've got business to attend to.'

'Seus wants to destroy the moon!' Quina shouted. 'He wants to destroy all this.' She waved an arm in the direction of everything.

Theus looked around, unimpressed. 'It's a dilapidated slaughterhouse, and' – he added before she could object – 'what's outside isn't much better. Less than a year ago you didn't know any of this existed. You'd never laid an eye on it, or this moon of theirs. You can go back to the ice and live out whatever pale little lives you people trudge through. I don't see why it matters.'

'If he crashes the moon all this will be miles deep in ice by the time you find your missing piece again, your Keot.

And you can't ascend without all of you.' Yaz wasn't sure if this was true – even 'whole' Theus was missing everything that was good in the original him – but Theus seemed to think that he could still ascend and that he needed all of him that remained on Abeth to do so.

Theus slumped with a series of clanks and an exaggerated sigh. 'Very well. Take me back. We'll need a wagon.'

'Back?' Yaz looked at Quina.

'Wagon?' Quina mouthed the word.

'Back!' Theus repeated. 'Back to where you abandoned me. Unless you've a better way of getting into the undercity? And yes, a wagon, unless you want me to walk through town and scandalize the peasants.' He shook his head. 'The mages were far better organized, I'll say that for them.'

'You can reach the undercity from those caves?' Yaz was amazed.

'They go down, don't they?'

'And the undercity reaches out that far?'

'How do you think I got caught? I didn't wander into this city wearing this . . . dog.'

Yaz shook her head slowly, adjusting to the idea. The nuns had had the entrance to their enemy's world beneath their feet the whole time. 'How do we get a wagon?' She'd no idea. Her impression of Verity's citizens was that they weren't the sort to just help out. Though perhaps two novices might get some charity . . .

'With money.' Theus hung Zox's large head and shook it slowly from side to side. 'They've told you about money by now?'

'Uh.' Yaz had heard the word but wasn't clear on what it was.

'Yes,' Quina said. 'It's little metal discs. I don't have any.'

'And you didn't kill anyone on the way in?'

'No . . .'

'Well, there's a corpse just outside. Don't bother with that one though. He'll have been looted already. The man on the floor just there' – Theus turned ponderously towards the archer who had fallen from the walkway – 'should still have what the mages paid him for his services. If that's not enough to hire a wagon then he was in the wrong business.'

Yaz was pleased that Quina went to search the body. The man had landed face down and one of his arms lay at a broken angle. Quina handled him squeamishly, preferring to reach under him rather than roll him over to reveal the full detail of what his reunion with the ground had done to him.

She cursed through clenched teeth. 'I can't find anything.'

Theus went over, one hind leg dragging a bit. 'He's not going to have it hanging off his belt in a handy-to-steal pouch.' One iron paw flipped the man over, spattering blood and mud; thankfully the leaking roof and the theft of flagstones had left sufficient mud to cover up the worst of his facial injuries. It didn't do anything for the smell, however.

'No need for delicacy.' Theus pushed out the black blades that served as Zox's claws. 'He's past feeling.' A lazy swipe reduced the man's jerkin to ribbons, also shredding the flesh underneath. 'Not that I'd be delicate if he wasn't.'

'There.' Quina's hand darted forward and in an eye blink had retrieved a flat leather package that she opened to reveal an assortment of silver and copper coins.

Quina was chosen to acquire the necessary wagon. On her way out she paused between the double doors and called back, 'There are people everywhere now!'

'Doing what?' Yaz asked.

'Watching, mainly.'

'They'll be watching the city guard arrest you if she doesn't get a move on,' Theus observed, then began to fold up into his customary cube.

It took a while, and with every passing minute Yaz expected guardsmen to barge in to take her into custody. None did, and instead Yaz grew both bored and more nervous. The slaughterhouse smelled bad. The corpse did nothing to improve the ambience. Things crawled in the shadows, up among the rafters, even across the soil, dark with the blood of generations of cattle. Yaz wasn't used to things crawling. It was at the same time fascinating and disturbing. She knelt to examine a black beetle busy about its own multi-legged business, oblivious to her inspection. On the ice it was just men and gods. She imagined that she had been like the beetle to the gods, just as oblivious. Even when she blocked its path with her boot the thing didn't acknowledge her existence, simply changing course. On the third try it scaled her foot and with a shriek she shook it off, imagining all sorts of horrors if it found her flesh.

Theus laughed. The sort of flat, cruel laugh that suggested he would enjoy putting a dozen of the creatures down her neck. Yaz's hot retort died on her lips when the doors shuddered. A moment later they grated open and Quina thrust her head between them.

'Got it!'

Quina's mastery of green-tongue left a lot to be desired but it turned out that money talks by itself and she'd managed to return with a man and a cart. Yaz could see a line of ragged children watching as the doors opened wide enough to admit the vehicle. The old man leading the draught horse was as skinny and dirty as the children, as if sixty years had done nothing to improve his lot.

'Is that going to be strong enough?' Yaz looked doubtfully between the cart and the iron cube.

'If the price is right.'

The old man's logic didn't stand up to scrutiny but he helped the two novices use the hook and pulley arrangement to load Zox, and clearly the price was sufficient for the cart merely creaked and groaned rather than splintering and collapsing.

Without delay or a second look at the gory corpse left in their wake, the novices and their cargo departed for Sweet Mercy.

CHAPTER 34

Yaz and Quina walked while the old man steered his over-loaded cart through the streets of Verity. The iron cube that was at once both Zox and Theus lay covered with a large square of sacking.

The slum dwellers either had too much respect for Sweet Mercy Convent to send any city guards after them, or perhaps too much fear. Or maybe they hated mages, or city guards. In any event, the novices eased through the crush at the city gates a second time without trouble. Soon they were free and clear of the city, back on the road to the Rock of Faith, passing hostelries and farms, retracing the journey they had taken with Sister Owl earlier that same day. On familiar ground again, the memories of the day's events weighed heavily on both of them. On more than one occasion Yaz looked back at the lump beneath the sacking and considered it a poor exchange for what had been lost.

'Take the left way.' The Rock of Faith loomed large, throwing them into shadow as the sun set behind it. Ahead of them a narrow, rutted track led off from the main road. The turn for the Vinery Stair lay a quarter of a mile further on and was much more travelled than this overgrown trail.

'Your coin, your call.' The man turned his horse's head. 'But I'm leaving you at the bottom. Couldn't even get my ownself up that cliff path these days, let alone a cart. And there's no place to unload. You'll need to be using the barrel hoist up in the convent. Not that I'm sure it could take the weight.'

'We'll manage.' Though Yaz hadn't actually thought through this part of the problem. Theus was going to walk Zox up the cliff path. But if they were to prevent the man from seeing the cube's true nature then she supposed they might lever Zox off the back of the cart and let it fall. Whether they had suitable levers and enough strength was another question, and the answer might well be no to both.

For a while Yaz was too distracted by trees to consider the matter further. She'd been in too much of a hurry crossing the Tacsis garden to pay any attention to the small wood she'd passed through to reach the mansion. Here, though, she walked with her head raised, staring in wonder at the interlacing branches, the complexity of leaves dancing in the breeze, breathing in the smell, bathing in the creak and rustle, finding some new surprise every moment.

'Got you!' Quina caught Yaz as she started to fall, tripped by a tree root that snaked out into the trail. 'I was like this the first time Wenna and Hell brought me down here.'

Yaz trailed her fingers through the leaves of a bush then reached up to test the strength and texture of a branch. 'And it's alive. All of it. Growing.'

'If you scoop up a handful of the soil' – Quina did it fast as thinking – 'there are . . . things . . . living in it. Look!'

Yaz saw four or five different types of thing, each so different from her and from the others it strained her imagination and for a heartbeat the two stars trailing the cart's progress began to fall from the sky. 'Uh!' Yaz recovered them. She shook her head in wonder again and returned her attention to the trail, just in time to avoid tripping once more.

By the time they came close to the foot of the cliffs the horse was struggling. The cart's wheels caught on a root from one of the many trees that spread their arms above the trail, and the horse strained, defeated.

'It's enough.' Yaz held up a hand. 'We'll take it from here.'

'Take it?' The man looked confused and glanced around as if expecting to see a team of nuns ready to drag his cargo off.

Yaz pulled the sacking clear and climbed up beside the cube. She gave it a shove. Nothing. Quina joined her and they pushed together. The planks beneath the cube sagged, creating a step of an inch or two to the next plank. The cube wasn't going to slide.

'Do you have a rope?' Yaz asked the man.

'Don't see how it'll help.' The man turned away and bent to get one from a hook on the driver's footplate, still grumbling. Yaz jumped down, beckoning Quina to join her.

'Move!' Yaz leaned in to hiss at Theus. 'Or so help me I'll give you back to the mages.'

There was a moment's pause. Theus somehow made it sullen. And then one of Zox's limbs unfolded until it lay flat against the deck, at which point the remaining cube began to tip. As it passed the point of no return the limb snapped back and the cube rolled forwards, splintering the last plank on the way to the ground. It hit with a dull thud that startled the horse forwards as the driver straightened. 'By the Ancestor's bal—'

Yaz made a show of rubbing her biceps. 'Just took a bit of muscle.'

The old man gave her a circumspect look and went off after his cart. He found a place to turn and came back past them without another word, creaking off down the trail.

Theus began to unfold. 'So, where are the other idiots?'

Yaz bit back her first reply. 'Erris, Thurin, and Mali are trapped by a time-star. A blue one.'

'Trapped?' Theus tilted his head. 'Interesting.' He started walking off up the steepening trail.

'How does he even know where he is?' Quina muttered and followed on.

They walked up the Seren Way, following its zigzag path up the near-vertical side of the Rock of Faith. Apart from the Vinery Stair it was the only way to reach the plateau for several miles if you didn't want to scale a hundred yards of sheer cliff.

By the time they came level with the cave entrance Yaz was sweating heavily. She would get used to the crowds and the animals and the noise and the green before she ever got used to the Corridor's heat. They edged across the rock face using ledges that looked too small even for children's feet. Yaz was first through the concealed crack that gave entrance to the caves. She brought the shipheart and the time-star down from on high and sent them ahead to light the tunnel before following. After a few moments she waited in the scarcely less hot tunnel for Quina, and then both of them waited for Theus to scrape and bang his iron body through the choke point.

'Where are they?' he demanded.

'Where are what?'

'The Watcher's eyes, of course! You need four shiphearts. Those are the pieces of a second one.'

Yaz sighed. 'I've tried to put them together. I can't do it.'

'Well, you're going to have to,' Theus said. 'But one thing's for sure. You can't build a shipheart out of them if you don't have them. So . . .' The pause seemed to be for him to push back his growing temper. 'Where the hell are they?'

'Path Tower.' Yaz had been hoping to avoid the convent. They would want to ask her about Sister Owl. They would want to take over this business with the ark. They wouldn't approve of Theus. At all. And, more importantly, she would get them killed. She had already got Kao and Maya killed, and Thurin, Erris, and Mali were trapped, Quina had been held with a knife at her throat. She didn't want to add to the death she'd already visited upon Sweet Mercy.

'I'll wait here.' Theus sat.

'Last time you said that you weren't here when we came back,' Quina said. 'I'll wait with you this time.'

Yaz bit her lip, studying the two of them. 'Don't do anything stupid.' And with that she squeezed past Quina, clambered over Theus, and went back out into the dying day. She left the shipheart and time-star where they were. They would stop Theus and Quina wandering any further in, and stop anything coming at them from the caves too.

By the time she reached the top Yaz's mind was already focused on how to deal with Abbess Claw, but as she saw Path Tower looming behind the abbess's house she realized that she would have to pass through the wall into the secret room again. Seus would be guarding the ways.

Part of her hoped that she might simply walk into Path Tower, collect the stars, and then leave. She knew from the start that wasn't going to happen. Yaz didn't see anyone on watch, but Grey Sisters do not intend to be seen.

She passed alone through the field of pillars. The setting sun skimmed the plateau now, throwing the column's shadows into the east. If the convent hadn't stood in their way the shadows might have stretched to the edge of the empire, spears set against the encroaching night.

A nun Yaz didn't recognize, in the black of a Holy Sister, waited for her at the far side, standing quietly in the space between the last of the columns and the convent. 'The abbess wishes to speak with you.'

Yaz was under no illusion that this was a request. She followed the nun to the big house, up the steps, through the doorway, and into a hallway far less grand than that owned by Wenna Tacsis's father but still large and imposing nonetheless.

Abbess Claw waited behind a paper-strewn desk in a room hung with portraits of old women, previous holders of her office to judge by their headdresses and croziers. Her window of many leaded panes looked out across the compound, where lights were beginning to blossom behind shutters. Somewhere down the corridor distant voices rose in plainsong, a high, haunting refrain.

'You'll be needed as a witness in the trial.' The abbess looked up from her papers. 'Did you see her die?' A hint of the hurt that she had kept out of her voice escaped with the last word.

Yaz looked down and shook her head.

'Did she say anything I should know?'

Again Yaz shook her head, seeing once more the small figure lying on the mages' floor in the dark pool of her blood. 'Will this make a war? Between priests and mages?'

'Not the kind you're thinking of.' Abbess Claw lifted her quill and blew on the page in front of her. 'This kind.' She tapped beneath the last word. 'The emperor has already summoned our high priest and the mage Atoan to stand before the throne.'

Yaz doubted that Atoan would be standing. Not with the

hole that arrow put through him, but she nodded and stared at her feet.

'Was it worth it?' Claw asked with sudden intensity. 'Did she die in vain?'

Yaz looked up. 'I got what we went for. One of the Missing. A kind of ghost of one of the Missing anyway. If I'm to join those stars and open the ark he's essential. His knowledge. Was it worth it though?' She drew a deep breath. 'No.'

'Time will tell. Sister Owl took you a step along your path. We owe it to her to see you to your destination.'

'I need to get my stars from Path Tower and then go into the caves.'

'I'll assemble a team,' Abbess Claw said. 'We've Reds and Greys close enough to call in. No Mystic Sisters, but I can send to Cannis Town for Sister Splinter. If I recall any sisters from Verity it will give the wrong signs. We'll have a lot more eyes on us as soon as Owl's death becomes more widely known. The emperor will send his brother, no doubt. The high priest will be here by morning. The last thing any of them want is the Church at war with the Academy. We'll have to be discreet, gather our forces without detection or someone will mistake our target and it will all go up in flames.'

'You could tell your emperor?' Yaz ventured.

'Ha!' The abbess managed a bitter smile. 'I don't know how much influence Seus has over him but it's certainly not none. Whether Edissat knows who's pulling his strings is doubtful but the sad truth is that he is compromised and indebted in numerous ways. To expect clear action from him in the common good would be misguided.'

'So do nothing. Don't risk war. Just let me and my friends do what we came here for. I can get my stars from the tower and be gone within the hour. I don't want anyone else to die.'

'Out of the question.' Abbess Claw set down her quill and wiped her inky fingers with a stained cloth. 'We are servants of the Ancestor. We don't stand by and let others take care of our concerns. Sister Owl has given her life for this cause and it was an illustrious life. If you only knew a tenth of what that woman . . .' The abbess shook her head. 'There's nobody in this convent who's taken holy orders that isn't ready to die to protect the Church and the empire, but above and beyond that to protect the children of the Ancestor, which is every man, woman, and child on the face of this icy ball we live on. Yes, we prioritize in favour of Church and state, but against an outside threat we stand for all.'

Yaz pulled her habit out to either side, displaying it. 'I'm part of this convent too. This isn't a disguise any more. I may not pray to the Ancestor but I'm part of this community. Sister Owl meant something to me and I would have stood between her and any attacker if I had been given the chance.' She let the habit fall back into its customary folds. 'Let me be your agent. If things go badly you can say I acted alone, an invader and deceiver from the ice.'

Abbess Claw sighed and pressed her lips into a flat, unhappy line. 'Go get your stars. I'll meet—'

A knock and the door opened without the abbess's say-so. Mistress Shade strode through, taking in the room at a glance, all business, her sharp-featured face a mask, not a single strand of her blonde hair escaping her grey headdress. She crossed to stand behind Claw's desk and bent to whisper in her ear.

Abbess Claw's frown deepened. 'We are going to have unexpected guests. It seems the high priest's meeting with the emperor has not gone well. The Inquisition are on their way, backed by the emperor's guards.' She looked at Mistress Shade. 'If you could rearrange things as we discussed, and have Sister Ring see to the library.' She returned her gaze to Yaz. 'Best be about your business, dear. Quick as you like.'

Yaz nodded, a novice to her abbess. She turned and made for the door.

'And, Yaz?'

'Yes, abbess?' She paused in the doorway.

'You are a part of Sweet Mercy. This place was built for souls like yours. And the Ancestor watches over you in dark places.'

Yaz nodded again and let the nun waiting in the corridor lead her from the house.

CHAPTER 35

Yaz could have sought out Wenna and the others in the dormitory or perhaps still loitering in the novice cloister. Part of her wanted to, wanted their company. But she turned away. Sister Owl had spoken of the Path taking many guises, not only as something to be walked in order to gain power but as something that would lead you through your life if you had eyes to see it and the heart to follow. Yaz had yet to see it that way but here and now she understood the sentiment. She had a path to follow and it was one she would end up walking alone, so the fewer people that started it with her the better. If she knew a way to save Quina and the others from sharing its dangers with her she would, but they too were bound to it for now.

Path Tower loomed against the thickening night, black against the crimson sprinkle of dying stars, the singular white light of the Hope star hanging above its spire. Yaz entered by the nearest door and found that the ground floor where the portraits hung had been lit by half a dozen lanterns, most of them clustered on the ground before the portrait of a young woman. A dozen novices sat cross-legged watching the picture, perhaps in the serenity trance, for none were weeping and none turned to see who had come in.

Like all the others, Sister Owl's portrait contained flights of fancy relating to her character and talents. She had a wild torrent of auburn hair, high cheekbones, a face full of energy and good humour. She looked to be just about to speak – so much so that Yaz found herself coming to a halt halfway to the staircase, waiting for whatever it was Owl had to say. A turbulent darkness full of wings and feathers formed the border, evoking images of violent destruction, and reminding Yaz that in addition to once, long ago, being young, Sister Owl had been a potent weapon in service to the Church. Offsetting this, though, and floating above both the darkness and Owl's own face, a pair of calm, dark eyes looked out, seeming to see all the world and more.

Yaz turned away, an ache in her chest that didn't fade as she climbed the stairs. Each turn of the spiral staircase took away some of the light, and by the time she reached the spot where the entrance to the third room should be she was in pitch darkness. She set her hands upon the wall. She could sense the stars in the space beyond through the shielding sigils. Despite her eagerness to claim them, she hesitated. Seus might be waiting for her in the gap between the two sides of the wall.

Yaz considered going in search of a sledgehammer. She shook her head. No part of her believed she would be getting to the ark without facing down the city mind in some form or other. If she did it here none of her friends would have to die by her side. And if she failed it would prove her unequal to the task and Taproot would just have to find another tool to use in pursuit of his ambition.

She reached for the threads of the stonework and saw them ripple in the current that would carry her through.

A further moment's hesitation and she let the flow take her. It wasn't really walking through walls but more a case of flowing. She thought that, perhaps, although the Missing and the quantals both saw the Path, the Missing might see it differently, more like she did, as a river rather than a path.

The blindness of the stairs was replaced by the soft glow of a hundred sigils and the blue-green luminescence of the stars that Yaz collectively considered as the Watcher's eyes. Once, long ago, those stars had been something singular and altogether more. Yaz ignored them all and turned to regard the wall behind her. Her body remained tensed, ready for a fight and, as her muscles slowly relaxed, a sense of anticlimax edged her relief at the ease of transition. Maybe Sister Owl had found time to strengthen the defences against Seus while Yaz lay unconscious after her failed attempt to save the proxim boy from the demon he'd carried to the Rock. It seemed unlikely, though.

She collected the Watcher's eyes, setting them orbiting her along with the blue-green star she had made by joining innumerable grains of stardust. She took a last look at the room, at Sister Owl's coffer that would be inherited along with its contents by the next sister to carry the title of Mistress Path, and then reached for the wall again, letting the Path, the river that flows through all things, carry her back through.

Instead of darkness, Yaz walked into an unnatural white light that stole her sight just as effectively. She covered her eyes and tried to find the stairs with her feet. The ground beneath her lay flat with no hint of an edge. Squinting through her fingers she saw enough to know that she wasn't alone. Her stars were no longer orbiting her but she could sense them behind her, beyond a barrier of some kind, very different from the sigiled wall she had passed through.

'If Seus intended you harm it would be a simple matter to drive a spear through you at this point.' An old woman's voice, speaking the ice-tongue.

'Jeccis.' Yaz spat the name. Through watering eyes she could see the priest now, still wearing her Church robes and the tree of the Ancestor in silver around her neck. Two large men in furs and leather and chainmail shirts flanked her, their hair stiffened with dried mud into alarming spikes, their beards braided, each braid ending in an iron cap. Both carried a spear taller than themselves with a broad-bladed head. Impalement hadn't been an empty threat.

'Come with me, girl. He wants to see you.'

Yaz lowered her hands and looked around. She was in a rectangular room with a single exit which was blocked by Jeccis and the two men. Behind her a haze-gate, three yards in diameter, leaned against the wall, the threadscape still turbulent in the encompassed space through which Yaz must have emerged moments before.

Even in her panic Yaz's mind found time to wonder how the gate had been brought into the room when the entrance was clearly too small for it to fit through.

'Now!' Jeccis barked the word.

Yaz eyed the gate, wondering if she might force a way back through it. The connection to her stars remained, a burning thread that might lead her back through the labyrinth of other destinations and strange corners.

One of the men lowered his spear.

'These men are Pelarthi mercenaries from the ice margins. It's where the ice meets the Corridor. It's where the ice grinds over homes and farms, castles and kings, forests and lakes. It's where you see what we become at the end. It's a misery that breeds cruelty and freezes hearts. And it won't ever end until the northern ice joins hands with the southern. In short, don't expect mercy from them, and don't force me to make them compel you.'

Yaz eyed the old woman, a lean twist of gristle, hardened by the years. Jeccis watched her in return, everything she'd attributed to the Pelarthi visible in her dark-eyed stare.

'I'll come.'

Yaz let them lead her. As Jeccis had said, she would be dead already if Seus wanted it that way.

The doorway led onto a brightly lit corridor. The light came from white rectangles on the ceiling and in it every colour took on new flavour absent in the red light of the sun.

'You'll see that reaching the ark without Lord Seus's permission is not an option.' Jeccis waved an arm in the opposite direction to the one she was taking.

Back along the corridor dozens of Pelarthi sat, tending their weapons and armour, some in conversation, others watching her with guarded stares. Most had fair hair that reminded her of Kao. The women painted their faces with designs in blue, some with rays of a cold sun stretching out across their cheeks and forehead. They seemed relaxed, as if they might be the reserve for guards further out.

'And these might be familiar.' Jeccis pointed through the doorway opposite the one they'd emerged from. In the unlit room beyond, the shapes that Yaz had taken for crates of some sort were in fact creatures very much like Zox, but in place of his mouthless head and modest claws they sported wide jaws full of gleaming steel teeth and talons fit for gutting whales. The priest led on.

'Were it up to me, girl, I'd see you dead for what you've done to us.'

345

'What *I've* done?'

'The Black Rock was my *home!*' Hatred dripped from her voice. 'You killed most of the priesthood. You destroyed Arges.'

Yaz bit her lip against any retort. What was the point of noting that half the woman's life seemed to have been spent in the comfort of the Corridor? Or that Jeccis was dedicated to destroying the home of millions? People fasten onto hatred for reasons that have little or nothing to do with fairness or reason. And neither fairness nor reason are tools that will prise them free from it. Jeccis had clearly fashioned herself Yaz's enemy and her enthusiasm to see her dead in the Church trial was in no way manufactured to serve her master's needs.

'Remember that, Ictha. The only thing keeping you alive is that you can open the ark. I've counselled Seus against letting you live. Better to seek another and give you an ending so cruel that it will serve as warning against any future refusal.'

Yaz refrained from adding fuel to the fire of the woman's hate. She kept her eyes ahead and her mouth closed.

A hundred yards on the corridor terminated in a white door. Jeccis walked forward without pausing and the door slid away to reveal a large white-walled chamber. Five more white doors stood spaced around the perimeter. A huge circular silver door had been set into the floor at the centre of the chamber, its single hinge thicker than Yaz's thigh. On the far side of it stood a man, taller and wider than any gerant, well over twice Yaz's height, his muscular body clothed in a white shimmer, his arms bare, his face handsome and ageless, though his beard and curling hair were as white as high cloud. He watched their approach through eyes that were blue from corner to corner and shone with the promise of lightning. The body that Seus had built himself in the world was not dissimilar to that which Haydies had worn back in the ruins of his undercity beneath the ice. Yaz supposed that the city minds could make themselves any bodies they liked, imagination the only limit, but instead they modelled themselves on the Missing, still slave to the memory of those who had abandoned them to the ravages of time.

'That's what needs opening?' She knew she should be intimidated by the giant would-be god in front of her but in the end she'd be no more dead if he stamped on her than if one of the mercenaries stuck a spear through her. The door, however, surprised her. It was impressive, but surely it wasn't beyond the capabilities of Seus to force it open or simply tunnel past it? He had lifetimes at his disposal, after all.

Seus set a massive foot on the portal.

'It's the most obdurate of metals.' Jeccis crossed to stand before Seus, leaving Yaz in the guards' care. 'Atomically compressed. A cubic inch of it weighs about the same as you do. But the door is, more than anything, a symbol. If Lord Seus were to prise it loose he wouldn't find what he wanted on the other side. For access to the powers of the ark the door has to be opened correctly, using key stars. Shiphearts from the invaders can serve the same purpose in suitably skilled hands.'

Yaz looked from Jeccis to Seus. 'Why isn't he speaking?'

'Gods do not speak to mortals.'

'You're not mortal?' Yaz remembered that the city mind in Vesta had never spoken, not even to Erris, over all those years. But Haydies had spoken in his halls. Maybe the more broken their minds the less they had to say. Though if Haydies, lurking in his handmade hell, was more sane than Seus, that was a worry.

'Lord Seus communicates to the faithful in dreams and in the space beyond the gates. I speak as his mouthpiece.'

'And why are you calling the four tribes invaders?' Yaz demanded. 'You're descended from them. This world was all but empty when they arrived.'

'I carry the blood of the Missing,' Jeccis said, proudly. Behind her Seus rumbled, like distant thunder. 'But spoiled and corrupted by that of the invaders,' the priest amended. She continued hurriedly. 'As I was saying, shiphearts from the invaders can serve the same purpose in suitably skilled hands.'

Behind her Seus looked into his own hands.

'But the Missing put the stars beyond the reach of city minds. A cruelty, really, when their consciousnesses are housed within the greatest stars of all. But the Missing feared to put too much trust in the mightiest of their creations. A separation of powers, they called it. And so to achieve Lord Seus's goals – to prove himself worthy of complete trust and to carry out the Missing's last directive to the fullest extent – he must use proxies, such as yourself.'

Yaz tried to fake the confidence she didn't feel. 'I'm not opening it for you. You'll destroy Abeth.'

Small lightnings crackled around Seus's fingers.

Jeccis scowled as if evidencing the displeasure that would otherwise have marred Seus's perfect features. 'It will merely be completing a process that is already a hair's breadth from being finished. You can return to the life you've always known. None of your clan or tribe will be in any way impacted. It's not a battle that concerns you.'

Yaz opened her mouth to reply but hesitated, imagining what the Ictha might say. Would any of them care that a place they had never heard of had ceased to exist, no matter how marvellous it was? To them the whole Corridor was nothing more than another world that might be imagined sitting like an island in the black sea, at such a remove that nothing happening there had any bearing on their lives. 'I care, though. I've seen the green lands. I don't want them buried beneath the ice. I care about the people too. They won't survive in the wind. Friends of mine died just trying to get here. I can't simply turn around and leave it.'

Jeccis scowled. The silence stretched, and one of Seus's great hands came down to rest, partially, on the woman's shoulder.

'Lord Seus wishes you to know that the Hayes gates can send you not only anywhere, but anywhen.' Jeccis seemed, if anything, even more sour as she said it, as though she was offering some much-coveted prize that she didn't feel Yaz was in the least bit worthy of.

'Why does that matter to me? I don't see how—'

'There are many futures and many pasts, girl. Time is like a tree, forever branching. If you go to the past that you have experienced then the price is always the loss of all memories and information from the time after the one you return to. But you can carry your memories to a branch you did not travel.' She looked at Yaz expectantly.

The priest's words lent a new meaning to the Ancestor's silver tree pendant about her neck but the appeal of her offer eluded Yaz. 'I still don't see—'

'With the power of the ark at his disposal Lord Seus can find you a branch where you died and your loved ones did not. Imagine the joy of returning yourself to them while in turn having them returned to you.' Jeccis managed to give the strong impression that it was a joy she herself could not imagine. 'Give him the ark and he will give you a new life with those you've lost.'

Yaz stared up at the being towering above Jeccis. Truly,

those were the powers of a god, to rewrite the truth, to toy with time. 'Why doesn't he just go to one of these branches where things worked out the way he wants them then?'

Jeccis curled her lip, anger edging her words. 'Most of the gates are damaged, stuck on their last setting or with limited range. To use them properly, access to an ark is required. But, in any event, Lord Seus is bound to service on the branch on which we find ourselves. His service to the masters demands he remain in this present.'

Yaz frowned. The Ictha had a saying that they kept for the gathering where once every four years they shed their broken children and had the chance to trade with all the known clans. *Ask yourself why.* Meaning that in any barter it pays to ask why the person offering the thing wants your goods more than what they are giving up. Generally the answer was an innocent one concerning excess and lack. But sometimes it would open your eyes and save you from a mistake that might prove fatal. But that was a question for a barter – this was extortion. Seus held Yaz under threat of death. She had no reason at all to trust him.

'Why should I believe you?'

'Because Lord Seus is going to let you go back now.' Jeccis pointed to the exit and the two mercenaries stepped aside.

'Also . . .' Seus spoke for the first time, his voice a rumbling menace. 'This.' His hand rose fractionally and closed around Jeccis's head, cutting off a thin scream. The lights dimmed to almost nothing and a crackling surge of energy ran through the old woman, sparking across her limbs. In the alternating brilliance and darkness Seus's flesh grew momentarily faint as a ghost's, revealing his true form beneath the illusion. A black metal skeleton, thorned and barbed, with lightning coursing through it, arcing between the joints.

The lights fluttered back to life and Seus released what

remained of Jeccis, a burned and blackened thing that fell into a smoking heap. The awful stench reached Yaz and she retched before turning and beginning to run. She passed the two guards and raced down the brightly lit corridor, expecting a spear to find her with every stride.

Yaz reached the room with the gate unharmed and grasped for the threads still tying her to the Watcher's eyes. She forced the panic from her mind. She hadn't been attacked. Seus had destroyed Jeccis as a display of good faith. He had murdered someone who wished to see her dead whatever the price. It was a frightening and callous display but intended to strengthen her trust in him. Yaz took a deep breath and focused, pulling on the threads, trying to draw the stars to her.

The gate lit with the same eldritch light it had held as she had stepped from it. The stars didn't appear but she could feel them pressing on the other side of a boundary that was at once both paper thin and miles thick. Stepping into it scared her, but less so than staying. She took the plunge.

A heartbeat later she was reaching for the wall to keep from falling down a set of spiral stairs with half a dozen ocean-coloured stars throwing shadows in all directions.

CHAPTER 36

Yaz hurried through the convent, knowing that her stars would draw many eyes. She hoped that she could escape the grounds before her friends heard of her presence and demanded to go with her into the undercity. The Inquisition would soon be arriving. Yaz had not been long among the novices but she had already heard enough whispers concerning the Inquisition to make her anxious to be elsewhere when they arrived. If her friends could honestly say they hadn't seen her since leaving the city, all the better.

She steered clear of the dormitory and dimmed the stars but still they glowed like blue embers in the night. She'd extinguished stardust before but felt less confident about quenching and igniting stars of this size, and besides, if she did, she would have to carry them all. Her path took her past Blade Hall and close to the edge of the plateau from where she could see a multitude of torches snaking along the Verity road. The forces that the emperor had directed towards Sweet Mercy were making no secret of their approach. The distant flickers blended into a line of fire that seemed to promise at the very least a small army on the move. Yaz offered a prayer to the Ancestor for the friends she was leaving behind.

She reached the pillars unnoticed save by a handful of nuns who let her pass without comment, each busy on their own urgent errands. She returned to the Seren Way. A fold of the plateau shielded her from the city road and she urged the Watcher's eyes to greater brightness now so that they could light the treacherous path. The darkness made the way seem narrower but also hid the true extent of the drop to the woods below.

The cave entrance, backlit by the glow of the shipheart, stood out on the rock face, announcing its presence to anyone who might glance up from the forest path.

'You locked us out, like children!' Quina came from the crack and greeted Yaz's return crossly. 'You left that star to stop us exploring!'

'Well, Theus did wander off last time and get himself captured.' Yaz returned Quina's glare. 'And you've just admitted you'd have gone in without me.'

Quina blew a dissatisfied noise through her lips and folded her arms. 'What's the plan? And where are the others?'

'I convinced them not to come.'

'Liar.' Quina shook her head. 'They wouldn't listen to you.'

Yaz frowned. 'I've seen what Seus has waiting for us before the ark. You wouldn't want Wenna and Hellma and the rest there. Besides – the abbess has problems of her own and having novices missing will only cause her more trouble and prompt more questions.'

'What's he got waiting for us?' Quina asked, frowning. 'And how do you know?'

'Too much. Pelarthi mercenaries are the least of it, and they're ruthless killers.' Yaz reached out and sent the shipheart further down the tunnel along with the time-star. The Watcher's eyes she kept at her back, far enough away not to trouble Quina. 'We need to go. There could be troops following us soon.'

'Troops?' Theus showed an interest for the first time, not having acknowledged Yaz's return until this point.

'And the Inquisition.'

'Oh hells.' Quina began to follow the shipheart. 'All the novices talk about them.' She shook her head. 'Why do people behave like this here?'

Yaz followed, shrugging. 'I think it's just what people are like everywhere if you give them enough to eat and some spare time. We build wonders and horrors in equal measure. Sometimes both at the same time.'

Theus brought up the rear with a grunt. 'From the mouths of babes . . .'

Yaz called a halt a hundred yards on in the first cavern large enough to allow space between the stars and her companions.

'How did you get to the undercity, Theus?'

'I followed my nose. Down is generally the way to go when seeking undercities.'

Yaz bit back an acerbic reply. 'Can you find the path you took?'

'Yes.'

'Good. Take us that way then.' She knew she wouldn't be able to retrace the route they'd taken through the caverns on the day of their arrival, but perhaps Theus shared with Erris a memory that let go of nothing. Yaz had been jealous of that when Erris first revealed it, but of late she'd changed her mind. There were plenty of things she'd seen in the last couple of days that she sincerely hoped not to carry with her through the rest of her life. Though given what Seus had shown her that might not be a very long time at all – unless she took his offer.

With the shipheart Yaz knew she would be able to find a thread that aimed her at Mali and the others. Whether that direction would be sufficient to reach them through a network of tunnels and chambers that did not cooperate was another thing. However, from her time in other under-cities, Yaz had learned that they were not constructed as labyrinths – rather they were either for living in, or for storage, or to house machines, and could be navigated relatively easily except where there were collapses.

'Did you see anything down here?' Quina asked Theus. 'Anything dangerous? Apart from the mages who caught you? No hunters? No Tainted?'

'Some of the stalagmites were quite pointy.'

'I don't like you.' Quina scowled. 'I think even if you get all put back together like you were before all this . . . you'll still be an awful person.'

'I do hope so.' Theus clumped along faster, as if encouraged by her scolding. 'From what I remember I did tend to rub a lot of people up the wrong way.'

'You should have said to bring some food,' Quina complained.

The descent through the Rock of Faith and into the cave system beneath had taken what felt like days. Tight squeezes, steep climbs, slick rocks, impassable tunnels, and all of it with Theus lumbering along in Zox's body, taking several falls, once rolling half a dozen yards down a sudden drop and smashing through an intricate flowstone veil that must have taken untold millennia to form. They'd been able to slake their thirst at various pools but their stomachs, particularly Quina's – more used to regular meals now – had been growling for some time. 'If you'd mentioned how long it

355

would take, Yaz could have brought supplies from the convent.'

'I enjoy your distress too much for that.' Theus led on relentlessly.

The natural caves had intersected the first of the undercity's passages an hour or two earlier and their progress had been much swifter ever since. Yaz had paused to select, with the shipheart's help, the threads binding her to Mali. These were easier to follow than those that connected her to Quina and provided a direction that proved relatively easy to stick to in the interlocked chambers of the Missing's ruins.

'It's all the same,' Quina spat in disgust. 'The same room after room. And the same city after city. I couldn't tell if I was in Verity or Vesta, and it took us months to walk less than half the way between them.'

'Because the ice is so varied?' Theus growled. 'Oh look, this bit of ice is a shade whiter than that bit ten miles back. Oh look, some snow! The excitement never ends.' He swung Zox's iron head from side to side. 'Besides, this is very clearly equatorial architecture, obviously distinct from the northern tastes.'

As if to prove him right, they left the last of a series of perfectly rectangular rooms that might have been intended to be packed to the gills with cuboid crates, and entered a vaulted chamber, oval in shape, with tiered stone seating rising on all sides of a wide central space.

'Do you remember this place? The undercities? What went on in them? Did people live down here?' Yaz couldn't imagine why they would. She'd seen the ruined spires of Vesta from back in Erris's time. Why would anyone burrow under the earth when they could live far above it in gleaming spires?

'I remember a bit.' Theus grunted and walked into the

room. 'A bit less than I did before the mages got hold of me and I had to reduce myself. I get flashes of memory. It was a hell of a lot better down here than what they have up top nowadays.' He paused. 'But it wasn't paradise. It was still just concrete and steel, crime and sorrow. Which is why they wanted to move on, I guess.' He looked back at Yaz and Quina. 'It's in our nature to be dissatisfied with what we have. We want the next thing, the greener grass, whatever the cost. We're only happy when we're moving towards something better. It's not getting the thing that makes us happy. Not for long. It's the progress. The same force that moved you from the ice to the Corridor moved my people from these places to the golden cities. They'll be complaining about their paradise now. Bank on it.'

Theus moved on towards the far exit and Yaz went after him. The thread she'd been following to find Mali had been slanting upwards slightly for a while now, but as they entered the chamber it began to angle more swiftly towards the vertical.

'They're above us. We just need to find a way up.'

'We haven't seen any stairs for ages,' Quina said. 'Maybe this is the top level.'

'How would that work?' Yaz stopped to gaze at the ceiling. 'They were in a tunnel. Under the ground.'

'Soil builds up over time,' Theus said. 'Particularly in cities. There's probably twelve layers of ruins and sewers over what used to be the surface when we built the original city.'

'So . . . we just keep searching for stairs and try not to move too far away?' Quina pressed her belly experimentally as if she expected it to collapse beneath her fingers.

'I could ask the city,' Theus said.

Yaz hurried after the iron dog. In her mind she'd taken to thinking of Seus and the city as the same thing, but

Theus's words reminded her that Verity was its own entity and the city that housed Seus's void star lay far away beneath the southern ice. The monstrosity waiting for her outside the ark was simply a body he'd constructed for himself and marched here. Perhaps decades or centuries ago.

'How far are the stairs then?' Quina caught them up.

'Still negotiating,' Theus said. 'Verity's even more degraded than Vesta. Lots of authentication needed.'

'How are you even communicating?' Yaz asked.

'I'm part of the infrastructure. All cities need maintenance. This base unit was pretty ubiquitous. There are probably some still functioning on the lower levels.' Theus took a sharp turn down a smaller passageway. 'Should be a shaft along here.'

Yaz sent the shipheart and the time-star ahead, spiralling around each other, filling the corridor with a red-gold light. About fifty yards further on they found the shaft, which, like many in Vesta, came down next to the passage and could be mistaken for a small room if you neglected to look up.

Yaz sent the Watcher's eyes spiralling up to illuminate the space above them. The shaft rose for fifty feet or so, ending in what looked to be some sort of rough stone ceiling at odds with the smoothness of the walls. A smaller square trapdoor was set into the ceiling and sealed with a slab of stone.

'Were your people very fond of climbing?' Quina asked.

Zox made no answer.

'So . . .' Quina gestured helplessly at the shaft.

'I've learned some new tricks.' Yaz motioned to the entrance. 'You'll want to stand back.' She waited. 'A bit further.'

Yaz called in the two largest stars that had gone on ahead down the passageway. She took hold of the shipheart, wincing, and with a grunt of effort threw it towards the ceiling. The strength of her arm played no real part in the resulting velocity of course, but the proximity allowed her to dramatically increase the acceleration she could impart with her mind. Experience had shown that the stars were essentially impervious to physical force. What had reduced them to dust and fragments in Vesta Yaz had never determined but it wasn't the grinding of glaciers. And hitting a slab of stone at enormous speed wasn't going to break a shipheart.

Chunks of shattered rock rained down, but Yaz had stepped back into the doorway and raised an arm to shield her face from flying shards. The crash had been louder and more violent than she'd anticipated and left her ears ringing. Dust billowed around her.

'Gods . . .' Quina muttered faintly from further back along the passage.

Yaz went back into the room, rubble shifting beneath her feet as she tried not to choke on the settling dust. She brought the shipheart down and took firm hold with both hands.

'How do *we* get up?' Quina shouted.

Yaz had no idea. 'I'll come back as soon as I've found them.'

'Wait, you can't go alone!'

But Yaz was already rising, her hands burning with a keen desire to let go while her mind forced them to keep gripping the star. By the time she had risen smoothly through the square hole at the top the whispers scratching away behind her thoughts were almost intelligible. Yaz released the star as soon as she had new ground beneath her feet. There was something about the whispering which made her think that once the voices started to make sense it would be hard to ignore them. She wondered what it was like for Theus just being Theus. For her the idea that she comprised a multitude was an abstract one. There might be many voices debating behind her thoughts but in the end they let her speak with one voice. Theus had been broken into his components and only by force of will had he dragged them back together again. Even now he was less than half made, and he knew it. He was base instinct, malice, jealousy, raw emotion . . . yet, somehow, he functioned. She shook off the sensation. Touching the shipheart always left her feeling strange.

She shouted down the hole, 'I'll be back!' Then she sent her shipheart ahead along the new tunnel she found herself in. Mali's thread gave her direction. She was close now. Yaz set the Watcher's eyes orbiting her and hauled the time-star up to follow.

The tunnel wasn't one of the Missing's. It was damp, circular in cross-section, brick-lined, and smelled earthy. Ten yards ahead the tunnel joined a second one at right-angles and there, glistening on the wetness of the walls . . . a blue glow.

'Found you.' Yaz hurried on.

She splashed into the larger tunnel, her shipheart a short distance before her, and immediately found herself hailed from the direction of the light.

'Yaz of the Ictha.'

Yaz shielded her eyes and dimmed the light of her star which hung between her and the speaker. 'Who's there?'

'You know me, *sister*.' Someone pushed out from the curve of the tunnel where they'd been resting against the wall.

Yaz recognized the broad shoulders and the heavy brow, from beneath which she knew two mismatched eyes were watching her. 'Krey.'

'*Mother* Krey.' The priest feigned hurt. Behind the woman Yaz could now make out other figures against the blue glare, the closest two holding spears aloft, ready for the throw, not aimed at her but in the opposite direction. Beyond those two the light was too bright to see much but there was at least one more person standing there. 'If you're going to present yourself in the habit of a novice then you should at least do proper honour to a priest of the Ancestor.'

'If I see one, I will.' Yaz lowered her hand and shifted from the green-tongue to the ice-tongue. 'I know who you worship and it's not the Ancestor. The one you've placed your faith in is no god.'

'He's salvation, and that's enough for me, girl. I'm a survivor. The Ictha are survivors too. This shouldn't even be a hard choice for you.'

'He wasn't Jeccis's salvation.'

Krey stiffened. She reached towards Yaz, fingers in a claw. 'If you've harmed—'

'Seus did it. He ran a lightning bolt through her, from head to toe. Nothing but blackened bones left.'

The snarl on Krey's face softened and became a sneer. 'And they say the Ictha don't lie.'

'We don't.'

'Well, one thing's for sure – you shouldn't try. You're really not very good at it.'

'I'm not lying. He said he did it becau—'

'The important thing here, child' – Krey spoke over her – 'is that these two gentlemen are going to throw their spears at your friends, who will all be dead before they know what's happening. And those spears will be thrown any moment now, unless you come with me to the ark immediately and do what Lord Seus demands of you.'

'I've already been. He let me go so I could get the shiphearts

361

that I need to open the silver door. The one in the floor at the middle of a big white room.'

Krey frowned at that, a moment of doubt twitching across her broad brow.

Yaz pushed on. 'That's where I saw Jeccis die. I've already been there.'

'No you haven't. I would have been told.' She shook her head violently as if ridding it of doubt and glanced back towards the Pelarthi spearmen. 'So Thom and Egol here are going to stay in order to ensure your good behaviour, while you and I go to the ark.'

Part of Yaz wanted to walk to the ark with Krey and watch as the priest's faith in Seus crumbled before her eyes. But she didn't want to leave Mali and the others at the mercy of Krey's hirelings, nor did she want to abandon Quina at the bottom of a hole with only Theus for company. It also occurred to her that she'd left Quina in the dark . . .

'If you kill them then you've got nothing to hold over my head.'

'I'll have them start with just one of them then.' Krey's face split in a slow smile revealing tombstone teeth. 'You can choose. The little novice? She's just a stray you picked up on your travels. No great loss there? Or perhaps one of the two from the pit? You like them, don't you? One of them's the reason you're here. Which one is it you're trying to get loose? Which one should I have killed?'

Yaz suppressed a shudder. It wasn't a choice she would or could ever make. A whisper at the back of her mind said that Erris had lived so long and Mali so short a time . . . She ground her teeth and willed it to silence, telling herself it was the voice of something that the shipheart had been chipping free, whilst worrying that in fact it wasn't, that it was just that undesirable part of her speaking into the silence of the moment. The same old voice that had always spoken unworthy thoughts.

Mother Krey wasn't as close to the shipheart as Yaz but she was closer than any of the mages or nuns ever got, with the exception of Sister Owl. Close enough for the golden light to illuminate her even in its dimmed state. She glanced towards it a few times and her face twitched in discomfort, but she made no move to back away.

'Though perhaps', the priest added, 'I should kill them all. That would make what Lord Seus intends to offer all the more valuable. He can open a gate to a future in which they remained alive. He can give them back to you, and more. Any friends or family who met an untimely end could be waiting for you out on the ice, untouched by whatever took them from you.'

Yaz bit her lip and regarded the woman with suspicion. Seus had indeed offered just that. He'd implied that the gates might take you to any possibility you desired – that it was all out there, unfolding simultaneously, every chance explored in some branch of an infinite tree. Something in Yaz rebelled against it. Not against the idea itself – if it was true then it was true – but against the notion that any one of these infinite variations held value to her compared to the path she'd trodden. To abandon what the gods had dealt you, the concrete reality in which your actions, good or bad, had mattered, for something in which you had no hand, to select from innumerable versions, to pluck one snowflake from a towering drift, seemed to lessen the currency of life itself. Either the life she lived had value or nothing did. It was a trade that might make sense to Seus's broken inhumanity: he clearly thought it a dazzling prize to dangle before her. But Yaz wasn't dazzled any more. She stared past Krey, clear-eyed. Mali had turned and stood frozen, looking at

Yaz, though her eyes probably hadn't had time to register her presence yet. Beyond her Thurin and Erris were caught in mid-step, advancing on the star. The space between Erris and the star lay crowded with other, earlier, victims, but the tricks of light and time disguised how many there might be.

'Come on.' Krey started towards her. 'Enough of this. With me now. And you two – if she or anyone else approaches without me, kill her friends.'

Yaz had saved Quina from Yelna's knife by pulling on the metal just as Atoan might have if he had been there. But this time there were two spears, mainly of wood, gripped in stronger arms. She could see no way to save her friends other than by obeying Krey.

'I'll come . . .'

'Good.' Krey's mismatched eyes watched Yaz intently from beneath the overhang of her brow. 'But I feel you need some additional motivation for the tasks before you.' Krey's mouth twisted into an ugly smile and she raised her voice, calling to the men behind her. 'Kill one of them now.'

CHAPTER 37

Yaz had no time to think. She accelerated the shipheart in a straight line that she hoped would strike all three of her enemies. Even if she missed, she knew that almost nobody could throw a spear with a shipheart in their immediate vicinity.

The short distance wasn't sufficient to build up the slab-smashing velocity she'd used in the shaft, but the star hit Krey in the side as she tried to throw herself clear. It hit the first of the spearmen in the back with a devastating crunch and knocked him into the second who was already starting to scream even before the impact.

Krey staggered drunkenly back to the centre of the tunnel, blood running from her mouth. A crimson stain that had nothing to do with the blow she'd sustained bloomed across the left side of her face, filling one eye. Her neck mottled purple. And, even though the priest stood exactly where she was, Yaz both heard and felt the pounding of her feet as the woman rushed towards her. It was Yaz's fault too. The ship-heart might have wounded Krey both physically and mentally but it had opened the Path wide to her.

Krey's charge along the Path stopped and she shuddered back into herself, echoing with power. Yaz reached for the Path too, knowing it was too late to save herself. She'd barely touched it before Krey threw out the vast energies that even with the shipheart's help she could hardly contain. She hurled them as a thick bolt of devastating power, a horizontal column of coruscating light.

In the moment that Yaz acknowledged her death some dark hand interposed itself, breaking into the instant, and the subsequent detonation took everything away.

Yaz surfaced as though from the depths of the Hot Sea into which she so often sank in memory, dragged by her brother and the beast that held him. The light returned, distorted at first as though through waves. She opened her eyes and saw a ceiling of rubble and earth through dusty air. She sat, anticipating pain, expecting her body to be a ruin. Instead the debris fell from her to reveal her habit beneath, dirty but intact. Pieces of bright metal and pulverized brick lay all around. Further down the tunnel in the time-star's ruddy light she could see that the brick lining had survived but here the walls were just the raw ground through which the tunnel had been bored. It was a wonder the whole lot hadn't collapsed.

Yaz stood slowly, realizing that she was still dazed, reeling from the blast. She turned slowly, remembering Krey, the bolt of Path-power, and the . . . something . . . that had blocked it. Yaz had barely touched the Path herself but what she'd taken must have been enough to protect her against the explosion of whatever had interposed—

'Zox?' The iron dog's head had been embedded in the wall. Smoke rose from the socket where one dark eye had been. The stump of his neck trailed coloured veins and dribbled a milky fluid. Jagged chunks of metal that must constitute the rest of his body littered the ground. 'Theus?'

Krey lay face down, motionless but not shredded. Like Yaz she'd been protected from the full force of the blast by her own Path-energies, but the men behind her were in scarcely better state than Zox.

'Mali!' But the girl was still standing where she'd been before. A dozen pieces of Zox were spinning towards her lazily on flat trajectories, slowing all the while. Yaz stiffened in horror, realizing that by the time they approached Mali they would be travelling so fast as to punch right through her, leaving her more holes than girl, becoming a red mist that obscured the carnage behind her as Thurin and Erris suffered a similar fate. She glanced back at the few remnants that were left of Zox and was struck by the awful thought that Quina might have been with him.

Yaz pushed away the idea and returned her attention to Mali. The silence felt wrong. Her ears still rang with the memory of the explosion, and its violence was still being wrought before her eyes. The jagged pieces of metal thrown in this direction and caught in the time-star's aura had made noticeable progress towards Mali, cutting the remaining distance in half. Yaz felt as if she should be able to run after them and push them aside but of course she would never reach them: the star would reduce her sprint to a far slower crawl than theirs.

'Mali!' Yaz wanted to reach out along their thread-bond but no warning could help her and such contact might snare Yaz into the star's embrace once more. Yaz chewed the inside of her mouth, frantic, needing guidance and finding none. She needed Sister Owl. What would the old woman say? Think. She would tell Yaz to think. To take her time. 'I have time . . .' The fragments were slowing. In their own frame they were zipping along faster than any arrow, but as they got closer to the star the slower they went when viewed from outside. 'I have time!'

Yaz drew her shipheart closer to her, close enough to become a discomfort. Then, just as she had at the slaughterhouse with Yelna's knife, she found threads relating to the largest of the pieces, threads that traced its trajectory through the air and could be followed back to the moment of detonation and beyond, back into the unity that was Zox and into his long history, most of it beneath the Black Rock. She bundled the threads together and pulled on them, not in the most obvious way as she had before, jerking the knife towards her, but in a more subtle, tangential way so that the threads tried to haul the metal mass to one side. The jagged object of bright and dark metal, glittering in the starlight, showed no reaction whatsoever, but Yaz understood that any change in trajectory would happen on the mass's own timescale. She didn't need to yank it aside, merely to deflect it sufficiently that by the time it drew level with Mali it would pass to one side of her or skim over her head.

Yaz turned her attention to the next piece, a shard half the length of her forearm, turning over and over as it flew. She hauled on that one, trying to deflect it to Mali's left. She had time, she told herself. Time both to pull on the many fragments individually and, just as important, time to see the effects develop and judge whether more effort was required.

The work proved punishing. The shipheart's closeness threatened to fragment her, working subtle wedges into invisible cracks. And pulling on the shrapnel exerted its own pull on her brain, helping to separate one part from the next when really all her efforts should have been devoted to clenching her mind like a fist against the star's corrosive aura.

All the while the fragments spun closer to Mali, reminding

Yaz that the novice's time wasn't frozen, merely slowed, and objects moving as fast as the pieces of Zox thrown her way were going to reach her within minutes or hours rather than days or weeks.

Worried that she might run out of time to do the necessary work, Yaz called Atoan's red time-star to her, dramatically increasing the differential between her and the objects she was focusing on. Now the shrapnel truly did appear to halt all progress, lit curiously, blue on one side, red on the other, with a purple middle ground.

As she worked Yaz became aware of a curious resonance between the two time-stars, one speeding time up all around it, the other slowing time down. The radiance of the two stars seemed to beat against each other. Atoan's star crackled beneath the blue light of the sewer star. Yaz wondered how long the blue star had hung where it was. Perhaps since its malfunction. Perhaps the city had grown up to meet it, layered its ruins about it, buried the thing, only to excavate it centuries or millennia later. Perhaps the labourers who had dug the tunnel were still digging, unaware that their shift had lasted longer than the lives of everyone they had ever known. She shook off the mesmerizing influence, aware that once again she had nearly been sucked into the timeless state that had held her captive for weeks in the convent.

'No.' Yaz found her focus and, with an aching head, returned to her work. Every now and then she would push back the red star and watch the storm of jagged metal advance, trying to judge if each piece had been sufficiently deflected before bringing the red star forward and making more adjustments, tugging here, pushing there. The red star's aura, she noted, was considerably smaller than the blue star's, which would start to slow you at quite a distance.

At last she was satisfied. Exhausted, she pushed back the

red star and took mental hold of the shipheart, intending to thrust it away to a less damaging distance. She paused, noticing that in the fierce embrace of the shipheart not only did the threadscape and the Path present themselves more clearly but also the time-star made more sense. She saw it not as the perfect sphere presented to the eye but as a pattern, supremely complex, full of motion, wheels within wheels, snowflakes of light rotating, meshing with each other like multi-dimensional cogs. The shipheart remained its perfect self but the other stars . . . she could see them now, see into them, truly comprehend them. The Watcher's eyes were puzzle pieces that fitted together. A difficult puzzle, to be sure, but at least she could see that there was a solution even if that solution didn't immediately present itself.

The shipheart's light burned on her skin and its song threatened to drown out her internal voice while all the time raising an answering chorus from parts of her being that were coalescing, forming voices of their own. She shuffled away from it and immediately Quina's name resurfaced in her thinking.

'Quina!' She accelerated into a broken jog, only to come to a staggering halt when she reached the place where Krey's corpse lay. The woman flopped an arm into her path and Yaz barely avoided tripping on it.

She stood, open-mouthed, as Krey shuddered, shifted, then rolled onto her back with a groan. Blood and grime covered her face. Her breath rattled out in a manner that suggested broken ribs. Under the dirt and gore a bruise ran from her forehead, down across her left cheek, black at the centre, haloed with shades of purple and sickly green. Her lips pulled back in a savage grin that exposed broken teeth.

Instinctively, Yaz reached for the Path.

'That wouldn't be a very nice way to say thank you.'

Krey spat blood and started to push herself into a sitting position.

Yaz paused, fingers tingling with the closeness of the Path's potential. 'Thank you?'

'You're welcome.' The priest coughed. 'Well, not welcome. What I meant is that you owe me.'

'*I* owe *you?*'

'Glad you see it my way.' The woman gritted her teeth and tried to stand. She let out a shriek, half expletive, half shock, and all pain. 'Ribs. Broken.' She gasped. 'I preferred being metal, if I'm honest.'

'Theus?' Suddenly the bruise made sense. Bruises don't form so quickly.

'Of course Theus!' The woman growled and got to her feet. 'You don't think I'd die to save you? You're my key and I need you alive, but a key's no good to me if I'm not here to use it.' He stamped one of Krey's feet experimentally. 'This body's useless. It's broken. It hurts. And she's fighting me all the way.'

Yaz frowned. She would normally have harsh words for Theus possessing a person, but he had just saved her life and Krey was her enemy. 'We need to find Quina.'

Theus shrugged. 'Probably where I left her.'

'And where's that?'

'Where you left us.'

Yaz started walking. Theus, in Krey's body, shuffled along behind, hunched over her injured ribs. Yaz left the shipheart and the time-star behind them, taking only the Watcher's eyes.

'How did you get here?' Yaz asked as Krey drew level.

Theus showed Krey's nails, apparently forgetting he wasn't still Zox. 'Claws. Maintenance units are built to be able to navigate these places even when the infrastructure isn't working.'

Yaz tried to imagine Zox hanging upside down by his talons, negotiating the transition between wall and ceiling, depending on three-inch talons driven into poured stone. She gave up. Together they returned to the top of the shaft Yaz had risen up while dangling from the shipheart.

The shifting light of half a dozen lesser stars revealed the hole through which Yaz had risen earlier. She called down, 'Quina?'

'Get me out of here!' A distant voice.

'Are you all right?'

'I will be when you get me out of here! What was that bang?'

'I had some trouble.' Yaz didn't want to explain everything at the top of her lungs. Fortunately Quina was more focused on being rescued.

'Get me out of here.'

'I'm working on it.' Yaz sent one of the eyes down and let it hang at the top of the shaft pouring out light so that at least Quina would be able to see. 'I've found the others. I'm going to try to get them free.'

'Can't you just push away the time-star that's got them trapped?' Quina yelled.

'I—' Yaz hadn't actually thought of that, though admittedly she'd been focused primarily on finding them. 'I'm working on it.'

'Can't Zox help?'

'Uh . . . Don't think so.' She knelt by the opening. 'I'm going back to get them free.'

Yaz and Theus left Quina and began to hurry back to where the others stood, time-locked in the blue light of the time-star that had held them for weeks. Theus was the slower of the two and continued to hold his side. Blood flecked his lips – Krey's lips – perhaps from a bitten tongue, perhaps from a punctured lung.

'These time-stars, they're broken,' Yaz began.

'A bit like this body, yes.' Theus spat blood.

'But your people must have been able to fix them,' Yaz said, slowing as they turned the corner and saw the light of the three stars ahead. 'I mean, they made them in the first place.'

'You can make a baby,' Theus said. 'But if you drop it on its head, can you fix it?'

'So . . . why isn't Abeth littered with shiphearts that became time-stars?'

They began negotiating the part of the tunnel that had been devastated by Krey's blast of Path-power. Theus paused a moment to consider Zox's head, still embedded in the wall. Yaz guessed it must be a strange experience given how long Theus had spent wearing that body.

'It's rare for a shipheart to overload in a manner that creates a time-star,' he said after a moment. 'But also, we *could* fix them.'

'Ah!' A sudden sense of relief washed through Yaz. 'How—'

'But not with our bare minds! We had tools. Machines for the purpose. You people have all manner of things that break but you don't fix them with your bare hands. You take a hammer, you take nails. And no – before you ask – the machines have not survived. You've seen the undercities.'

'Then how . . .' Yaz trailed off. Beneath her feet the tunnel's brick lining was mostly re-established, the worst of the damage lying behind her, but she both felt and heard something. Beneath the songs and heartbeats of the stars a deep vibration reached her through the soles of her feet. She started to turn. 'There's something—'

The head of a monstrosity burst through the ground

spraying earth and stones. Multiple rings of gleaming metal teeth rotated in alternating directions on top of a thick, segmented body, the whole thing reminiscent of an ice worm but manufactured rather than born.

Even as Yaz reached for the Path the worm was retreating back into the ground on the same line along which it had emerged.

'What in the hells is that?' Yaz found herself shouting over a now-absent whirring and crashing of teeth. 'Or *was* that?'

Theus shot her a disparaging look as if the question didn't merit a reply.

'What's it doing here?' Yaz amended. She could still feel it burrowing beneath her.

Theus answered this one. 'My guess . . . Seus reckoned you might try to free your friends and sent it to collapse the tunnel.'

'But he wants me alive!'

'Not on you. On them.' Theus pointed towards the blue light. 'If he's trying to buy you with a gateway to somewhen where people you love are still alive, and you're not biting his hand off to accept the offer, then killing more of your friends to sweeten the pot is the obvious move.'

'What can we do?' It seemed hopeless. The relief that Yaz had felt on hearing that time-stars could be fixed was a distant memory now, buried by Theus, just as her friends were about to be buried by Seus.

'Get them out of there!' Theus said.

Following Quina's earlier suggestion Yaz tried to move the blue star that held her friends time-locked. She felt no more give in the thing than if she had set her shoulder to the Black Rock and tried to shove it aside. 'I can't move the star.' Yaz tried again, straining with effort and finding that her mental command slid from its target, gaining no purchase. The red star could be moved from outside its aura but not from within. The blue star seemed impossible to move from outside, but Yaz had an intuition that if she hurried towards it and tried to move it from close by, inside the aura, then she would be able to. The stars were opposites. If it were possible to move the red from inside or the blue from outside then both would be extremely potent weapons. But by chance or design, neither could be done.

If Yaz were to rush up to the blue star then to her it would seem only a matter of moments, but while she worked, centuries would roll by for the rest of the world. Also the roof would collapse and crush her before she got close. 'I can't move it,' she repeated.

'So fix it!' Theus shouted. All along the wall beside him bricks began to fall as the worm bored its way upwards just below the surface.

'You said it couldn't be done without a machine!' Yaz shouted back above the din.

'I said I'd need a machine. I said we, the Missing, used machines. But your talent is special, girl, even among the Missing. It's something in your bloodline. Rarely seen. So try it.'

'How?'

'I don't know! Just try!' The bricks stopped falling as the worm reached the ceiling and went deeper. They wouldn't have long before the worm brought the lot down.

Yaz focused on the red time-star before her, Atoan's star. 'You really think I can do it?'

'No.' Theus wiped blood from Krey's mouth. 'But I really think you should try!'

CHAPTER 38

It didn't matter that Mali, Thurin, and Erris were time-locked. If the roof fell it would crush them just as inevitably. Once countless tons of earth and rock had begun to fall, then fast or slow – depending on where you stood, it would kill them. And if Yaz managed to make the time-star whole again after that, it would make no difference.

So, with the muted grinding of the worm tunnelling away above them, Yaz studied the two time-stars, the red and the blue. She brought Atoan's shipheart as close as she could while still leaving herself able to concentrate. Its light showed the time-stars in new ways that remained hidden when it wasn't close. Like a magnifying lens suddenly revealing important new detail.

The first new thing Yaz saw was that both time-stars were broken in a way that mirrored the other, in some senses opposite and equal, as if under the pressure that had damaged them one had buckled to the left and one to the right.

'Hurry!' Theus hissed.

'Why do you even care?' Yaz hissed back, not taking her eyes from the red star before her. 'You just want the ark open so you can chase yourself through it. Why does it matter to you if I save the others?'

'It doesn't. But you need four shiphearts to open it and in case you hadn't noticed, your friends are standing next to one of those. If you fix both time-stars you'll have three of your four shiphearts.'

'I'm trying.'

'Try harder. Or I might just let Krey do the things she keeps threatening to do to you back here.'

Yaz just shook her head, ignored him, and kept working.

Theus continued his complaints. 'I'm telling you, there's not—'

Yaz moved into the red star's aura and that shut Theus up. It stopped the worm's progress too, freezing it in place as it chewed its way through the rock above the tunnel, trying to weaken it sufficiently for a collapse. Yaz now had as long as she wanted to study Atoan's time-star.

It was a puzzle. A complicated, multi-piece, moving puzzle. She didn't know how long she stayed in the red star's time bubble – long enough to grow hungry and tired and thirsty, long enough for her headache to deepen into something vicious that threatened to undermine her concentration. Long enough to realize that this was simply not something she could solve . . . not in isolation.

Yaz needed to study the blue time-star but she needed to do so out of the red star's aura. This was about motion, about how the moving pieces meshed, interacted, divided, and joined. The stars' own weird effects on time did not disguise their internal motion but viewed from within the red star's aura the blue star was static. She stepped clear of its effect and, as the gap between her and the star widened, Theus's voice accelerated towards normal speed, and he finished the sentence he'd begun seemingly on the previous day.

'—much time left. You have to work faster!'

She ignored Theus and, free of the red star's influence, she tried to study the blue star. She wanted a clear view of the time-star but it hung in the air at a height not much above her own, and her line of sight was partly blocked by the people standing in the way no matter where she moved.

'Lift me up!'

Theus stopped in mid-complaint. 'What?'

'Lift me up.'

'Lift yourself. Broken ribs, remember? You should do – it was you who broke them.'

Yaz ignored Theus and summoned the shipheart to her, sending him reeling away. 'Careful, damn you. You'll push me out and then this madwoman will be free to throttle you with her bare hands. It's pretty much all she wants to do right now.'

Yaz grabbed hold of the shipheart and let it lift her to the roof of the tunnel. Once more she could hear the worm relentlessly weakening the ground so that it would become a burden the brick shell of the tunnel had to support. She knew it must be doing its work quite high above, in order to keep out of the star's aura. It gave her more time but how much she couldn't say.

She could see over Mali now, over Thurin and Erris, but a figure even closer to it, a narrow silhouette in the sapphire blaze of the time-star, still partly obscured her vision. She made the shipheart drag her to one side, scraping her knuckles against the brickwork ceiling while her palms burned with the star's fire. Now she could see the time-star directly. It was a good ten or fifteen yards off but while the shipheart filled her head with fragments of her own inner voice it also, at this proximity, made a wonder of her eyes, allowing her to see the blue star's workings, the patterns it projected into the space around it, the motion of wheels within wheels, spinning in more dimensions than thought allowed. She could see the damage. She could understand how it was broken. And again, as with the red star, she knew that even if the shipheart could boost her mind's ability to the point where it had the strength to fix the problem, her skull would shatter and her brain boil under the pressure. Theus was right. This was like trying to hammer in nails with your fist, or work metal with your fingers when it came red from the forge fire.

The ceiling groaned and in three places close by bricks began to fall, their descent slow as the creep of ice.

'Hurry!' Theus urged, as if she was somehow unaware of the need for swiftness. As if his pressure might help rather than panic her.

'You might make some useful suggestions. And "hurry up" is not one of those.' Yaz pushed and pulled at the red star in various different ways, straining her mind to try to change its underlying configuration. Nothing happened, despite the precision of her efforts and the force applied. 'You're always telling us how primitive we are and how you're older than the ice and how you sailed the black sea and were there to see the cities built. So tell me what to do! Tell me how to fix this!'

Theus snarled through Krey's bloodstained teeth: 'In my day there were two things we always did to any sophisticated piece of equipment that malfunctioned . . .'

'Yes?'

He frowned. 'We tried turning it off and then on again.'

Yaz forced the red time-star to sleep. It was infinitely harder than putting stardust into the grey quiescence that Eular had imposed on hers. It was much harder than sending to sleep any other star she'd tried it on before. But she managed it – in part because it was close at hand; she forced it down into a lightless sleep. Then woke it again. The light flickered within it, a red ember, growing into the same redness accompanied by that same sense of retreat as if the star were streaking away from her despite its immobility.

'Didn't work.' Yaz wiped a trickle of blood from her nose. She knew she had no chance of doing the same to the blue star without getting just as close. 'The other thing?'

'Give it a thump.'

'A thump?'

'Hit it.'

'Hit it?'

'You'd be amazed how often it worked.'

'I'm amazed I'm wasting time on this.' Yaz reached for the red star with her mind and threw it against the wall as hard as she could. The star pulverized a brick and bounced back a handspan. The dust that should have hung in the air between it and the wall fell almost faster than the eye could see. 'Nothing.' She couldn't keep the bitterness from her voice.

A rumble cut across any reply Theus had. It cut through Yaz too, so deep as to reverberate through her whole body, the sound of an untold weight shifting, restless, eager to fall.

She drew the red star towards her again and stepped into its aura, buying useless time. If she could only move the blue star the same way, but each seemed the opposite of the other and the difference was never in her favour.

Seized by an idea, Yaz stepped clear on the far side and drove the red star towards the blue. Perhaps mixing their auras would be dangerous but the time for caution had long since passed. She pushed the red star towards Mali and, as it approached her, she began to move, slowly at first and then in a blur, crossing from one side to the other, running towards Yaz until she left the red star's smaller area of effect; then she slowed and ground to a halt on the closest side. In her own mind Mali wouldn't have noticed any effects except for the sudden arrival of the red star and the instantaneous appearance of Yaz and 'Krey' in the tunnel. She would still be running towards them as fast as she could.

'You could move the star with her and bring her out,' Theus said.

'I could.' Yaz pushed the star on and miraculously Thurin began turning as the red light swelled behind him. He spotted Mali frozen ahead, then Yaz and Krey further on. The red star moved on, relinquishing him to the glacial time of the blue. 'But I don't know if they have that long.'

'What then?'

'This!' Yaz swerved the red star around Erris as he too came alive and turned to face her. He glanced worriedly at the ceiling before the star left him behind. More people appeared, came to life, then froze again, tight-packed but not interacting with each other, as if this close to the time-star they were hardly in the world any more. With the others moving aside to get out of the red star's way, Yaz now had a clear line of sight to the blue star. Pushing as hard as she could she slammed the red star into the blue.

Theus had inspired the plan. She was giving both stars a thump, simultaneously. Smashing them together wasn't the whole of her plan but it was certainly a necessary part of it. She'd seen that the two shiphearts were broken in complementary ways and that the possibility existed for each to be the tool to fix the other. Her strength wasn't sufficient to repair them, but using one as a lever on the other, using its fault to mend the other's fault, might work. It had to be done at the same moment. An undamaged shipheart was too perfect, too self-contained; it had no faults with which to manipulate another star.

The moment of impact sent out a shockwave that Yaz felt throughout her mind. Had it been physical it might have brought down the ceiling. As it was, Yaz fought not to be brought down instead. She threw herself into the timeless moment of impact, visualizing the two stars' patterns and how they could be brought together, each filling the gaps in the other. In the next moment she tore the two stars apart, leaving both whole. The beauty of the solution filled her with a moment of wonder. Then suddenly everything was shouting, running feet, and falling bricks.

CHAPTER 39

Thurin

Thurin had been about to comment on the strange deepening of Erris's voice and the higher pitching of Mali's when a red glow grew rapidly behind him and several somethings whickered through the air around him. One passed just above his head and hit the side of the tunnel a little beyond him. Brickwork exploded into dust and shards where it struck, but a greater blast came from behind, nearly flattening him.

Thurin flung up an arm and, as he started to turn, a crimson star of enormous size floated past him. He spun swiftly, ears ringing, and was amazed to see Mali frozen in mid-stride, apparently as she raced away from him. Beyond her, to his even greater surprise, a golden star lit not the tunnel he remembered but a section shattered by some terrific detonation. And there, beneath the golden star, amid the static swirl of the Watcher's eyes, stood Yaz in a novice's habit, with the priest Krey at her shoulder also frozen in the moment.

'Yaz! Watch out!' Thurin reached for the priest with his ice-work, intending to slam her into the wall. But the red star moved away and in the next moment everything was shouting and falling bricks.

'Run!' Erris powered past him. Ahead, Mali was moving again, running towards Yaz and the priest, both of whom seemed to have moved position with impossible swiftness.

Thurin needed no encouragement from Erris. The roof above him was crumbling. A brick struck his shoulder a glancing blow. And as if the threat of being buried alive weren't enough motivation, he felt behind him the aura of some star far greater and more awful than any he'd experienced before, tearing at his mind with invisible claws.

Knowing his legs couldn't match Erris's speed, Thurin used his ice-work to fly through the rain of debris. His power came stronger and more easily than it ever had before, propelling him forward like an arrow, overtaking Erris. He covered his head as best he could with both arms and snatched up Mali with his ice-work as he passed her. Both of them shot past Yaz. The presence of the great gold-white star kept him going but Thurin gave the priest a mental shove, hurling her into the wall, away from Yaz.

Thurin brought himself and Mali to a halt at the far end of the blasted section, turning in time to see the tunnel where he'd been standing vanish in a thunderous collapse, blasting dust towards him in an all-consuming cloud. The last glimpse he had before the darkness swallowed him was of Erris diving clear, two balls of light at his heels, one a virulent green and one the deep red of iron just as it starts to glow.

For an age Thurin could see nothing and make no sound for fear of choking on the required breath. The crash of falling earth and rock quickly faded into the much deeper sounds of a great weight settling, a noise more felt than heard, peppered with the fall of stray bricks. Thurin pulled

Mali to him and found her hand at his throat before she understood and held to him with the fierceness unique to people lost in darkness.

The light returned as a diffuse glow, lighting the dust but revealing nothing. The three great stars reappeared slowly, first the golden one, then the unnaturally green one, and finally the crimson one, whose light was nothing like that of the red star whose appearance had begun this sudden and unlikely turn of events. The Watcher's eyes became apparent next, and then three figures. The two standing together had to be Erris and Yaz. The one groaning and using the wall to slowly regain their feet was Krey.

'Yaz!' Thurin started forwards, eyes on the priest. He started to warn her but broke off, choking on dust.

Yaz and Erris came to him, both of them coated in the reddish dust. As Thurin raised his arm towards Krey, Yaz pushed it down. 'That's Theus.' She coughed. 'I mean, Theus has her.'

Thurin was still eyeing the priest suspiciously when Yaz caught him in an unexpected hug, and then broadened her arms to include Mali. 'I missed you!' She squeezed and belatedly he put his arms around her. 'Both.'

Thurin remained confused. He could understand and share her relief that they'd not been crushed. But he'd seen her the day before. He wasn't arguing though. She felt good in his arms, the strength of her somehow calming and exciting at the same time. 'We only left—'

'It's been a while.' Yaz raised her face to his, her white-on-white eyes held enough colour that this close he could see her irises, the faintest of blues. 'There are things to do before we talk.'

Thurin released her reluctantly, exchanging a puzzled glance with Mali, who seemed less confused than he felt.

'Where's Zox?' Mali looked strange in her new brick-red skin. All of them did. Like one new tribe.

Yaz waved an arm around, indicating the shattered tunnel. 'Everywhere.'

'He's gone?' Thurin had liked the dog. More than liked him. Even though he was made of metal and never once spoke during all the length of their journeying.

'Saved me.' Yaz coughed again. 'From her.' She gestured towards Krey, who was stumbling towards them, cursing and spitting black stuff from her mouth.

'What . . . what happened?' Thurin couldn't condense his questions into anything sensible. Everything had changed in a moment. The stars, pressed back against the collapse, were still too close for comfort and frayed his thinking. 'How are you here?'

'You were trapped by a time-star,' Yaz said. 'It's been ages. Weeks.'

'Weeks?' Thurin laughed. 'No, that makes zero sense.'

'The blue star . . .' Mali nodded. 'I saw myself old.'

'You did?' Thurin looked down at her and blinked. 'I was just following Erris and then . . . this.'

'That's how it was for me too.' Erris nodded. 'Where's the time-star now? Buried?' He looked back at the mass of rocks and soil.

Yaz pointed to the great stars. 'There. I fixed your slow time-star with a fast time-star. We have three shiphearts now.'

Krey reached them and Thurin joined Mali in stepping back from her. The woman was dangerous and wanted them all dead. The fact that she was now possessed by an evil spirit wasn't a great comfort. Thurin had carried Theus in his mind, both unconsciously and while under his control, and the memory still made his skin crawl, but any measure of sympathy he might have felt was crushed under the heel of what the priest had tried to do to them and what she wanted to do to the world.

Krey gave him an ugly look, snarling over broken and bloodied teeth. 'Watch yourself, boy. I'm in the market for a better body and with a market this bare, yours might be the best on offer.'

Yaz moved between them, turning her back on Krey. 'We need to get Quina. Then I'll explain where we stand and what comes next.'

Thurin lifted Quina from the depths of a shaft that seemed to be part of the true undercity, built by the Missing in the long ago. Quina rose towards them, thrashing her limbs in agitation and attempting to both complain about her long incarceration and ask a dozen questions at the same time.

Finally she rose through the trapdoor hole looking so furious and so like a novice that Thurin almost dropped her. On Yaz the habit looked like a costume. On Quina it seemed like a second skin. The nuns had even tamed her hair.

With her trademark swiftness Quina slammed into Thurin in the same instant he released his mental hold on her. For a wild moment he thought he was under attack and that, like Krey, Quina had been possessed by some malevolent spirit. But no. She was hugging him tight enough to squeeze the air from his lungs.

'When did you get so strong?' Embarrassed, though strangely pleased, he tried to prise her loose. Yaz had told them it had been weeks since they left the convent, but to Thurin it barely seemed days, and the fierceness of Quina's embrace seemed to claim it was months.

Quina released him, bright-eyed, her grin wide enough to show every tooth. 'I've been training with the nuns. I could put Erris on his back now!'

Thurin found himself returning her grin. She looked older too, somehow, though he wasn't sure how or if she'd even reached sixteen yet.

'Erris! Mali!' And Quina was past him, trying to hug both the others together. She released Erris first and bounced in a circle around Mali, holding the novice's hand in both of her own. 'I can speak your tongue now!' And with that she began to spout gibberish that did actually sound rather like the green-tongue.

Thurin sat around the shaft head with the others while Yaz recounted the events of the past month, much of which, it turned out, she had spent in the same timeless state as he, Erris, and Mali had, thanks to her strange connection with the novice. Erris also told Yaz and Quina of the successful recovery of Taproot, or at least the part of him needed to reinforce the ark.

From Yaz's report Thurin learned that the old marjal nun with the big eyes had been killed in the city. He had met her only briefly, but it seemed to be a personal tragedy for Quina, who bowed her head in silent tears, and for Mali, who sucked in a great breath as if struck by sudden agonizing pain and fighting the need to cry out. He learned that Seus now knew that Yaz was his key to the ark and had changed from trying to kill her to trying to force her hand. Thurin and the others were now viewed as potential hostages against her cooperation, or, failing that, it seemed Seus was happy to kill them so he could tempt her with passage to realities where they were still alive. Thurin found no comfort in the idea that if Seus killed him a replacement could be found in some other nearly identical world: it sounded like the 'simulations' with which Erris had dazzled Yaz back in Vesta. Pretend worlds that fooled the senses yet lacked some fundamental value intrinsic to this one. Thurin knew that if challenged to defend his point of view words wouldn't suffice. It was something his gut told him, his heart, not an argument in logic.

'So,' Erris said when Yaz ran out of words. 'If you want unfettered access to the ark we have to clear a path through a hundred or more of these mercenaries, two weaponized Zoxes, Eular if he's around, whatever else they have, and then Seus's avatar?'

Yaz nodded. 'Or I pretend to agree and go there alone.'

'And then what?' Mali looked horrified.

'Try to get Taproot into the ark before Seus can get in, and then hope Taproot can hold him off,' Yaz said.

Erris shook his head. 'Taproot said he could reinforce the defences if he got inside, but I don't think he was imagining doing it with the door wide open and a head start of half a second.'

'You don't have four shiphearts.' Theus wheezed, more blood flecking Krey's lips. 'That's the first step.'

'Because you just want to get in.' Thurin found it doubly easy to hate Theus now that he was hiding behind Krey's eyes rather than Zox's. 'You don't care what happens after!'

Theus sneered. 'You forget. Yaz stupidly managed to all but destroy an important fragment of me. I can't use the ark until I get it back. That could take years. Decades maybe. I want the ark open but I need to know that whoever controls it will let me use it when I'm ready.'

'He's thinking he can strike a deal with Seus.' Thurin looked to the others. 'You know you can't trust him!'

Yaz frowned. 'Theus needs the Corridor and the people in it. Part of him is waiting at death's boundary now. The only way he'll get his fragment back is if it can hitch a ride on someone in this area who comes close enough to death for it to . . . infect.' The last word looked to have left a bad taste in her mouth.

'And *he* told you this, did he?' Thurin laughed. 'He invented lying.'

'He did. But Sister Owl agreed it was true.' Yaz folded her arms.

Thurin sensed there was no mileage in arguing with the dead nun's judgement.

'So, what do we do?' Yaz looked around the group.

'You're not going in there alone!' Thurin felt foolish trying to protect her. She'd looked after herself in this new world for weeks while he took half a step. She'd survived the church, Eular and his priests, mages, even close encounters with Seus. And yet now he *was* able to act he was damned if he'd see her walk into the enemy's arms without him. 'You've got the shiphearts. Nobody can go near them except you. You can drive any number of these Pelarthi away.'

Yaz quirked her mouth. 'It's hard to move two. I tried moving the three we have together. It's like dragging a family sled on my own. While I'm struggling with them someone will just throw a spear through me.'

'But they need you alive!' Thurin said.

'If it's clear I'm not going to help Seus whatever the price then he may as well go back to the old plan: kill me and keep chewing at the defences until he finally gets in.'

'So we take one shipheart, and scare off the Pelarthi with that,' Mali said.

'Then Seus will just use that worm to bury the shiphearts I leave behind.'

'And we don't even know how to get to the ark,' Quina said.

'Theus?' Yaz turned towards the priest, who lay in the

curve of the wall, easily mistaken for a corpse if not for the slow rattle of her breath.

Theus shook Krey's head. 'I only had plans for the under-city proper, not these old sewers. And those plans were in Zox's memory, not mine. Anyway, the fourth shipheart is your next step. There's no opening the ark without it. You can decide how to use it once it's made.'

As the debate continued Thurin became aware of a tingling sensation around his left collarbone. His fingers were there, exploring the area before he realized what he was doing. 'Hey!' He jerked his hand back. Something had stung him.

'What?' Quina and the others were looking at him now.

Feeling foolish, he pulled free from the collar of his soiled finery the needle containing that part of Taproot selected to defend the ark. It vibrated again between his finger and thumb. 'This. It's buzzing.'

Quina plucked it from his grasp, faster than thought. With hunska dexterity she spun it around her fingers, walking it across her hand and somehow whirling it up to balance on the tip of the longest one. Its rotation stopped suddenly as if the needle were anchoring itself to a direction.

'Perhaps it's pointing the way to the ark?' Mali suggested.

The needle buzzed off Quina's fingertip. 'We should scout the way ahead while Yaz works on the fourth shipheart.' She picked it up again.

'Splitting up would be a bad idea,' Erris countered. 'What's the rush?'

Quina shot him a narrow look. 'You might suck all the power you need from the undercity but some of us have got to eat! I've been down here forever and I'm hungry.'

'Hungry to die?' Thurin spoke half in jest, but an empty belly did seem a poor reason for racing into danger.

'Your last meal might have been weeks ago but your stomach doesn't know it.' Quina folded her arms. 'And in case you missed it, there's nowhere safe for us above ground any more. My friends at the convent are dealing with the emperor's army and the Inquisition. The city guard and half the mages are after us. For all we know Seus has spies watching us, spies who will carry our plans back to him. And Mistress Blade teaches that you never let your enemy find their footing. You strike first and you strike fast. You don't let them regroup. You don't let them think. You take away their time. You—'

'All right! All right!' Erris couldn't keep a grin from his face. 'Our warrior nun here has some valid points. Perhaps it would be good to know the way to go once Yaz is ready to move. If it's going to be as hard as she thinks it is to bring four shiphearts with her we could do with a direct route.'

'Obviously I'm going.' Quina stuck the needle into the hem of her habit's collar.

'I'll go.' Thurin wanted to spend time with Yaz but if she was going to be working with the stars he wouldn't be able to get close enough for any conversation that wasn't shouted, and she'd probably be concentrating too hard to focus. Spending time with Quina was also good, and she at least needed him.

'I'll go.' Theus clambered slowly to his feet, mouth twisting in a silent snarl against the pain of his injuries.

'No!' Thurin objected reflexively before realizing he didn't want Theus staying with Yaz either.

'You'd rather this be my choice when my current body dies?' Theus swung an arm to encompass Yaz and Erris.

'You're not coming with us, Erris?' Quina asked.

Erris shook his head. 'Someone has to watch Yaz's back

while she's working on the last shipheart. And I'm more tolerant of stars than the rest of you.'

Thurin couldn't fault the logic, though he noted that even Erris shied away from getting too close to the shiphearts.

'We should go,' Quina said.

'But . . .' Thurin wanted the reunion to last. 'We could—'

Quina's belly rumbled loudly as if on cue. She looked down at it. 'I have spoken.'

Mali nodded. 'She's right, Thurin. The longer we wait the more time Seus has to learn what we're up to.'

'*We* don't even know what we're up to!' Thurin raised his empty hands to show how little they had to work with.

'Whatever we decide, we're going to need to know how to get there.' And with that, Quina walked off into the darkness.

Mali and Thurin exchanged glances and waited.

Quina's voice came back to them a moment later. 'We're going to need a light though.'

CHAPTER 40

Mali held aloft the small star Yaz had given her. Blue-green light reached both sides of the tunnel and illuminated five yards or so of the way ahead. It was one half of a star that Yaz had divided while they watched, breaking the sphere into two smaller spheres, each perfect, as if it had been a water droplet held in shape by surface tension rather than an impenetrable ball of light and energy.

Thurin and Quina followed, side by side, with Theus bringing up the rear, labouring along in Krey's damaged body. Whenever a choice presented itself Quina took out the needle and let it guide her.

'Taproot should just tell us. I mean using his voice. He did it before with that box.' Quina put the needle away and motioned Mali down the left-hand passage, ignoring the drier tunnel that veered to the right.

'Maybe the needle wasn't intended for this purpose,' Thurin speculated. 'Perhaps he's pushing it to its limits. There's not much left from the Missing that still works.'

They walked on in silence for a while, the only sound the

splashing of their feet in ankle-deep water and the slow but constant patter of droplets falling from on high.

'This thing Seus is trying to bribe Yaz with . . .' Quina began. 'It doesn't make sense to me.'

Thurin shrugged. 'Perhaps that just shows how little the city minds understand us. How different they are, or they've become.'

'I mean . . . if these gates can lead to endless maybes . . . versions of our world where this person died or that person didn't . . .' She shook her head. 'If you thought they were *real*, wouldn't it just make everything seem worthless? If you could watch someone die only to take your pick from a thousand identical versions in identical worlds. It makes my brain ache. This Quina here.' She patted her chest. 'This one has to matter. This one has to be the real one.'

'You do matter,' Thurin said, surprised at how much he meant it.

'But I matter more than any other Quina Seus might offer you with his tricks, right?'

Mali answered without turning her head to look at them. 'It's hard to answer that question until you've lost someone really important to you. Then the balance in the scales shifts.'

'But—'

'But, yes.' Mali spoke over Quina. 'I agree with you. Now. But if the convent burned and all my sisters with it . . . who can truly say?'

'It wouldn't feel real,' Quina concluded. 'Sometimes all this doesn't seem real either.'

Thurin frowned and glanced around.

'Not the tunnels, stupid,' Quina said. 'The Corridor. All the green. All the plenty. The still air. The heat. It must be the same for you, Thurin. You weren't on the ice long, but the pit was a world away from the green lands.'

Thurin nodded slowly. 'I suppose so. I'm still new to it. You've had much longer.'

'That's why she's going back,' Quina said.

'Who?'

'Yaz.'

'To the ice?' Thurin stopped walking, astounded. 'She said that? She told you she's going back?'

Quina turned to face him. 'It's in her eyes. You can see the ice there.'

'And you?'

'I'm staying. I love this place.'

'But Yaz? You think she wants to go back?' Thurin didn't believe it.

Quina frowned. 'She's Ictha. I don't think she wants to. But I think she will. It's in her blood. This place is too easy for her. She's a visitor.'

Thurin shook his head, as if denial could push away the worrying sense that Quina was right. He walked on, not seeing the ground before him.

'Will you follow her back?' Quina's voice had that strained quality of someone trying too hard to sound uninterested.

'What?' Remembering the ice made Thurin shiver. It seemed impossible that he had endured that wind, day after day, week after week. 'Why would I?'

'You left the Pit of the Missing to find me?' Quina arched a brow, keeping her gaze on Mali's back.

'I . . .' That endless escape haunted his dreams. 'I left for me.'

'Ha!' Theus barked a laugh behind them. Thurin had forgotten he was there. 'That's a lie, boy. Lifting yourself out of that hole nearly killed you. I thought I'd have to reveal my hand and force you on when the pain became too great and you gave up. But no. You just kept on going.'

Thurin whirled round, raising an arm and seizing Theus with his ice-work. He lifted the priest's body from the ground. 'I'm stronger now, so watch your mouth, parasite.'

Theus merely sneered. 'The truth stings, doesn't it? I wasn't the only dog following sweet Yaz. And if you all live through this we'll get to see if the leash she has on you will drag you back to the ice to die.'

Quina placed a narrow hand on Thurin's arm. 'Leave him. He's got a hole through him and he's just trying to fill it with your pain. You know what he is.'

Thurin lowered Krey and her passenger roughly to the floor, then turned away sharply and walked off, letting Quina's hand fall. 'Why are we all standing around?'

The way ahead was anything but straightforward and Taproot's choices via the needle soon made it apparent that he was working on a direction rather than a map. Half a dozen times they came up against dead ends or looped back through a complex series of climbs and falls to some section they'd passed through earlier. Many of the tunnels had collapsed over the years and several incarnations of sewers threaded each other at various levels. In places more recent work was evident, some clearly the labour of men with mortar and stone and even timbers, in other cases it looked more like the work of something else – perhaps the metal worm that had nearly buried them earlier.

While they searched, stumbled, backtracked, and sought new ways forward, Thurin did much the same in the darkness of his own mind, following Yaz endlessly across the ice. She was special, obviously. The rarest of talents, precious to the world for what she might achieve in its defence. But already he was thinking of the Corridor as the world, of the thin circlet of green, packed with life, as all that mattered. But Yaz was from the ice, from the harshest extremes of the north. If the Corridor closed it would just be the smallest addition to a white realm in which she had spent nearly all her days.

And was what made her special to the world the same thing that made her special to him? In the stories it was so simple. Even in Yaz's tales: Zin was made for Mokka. There was only Mokka. Had it been Yaz that drew him out of the pit, or had she simply shown him the way? Had it been inevitable as soon as he discovered he could lift himself from the ground that he would see the sky? He'd told Quina that he had left the pit for himself. Maybe it was true. Yaz had a great weight to carry now. To add to that the burden of his desires wasn't the act of a friend, let alone someone who loved her.

A shelf in the rough floor tripped him and Thurin, too deep in thought to save himself with his power, crashed to the ground, reflex interposing his arms and earning him grazed palms in place of a broken face. 'Ouch!' But it wasn't the impact that occupied his mind, even as Quina helped him up and Theus laughed. It was the sudden realization that had hit him harder than the floor. He wasn't going back to the ice. He wasn't ever leaving the warmth of the Corridor. He would fight for it even though he had just arrived. And if Seus's strength proved too great – he would die for it.

'You all right?' Quina released his arm. 'Falling down isn't what you do. Falling up is your thing.'

Thurin managed a grin. 'Wasn't concentrating.'

'Well, concentrate.' Mali turned back, unsmiling. She looked at Quina – 'Clarity. Like Sister Owl teaches.' Then she led off again. 'We've got trouble waiting for us this way.'

Thurin shrugged. 'Trouble that's likely to kill us.' He kept his voice low, intended for Quina. 'You've had longer than I have to get used to the idea.'

'Catching you up in age too,' Quina said. 'If you'd managed to take a few more steps towards that star I'd have been an old woman.'

Thurin sighed. 'I just thought I'd have more time. We came all this way to reach the green lands. And I walked from the Rock to the city. That's all I've seen of them. And now I'm probably going to die in a hole not much different to the one I came out of.'

'Keep me safe and I'll show you around properly when we get out of here.' Quina took his hand.

Thurin opened his mouth but found he had nothing to say. Quina's hand was warm in his, small, her hold firm, comfortable. Thurin closed his mouth and walked on in silence. After ten paces he realized he was smiling.

CHAPTER 41

Yaz

'So it's like fitting the parts of a broken jug back together to remake it?' Erris asked.

'Yes.' Yaz nodded. Focused on the Watcher's eyes. 'Except that all the pieces have to be snapped in place at the same time. And it all takes place in my head. And the pieces are rotating. I mean tumbling around all their axes. And none of the pieces want to be anywhere near the others.'

Erris caught one of the eyes as its orbit took it close to him. 'Does it help to have them circling you? I'd want them still. Like jigsaw pieces.'

'It doesn't work like that.' Yaz watched the star burning in Erris's hand, too big to be lost in his grip. 'Doesn't it hurt you?'

Erris met her gaze, smiling but with sadness at the corners. 'I tried to build a body like the one I had, only better. But it didn't turn out very human, did it? Hurt and effort are the least of it. I don't strain. I either can lift something or I can't. I don't hurt, I feel. I feel a blade or a blow, but it's not the same distress I remember when it was the flesh I was born into. Which is all a long-winded way of saying: Yes, it hurts, but that just means I know it's doing me damage.' He let the eye go and nodded towards the three shiphearts further along the tunnel. 'Those would break me.'

Yaz said nothing, just stared at the stars, trying to see solutions to the puzzle they presented. Soon she would call in the shiphearts to sharpen her perception and enhance her powers. She would burn like a candle lit at both ends, spilling her fuel with abandon. But the price she paid would purchase her the clarity that might show her what she needed. For now though, she worked alone. The fact was that she was frightened of bringing the three shiphearts to her together. This – the ability to withstand the stars – was what made her special. This was why so many hopes were piled upon her. But it was hard. So hard. And she was scared.

'We don't have long.' Yaz muttered the words as if the louder she spoke them the more true they might be.

'No,' Erris agreed.

'That worm could go back to Seus. Maybe it can tell him what's happened here without even going back.'

'Maybe.'

'And then he'll be sending his mercenaries and monsters to kill everyone I care about.'

Erris nodded.

'Say something, dammit.'

'I can say "no" and "maybe". If you want me to panic or blame you I could try.'

'I should have used the time-star to give me however long I needed to put these pieces together. I was an idiot. I could have taken months and inconvenienced nobody.'

'Sometimes more time isn't what you need,' Erris said. 'Some tasks always come down to the wire. It's that pressure which makes you take the necessary risks, accept the necessary pain.'

Yaz freed the Watcher's eyes from their orbits around her, directing them in front of her where they swung around each other instead. Half a dozen ever-changing paths, each star threading in and around the others, never touching but unable to stray too far. It seemed to Yaz a fine metaphor for herself and Erris and Thurin, and even Quell, who, although he had stayed behind, was also somehow with her, carried across thousands of miles of empty ice. She'd left the north but it hadn't left her. The ice and the wind wouldn't ever leave her, not even if she took sail across the black sea until Abeth itself was just another star hanging in the void behind her.

Yaz turned from the glowing mass to face Erris with the light at her back. 'It's true,' she said. 'Some things we put off, we avoid them until there's no time left, until the only choice is to act or lose the chance forever.' She took a step towards him, another, each against more resistance than she'd fought in the teeth of Yelna's mage-wind. She was too close now, pressing against that same barrier two stars had to overcome before attraction took over and they became one. Erris's closeness prickled on her skin, and as she raised her face to his the dark eyes that met hers burned with more than just the reflected glow. Her heart had been racing even as she turned – now it hammered within her chest as if she'd run a mile.

'Yaz . . .'

'Erris?' She bit her lip, released it, and leaned towards him, so slowly that she could convince herself the distance between them wasn't changing.

'I'm not made—' His hands were on her upper arms, gentle enough that she could almost imagine he wasn't holding her back. Almost.

'Like a man?' She'd passed the point at which pride could be salvaged and she didn't care.

'I'm so old, Yaz.'

'You don't look old.'

'I died before the ice came to Vesta. I'm older than these tunnels. I won't age. I don't look old . . .' He released her and raised a hand to his face, drawing his fingers down across forehead, cheek, and chin. A very human gesture. 'I don't look old but I'm dragging too many years behind me to be what you need.'

'And what do I need?' Yaz frowned up at him, a strange mixture of emotions bubbling through her.

'Someone who can marvel at the newness of each experience with you.'

'Now you're patronizing me.'

'Someone who can make life. Someone who can change with you. Someone who doesn't have to watch you grow old, then wither, then die, all the while staying just like . . . this—'

Yaz lifted onto her toes and pressed her lips to Erris's. He didn't turn away – some small but precious thing might have died inside her if he had. His arms closed around her, not with passion's strength but close, protective. When she had kissed Quell out on the ice in the darkness and temporary shelter of two hoods coming together they had opened their lips, never knowing which of them initiated the action. Erris did not. And Yaz, feeling that the mouth beneath hers was neither as warm or as soft as it should be, made no move to either. The thing that passed between them needed neither words nor tongues; it was an understanding steeped in old sorrow, but the tightening of their hugs as each slid their head to the side of the other spoke of something else: affection, respect, a different kind of love.

They stood holding each other for some while, and when

it was time for her to return to the labour before her, neither needed any prompting.

The inspiration that struck Yaz as she stared at the glowing puzzle of many moving parts rose – as all truly novel ideas do – from the hidden depths at the back of her mind where thoughts framed in words and images never travel. It rose from the place where primal fears and gut instinct wrestle with darker emotions, the battle from which on rare occasions a bright epiphany bursts out. She called her blue-green star to hand, the dust-star she had laboriously manufactured back in the convent. What remained, after the half she had given to Mali, was scarcely larger than one of the peas the novices were sometimes served at table.

Yaz could have given the whole star to Mali. She should have, but it had felt too precious to part with entirely, its light and lustre the product of so many hours of labour. It was the battleground on which much of her understanding of the stars had been founded. She had freed Eular's army from servitude with grains of stardust and learned since that there was much to see in a handful of dust.

Gripping the star between finger and thumb she spoke a word of undoing and squeezed. The star's light shifted, becoming in moments a mottled rainbow glow from the dust that now coated her fingers.

'What have you—' Erris fell silent as, with utmost concentration, Yaz lifted the grains in a growing cloud of sparkling motes and sent them to join the dance of the Watcher's eyes. Each grain followed its own course, spiralling through the air into one of half a dozen bright threads, each thread following in the wake of one of the eyes. For several moments the whole ensemble continued along their interweaving orbits, each large star now trailing a thin tail of dust. And grain by grain she joined the motes to the eyes, growing each eye by the tiniest fraction, not enough to be noticed or to change the quality of their light.

'I've added to each of them parts of something that used to be singular and that I made and understand,' Yaz said. 'The threads that still bind those grains of dust to the memory of their previous unity will help guide the larger pieces into a greater whole.' She drew in a slow, deep breath. 'Or at least that's my theory. And now you should probably stand back because if this goes wrong there's not going to be much left for quite some distance. Probably best to run.'

'Yaz . . . Maybe you should—'

'Waiting's not the answer. Not for something like this. You said so yourself.'

The real trick, Yaz decided, was not in finding the precise solution and then gathering your resources to act, although it was necessary to see a possible solution. The real trick was to act in the moment as it presented itself. The potential for joining the Watcher's eyes into one great star seemed to appear and reappear like a fish glimpsed beneath the waves, sometimes swimming closer, sometimes diving from view, but never still, never perfect. Every Ictha knew that if you waited for the guaranteed shot before thrusting your spear you would starve in your boat or the sea would freeze. There was no such thing – just chances good enough to take – and those chances had to be seized, not agonized over as they faded away. That was a lesson for life too. One Erris had reminded her of.

Yaz reached out with a grunt of effort, dragging in from behind her the three shiphearts. The resistance was so great that she relented and tried to bring forward just one. It seemed that simply the presence of the other two somehow anchored the third to its place in the world, and that the task would be scarcely easier one at a time. With a straining cry she hauled all three forward, and Erris retreated from their aura.

The combined light of the trio burned on her skin and made even the walls of the tunnel translucent to her sight, revealing the raw earth behind the bricks. The voices in her mind swelled rapidly, whispers becoming mutters, mutters turning into opinion. And in that light the Watcher's eyes revealed their secrets, the swirl of their mystery unfolding.

Yaz reached for the river that flows through all things and thrust her arms into it past the elbows. The fierce rush of its flow promised to take her everywhere, to tumble her through strange new worlds even as it stripped the flesh from her bones, and unwound each constituent that combined to make her.

A shriek escaped her as she drew back her arms, both shining with an unbearable brilliance as if dipped into the light of the whitest star. The power of the Path flooded her body. At her bidding the dance of the Watcher's eyes accelerated until no single star could be seen, just a whirring pulsation, a hard bright core surrounded by a haze of elliptical orbits. Streamers of energy trembled in the air, reaching from Yaz's incandescent body to be drawn into the maelstrom of stars, the power leaking from her into the mix.

Yaz threw her arms wide as if struck by an arrow between her shoulder blades. And then, with a growling moan that grew steadily in volume and pitch, she began to bring her open hands in towards the whirl of stars.

For one instant the stars simultaneously reached the farthest-flung points on each of their orbits, and then with a crash louder than the collapse of the tunnel they swung towards their inevitable collision at the centre. Yaz's hands arrived at the precise moment required to contain the impacting stars and pour into their reunion a vast amount of energy – more than she had ever owned – enough to turn an entire forest to charcoal.

The flashback forced her hands apart and hurled her, flaming, into the opposite wall.

Armoured in the Path, Yaz lay among the rubble of pulverized bricks and gazed up at the thing she had wrought.

Unlike the other stars – the white-gold of Atoan's ship-heart, and the virulent green and forge-red of the former time-stars – this shipheart was dark, sometimes deepening to the blackness of the space between true stars, then flaring erratically with eruptions of indigo that brightened to a painful violet before once again submerging in the darkness of the sphere.

Yaz stood and in her mind a cacophony of voices rang so loud that she could barely hear her thoughts. For now, however, one voice dominated: *I did it. I've got four shiphearts.*

CHAPTER 42

Thurin

The ancient sewers and buried passages were far from dry but Thurin could still, with less impressive results, extend his water-sense as he had back in the Black Rock beyond walls and into the darkness where Mali's light had yet to reach.

'People up ahead.' He reached for Mali's shoulder and she closed her hand about the small star Yaz had given her, quenching the light.

Thurin strained his sixth sense, trying to filter out the dampness in the soil, the water trickling between rocks, the puddled floors . . . 'There's a space. A chamber. Five . . . maybe six people, just waiting.'

'Keep moving,' Theus grated. 'Kill all except for the one we're going to question.'

'Can we take six?' Mali held up her stump to remind them of her weakness. 'Quina's fast but untrained. Theus can barely walk—'

'I'm trained!' Quina snapped off an impressive kick that came within a finger's width of Mali's nose.

Mali seemed less impressed than Thurin. 'It takes years to

be good, and even then hands and feet against swords and spears is an uneven contest.' She returned her gaze to Thurin. 'It's down to you really. Can you kill them before they kill us? Quicker, if possible, because more will probably be coming if it gets noisy.'

'This is what we're doing?' Thurin frowned. 'Clearing a path to the ark for Yaz?'

'She's going to be busy with four shiphearts, assuming she can actually make a fourth,' Mali said.

'But Yaz said there were a hundred of these Pelarthi, maybe more, and other things too.' Thurin looked at his hands. 'You're asking me if I can deal with six. Maybe. But not a hundred. We can't do this.'

'It's not going to be easy,' Mali agreed. 'But if we don't do it, what's the alternative? Waiting's not going to make it any easier. Besides, I can walk the Path. But if I'm going to do that it's got to be for more than six. Six would be a waste.'

'Can you, though?' Thurin asked. 'Didn't you just blast that shaft open when we were escaping' – he waved an arm at the priest Thurin occupied – 'her?'

'That was weeks ago,' Mali said.

'It feels like it was an hour ago. Two at most.'

'I suppose we'll find out when we need it.' Mali crossed her arms and fixed him with her dark eyes.

Her resolve shamed him. 'I can handle six.' Thurin straightened himself and gathered his resources. He flexed his ice-work muscles. 'We need to think this through – plan our attack – hit hard and fast so th—' He broke off. Something was tickling the outer edges of his water-sense. 'There's more coming!'

Quina drew her knife. 'How many?'

'Hard to s—' Thurin closed his eyes and pressed the heel

of his hand between them. 'Lots! More than a dozen. Moving fast.'

'If they're being reinforced we should go back and look for a way around,' Quina suggested.

'We can't.' Thurin shook his head. 'They're coming up from behind us!'

'What do we do?' Quina stared back at the darkness, fear making her eyes wild.

'Forward,' Mali said. 'We go forward.'

Thurin felt closer to Quina's fear than to Mali's determination but she was right. The newcomers would have to navigate quite a few twists and turns to reach them. Better to deal with the smaller group on its own while there was time. And perhaps the second band were bound elsewhere. He hoped they were not heading for Yaz. 'Let's go.'

Thurin took the lead, moving ahead into the dark, relying only on his water-sense to know where the enemy stood, and on his hands to follow the wall. He could smell their smoke now.

Another branch of the tunnel revealed the glow of lanterns ahead. 'Seven,' Thurin muttered as one body of water resolved into two close together.

'Easy,' Quina hissed at his side.

Thurin reached out to find her and moved his hand to her shoulder. He could feel the tremble in her. 'Let me do my thing. It'll be harder if you're in the way.' He pressed on as she drew breath to object. 'You can step in to save me when I need saving.'

'I've got your back.'

With a confidence he didn't feel, Thurin marched towards the light.

He laid eyes on the Pelarthi before they spotted him

emerging from the darkness. There were seven of them arranged around a crumbling chamber with a roof that vaulted a good ten yards and a floor that lay littered with fallen sections of fluted columns, half as wide as he was tall. A temple to some out-of-favour god perhaps, one that had been worshipped in an incarnation of Verity built before the faith of the Ancestor came to dominate.

Four men, three women, all tall and sturdy, armoured in mismatched pieces, a breastplate here, a chain shirt there, a round shield blazoned with an eye, a kite shield sporting the tree device seen on nuns' outer coats. The women wore face paint and carried spears. Two of the men held bows, one a sword, another a battle-axe.

The archers were furthest back, hardest to reach, but he went for them first, sending one tumbling across the floor, the other striking a fallen pillar and reeling back, bow lost, arrows scattered.

Thurin kept walking towards them, unarmoured and empty-handed, praying to the Gods in the Ice that his strength wouldn't fail him.

The women came to the fore, arms back for the throw, spear tips catching the torchlight. Thurin caught hold of all three as the first began to launch her weapon. He pulled their feet out from under them, setting them onto their backs.

The man with the sword and the one with the axe charged him, their braided beards bouncing on their chests as they ran, shouting challenges. Thurin fought off his instinct to fell them at a distance. The focused ferocity of the pair, the light in their eyes, the eager anticipation of slicing his flesh, spilling his blood: all of it ran a cold terror through his veins. But he waited, raising his crossed arms before him as if to ward off their blows.

They were almost on him, the axeman in the lead, when

411

he reached for them. At such close range Thurin had the strength to do what needed to be done. He threw his arms outwards with a fierce cry of his own, and the two men shot to either side, torn from their path, to hit the walls with bone-crunching force. One managed several convulsive twitches before exhaling his last and lying still like the other.

The archers and the women with the spears were on their feet again. Thurin yanked their legs from under them a second time and ran towards them. Already his stomach was churning from the sight of the damage he had wrought on the first two men. He had no appetite for more killing but even if he could speak their language these did not look like people he could talk out of a fight. And if he were to let them go how long would it be before he faced them again? Or worse: how long before they crept up behind him?

This time his cry was more despairing than fierce. The first of them to regain their feet was a tall blonde woman clutching her spear. Thurin slammed her into the ceiling with an effort that made his brain ache, then guided her descent so her broken body hammered down onto one of the archers as he rose.

The other man tried to loose an arrow from the floor but Thurin yanked him across the ground into a section of pillar, scything down another woman as she stood. For a second she lay where she'd fallen, weaponless, clutching her leg.

'Don't make me do this.' Thurin spoke through gritted teeth.

The woman's fierce eyes met his through the wild tangle of her hair.

'Stay down.'

Instead she reached for her knife and screamed with rage. Thurin shoved her. Hard. Smashing her back into the chunk of shattered pillar behind her. Her head and neck hit first with a fatal crunch.

The last woman he slammed into the nearest wall.

For a long moment a blessed silence reigned. Thurin hung his head, unable to look back to see the expressions on Quina and Mali's faces. Then the man he'd crushed beneath the woman's falling body began to groan, one leg moving as if trying to drive himself out from under her.

'Dear gods, let it end.' Thurin didn't want to kill the injured man, or leave him to suffer, or listen to his pain. He didn't want to be where he was, doing what he was doing. Remembering the second party coming up behind them, Thurin reached out with his water-sense to see how long they had. Not long – they were coming fast.

'We have to keep moving. The second band will be here soon.' Thurin had to raise his voice above the injured man's increasingly loud moans.

Theus limped past him, clutching a sword taken from one of the Pelarthi. Almost casually he stuck it through the neck of the injured man.

'With any luck nobody heard—' A shout from the direction they were facing cut across Theus's words as the first of a crowd of Pelarthi mercenaries burst into the chamber at a run. 'Shit.'

The tunnel down which the Pelarthi advanced glowed with the light of lanterns and torches. It seemed that scores of them were on the move. Perhaps the entire force Yaz had seen. If so, it meant they were closer to the ark than Thurin had imagined, and in no end of trouble.

The torches' naked flames tugged at Thurin's mind, and even at this range the closest of them began to flare, the fire appearing to his gaze like holes punched through the world into an inferno normally hidden beneath the surface. His flame-work had once melted a miles-long shaft to freedom after being banked within him his whole life. That had been months ago and Thurin released in one burst everything that had built inside his bones since then. Torches blazed so high that their flames roared against the ceiling. Lanterns exploded in blossoming flame, the oil so eager to be consumed that few drops reached the Pelarthi but every one that did immediately set fire to what it touched, be it flesh, clothing, even iron.

For a few bright moments the far end of the chamber became a firestorm from which Pelarthi staggered, howling and in flames. Dozens of them dying, some screaming, others unable to. Tears filled Thurin's eyes. Some large piece of him wanted to say sorry, wanted to take it back.

To Thurin's amazement the Pelarthi to the rear came on even before their comrades had stopped burning, leaping over blackened corpses, the smoke and stink swirling in their wake. The fierceness in their eyes prompted Thurin back into action. He reached into the mass of their attackers with his ice-work, heaving them to one side. The combined weight of the foe meant he couldn't manage the killing force he could apply to a single body, merely enough to send them stumbling, falling over each other, causing bruises, a twisted ankle or self-inflicted injury. Several of the forerunners kept their feet and came on at speed. Quina flung herself among them, blurring under the swing of a sword and rising in a flurry of stabbing. The warriors, already off balance, fell, clutching their wounds, blood spurting between pale fingers. But more were already coming, a second, thicker wave detaching itself from the entangled crush of figures on the tunnel floor. A spear hissed out of the crowd, perhaps targeted at Quina – but she was no longer there and it flew wide of Thurin.

'We can't hold them!' Thurin lifted four men and hurled them back into those behind them. A handful still managed to come on, jabbing at Quina with spears, forcing her to focus on evading them rather than fighting back.

'How many are coming behind us?' Mali shouted from back where she stood with Theus.

'Lots!' Thurin felled a swathe of Pelarthi but they would all rise again and he was weakening already. 'Not this many though!' The hairs on the back of his neck tingled – a warning that Mali was close to the Path, about to call on its power. If she blasted those in front of them more would come and she wouldn't have a second blast to clear a way through the band at her rear, leaving them all trapped.

Quina screamed and spun clear of two women with spears.

'No!' Thurin's blood ran cold.

Quina clutched her side with one arm, down to a single knife, the fierceness in her eyes replaced once more by fear. Suddenly, protecting her was the only thing that mattered. Thurin reached out an arm, shoving both women away, but with an unreal, almost magical swiftness an arrow sprouted from the back of his extended hand, the point coming to a halt just inches from his eye.

'Theus! Use the Path!' The pain from Thurin's wound had yet to reach him. He waved the other hand, slapping down two axemen closing on Quina. She pushed away her shock at being injured, dropping beneath a spear thrust, spinning as she did so to sweep away the attacker's legs.

'I can't.' Theus reached Thurin's side, snarling through Krey's mouth. 'It's just her body I've got. Quantal talents are harder to use than marjal ones. I'd need her mind to—' An arrow hit Krey's shoulder, spinning her round and Theus broke off into cursing.

More Pelarthi spilled over their fallen comrades, charging towards Thurin. The feathered end of the arrow rested in Thurin's palm as if growing from it like some strange flower. The red shaft protruded from the back. Suddenly it hurt. Still not as much as he thought it should – but a lot.

'Run!' Quina passed him, favouring one side but still faster than her pursuers.

Thurin turned from the flood of attackers towards the darkness of the tunnel that had brought him to the chamber. Theus was already hobbling towards the exit but Thurin's water-sense told him more were rushing at them and would break from the shadows before he even reached them.

Thurin drew level with Mali and grabbed her shoulder with his good hand. The shock that ran up his arm nearly threw him clear – she was so close to touching the Path that she practically glowed with it. 'Blast them!' he shouted.

'Which way?' Mali kept her eyes on the Pelarthi chasing him.

'I . . .' Thurin knew they were lost. Terror took his voice. This was the end that had been waiting for him the whole length of his journey. The fight that could not be won. Yaz wasn't here to see him die. He reached for Quina with his ice-work just as she entered the darkness of the exit. He pulled her back as figures began to emerge. He wouldn't watch her be killed. They would fight side by side. Guard each other's backs. Go down together. As she slid back to him, swearing loudly, the fear that had been in him vanished.

'It's over.' He turned her towards him. 'Let's give them hell.' He turned to face the charging Pelarthi with Mali. 'Keep them off my back, Quina.' He swept his arm – he didn't need to, but somehow it helped focus his power – and hammered the foremost warriors back into their comrades. It wasn't enough.

Mali glanced back.

'Mali! Hit them now!' Thurin picked up an armoured warrior without touching him and swung him like a club. The effort drove a spike of pain behind his eyes. A spear found the narrow gap between him and Mali and passed between them, ruffling her habit. Another flew over his head and he silently thanked the gods that the Pelarthi's aim wasn't anything like as good as he imagined it should be. 'Mali!'

Still she didn't turn.

We're dead. We're dead. We're dead.

A gerant warrior, over seven feet tall, clad in chainmail with a battered iron helm on her head, leapt over the man Thurin had felled last, behind the swing of the Pelarthi he was using as a weapon, and brought her broadsword down in an overhead slash.

Frozen, Thurin waited for death, only for an explosion of sound and flashing metal to detonate just above his forehead. The gerant's blade slid off another and deflected to the side, just missing Thurin's shoulder. Figures in habits passed him, swords flickering. Any Pelarthi not on their feet slumped to the ground with mortal wounds. The rest fell back to the rear of the chamber where the continuing flow of reinforcements was massing.

'Nuns?' Thurin looked around at the newcomers. Many of them had their hair flowing loose like Mali and Quina. 'Novices?'

At the head of them strode a nun as tall as Thurin, a woman with blue eyes, so pale that she might almost be Ictha. She was old, maybe fifty, but the scars seamed across her hands and face hinted at the lessons the years had taught her.

'Mistress Blade of Sweet Mercy Convent,' Mali whispered.

Quina came to stand at Thurin's other shoulder. 'Now you'll see something.'

At the front of the Pelarthi a lean man of uncertain age stepped from the ranks. His polished breastplate and thick furs hinted at seniority. A livid scar tracked from the black thicket of his beard up past the corner of his left eye. He held a small iron buckler on one arm and in his left hand a curved blade half his height. He called out to the nun in a language that was neither that of the north nor that of the Corridor.

'No,' Mistress Blade replied in an even voice. 'Leave while you still may.'

The man sneered and replied in a harsher tone, indicating the scores around him. Many held spears ready. Some had their bows raised, arrows halfway back to the point of release.

'The Ancestor teaches us to love, and that all men and women are our brothers and sisters.' The convent's sword-mistress stood with two other nuns in red habits. Behind them were a dozen novices around Mali and Quina's age, two a little taller than Thurin and more heavily built, though something about their faces suggested they might be gerants of an age with the others. 'The Ancestor teaches love, but we are imperfect vessels and to my shame I must admit that I want to fight you. So please, take your wounded and go. My soul is stained enough as it is.'

The man laughed and barked a command. A bow twanged and too quick for thinking Mistress Blade had an arrow in her hand, not through it like Thurin but captured, held a few inches from her throat. In the next moment more archers loosed and spears sliced through the air. The nun moved like Quina but faster, somehow consuming the space between her and the enemy as if it were a single step. Spears and arrows missed their mark, deflected, divided, defeated in the air, and the woman was among the Pelarthi, a whirling dance of death punctuated by bright arterial sprays and sliced-off screams. Her two Red Sisters followed in her wake, scarcely less deadly.

CHAPTER 43

Quina and Thurin

'Wenna! What are you doing here?' Quina chased after the blonde novice as she advanced behind the three nuns.

'Got out before the Inquisition arrived.' Wenna kept focused, sword raised, ready to cut stray missiles from the air or engage any Pelarthi who got past the Red Sisters.

'We left to help Mistress Blade investigate Mistress Path's death,' said Hellma, towering beside her.

'Officially,' Niome said, dark hair trailing as she ducked quick as lightning to run through a wounded Pelarthi on the ground.

'Where's Yaz?' This from Gully. The skinny novice was the only one of them to look scared, her long mousey hair in mud-splattered disarray.

'Gully!' Kola yanked the mousey girl aside with a gerant's strength as a Pelarthi came at them, spear levelled. Wenna dived forward and to the side, slashing the Pelarthi woman's thigh.

With Mistress Blade and the two Red Sisters to the fore, the convent party carved a deep line into the Pelarthi ranks.

Soon the novices began to engage the mercenaries spilling out on the flanks of the three nuns' attack. Thurin knew next to nothing about armed conflict but he had watched the Broken's warriors train in the ice caves and could tell that the mercenaries here were far more deadly. Unlike the Broken, the Pelarthi were veterans of life-or-death conflicts against armed foes, something that even the convent's training was hard-pressed to match. The novices did, however, have a much higher concentration of gerants, hunska, and marjals among their number. Their innate talents, combined with the serenity trance in which they fought, and the years of relentless training under Mistress Blade's uncompromising eye, meant that even these half-complete nuns could hold their own. At least for a while.

One girl fought wrapped in a seemingly razored smoke of darkness. Another, with red hair shaved almost to the skin, exploded the Pelarthi's lanterns and sent the fire coiling up around men's bodies in bright spirals, her power better controlled than Thurin's. Quina followed, despite being told to stay back, cutting injured Pelarthi's throats with none of the squeamishness for killing Thurin had suffered.

Mali stayed at Thurin's side and Theus rejoined them, surveying the carnage with a grin.

'We're both one-handed,' Mali observed.

'Let me.' Theus reached for the arrow still impaling Thurin's palm.

Thurin pulled his injured hand back, but too slow to stop Theus catching the bloody shaft.

'Don't pull it through!' Mali shouted. 'They smear stuff on the feathers. The wound will sour!'

Theus rolled his eyes and grabbed both ends. 'Bite down. This is going to hurt.' He slid the shaft back through the hand a little and without warning brought his knee up to

snap it. Before Thurin's scream had time to escape Theus
whipped out the broken half still transfixing his hand. 'Now
do your work!'

The agony in Thurin's palm only eclipsed the pain in his
head for a few breaths. Thurin's head felt as if it might fracture if pushed with his ice-work even a little but he squinted
at the battle and began to shove any Pelarthi who looked
like they were gaining the upper hand on a novice. With the
Red Sisters it was too hard to tell: every engagement was
over before it started. The trio of killers flowed through the
battle as if they owned it. Even with the novices it was difficult, especially to his untutored eye, to tell who was in
immediate danger. But some cases were clear-cut. A man with
an axe looming at the unguarded back of the blonde girl.
Perhaps another novice would have saved her, but Thurin
shoved the man into the swing of a nearby woman's sword
and saved that hypothetical other novice the bother.

The fight raged, a bloody and ugly thing, despite the grace
of Mistress Blade and her sisters. Whatever skill was on
display, the net effect was the lethal application of sharpened
metal to flesh, and as they advanced the nuns left butchery
behind them. One of the gerant novices fell too, the red-
haired one, and Quina, lacking the discipline of the other
girls, went to cradle the big girl's head amid scores of scattered Pelarthi corpses.

'Kola! Get up!' She forgot her green-tongue and tried to
lift the girl. She would have been speared by a tall mercenary
had Thurin not slapped him down with the invisible hand
of his ice-work.

More novices fell back, wounded, three at least, but the
Red Sisters were still carving a crimson path through the heart
of the Pelarthi and it seemed even hardened warriors such as
these could not fight on much longer in the face of such losses.

Thurin, Mali, and Theus advanced through the carnage, still behind the line of battle, until they drew level with Quina.

'She's gone, sister.' Mali reached her hand down to draw Quina up, leaving Kola lying in her blood. 'The Ancestor has her now.'

Back down the tunnel it seemed that the Pelarthi were breaking, pulling back. The victory had been hard won and Thurin slumped in relief. He knew he couldn't have fought on much longer. Without the nuns' help there would have been no chance.

'I think we've done it.' He looked down at his almost pristine finery, cast-offs from Mali's near-royal brothers, feeling that despite his efforts it looked as if Quina, torn and bloody in her habit, had made the greater contribution. 'I think they've done it. Those Red Sisters are magnificent . . .'

But, even as he spoke, something thundered through the midst of the conflict, scattering both Pelarthi and nuns. The novices fell back, breaking from their melee with the few mercenaries left in the nuns' wake. The thing charging towards them was like Zox but far more fearsome. Just as Yaz had described, an iron hound of similar design but with scythes as claws where Zox had daggers, and with a gaping jaw whose most fearsome contents were not the rows of gleaming steel teeth but the gory remains of one of the three Red Sisters. A second hound, equally large, thundered along behind it, ignoring a rain of blows from Mistress Blade's sword.

CHAPTER 44

Thurin and Quina

Thurin stood paralysed in the path of the charging hounds. He could find no water in them to take hold of and would have lacked the strength to lift them even had they been filled with it. In an ice cave he might have brought the roof down on both but not in these tunnels through the earth.

The two metal beasts, one still champing on the torso of a Red Sister, came straight towards him, effortlessly shouldering aside any of the novices too slow to clear their path. The tide of the battle had turned in a moment: even though their swords had left deep cuts on the thick iron bodies, Mistress Blade and her surviving companion had nothing that could hurt the hounds.

For the second time in the engagement Thurin knew himself to be moments from death. With the hounds scant yards away he got hold of himself and lifted his body smoothly from the dogs' path, drawing Mali with him. Quina he abandoned to her own quickness. Theus he just left, lacking the strength to easily lift him too or the inclination to risk damaging himself in the effort.

424

'No!' Without warning he lost his hold on Mali while she was less than a yard above the ground and well within the reach of those jaws. It was as if she had simply vanished as far as his ice-work was concerned, though he could see her drop to the rocky floor. He focused all the strength not being used to keep himself aloft and tried to close the hand of his ice-work about her, but it was like trying to hold air.

Mali hit the ground with an impact that reverberated through the chamber, as though she were a vast boulder rather than a slightly built girl, and as if she had fallen from some great height. Her flesh shone with the power of the Path she had just walked, its radiance bleeding through the darkness of her skin. Her face, often smiling, always in control, now lit with fierce emotion, her eyes becoming beacons.

'Just run!' Thurin shouted. He knew that Krey had destroyed Zox with a blast of Path-energy but he'd also seen the devastation. None of them would survive the explosion.

And Mali did run. But directly at the foremost hound. With remarkable speed she threw herself at her foe – only to be snatched from the air. She vanished into the beast's cavernous mouth. A heartbeat later the second hound crashed into Theus, scooping him into its jaws.

'No!' Thurin dropped to the ground, overburdened by defeat. 'Mali!'

The lead hound swivelled its head towards him. Its outsized jaw clamped shut, presenting an interlocking mesh of bright steel blades, blood leaking between them. Quina attacked it, her daggers hitting so fast that they almost made a continuous note rather than a series of clashes, but they did nothing more than scratch the creature's armour.

The second hound also turned, two severed legs falling from the corner of its mouth. It cocked its head to one side, as if wondering what possible threat Thurin could pose – a very human gesture.

Once more Thurin prepared for the end. He could neither fight nor outrun these creations of the Missing that Seus had corrupted. Quina fell back, panting, to stand at his side. Behind them the sounds of fighting lessened as one of the two forces involved began to run out of bodies.

'I'm sorry.' Thurin reached for Quina's shoulder.

The closer hound's jaws opened a fraction with a metallic squeal of protest. Brilliance bled out between the teeth. A moment later a bright fist punched out through them, sending steel shards tumbling through the air. With blinding speed Quina deflected an unknown number of them. Thurin felt the wind on his throat as her hand snapped past him.

The hound's jaws squealed again and its maw opened wide, revealing Mali with her feet just inside its lower teeth and her shoulders against the roof of its mouth, head bent, as if carrying the weight of the world. One more straining heave and the lower jaw snapped off. Mali reached down the dog's throat with a burning white arm, her hand clearly grabbing something vital and tearing it loose. In the next moment the mechanism collapsed, rolling almost gracefully to its side.

Mali stepped clear, the Path's glow fading from her.

The second hound turned its head towards her, blood still flowing out between its lower teeth. Whatever power remained in Mali it wasn't going to be enough to repeat her destruction of the first one. Thurin braced for action.

Instead Mali met the hound's dark gaze, her own eyes returning to their usual blackness. 'Theus?'

The dog opened its mouth and shook out Krey's gory remains. Its jaw snapped shut again.

'Is that you, Theus?' Mali asked.

426

And without speaking the dog gave a slow nod.

Behind him the last of the Pelarthi broke and ran.

Mali felt it first. The two surviving nuns were helping the novices bind their wounds when Mali turned from her one-handed attempts to help Quina deal with the spear slice across her side, and stood to face the tunnel by which they had reached the chamber.

'She's coming.'

'Yaz?' Thurin asked.

A nod.

'Best be ready to move then.' Thurin forced himself back to his feet, using a section of pillar for support.

Quina, with her wound half-bound, returned to the trio of novices laid out at the far side of the chamber, each on her back with her hands folded across her chest. Thurin glanced at the dark tunnel where Mali watched for Yaz and then went to join Quina.

'Friends of yours?' He still found it hard to feel that a month had passed for her while he took two strides towards the time-star. He believed it but he didn't *feel* it.

Quina nodded, lips pressed into a pale line, tears cutting two clean paths down through the blood spatter on her cheeks. Not trusting herself to speak she pointed first at the biggest, the novice called Kola, and then at a slight girl with long brown hair, sticky with dark blood on the side where an axe had caught her between neck and shoulder. Quina made a noise that might have been a name or a broken sob: 'Gully.'

'I'm sorry.' Thurin set a hand to her shoulder. He knew enough to know that he had nothing useful to say.

'There!' Mali called from the tunnel mouth, but when Thurin looked he could see nothing.

A moment later Erris emerged into the light of scattered lanterns, the tunnel still dark behind him. 'Yaz is coming. She needs a clear path.' He surveyed the carnage, his face hardening. 'Do you know the way?'

Mistress Blade stood. 'A hundred Pelarthi came here to stop us. If they came from the ark then we have our trail.'

'They did,' Quina said. 'Or at least Yaz saw scores of them waiting there.' She paused, looking worried. 'I hope that's the same group, not *more* waiting for us.'

The iron dog closed its grinning jaws and began to stomp towards the rear exit from which the Pelarthi had emerged.

'Theus?' Erris asked, raising a quizzical eyebrow.

Thurin nodded. 'Theus.'

Behind Erris a hard, shifting light cut through the darkness. 'Better go – she's coming.' He cast an eye over the novices before approaching Mistress Blade. 'We need to protect Yaz's back. She's vulnerable to a Pelarthi spear or anyone who comes at her with a weapon of sufficient range.'

The nun favoured him with a steely, appraising stare and then gave a sharp nod. 'Sister Tower.' She pointed to a side corridor. 'Wait until Yaz has passed then follow on. If anyone comes at her – kill them. No retreat. The novices will go with you.'

For a moment it looked as if some of the novices might protest, but none did, not even the blonde girl spattered with blood, one of the few whose eyes still held the same eagerness they did when Mistress Blade first led them into the fray. Frowning, Mali began to cross the chamber to join her class.

Quina glanced back and forth between Thurin and the novices gathering by Sister Tower, seemingly unsure whether Mistress Blade's instructions extended to her and similarly divided about where her loyalties lay. Thurin wanted to ask her to stay but somehow his mouth was too dry to say the words.

Quina felt Thurin's eyes on her. She wanted him to tell her to stay but instead he just stood there seeming to wrestle with his doubts. Her gaze came to rest again on the three dead novices. Kola had been so fierce in the battle and Gully so scared, but they'd both died the same, surprised, and then alone, and then gone. Quina wanted to be with Thurin, not with the green-landers. Even if they couldn't save each other she wanted to be with him at the end.

'I'll go with Erris and Thurin and Theus. This is what we came to the Corridor to do. We might not have known it at the time. But it is.' She looked back at Mali. 'Mali too. She's bled on the ice, Mistress Blade. In this, she's one of us. Besides, we need her.' She met the nun's eyes, her tone had been respectful but she let her determination show on her face, promising a fight if she didn't get her way.

Mistress Blade let her raised eyebrow settle and gave a grim smile. 'On your own head be it, Novice Quina. You're untrained and somewhat of a liability. But the high priest did declare you blessed and, as such, if you demand it I will give you sufficient rope to hang yourself. Please use it for another purpose.' The nun turned to face Mali. 'Novice Maliaya, you have proved my oldest friend correct in her final judgement. As Sister Owl said, you are, my dear, a formidable force of nature, and though the Ancestor may speak through all of us at times, down here it is through you that the Ancestor speaks loudest. I have no doubt we will need you to the fore when we face what lies ahead.'

'We're agreed then.' Erris inclined his head in thanks and then indicated for the rest of them to go after the dog.

Quina wanted to ask how Yaz was coping, whether she

needed help, what she could do – but the edge of the ship-hearts' combined aura scraped against her mind and suddenly she was following Theus. Whatever stresses and strains Yaz's load was placing on her, they were hers to carry alone. Some burdens can only be borne on one pair of shoulders, just as some hurts can never be shared, and some worries must be endured in silence.

Thurin watched as Yaz advanced behind them, wrapped in the light of the stars, unapproachable, unique. She'd been elevated by her gift and by the destiny that had been imposed upon her, elevated to a level that was both more and less than human. It was hard to think about her as the girl who had fallen into his world, or who had drawn him from it into hers. It was hard even to look in her direction. So many hopes rested on her even if the millions who would suffer didn't know her name or even that she existed.

Thurin focused on what lay behind him, his mind full of feelings both too complicated to untangle and yet easy to understand.

Quina hurried to stand beside him, her torn habit flapping, a symbol of a faith that said everyone was connected, all of them branches on a great tree of life. Thurin supposed that might be true, but it hadn't stopped him feeling very alone during the moments in the chamber he was just leaving. Moments when he felt sure he was going to die. He glanced at Quina and she favoured him with a nervous smile, lacking the fierce confidence she'd had before the battle. He tried to smile back. He might have been alone at the sharpest end of things, but even so, he was glad to have had Quina with him.

Mistress Blade proved equal to her promise, tracking back along the hasty advance of the hundred and more mercenaries.

The muddy trail of their boots provided a clear path to follow along much of the route. In other spots more skill was required to find the exit point from a half-flooded tunnel or to trace their path by lantern light across a slope of crumbling debris.

Erris went to walk beside Theus, and Thurin followed behind the pair with Quina at his side.

'Back in steel.' Erris eyed the jaw-hound's fearsome teeth.

'Anything would be an upgrade on Krey.'

'Steel is better than flesh?' Erris sounded doubtful.

'Better than broken flesh.' Theus worked his jaw. 'I'll trade this box of bolts in once the ark's open and I can get back in my own body.'

'Your own? Aren't you a copy, just like me?' Erris held his hand before him, studying his fingers as he flexed them. 'They copied you, carried you between the stars and printed you on a clone. Isn't that what you said?'

Thurin was about to speak, to tell Erris that it no longer mattered what his water-sense told him. They were friends and a man stood before him, whatever he was made of. But Quina raised her hand to his mouth and gave a quick shake of her head.

'It's all relative,' Theus growled as they walked on, negotiating the rubble-strewn floor.

'But—'

'Don't ask me for answers, boy. Are we *real*? Did we die? I was a king once – did you know that? An emperor . . . briefly. In a time even more primitive than yours. My bones are in a vault on a different planet under a stone statue of me. I didn't even make it to twenty-one.'

Erris raised his brows. 'I was twenty-one when—'

'I threatened the first computer I met. With a sword. So don't come to me for science.' He looked up at Erris. 'Do

431

you feel real? To you? That's all that matters. *I think, there-fore I am.* Well, here we are. What do you think?'

'I think we should do our best to—'

'We're going to find this Seus and fuck him up. We're going to leave his ruin in our wake, rub his name from the histories. Don't waste your time angsting over whether your heart's made of muscle or steel. Anger's real. Want's real. We make real. It doesn't make us.'

Thurin exchanged a glance with Quina. Whatever Theus had lost when the Missing divided him he clearly hadn't lost all humanity. And Quina had been right: Erris needed to hear these things from someone who shared more of his path than she or Thurin did. Thurin might have talked about friendship or love proving Erris's essential worth, but anger worked too.

The group wound on through a labyrinth of crumbling passages until in time they came to tunnels of much better construction and then to a large iron-bound door that, when broken open by Theus, gave onto the white-walled corridors that Yaz had described – ones with perfect corners and panels of white light in the ceiling.

'This is the outer ark,' Erris said. 'We're in the upper levels of the undercity again.'

'Who's waiting for us?' Mistress Blade asked. She fell in beside Thurin and Erris, apparently unwounded despite her habit being sliced and torn in a dozen places.

'Yaz saw Seus there, wearing a body three yards tall. So there's that,' Erris said. 'If we're lucky then you've already dealt with everything else she saw and there's no more.'

'I'm not feeling lucky,' Thurin said.

'And he'll be out to kill us?' Quina asked from behind them.

'He wants everyone but Yaz dead,' Erris said. 'And if it

looks as if he can't win he's going to try to kill her as well. We want the same thing he does – free access to the ark, only he needs Yaz for that. But by now he might have decided to go back to his earlier plan: kill her and force the ark open on his own, however many more years that's going to take.'

Thurin sniffed and wrinkled his nose at the familiar human stink. The corridors that Mistress Blade now followed had clearly been home to Seus's mercenary force – who, unlike his mechanical servants, required both feeding and sanitation. A long gallery bore many signs of recent occupation, including scores of bed rolls and packs. Their owners either lay dead back in the chamber of broken pillars or had fled.

The area previously occupied by the Pelarthi extended several hundred yards but eventually gave onto a corridor less sullied by the passage of muddy boots. The whiteness of the walls made Thurin feel like a stain, acutely aware of the dirtiness of his limbs, the wild tangle of his hair.

To either side of the passage, entrances gave onto small chambers offering no other exit. In the distance the corridor appeared to terminate in a dead end.

'I don't like it,' Quina muttered. 'We could get trapped here.'

'This whole place is a trap,' Thurin said. 'We've come five thousand miles to stick our heads into it. Best get it done.'

Ahead of them Mali, walking with Mistress Blade, paused at one of the entrances. 'Look. Yaz's gate.'

The haze-gate lay slightly tilted, just as Yaz had described it, leaning against the rear wall of a chamber scarcely large enough to house it. Thurin deduced that the dead end must in fact be a white door, behind which lay the chamber with the silver-steel door to the inner ark set in its floor.

They advanced cautiously, Mistress Blade in the lead, followed by Erris and Mali, then Theus in the body of the jaw-hound, then Thurin and Quina. It felt like too few to bring against a creature such as Seus. Even Mistress Blade, who could cut a red path through an army, had had little to offer against jaw-hounds.

The remaining yards of the corridor vanished beneath their feet with a feeling of inevitability. Mistress Blade set her hand to the door and then struck it with the hilt of her sword. The effect didn't appear noticeably different than if she had hit the wall instead.

Theus moved up, squeezing Erris and Mali to either side. The dog dipped his over-sized head and brought his steel snout to within six inches of the barrier. Then with a violent thrust of his legs he butted the door. The impact left no mark but as he drew back for a second attempt the door slid smoothly upwards, revealing the room beyond.

The chamber was bigger than Thurin had imagined, with five other doors at regular intervals around a circular perimeter. Seus stood before a huge silver-steel door set into the floor at the centre. Just as Yaz had described, he stood head and shoulders above the tallest gerant, a perfectly muscled specimen of humanity, clad in a white tunic, his curling hair and short beard equally white. His eyes shone with an inner light such that even at this distance Thurin could tell they were a startling, dangerous blue. Beside him Eular looked like a small child, hunched in the blackness of his robe.

Seus folded his thick arms and Eular stepped forward as if to bar the newcomers' passage. 'Neither of us expected you to get this far. Truly, you would have made a formidable army.'

'You.' Mistress Blade stepped through the doorway, sword before her. 'You are no priest of the Ancestor.'

'Of course I am.' Eular seemed to study the woman with his empty sockets. He made the sign of the tree in the air before him. 'You think I have to agree with your abbess on matters of policy just to qualify as faithful?'

'You serve a false god.' The nun angled her blade up towards Seus's head.

Lightning cracked the air, arcing all around Seus to strike the silver door and half a dozen spots across the ceiling and floor, thick streamers of power dazzling as they seared out from his fingers.

But Eular just smiled that same warm smile that Thurin had grown up knowing – the smile of a kind man, a wise man. The storm behind him died down. 'We spend all our years on the short journey across the Path, from life to death. You and I journey across the width of the Path, but as a people we follow its length. The Ancestor stands at both ends. The Ancestor watches us from before the flight – before the shiphearts first beat their rhythm. That is the Ancestor of singular form, the origin, the alpha. And the Ancestor watches us from the end, from beyond the death of stars. That is the Ancestor of singular mind, the destination, the omega.'

'Don't dare to quote the scriptures at me!' Mistress Blade snapped, but the venom had drained from her voice.

'A priest may quote the scriptures, surely?' Again that smile, full of warmth and humility and humour. 'But did you listen to the words? Do you ever listen to them now or have you repeated them so often that they have divorced from meaning, becoming mere sounds? The Ancestor is the alpha and the omega. There is no start without an end. Seus has come to give us that ending, to show us the omega, to bring our journey to its close. There's no value in anything eternal. It's the very fleetingness of our lives that makes them precious.

435

All leaves must fall in time. Seus is the reaper – the Ancestor's blade.'

Eular turned his eyeless gaze on the rest of them as they came through the doorway behind Mistress Blade. 'The truth is that I wore my priestly robes today in case any of Abbess Claw's coven slipped out beneath the descending heel of the Inquisition. I reasoned that, together with the serenity trance that the good sisters carry into combat with them, my robes would win me the time I needed.'

Thurin saw it then, the slight twitching in Eular's fingers as he talked. As if they were being restrained from plucking at invisible threads.

'Really,' Eular said. 'Mistress Blade would have been better served by some more of that righteous anger, and by flinging two handfuls of throwing stars the moment the door opened. She teaches to strike first and to strike fast. But she hesitated and was lost. In any event, it's been a long journey but you have reached the end, the omega.' He reached out, grabbed a handful of nothing, and twisted it. 'Show them, sister.'

And faster than blinking, swifter even than Quina, Mistress Blade spun round, driving her sword through Erris's chest.

CHAPTER 45

Yaz

The weight of four shiphearts was nothing like four times the weight of one. It felt closer to four hundred. Each seemed to drag on the other, a multiplying effect that meant simply keeping them aloft proved so taxing that adding the business of walking on top became nearly impossible. The weight rested on Yaz's mind. The closer they were to her the easier it was to lift them. She could have taken all four in her arms and carried them in a basket with relative ease, but to have them so close would break her. She needed the distance between her and them just as ice needs distance from a flame if it's not to melt.

In the shifting glory of their combined light the drab tunnels became a playground for the imagination, a many-coloured dreamscape. She walked on, with the stars closer than she wanted them but far enough away that maintaining their orbits took all her strength. Ahead in the distance she could see Erris, guiding her through the maze of passages. The voices talked about him. They weren't inaudible mutterings now, or even pervasive whispers, they were loud, clear, and speaking every unworthy thought she normally kept buried down in the voiceless blackness at the back of her mind. These were the thoughts that might escape in rare moments of weakness but were always swiftly stamped upon. Now they sounded reasonable, speaking over her own protesting narrative and claiming that they too were her, just different aspects of her personality, no less worthy of respect or audience.

Yaz set her focus on the business of putting one foot before the other, employing the same tenacity and endurance that had seen her across countless miles of open ice. She didn't need to see Erris in order to follow him. The four shiphearts opened the threadscape to her as never before and everything she needed to know lay written there. She could see Erris's threads and knew that they had joined those of Thurin, Mali, Quina, and others. She could see the record of a battle as she passed through a large chamber, not just in the corpses scattered among fallen pillars and the broken shell of a jaw-hound – she saw the details of the fight: who had died, where, when, how. Burned flesh, blood gushing, the stink of death: nothing was concealed from her save by her need to focus on moving forward. If she let them, the threads would tell her tales so vast and interlaced that she would be lost among them, no more than the wind following the ice in an endless chase.

She came in time to the white and unnaturally regular corridors of the outer ark and walked again down passages that Theus's people had made, towards one of the centres of her own distant ancestors' power. The threads told her what lay ahead. They showed her Theus hammering his stolen steel head into the white door. They showed her Seus and Eular beside the door into the ark, the one she intended to open. The threads had so much to tell her, a flood of knowing, enough to drown in. She saw Mistress Blade as a fierce-eyed child, staring defiantly up at the Dome of the Ancestor on the day some previous abbess had brought her to the convent. Her name had been Elli Shoesmith. Novice Elli. Sister Leaf. Mistress Blade. That abbess had been Abbess Quartz, it had been her birthday, she'd broken her fast on oatmeal and— Yaz forced herself back to the present, forced herself to take another step.

She passed the gate through which she had arrived on her only previous visit. The threads pulsed with information – too much even when she filtered out everything but the present.

They showed her Thurin Ice-Spear of the Broken, true to his name, sharp and fractured, and they showed her friend Quina Hellansdaughter, and they showed the bond that had grown between Quina and Thurin, the bond that had always been growing.

She saw Mali without seeing her, and saw through her. Even as the shiphearts were breaking her mind apart they were giving her a glimpse through the eyes of the gods. Mali, Maliaya, she who would be Mistress Path of Sweet Mercy Convent if she lived past all the futures that saw her die this day. She who would carve her own legend across so many years. Yaz saw the day her friend was born and the day she died.

The threads sang with the story of Lestal Erris Crow, the echo of a boy who had died so long ago, but who was so much more as well. They showed her how Eular had twisted Mistress Blade's perception and caused her to drive her sword through Erris's chest, a foot of gleaming steel emerging between his shoulders, black with his inner blood.

'No . . .'

Seus came forward. Yaz didn't need to look over the heads

of her friends just beyond the doorway a hundred yards further on: the threads gave it all to her. Erris falling, Mistress Blade's sword flickering free. Eular following at Seus's heels, pulling the nun's strings, Quina shocked into stillness . . .

The gate. The gate in the side room to her left. By the light of four shiphearts it looked like a bottomless well painted in swirling colours for which there was no name. It hauled at her with the same pull any fatal fall exerts on the eye. Just as the threads wanted to drag her away down myriad paths with no end, the gate also promised an infinity of destinations.

The conflict in front of the ark's silver-steel door was tumbling back towards her. Even now Seus was bowing his head to pursue her friends into the long passage. Shouting reached her, cries of pain, or anger, or both. The sounds cut off the moment she stepped into the shimmer of the gate. With a grunt of effort she drew the shiphearts forward to join her in the no-space behind the gate.

Instantly hundreds upon hundreds of exits beckoned. Every gate on Abeth still able to receive her offered its hand, eager to draw her across such trivialities as distance and spit her out in a new location. The shiphearts began to orbit her and in their light she saw that each gate cast a legion of shadows, all threaded together, the whens overlaid upon the wheres, and behind those a legion of fainter ghosts, an infinity of maybes. Somewhere out there was a maybe in which Erris had not just taken a sword through his ribs. One of those gates opened onto a world where her youngest brother had never been taken from the boat, a world where the regulator had passed her into adulthood without comment, maybe even a world where there *was* no Pit of the Missing.

Yaz ignored the possibilities. The sheer scale of choice weakened their temptation. To leave behind what she'd been given would dilute every experience she'd ever had, make every choice seem arbitrary, something that could be undone, rewritten. Life wasn't a game. To play it like one just cheapened . . . everything. Besides, to navigate those possibilities successfully required more skill and more strength than she had.

'Show me.' Taproot had used his gates as an eye on the world, their sight opening in any place he commanded. 'Show me!'

Yaz pulled the shiphearts closer until her skin screamed and her mind roared with so many voices that she could hardly hear her own. Even so, the image she'd sought swam into view. The ark's silvery door, the wide six-doored chamber.

Yaz had pulled Mali from the open ice using a haze-gate and a single star far smaller than a shipheart. Now, with the power of four shiphearts, she attempted to push herself through without needing a gate. She had passed through walls before using the paths left by the Missing. Now she was making her own path.

The pressure built behind her, thrusting her forward into something that refused to yield. More pressure, and the pain grew. It was as if she felt the rock itself grating away at her flesh as she forced herself through the space it occupied. Every instinct screamed at her to stop – just as the body refuses when a hand is pressed to a fire or to the point of a blade. One advantage, though, of a mind that is already filled with voices, each howling for attention, is that instinct must wait its turn to be heard. Yaz pressed on, her insistence growing even as the rock resisted her with greater force.

She tumbled forward, crying out her agony, and fell to the ground, resting her face against the coolness of a white stone floor. Her blurred vision cleared and across the chamber, through a doorway, she could see Seus's back, hunched in a corridor too low to accommodate his full height, smaller figures fighting around him.

Above her, filling the chamber with the changing patterns of their light, four shiphearts followed slow orbits around a common centre.

Straining not to cry out, Yaz pushed herself to her knees, and then stood up. She'd made it. She was at the doorway. The next part would be hard.

CHAPTER 46

Thurin

Up close, the speed with which Mistress Blade fought proved so terrifying that it robbed Thurin of the ability to move even at his own sluggish pace. The nun had turned and thrust her sword through Erris in a single fluid move occupying less time than a finger snap. In the next beat she whipped the sword back out and leapt at Thurin. If not for Quina's blindingly fast dagger throw the nun's blade would have taken Thurin's head. As it was she somehow understood her peril, rotated in the air, and knocked the tumbling knife aside with her sword. Instead of being decapitated Thurin found himself flying back from the impact of an iron-hard foot in his solar plexus.

Only Thurin's ice-work saved him from being wrecked by his collision with the wall. He would have slid helplessly to the floor but for his mind's ability to support him without help from the muscles usually tasked with the job. Black dots swarmed before his eyes as he tried and failed to draw air into lungs that had been rapidly emptied by Mistress Blade's kick.

Quina ran suicidally at Sweet Mercy's weapons instructor while behind the nun Seus loomed larger than the nightmares that he'd so often inspired in Thurin. Fast as Quina was, lightning was faster. A searing blue-white bolt crackled from Seus's fingers and Quina's arms flew wide. She toppled with a short, unnatural scream, making no attempt to cushion her fall.

Mistress Blade came at Thurin, her single-minded intensity terrifying. Thurin wanted to protest – he wasn't the most dangerous of her foes – but perhaps it was easier for Eular to turn her against a man she hardly knew than against novices she had taught. She might even think she was protecting them.

Theus interposed his iron bulk but the nun didn't waste time pitting her blade against his armour again. Instead her speed made a mockery of his fearsome jaws as she leapt, set a hand to his snout, and vaulted the length of his body to reach Thurin.

Ice-work saved him again. Still unable to draw breath and rapidly losing his grip on consciousness, Thurin managed to grab hold of the nun as her feet touched the ground and thrust her violently at the ceiling. Even as she accelerated towards the stonework the nun twisted, managing to interpose her sword arm to brace against the impact while at the same time pulling a handful of gleaming throwing stars from inside her habit.

Thurin saw his death on the wicked points of those jagged projectiles. He tried to pin her throwing arm but the blood was thundering in his ears and the world was growing dim.

'Mistress Blade!' Mali's voice, not pleading but sharp with reprimand.

Thurin's breath began to hiss back into agonized lungs. He realized that he had dropped the nun and that she stood above him, sword in hand. He'd blacked out for a moment. Amazed that he wasn't dead yet, Thurin lifted his head.

Seus had passed by Erris and Quina, who lay in an untidy sprawl, a dark stain on the white floor, unmoving save for the smoke rising gently from her. Eular, worryingly, was nowhere to be seen. The giant avatar had come through the doorway, bowing his head to fit inside the corridor whose ceiling was a good ten feet above Thurin. Theus was charging at him. Mali stood close to Mistress Blade, looking towards Seus rather than the woman who had killed Erris. Though now he looked, Thurin realized that Erris was starting to move. Thurin wheezed and used his ice-work to haul himself upright, gathering his strength to throw Mistress Blade back, but instead finding that she was helping him up.

The nun held him by his wrist rather than his injured hand. 'Your pardon. The false priest had my mind until Novice Mali broke his hold.'

A deafening clang rattled the corridor as Theus's charge met Seus's swinging leg. Before he knew what was happening Thurin was shoved violently back against the wall. Mistress Blade dropped into a leg sweep, cutting down Mali. Thurin might have thought her under Eular's control again but for the blurred passage of the jaw-hound passing through the space all three of them had occupied some small fraction of a heartbeat earlier.

Back beyond Seus, beyond Erris, now jerking brokenly to his feet, and beyond the unmoving Quina, an awful light appeared out of nowhere. Four stars revolved in a halo of poison-green, forge-red, white-gold, and black-violet, and beneath them stood Yaz beside the great silver door. How she had bypassed their battle Thurin couldn't say, but he knew she needed every second they could buy her.

The heavy thud of Seus's approaching footsteps filled the space left as Theus's metal body clattered to a halt somewhere down the corridor. Mali backed away before the giant, horrified. Mistress Blade threw herself forward, slashing left and right. Her sword cut effortlessly through Seus's illusionary skin to strike what must be the blackened metal skeleton that Yaz had seen beneath. Whether or not her weapon caused any damage Thurin couldn't see, but certainly Seus didn't seem hurt by the blows. He reached for her with a hand large enough to close around her head and shoulders. She sliced at his fingers and dodged back.

Thurin still had difficulty breathing and the agony in his chest made him certain that the flying kick had, at the very least, broken some ribs. He let the wall support him as he tried to suck in the air he needed. Past Seus's advance he kept getting glimpses of Quina still lying where she fell, and of Erris, now standing, unsteady on his feet. Thurin tried not to think about what Quina's immobility meant. The thought that she might be dead kept finding different ways past his barriers, threatening a hurt much deeper than any kick could deliver. He knew he ought to be angry: a foaming rage should be driving him into the fray with greater vigour than ever, but all he could feel was a sorrow that threatened to drown him and rack his aching lungs with sobbing. More to focus on something else than in any real hope of success, Thurin extended his water-sense in a search for anything he could use. Even Pelarthi bodies could be used as missiles. But none lay in range. Only abandoned waterskins further down the corridor. He reached for those instead, starting to haul them towards him.

For a time, while Thurin pushed himself away from the wall and managed to support his weight using just his legs, Seus and the nun fought in the corridor. The giant lunged for Mistress Blade several times and twice tried to stamp on her, but her speed meant that she was never in any real danger. For his part, Seus paid little attention to her swordplay, enduring the cuts and thrusts with no obvious discomfort.

Worryingly, as the fight continued, sparks began to build around Seus's hands, growing in intensity and frequency, arcing between his fingers, crackling through the air. Several times lightnings crackled along the nun's blade, causing her to cry out and drop the sword, only to recover it an instant later before it hit the ground. The discharges were clearly taking their toll on Mistress Blade but were also slowing the build-up of the lethal bolt Seus was working on.

Erris, who had earlier equipped himself with an axe from one of the fallen Pelarthi, now came running at Seus from behind. He moved awkwardly, but less so than almost anyone else would after having a yard of razored steel rammed through their chest. Thurin tried to call out for Erris to keep back, tried to tell him this foe was beyond them. Wherever Erris kept his heart and whatever he was made from Thurin considered him a friend – that bond had been forged across so very many miles on the ice – and Thurin had lost too many friends.

Erris came on, swinging his axe. The weapon struck Seus in the spine, driven by a strength many times that of even the largest gerant. Thurin couldn't see the impact but he saw the bright shards of the blade as they came spinning through the illusion of Seus's flesh. For a moment the whole projection flickered, revealing the blackened metal skeleton within, barbed bones wreathed with electricity.

Back along the corridor Theus raised his iron body, accompanied by a loud grating sound as the joint on a damaged leg ground metal against metal, making sparks. On both sides of the jaw-hound half a dozen Pelarthi waterskins came slithering down the passage towards Thurin, drawn by his will.

'Enough.' Seus spoke for the first time. His handsome face flickered briefly out of existence, revealing the grinning skull beneath. He extended his arms towards Thurin, Mali, Mistress Blade, and Theus, hands splayed and full of lightning. In the arcing light his fingers were bones one moment, flesh the next. 'Time to die!'

CHAPTER 47

Quina

Quina had thrown herself towards Mistress Blade without any expectation of surviving the encounter. But the woman had killed Erris and was one broken moment from doing the same to Thurin, and the denial that filled Quina outshone her anger and her sorrow, both of which were vast and growing. A 'No!' had been about to burst from Quina's mouth, but more than that, her whole body was that 'No', and the fact that the nun was unstoppable was not going to prevent Quina from placing herself between her and Thurin.

Deep in her quickness she sensed rather than saw the lightning. She felt its promise tingling across her back and heard the fierceness of its crackle building around Seus's fingers. She even tried to throw herself out of its path.

The bolt struck her and Quina lost all sense of her limbs. Mistress Blade's advance on Thurin was replaced by a midnight laced with thunderbolts. Bright streamers of electricity filled her vision, arcing across her sight again and again, then once more, after which a velvet darkness claimed her. There wasn't any pain. Her worries left her. Memory waned. All that remained was a fading sense of being.

And that had been that until, when she had all but gone, a single golden thread snaked across her blindness, bright but paling even as it drew its path. Anything that offers direction in such a place carries a certain compulsion, but Quina had sunk deep into the numbness that might, she decided, be all that forever was. Had it not been for her defining curiosity Quina would have let the thread fade away, but it niggled at her, and before it could vanish entirely she followed it.

'Yaz?' Although it was just a thread it felt of Yaz. The Ictha had led her out of darkness before. Had Yaz reached into this ultimate darkness to draw her out once more? Perhaps she had even stolen the power from Seus's bolt, or how had it failed to kill one girl?

The thread became a cord, a rope, a road, and suddenly an awful light. Quina jerked back into consciousness with a scream. The pleasing numbness of forever was replaced by the agony of burned flesh and the pressing madness of ship-hearts so close that her mental anguish competed with her physical distress.

She crawled. Away from the light, towards the doorway. She could see little but her scorched hands against the floor, clawed in pain. Her limbs twitched and trembled, trying to support her weight and drive her forwards.

As the distance from the shiphearts increased, Quina's blurred vision began to resolve the objects before her. Erris was somehow getting back to his feet, clutching an axe. Seus had moved out into the corridor and was stooping over someone. It was hard to see who was standing up to him but Quina doubted they would last long.

A blur at the corner of her eye made Quina swing her head. Eular was there, close to the doorway but to one side so that nobody on the other side could see him. Erris didn't appear to have noticed him either, though robed in black and pressed to a white wall, the priest seemed hard to miss.

As Erris closed on Seus from behind, raising his axe in both hands, Eular lifted his own hands. Quina had seen the gesture before. Quantals used it when preparing to gather power from the Path and fling it at their target.

Quina couldn't ignore the searing agony of her wounds so instead she channelled that pain into action, convincing her legs that the hurting might be outrun if only they could drive her fast enough. She rose from her crawl into an uneven sprint. Abandoning the lessons she'd learned in Mistress Blade's class, she simply hammered into Eular, sandwiching him between her speed and the wall.

Both of them recoiled and fell, both crying out. Quina, who truly had outrun her pain, now found that it had caught her up again, returning with a vengeance that was beyond belief. Eular, showing his years, clattered to the ground awkwardly, groaning, his robe flying.

Quina rolled with a groan of her own and managed to kick the old man in his eyeless face. It was his turn to crawl, making for the doorway where Erris now stood holding the haft of his axe, the blade shattered and gone. Quina reached out and snarled her fingers in Eular's robes. He tried to pull away but she hung on. It was all she had left in her after her charge.

Blood poured from Eular's broken nose. He wriggled free of his robe, and crawled away from Quina. He got to his feet, using the wall as support, abandoned by the calm he needed to reach the Path. Instead he sifted his fingers through the air as if gathering gossamer floating just beyond sight. And as he did it, he too became somehow beyond sight, not transparent like ice or colouring himself to camouflage his body against the whiteness, but just avoiding notice. He succeeded to such a degree that despite Quina knowing he was there she couldn't manage to focus on him and found herself instead staring at the wall and the memory of him as he'd been standing there.

In the corridor Seus's flesh shuddered, there one moment and gone the next, leaving only his nightmarish skeleton. In those instants Quina could get a clearer picture of her friends. Mistress Blade seemed to have regained her senses and to be pitting herself against the giant, if that could be called sense. Thurin and Mali stood just behind her, and Theus was, for some reason, a dozen yards further down the corridor, but pounding forward. Overlaying all this were the streamers of lightning arcing from Seus's hands as he prepared to hurl a bolt that would bring them all down.

Quina cast about for any weapon she might throw, any action she could take to help them. She was about to scream for Yaz to abandon her great task and save the others when she saw lying on the floor, close to the black sprawl of Eular's priest-robe, a white box. A bone-white box, a cube with rounded corners. Taproot's white box. She snatched it up in her burned hand, flipped open the lid and rasped through her damaged throat, 'Help us!'

Taproot's image shuddered into being above the mouth of the box, a miniature version of him, wild hair, sharp, dark eyes, eloquent long-fingered hands given to plucking at the air like a quantal thread-worker. Whatever he had to say, though, was obliterated by the crash of an almighty thunderbolt resounding in the corridor.

CHAPTER 48

Thurin

The water tore itself from a dozen skins, flying through the air in glistening ropes at Thurin's command. If only the blood inside people's bodies obeyed his will so completely Thurin would have been able to kill scores with a glance.

Thurin threw the contents towards the dazzling energies arcing in Seus's hands. As he did so Mistress Blade hauled Mali out of Theus's path. The jaw-hound came on less rapidly than before but still far faster than Thurin could have run on his best day.

Thurin had no idea if water could extinguish lightning but the stuff seemed to have something in common with fire, and since moving water was his only relevant skill, he determined to try. With a yell he poured it all forwards.

Seus released his lightning in one thick bolt that made what had hit Quina seem a mere spark. The blinding flash of energy looked set to reduce all of Seus's enemies to stains on the walls. Somehow, though, mere water seemed to divert the great majority of the bolt's force from its path, causing it to seek the ground through Theus as he thundered through the liquid ropes towards his target.

The blast of sound convinced Thurin that the roof had fallen in, but in truth it was the force of the thunderclap that threw him to the floor. Stray forks of lightning struck all of them, but Theus took the great bulk of it and what crashed into Seus's legs was a smoking iron shell.

Lightning arced through Mistress Blade's sword and she dropped it, cursing. But somehow, despite miniature lightning bolts burning half a dozen holes in her habit, she caught the weapon in her other, unburned, hand before it hit the floor. Mali flew back, shocked, twitching, and fell without trying to brace herself. Thurin, also on the ground himself and also burned, drew what water hadn't been turned to steam and soaked himself in it. For a moment, while lying there in the water's cold embrace, gazing half-stunned back down the length of the corridor, it seemed to Thurin that he could see Eular. The priest was disrobed and hobbling away, smoke rising from scorched patches on his tunic. While Thurin watched, Eular began to fade away like a vision as he turned towards the entrance to the room where the haze-gate lay.

'Thurin!' Mali was trying to pull him to his feet. He sat up, groaning, and through the fog he could just make out Seus still fighting to keep his balance after the jaw-hound's mass struck his shins. The ruin of the jaw-hound had wrapped inconveniently around one leg. A figure that had to be Erris caught hold of Seus's other ankle as the giant shifted his weight. With unnatural strength Erris hauled upwards. In the next moment Seus fell to his knees.

The giant reached back, caught Erris around the chest, and dragged him to the front, lifting him off the ground one-armed.

The warning glow beside Thurin was enough to let him know that Mali had somehow found the centred calm she

454

needed to reach the Path for a second time in the same hour. In part it was testimony to the supreme quantal talents that had drawn Taproot's eyes to her in the first place; in part it reminded him just how close they were to four shiphearts that had been boosting every blood skill, from the hunskas' speed to his own ice-work.

'Let him go!' Mali released her power and Thurin turned away to avoid a face-full of shrapnel.

The blast filled the corridor with even more sound and light than Seus's thunderbolt had. A shockwave sent Thurin back to the floor yet again. He rolled and lifted himself, trying unsuccessfully to shake the dizziness from his head. Through the clearing mist Thurin could see that Seus had been thrown from his knees to his backside but, horrifyingly, he still had hold of Erris and there was no sign of damage on him anywhere.

The self-declared god showed a fierce grin amid the white curls of his beard and yet again his blue eyes lit with electric fire. Only when he tried to rise did Thurin see that he had at least been injured, his right arm hanging limp. Behind his head, like a distant halo, the four great stars made slow circles above the centre of the chamber. Seus flickered and for a moment his flesh vanished, showing the sparking metal structure beneath, one arm still glowing red hot where Mali's blast had hit it. Past the god's black bones Yaz could be seen, a small dark figure amid the glory of the shiphearts' radiance, still struggling to unlock a door that had been sealed before any of the ruins layered above it had even been thought of.

CHAPTER 49

Yaz

Where rebuilding a shipheart had been a mind-bendingly complex puzzle of many moving parts, the opening of an ark appeared to be a fairly simple thing. Each shipheart was a key. Using the eyes of a Missing the four locks were self-evident. The task then was to insert each key and to turn them together. It wasn't a task that was difficult because of intricacies. It was a task that was difficult because it required enormous strength.

Mage Atoan had possessed almost none of the talent needed to control a shipheart. He had moved both his shiphearts, the functioning one and the time-star, using ingenuity. His chains allowed even someone called off the street to drag a shipheart if required. Mere mechanics, however, would not suffice in the matter of opening the ark. The turning of the keys was not a matter only of physical rotation but of internal manipulation, not a subtle one but a brute force revolving of the stars' internal state.

Yaz struggled with the burden of the shiphearts, struggled to turn them, struggled to retain her sanity as their combined aura threatened to tear her mind into a dozen warring fragments.

All of this to the accompaniment of the screams and cries and clashes of a fight in which her dearest friends pitted their vulnerable flesh against the cruel metal avatar that Seus had built to oppose them and now wore to battle.

Out of the corner of her eye she saw Erris impaled on Mistress Blade's sword. She didn't even need to look: the threads relentlessly poured the details of the fight into her breaking mind. She saw the present, endured repetitions of the past, and was horrified by the possible futures in which Seus variously ripped apart, fried, and bludgeoned her friends to death.

While she fought to position and turn the keys her attention was dragged towards a building threat against Quina. She somewhat weakened the bolt of lightning that felled the girl but had to focus on her task thereafter. A booming crash as Theus got kicked down the corridor punctuated her efforts. Seemingly only moments later a deafening thunderbolt shook her concentration, hollowing the returning jaw-hound and felling the others but somehow failing to kill them, as if Theus's final attack had channelled away most of the power.

Each interruption set Yaz back. At the cold core of her shattering mind she knew that she should ignore the fight, abandon her friends, and focus on the greatest good. Some of the voices in her mind actually screamed that message into the face of her denials. But Quina wasn't moving, and even with her sanity crumbling Yaz held to the truth that had brought her out of the Pit of the Missing. Some sacrifices may be acceptable in a morality of weights and scales, but any success gained through such acts will rot from the heart outwards and you will ultimately have lost what you sought to preserve. And so, letting her progress slip, she turned towards her friend. Boosted by the power of four shiphearts, she reached into Quina's smoking corpse and caught hold of her spirit, showing it the way back to the flesh. As the girl drew an agonized breath Yaz returned to her work.

Yaz repositioned the stars above her, ready to send out once more towards the four locks set high on the chamber walls at the compass points. She began to move them, twisting as she went, using the whole of her being as a lever with which to apply the necessary mental force. She knew she couldn't afford to get involved in the fight with Seus. If they couldn't defeat him then these moments, while he was engaged in combatting the others, were all the time she would have in which to unlock the ark and allow Taproot in to ensure that the defences would keep the city minds out forever. She would need the needle from Quina. The required elements of Taproot – his expertise in matters of the ark – were held within it. But that problem would have to wait till the door was opened.

A blast in the corridor tore Yaz's attention back to her friends despite her resolution. She recognized its signature. She had felt Mali's feet pounding the Path. In a last desperate defence Mali hammered Seus with a coruscating beam of Path-energy that knocked him onto his back. But slowly, horrifyingly, the avatar managed to sit back up even from this devastating blow.

Quina was on her feet again, but barely able to stand. Erris had similarly managed to return to the fray despite his injury, but was now in Seus's vice-like grip, his body being crushed by forces that could reduce boulders to powder. Seus stood, smashing Erris against the wall as someone might brain a fish against a rock. Yaz's friends were spent. In moments Seus would kill them all. She had time for one great effort to press the keys into the locks and turn them. Just enough.

Then Erris cried out. He didn't open his mouth. He didn't

make a sound. But Yaz heard his pain, carried by the threads that joined them. Not the pain of nerve and bone but the pain of impending destruction, the pain of a long life rapidly terminating, the swallowing of sorrow and defeat.

Yaz let the stars fall.

The Path lay all around her. The river that flows through all things had become an ocean and the power it offered was limited only by the ability of her body to channel it into the world of things, the world in which such energies would reduce steel to scrap, rock to rubble, and men to mist. Yaz, who had once feared to touch more than the palms of her hands to the river, now dived into the ocean. She rose from the bright depths, gasping, shuddering back into the world, potent with power, pregnant with it. The four ship-hearts that lay around her acted as a wall, a barrier that confined her, allowing her to own the energies she had taken and not fly apart into every possibility that presented itself.

With a cry of release Yaz threw all that she had taken at Seus's back. The strike erased all illusion, leaving his grim skeleton to fall in burning pieces.

Trembling, she hoisted the stars again, raising her arms as if she were pushing them back towards the ceiling. Once more she resumed the struggle.

'*I am Ictha.*'

CHAPTER 50

Quina

Seus's thunderbolt filled the corridor with smoke and for long moments Quina could see nothing but grey, billowing clouds. She hobbled forwards, curled around the pain of her burns, her ears ringing from the clap of thunder. Taproot's ghostly image was saying something but she couldn't make out the words.

As the first thinning billows of smoke reached Quina she realized that it was wet – not smoke at all but mist. Figures resolved ahead of her in the fog. Seus was on his knees but he had hold of Erris and swung him violently into the wall. A blinding bolt of Path-power burned through the mist, hitting Seus and throwing him back. Quina saw the metal skeleton, its bony fingers still clutching Erris. The illusion of flesh reclothed him and amazingly the avatar started to rise again.

A second, far more powerful blast of Path-power seared over Quina's shoulder, exploding into Seus's back and leaving her temporarily blinded. By the time she'd blinked away the bolt's after-images all that remained of the mist was shreds hanging in the air. Seus's bones were scattered and smouldering around the wreckage of the jaw-hound that had housed Theus.

Erris still had the cage of black metal fingers around his chest and lay slumped not far from the sprawled and motionless figure of Mistress Blade. Thurin was on his knees clutching his bloody right arm, perhaps torn by flying metal. Only Mali remained standing, still glowing faintly from her last contact with the Path.

The momentary silence was broken by a grinding sound. Not far from Quina the closest of Seus's bones appeared to be joined by a thin grey network of root-like extrusions that were now, against all sense, slowly contracting, and in doing so were drawing the two pieces together. Quina looked out across the field of debris and saw with horror that the grey roots were spreading everywhere, reaching out from every bone, questing across the stone floor in search of other bones. She picked up a shard of Erris's broken axe and hacked at the closest roots, trying to sever the connection between two pieces of Seus's leg. The stuff resisted her efforts. Threads of it even tried to cling to the steel shard, leaving its bright surface etched with attempts to burrow into the blade.

Quina looked back towards Yaz but she had already returned to her work with the shiphearts and the strain on her face was awful to behold. Perhaps it was a trick of the shifting light but Yaz also looked more bruised than could be accounted for by the fist fight days earlier . . . something Quina knew from bitter experience to be the first outward signs of inner demons emerging and finding their own voice.

Taproot was still talking. '. . . reassembling himself. This is the Missing's technology – primitive drawing on the source won't defeat it. It's point—'

'What will?' Quina shouted, holding the little man just inches from her mouth.

Taproot blinked as if she'd soaked him in spittle. 'As I was saying: If you look at the bottom of this storage unit—'

'Box! It's a box. Why do you have to complicate everything?' Quina turned the box upside down, aiming Taproot's projection at the floor. Jutting from the centre of the box's base was a silver needle, twin to that she still had stuck through the collar of her habit but firmly part of the box. She inverted the box again and barked at Taproot, 'What do I do with it?'

'Quickly – as I've been telling you – find any part of the structure—'

'His bones?'

'Yes.' Taproot sighed. 'If you like. Find any bone that still has the core exposed . . . the marrow, if you like . . . and insert the needle. This box contains many things besides me, including some ancient but still potent algorithms with which I can arm myself, and if we invade en masse we should be able to overwhelm him locally.'

Quina was far from sure what Taproot was talking about but 'overwhelm' sounded good enough. She ground her teeth in anticipation of agony, then with a scream of determined rage, sprinted as best she was able into the midst of Seus's wreckage, stepping with rapid precision to avoid tripping on the roots that were even now drawing the bones back together.

She saw that not every part was being salvaged. Some bones had been melted into a brittle black slag, others broken into complicated shards. On these she saw what Taproot had been talking about. Beneath a thick exterior of black metal each bone had a core of liquid silver that in some places had run from the shattered ends to form gleaming droplets on the floor.

Some of the roots were even questing towards Erris where he lay, motionless and at broken angles. Some instinct told

Quina it would not be good if those roots reached him and fed on his essence. 'Get Erris clear!' She shouted the words at Mali and Thurin. Fast as she was, there wasn't time for two tasks. She had to stop Seus's resurrection.

Quina reckoned that she was injecting Taproot as a kind of poison to disable Seus's healing process. She needed to find a bone with an accessible core that was being incorporated into the new structure. Even as she looked, though, the damage on individual bones in the rooted mass was being repaired. Rents in the armour were being knitted over by the grey tendrils and hardening back into the blackness of the original. She darted at one candidate only to have the wound she planned to infect close as she got there.

The bones were mending themselves rapidly. All around her Quina heard the grating of metal on stone as the grey threads tightened, pulling each bone to its partners, reconstructing Seus around her. Some leg bones were already standing, supported by tented threads. Thurin had righted himself and stared at her helplessly. Mali shouted for her to get clear as the threads tightened around her in a web that was rapidly becoming inescapable.

'No you don't. I'm not letting you win!' Quina's eyes flickered back and forth, hunting for any fracture not yet closed.

She leapt as if her burns were nothing, angling herself over the slanting threads and landing hands first, careless of how the rest of her body crashed back to the floor. She'd seen her chance, a long gash in a thighbone, knitting closed all along its length but still revealing the faintly gleaming marrow. She slammed Taproot's box against the wound even as the last fractions sealed shut. Whether the needle had found its mark or crumpled against the iron-hard exterior, she couldn't tell.

Quina hit the floor hard and cried out, losing her grip on the box. For a long moment the pain was too intense for thought or movement. When she managed to stop groaning the first thing she noticed was the silence. She forced open an eye and rolled her head to the side. The threads that had been drawing the bones together now hung loose. As she watched, one of the threads broke and fell to the ground. Two leg bones that had been standing up now swayed within their slack supports, then toppled, hitting the stone with a clatter.

Thurin reached Quina's side, helping her to stand.

'You should bind that arm,' Quina scolded, shaking him off, angry because being angry was better than being scared about how badly he was hurt, scared too of what she'd find beneath her habit when she inspected her burns.

'Blood's my element. I'll just push it back in.' He looked around at the scattered bones.

'The box!' Quina found it quickly enough: it lay on its side, the white material stained black and grey as if it were cloth that had been dipped in contaminated water. The glow it once held was gone.

'Look!' Thurin pointed. A faint smoke had started to rise from the fracture where Quina had stuck the box's needle. Seus might have infected the box but it seemed that the box had infected his bones in its turn.

'All of them,' Quina whispered.

It was true. All of the bones had started to smoke, as if being burned from the inside.

'Yaz!' Mali strode past them, squinting at the harsh light from the chamber at the corridor's end.

Quina felt a moment's shame. All this while Yaz had been fighting a greater battle. Mali led the way towards the chamber; Quina followed with Thurin, already feeling the shiphearts trying to pull pieces of her mind loose.

With a cry of effort Yaz sent the four great stars to evenly spaced points about halfway up on the chamber's walls and half embedded them in the stone. She stood there in front of the silver-steel door casting four shadows, locked in some invisible struggle. Yet even as Yaz's fight seemed to reach a climax Quina suddenly became aware that the dreadful influence of the stars had diminished to almost nothing, perhaps because Yaz was somehow channelling all their power into the task of opening the door.

'Holy Ancestor . . .' Mali fell to her knees between Quina and Thurin.

'What?' Something in the girl's voice scared Quina badly. 'What is it?'

'She's so close to breaking. It hurts her . . . so much.' Tears were rolling down across Mali's cheeks in great drops.

Quina could see it now, just a hint of what Mali must be able to see with her witch-sight. It looked as if a black line had been drawn to divide Yaz's face in two, running across her forehead and along the bridge of her nose to the bottom of her chin. Bleeding from it in opposite directions were stains, all of her demons being slowly torn from each other.

'She's dying!' Thurin raised his hands. 'I've got to get her out of there.'

'No!' Mali gasped, as if in great pain herself. 'She won't let go. You forget who she is. Pull her out and you'll break her in two. I have to help her.' And like that Quina knew that Mali had gone. Her eyes still stared at Yaz but they were empty.

'Maybe the two of them can do it together . . .' Thurin stared at his hands as if he could see his power gathered there, potent but useless.

Quina shook her head. Mali's whole body was trembling, the tiny veins in her eyes had burst, turning the whites

465

crimson, and blood had started to trickle from her nose. 'It's going to kill them both. Neither of them has the sense to quit.'

'What can we do?'

'We can be ready.' Quina was already sprinting towards Yaz.

She reached the Ictha girl in moments. The demon stain covered the middle third of her face, a slow, ragged spread as if they were being torn from the central divide with invisible hooks. Yaz seemed to be staring at her but whether her white-on-white eyes could see her Quina couldn't tell. It was almost as if she were staring through her . . .

Quina spun round and there behind her the air above the silver door was shimmering, twisting the light. The whole chamber felt as if the space filling it were stretched to the snapping point. Even filling her lungs proved hard, as if the air were too busy to comply, too thick with the energies raging through it.

A hand caught hold of her and Quina nearly screamed. She turned, expecting to see Thurin. Instead Yaz held her in a convulsive, unbreakable grip. Something flowed between them, changing Quina's vision. All at once the air wasn't merely shimmering, it was a great vortex of countless threads, not like those that grew between Seus's bones but something fundamental, as if the world were woven from them. The vortex centred on the door, and the door that had seemed utterly unmoved now appeared to tremble. The line dividing Yaz's face was echoed in a bright line that stood in the air with the vortex growing about it, rotating around it.

'Not a line . . .' Quina muttered. 'A crack.'

Yaz strained, every limb trembling, and the crack lengthened, widening at its midpoint. The door beneath also shook, the chamber shuddering with it. With Yaz's senses augmenting her own Quina could tell that they stood on the edge of an invisible knife. They were at the start of the beginning, where the door might open given just one more powerful shove. Yaz gasped her agony and the crack narrowed, shortened, until that other-worldly light bled through it only in the shortest section and then was gone.

'No!' Too late Quina remembered that although Taproot's box lay in ruin she still had that vital fraction of him which could defend the ark from the inside. She snatched the needle from where it had been this whole time, stuck through the collar of her habit. But the crack was gone and she clutched at empty air. 'Yaz?'

Blood ran crimson from Yaz's eyes. Even her pale irises were stained with it. She walked in that dark place where she had gone to out on the ice at the end of all extremity. The place where only the Ictha could go, beyond endurance, held to their course only by a stubborn refusal to die. When Quina and the others had lain in the boat-sled, dying, Yaz had marched on, her vision narrowed to a point.

With a groan that sounded like a last breath, Yaz shuddered, hunched, and once more the crack appeared, smaller than before but there; once more the door trembled but failed to open.

This time there was no hesitation. Quina understood that Yaz had cracked the ark's defences for a moment. Seus had been banished, perhaps to another avatar nearby, perhaps to the distant ice-bound ruins of the city whose beating heart he once was. Either way, he was too far off to take advantage of the weakness. Quina, however, was not. She reached out, driving the needle into the crack even as it winked out of existence.

Across the chamber Mali collapsed. The light of all four stars dimmed. Yaz fell as if her legs had been cut away, and only Quina's swiftness saved her head from striking the silver door.

Thurin, who had across all these fractions of a heartbeat been running to catch up with Quina, now reached her as she stood from lowering Yaz to the ground.

Nobody else was left standing, and perhaps if not for each other's arms, Quina and Thurin would have dropped too, beneath the heavy silence that fell across them.

CHAPTER 51

Yaz

Yaz opened her eyes to find her friends all around her. Thurin knelt at her side, pale, his arm heavily bandaged with strips from a habit, the hand a bloody fist. Mali sat close by, head on her knees, exhaustion in every line, but she looked up as Yaz turned her way. Mistress Blade, cut and torn, was tending to Quina's burns, applying a salve from a small jar. Erris lay beside her, his limbs straightened out. He was the first to speak.

'Stay still,' he advised. 'Let your body take a moment to recover.' He turned his eyes down across the length of his own. 'I'm following my own advice. Might take a while for me, though.'

'I'm sorry.' Yaz's voice sounded raw even to her own ears.

'For what?' Thurin asked.

'I couldn't open it. I couldn't do the one thing everyone needed me to do. The thing I was for.' Yaz's eyes blurred with tears. 'I was supposed to be the one who could. I was supposed to be like the Missing. But there wasn't enough of them in me.'

'You opened it a crack.' Thurin set his good hand to her

shoulder as she tried to rise. 'Quina said she saw a crack in the air and she thinks she got Taproot through. Some of him at least.'

Yaz hadn't seen that. She dimly remembered Quina being there. Seizing hold of her for support. 'A crack? Was it enough?'

Thurin frowned. 'We were hoping you could tell us th—'

'Is . . . it . . . done?' Quina panted past the nun's attentions and her own pain.

'It . . .' Yaz tried to focus on Taproot and find his thread. 'I think . . .' She attempted to sit again and regretted it. Instead she pointed. 'The needle.'

Thurin shuffled across to the centre of the room and after a bit of hunting found the needle lying up against the door. He came back and handed it to her. 'Here.'

'There's a lot less of him in here than there was,' Yaz said. 'And his threads lead to where the crack was.'

'It's done then?' Thurin asked.

Yaz bit her lip, concentrating. 'Some of Taproot got inside the ark. We'll have to hope it's enough to keep Seus out. Theus could tell us more maybe.' Yaz turned her head, looking for him. 'Where is he?'

'Who knows?' Thurin made a grim smile. 'He could have been burned out when Seus fried the jaw-hound. But we've thought him gone too many times before. Maybe he's back in here.' He tapped his forehead. He frowned. 'This doesn't feel like winning.'

'We're alive,' Yaz said. She might have added 'barely'. Her head felt like a bag of broken pieces. The demons that had been tearing from her mind were reintegrating, and it hurt. The shiphearts embedded into the compass points on the walls seemed distant, her connection with them weakened and frayed. Something had snapped inside her with that last push. Some part of her power had broken and it didn't feel as if it would come back.

'Eular?' she asked.

Thurin shook his head. 'I think he used the gate.'

Yaz forced herself into a sitting position, grinding her teeth against the effort required. Taproot's ruined box lay beside her. She picked it up absently and put it in a pocket. 'We need to go after him.'

'You don't even know where he's gone.' Erris watched the ceiling, not shifting from his back.

'I've a suspicion and I think I've learned enough about the gates to be able to tell for sure – at least if I get there soon enough.'

'Really? You want to go now?' Mali lifted her head from her knees. 'Can't we just rest a bit?'

Mistress Blade turned from her ministrations. 'These novices are in no fit state to go anywhere. Quina needs to be carried back to the convent, preferably without anyone touching her.' The nun looked at Thurin meaningfully.

Mali stood. 'Thurin, use your ice-work and get Quina back to the convent sanatorium. Sister Wheat knows burns. I'll go with Yaz.'

Mistress Blade stood too, despite her own obvious exhaustion. She frowned, then opened her mouth, but Mali forestalled her.

'Erris is going to need guarding while he recovers. The convent owes him a debt. You should stay, sister. Swords are not what's needed in matters of gate-travel or to battle Eular.' Mali didn't mention how the priest had seized control of the nun but the unspoken reminder clearly stung.

Mistress Blade nodded slowly. 'We owe him a debt. I will stay. Be careful out there, novice. The Ancestor will be with you.'

Yaz could tell by Quina's silence and the shuddering of her body that the girl's injuries were catching up with her. Thurin had seen it too. It was perhaps the only argument that would have kept him from coming with them. He lifted a hand and Quina rose gently. 'I'll take care of her.' He bit his lip and forced a smile. 'You two take care of each other. That Eular is—'

'We know what he is.' Yaz crossed the distance between them and wrapped her arms around Thurin's lean frame. It felt like goodbye though she couldn't say why. She let him go, blinking away foolish tears. 'Erris—'

'I'll be here if you need me,' Erris said from the floor. 'Well, not right here, but in the city.' He smiled up at her. 'If you need me. No rush. I've been known to be patient.'

Yaz went across to where Quina hung in the air and took her hand, avoiding the scorched side.

'Is this . . . what . . . winning feels like?' Quina winced.

'Maybe.' Yaz frowned. Her failure gnawed at her. She'd been unequal to the task. If she'd had more Missing blood the stars would have aligned for her, the door would have opened, the moon would have been theirs. 'I guess it will have to be.'

'I'm glad we didn't lose then.' Quina grinned, teeth gritted, sweat beading her brow.

'I'll bring Eular down,' Yaz said. 'That will help.' She was still frowning. They'd beaten Seus, protected the ark and thus the moon and thus the Corridor. But even so it felt like half a win at best. Seus was still out there, plotting, patient, immune to the years. Sooner or later he'd get his way and tear the moon out of the sky. If he really had to he could simply wait until Yaz and her friends were dead and try again with whoever came after them.

'Thank you.' Quina squeezed Yaz's hand.

'For what?'

'You know.' Quina smiled, eyes bright.

Yaz tried to answer but found her mouth dry of words. Everything felt like goodbye. She didn't know why. Perhaps something in the threads whispered it. 'It was an honour,' she managed.

Yaz followed Mali from the chamber, burdened with a strange sorrow that made it hard to breathe. Mali felt it too. Yaz knew she did. They were bound. Each step she took put Thurin and Quina further behind her and something in the threads seemed to sing that they would never meet again. She wanted to go back. To tell both of them that she loved them. To tell them to be happy. But instead she set one foot in front of the other and let the tears run down her face.

Mali waited for her before the great circle of the gate.

'I couldn't open that door again,' Yaz said. 'Not even a crack.'

'I know.'

'I'm not sure I could even get those shiphearts out of here one at a time. I think I broke something in me.'

Mali nodded. 'Maybe.'

The gate loomed above them, seemingly an empty ring. Mali cast a dark eye over it. 'Can you tell where he's gone?'

Yaz defocused her eyes and gazed at the centre of the gate, looking for Eular's thread. When she had passed through the gate with all four shiphearts burning holes in her mind Yaz had learned many things very quickly. The gate had unfolded its secrets before her. She had seen that she didn't need a star to open it, how the gates connected, and how many layers there were to the network. 'He's gone back to the Black Rock.' Yaz would have put money on it if she had

473

any. But now it was more than a sure guess: she could see his trail. 'Come on.'

Yaz set her hand to the space encompassed by the gate and, like the surface of a pool, it rippled, then gave. She reached for Mali's hand, and together they passed through.

A moment later and they stood a world away, a vast emptiness of ice crossed in a single step. It felt so profoundly like a cheat that Yaz trembled with faint disgust at herself. The theft of all those white miles echoed in her legs.

'Where are we?' Mali gazed at the rocky ceiling, the walls caked in old mud, all of it illuminated by the star that sat in a niche on the wall before them, a star the size of Yaz's fist, its surface smoke and gold in slow and constant interplay.

'The Black Rock. We're in one of the natural caverns below it that link to Vesta's undercity.' Yaz wondered how the Vesta city mind had managed without Erris. Perhaps on the city's timescale he had barely left.

'Eular.' They said his name together, remembering their quest, which had been momentarily dislodged from their minds by the strangeness and suddenness of the journey.

Yaz sniffed. Her sense of smell had been dulled by the Corridor's plenty, or perhaps just changed. Under the faint reek of old mud was something else, something that took her back to the day she dropped into the Pit of the Missing. 'Blood.'

Mali and Yaz turned together and found themselves facing an old nightmare through the empty circle of the gate. There, in the mouth of the tunnel that led off from the far side of the cavern, Hetta crouched. Nearly ten feet of her, bulked with fat and muscle, wrapped in what looked to be dog-furs, her chin and neck crimson with blood that did not appear to be her own.

'Hetta . . .' Yaz raised a hand, her whole arm so heavy with weariness that she could barely lift it. The day when she'd had the strength and fire to stab the gerant in the foot and escape between her legs seemed very far away. 'We don't have to fight.' Thurin had told them how he'd found Hetta beneath the mountain, free of the demons from the black ice that had ridden her for so long. He'd said she saved him from Arges's star-eyed minion, only to lose her sanity again beneath the creature's stare. Perhaps Yaz could appeal to some spark of humanity still burning inside her.

Mali stepped to stand at Yaz's side, close enough that their arms touched. Yaz didn't blame her. The woman was terrifying.

Hetta lowered her head, staring at them from beneath her heavy brow. A growl emerged, a sound more frightening than a hoola's guttural threat. She bent over and reached behind her. Part of Yaz's mind screamed at her to attack while her foe was at her most vulnerable. She could take the star and hammer it into—

Hetta snagged something and tossed the object into the space between them. Something black and flapping. It landed with a dull thud. For a moment Yaz thought it might be a child's body. But she realized that Hetta made everyone else look tiny.

It was a man. Hetta grunted, turned away, and lumbered off down the tunnel, favouring her left leg.

Slowly Yaz followed with Mali, circling the gate as she tried to get a better look at Hetta's 'gift'. She cleared the gate and stopped dead.

'Eular.' He lay with his face to the ceiling, his black vestments hiding the blood that had poured from the gaping wound where his throat should be. Hetta had been the darkest price paid for his experiment in the pit. She'd served as the sharp edge of the threat with which he whittled the army that would serve his ambition. And in the end she had come back around to bite him.

'I don't feel anything.' Mali approached the corpse and stood staring down at him.

Yaz sighed. She felt sad more than anything. Eular had been the kind of evil that thought itself justified, the kind that thought it was facing the truth of a hard situation head on and acting accordingly. She found it hard to hate him and was glad that she had not had to kill him.

Another sigh escaped her and she turned away. They'd won as much as they could win. But in the end they'd just inconvenienced an immortal. Seus would outlast them. His plans would outlast them. And in the end he would win.

CHAPTER 52

'Should we go back now?' Mali asked.

'Ah.' Yaz had been waiting for the question for a while. Her silent examination of the gate had stretched out and stretched again, all with Eular's corpse their only company. Rather than face giving the unwelcome answer Yaz replied with a question of her own.

'Why do you think it's so muddy here?'

'We're underground.' It was a sensible answer where Mali came from.

'It's all ice above us.' Yaz wasn't entirely correct – the heat from Vesta and from the Black Rock did melt a certain amount of ice and that water did make its way down through the rock, but the caverns were overwhelmingly dry, and certainly there weren't rivers capable of depositing so much mud at this elevation.

'I don't know.' Mali folded her arms.

'Because from this side the gate connects to a place that's underwater.' Yaz frowned and moved her hands slowly along the gate's perimeter. 'And . . . apparently nowhere else.'

'Can't you change it?' Mali looked less worried than Yaz felt.

'I thought I'd be able to. But it's proving tricky. It's very strange. It seems to point back to the Corridor . . .'

Mali sighed and sat down. 'I'll wait then.'

A long time passed. Yaz tried everything she knew and experimented with things she suspected. The gate resisted her. Once more she began to ponder her inadequacies. The Missing had built these gates. For one of their breed the thing would work, the ways would open. A Missing wouldn't collapse under the burden of four shiphearts. But the load had broken her, and now she was trapped in a muddy cave enormously far from everyone she cared for.

'Do you know the way to the Black Rock? I mean the bit where all the priests lived and some of your friends might live now?' Mali stood, rubbing at her legs where the hard floor had numbed them.

'No.' Yaz leaned her forehead against the gate's warm metal. 'This place was underwater when I learned about it. Only Thurin came down here and he floated back out.'

'That Hetta survived the flood. She knows the way up,' Mali observed, not sounding enthusiastic about the prospect of asking her.

'She must do.' Yaz frowned and leaned away from the gate. 'What was she doing down here anyway? It doesn't make much sense.'

'Unless she knew you were coming.' A stranger's voice speaking from behind them.

Yaz turned to see Hetta had returned, stealthy on her feet, the sticky blood drying on her chin, a smile revealing those terrible teeth filed to points. It wasn't Hetta who had spoken though. That was one of the two fearsome old women she was leading in, holding one of their withered claws in each of her own massive hands.

Like Eular neither crone had eyes, just empty sockets. Their filthy rags hardly covered bodies so bony and emaciated that they looked considerably more corpse-like than the old man on the floor. Their wild grey hair straggled in all directions, adding to an impression of madness.

'You haven't seen our sister, have you?' the other asked before Yaz could exclaim. 'We seem to have lost her.'

'N-no.' Yaz watched in amazement as the two women let go of Hetta and started to meander towards the gate, led by Yaz's voice.

'Did you bring the boy?'

One of them stumbled near Mali and, as instinct drew the novice forward for a moment, gnarled fingers snagged hold of her habit. Mali cried out in revulsion before cutting off the sound and managing to control herself. She glowered as the eyeless woman ran her hands over her body, her face, her hair, even the stump of her hand.

'Well?' demanded the other in the harsh rasp that ancient throats often produce.

'She didn't bring the boy, just most of a girl.'

'Unless the boy's hiding from us?' The other woman reached out, sweeping the air.

The first one released Mali and wiped her hands together. 'I was sure I saw the boy come back. I saw him go through the gate. Did he faint yet?'

Yaz wasn't sure how to answer that. 'You mean Thurin?' She supposed he might have fainted. He'd certainly been knocked about a lot. 'I left him behind.'

'The lovers' gate,' crooned the other old woman. 'Hand in hand to the promised land.'

'But where's the boy?' the first complained. 'I saw a boy.' She turned her eyeless stare accusingly in Yaz's direction. 'Haven't you chosen yet? Why not? What're you waiting for? You want to be old and alone like me?'

Yaz exchanged a quick, confused glance with Mali. 'You're not alone – you've got your friend . . . friends . . . did you say sisters?'

The woman hung her head, a grey curtain hiding her face. 'We call each other sister but we're all me. All me. All Agatta. It's the gate, you see? Tricksy things, these gates.'

'Where does it go?' Yaz asked, impatient with the women's riddles. Her gaze returned periodically to Hetta, who hadn't moved since the sisters released her hands. 'I can't change it. I need to send Mali back.'

'It leads where it has always led. And it can't—'

'—be changed. It's broken,' the second woman finished for her sister. Her twin perhaps. Under the dirt they looked the same.

Mali gave Yaz a narrow look. 'We're going back together – you can't stay here.'

Yaz wondered at her own choice of words. She might be far beneath the ice but somehow she could feel it up there, calling to her like Zin to Mokka in the old tales. Rather than answering Mali, she asked the old women another question. 'And where does it lead? Perhaps somewhere close to another gate we could use?'

'It leads where it has always led. To a cave beneath Sweet Mercy Convent.' The old woman gave a smile that might be mocking or perhaps pitying.

'You're lying.' Yaz shook her head. 'This place flooded when Thurin opened it.'

'Such a nice boy,' one of them said.

'We knew he liked water,' the other added.

'Wait . . .' Mali took a step forward, fingers pressing at her forehead.

The twins waited. Hetta waited, glowering at the girls.

'When does it lead?' Mali asked. She glanced back at Yaz. 'You said they lead everywhere and everywhen. When does it lead?'

'Right question.' Both women smiled, showing yellowing teeth and dark gaps in equal measure. The closest woman shuffled towards Mali, who stood her ground. She raised a withered hand to Mali's cheek and stroked her with a strange tenderness, making a shushing sound as Mali flinched away. 'It leads forwards a hundred and one years. When your friend opened it, it led to a day when many people die, Maliaya. Many people. Count the days since then and add them to that day. That's when it leads now.'

'It led to a time when those caves under the convent were flooded?' Mali asked.

The woman nodded. 'There was a lot of water.'

'And now?'

'Perhaps it has all drained away.' She gave a bony shrug.

'Dry or flooded, it's no good to us,' Yaz said.

Mali looked puzzled. She went and stood beside the gate, her hand on the curiously warm metal of the ring. 'We could go to Sweet Mercy. But it would be Sweet Mercy a century from now?'

Yaz looked at the women. Both nodded as one as if they saw her.

'It's a gift,' said the first.

'Of time,' said the other.

'Just remember, that if you do decide to come back you won't—'

'—won't remember.'

'You can't bring memories back.'

'Not without ending up like us.'

Mali stretched out her fingers towards the gap enclosed by the ring, as if expecting to meet some resistance, to feel the door through which they could pass. 'I've been there.' She didn't look at Yaz, only at some distant point in the darkness of the opposite tunnel. 'I've seen it.'

'What are you talking about?' Yaz wondered if the old women's nonsense was catching.

'While I was in the time-star. It's hard to remember now.' She knuckled her forehead. 'I saw myself there. In a Sweet Mercy years from now.' She turned to stare at Yaz with dark-eyed intensity. 'I was so old, Yaz.' Her voice broke. 'So old.' A shake of her head. 'I saw you there. I'd swear it. Only your eyes were wrong and your name was Zole and you hadn't aged a day.'

Yaz found herself taking a step back from Mali, with a smile on her face that didn't know if it was amused, appeasing, or horrified. 'That wasn't me . . . and no Ictha have dark eyes.'

'She knew your name though,' Mali said. 'It made her cry. Like . . . I don't know . . . almost as if it were holy.'

Yaz looked away, through the gate. A gift of time? A different her? Wasn't that why their victory over Seus had been ultimately hollow? It hadn't been enough. *She* hadn't been enough. He would just wait out their short lives.

In the darkness of the opposite tunnel something glimmered, briefly. A green spark. There again. Gone again. It returned and stayed, a pinpoint of green light. Slowly moving. Slowly growing bigger.

'Someone's coming.' Or something. Yaz heard the faint song of a new star, unlike any she'd heard before, but also familiar.

Rocky walls revealed themselves in the emerald glow, a

band of illumination moving closer. Two figures visible now, almost erased by the starlight, one frail, one broad, both strangely familiar, like the star song.

'Sister,' whispered one of the old women behind Yaz.

'She has our eye,' said the other.

'And our tooth,' said the first.

Yaz could see now that the star was set in the socket of a third ancient who might be a triplet to the other two, just as Thurin had described many times out on the ice. She would be carrying a knife made from a dagger-fish tooth. The figure a pace behind her at her shoulder was still hard to make out.

'Ah,' said one of the sisters. 'The boy.'

'I saw her going with the boy. Yes.'

'I saw three. But one,' the first said.

'Like us,' the other cackled.

'One of three,' the first agreed. 'And it turned out to be this one.'

Yaz saw him then – even though the light still blinded her – and she wondered how she hadn't before. 'Quell? Gods in the Sea! Quell!'

She rushed forwards and in moments he'd caught her in the thickness of his arms, squeezing her so hard she almost couldn't breathe. Emerging from the gate had felt nothing like coming home although she had eaten five thousand miles in one step. The yards she'd covered reaching Quell – that felt like the journey home.

'Yaz.'

He was the same. The same solid, handsome, smiling Quell. But different. As if the months since they'd last met, the months that had thrown a thousand changes and challenges at Yaz, had also wrought some invisible transformation on Quell. Perhaps the wind had continued to sculpt him in her absence, but he seemed somehow more . . . necessary.

'How are you here?' she asked.

'The same reason as you, I'm guessing?' He cast his eyes over Mali, then Hetta and the three ancients who now stood together, arguing in whispers. 'The sisters called me.'

'The sisters didn't call m—' But as she defocused her gaze and looked upon the threadscape Yaz saw the threads of her future and Mali's and Quell's all twisted together and spiralling towards the sisters' hands, which were now in constant motion, as if weaving an unseen tapestry.

'What are you doing?' Yaz called out. She detached herself from Quell and strode towards the old women. 'If you've been controlling us . . .'

'Never that!' said the one with the eye, not looking up from her work.

'Against the rules,' the second added.

'Reality's too fragile for rough handling,' said the third.

'We encourage possibilities, dear.' The first raised her head and dazzled Yaz with her green stare. 'But you'll have to put the pieces together yourself.'

'Or not,' said the second.

'She's almost there,' said the third. 'She can taste the answer.'

'She just needs to bite.' The first ceased her weaving and brushed her bony hands together.

As one the three ancients turned their backs on Yaz and the others. Without so much as a goodbye they began to shuffle off, with Hetta looming at their heels.

'Wait!' Quell called. 'You're just going to leave us?'

'I've never had much time for the present.' All three of them spoke together, none looking back.

'Such a thin slice between what was and what will be,' said the leftmost.

'And yet always so much going on in it,' said the rightmost.

'Agatta's going back,' said the middle one.

'To the north,' said the leftmost.

'To the past,' said the rightmost.

'A long, long way,' said the middle one.

The green star dropped to the ground. Abandoned as they walked on.

And the darkness of the tunnel began to swallow them.

'Quell, this is Mali, a green-lander and a true friend,' Yaz introduced them. 'Mali, this is Quell of the Ictha. My . . . a . . . I've known him all my life. He came down the Pit of the Missing to save me.'

'You didn't need saving.' Quell smiled his old smile and it warmed her. He might seem changed in some indefinable way but he was still the same Quell who when she had announced her journey to the south had known himself well enough to stay and known her well enough to let her go. He faced Mali and nodded. 'Welcome to the Black Rock.'

'I'm glad to meet you.' Mali inclined her head. 'Do you know the way out?'

Quell frowned. 'I could try. It's a long way with lots of choices.' He glanced at the tunnel down which the mad sisters had vanished. 'I wasn't expecting to have to retrace my steps.'

'What were you expecting?' Yaz asked. 'Why are you even this far south?'

'The Hot Sea didn't open.'

'The Hot Sea always opens!' Yaz was aghast.

Quell shook his head. 'It's been colder since you left, Yaz.'

'How bad?' Yaz couldn't keep the tremble from her voice. For an Ictha to speak of the cold meant that things were at an unheard of extreme.

Quell shrugged. 'Without the stardust Zeen brought from the Black Rock many more would have died. We decided to come south for a while.' Something about the way he said it made Yaz suspect that his opinion had played a central part in the decision. 'The clan is camped within sight of the mountain. I woke in the night and . . . well, I can't explain it. I followed a crack in the ice by starlight. And it led me to a cave at the base of the mountain. She was waiting for me there – Agatta, the ice-witch.'

'Ice-witch?' Yaz blinked.

'She was on the ice, in those rags.' Quell didn't have to say more. He paused, started to speak, stopped as if worried he might seem foolish, then started again. 'I wondered if Agatta might not really be her name at all.'

'Yes?' Yaz asked, puzzled.

Quell set his jaw. 'I think Mokka called to me and led me here.' He folded his arms as if expecting ridicule.

'Zin and Mokka are just—' Yaz shook her head. Just what? Just stories? She'd learned so much since she left. Zin and Mokka were stories but they weren't *just* stories. They were the Missing, they were Mali's Ancestor, they were who Yaz needed if she were ever to see an ark opened: full-blood Missing who could master four shiphearts with ease. She smiled. 'Maybe it was Mokka.'

She reached for Quell's hand and he gave it into hers. She saw it then, the plan that could defeat Seus. She had been thinking that, after her failure, time was on his side. He was immortal. He could wait. Eventually the ark would fall to him and then the moon and then the Corridor. An individual spent a lifetime crossing the Path, moving from the side that lay before life to the side that lay after. But an immortal followed the Path, moving from the alpha to the omega.

The sisters had said that the gate was the gift of time, but

486

the Ictha didn't need the gate for that. Not as a people. It was in the scripture the nuns of Sweet Mercy taught. A person crossed the Path – a people followed the Path.

The Ictha would move south as Abeth continued to cool, and generations would come and go, and in time another girl or boy would be born who could hear the stars sing, a dark-eyed child closer to the Missing even than Yaz was. And that child would open the ark. In fact, now that they knew what to look for, the clan might even arrange matches to strengthen the required bloodlines. Quell had withstood the stars' aura better than anyone she knew save Mali.

'I know who Zole is.' Yaz spoke before she could stop herself. 'I know why she knows my name.' Yaz realized now that she was the girl's ancestor. Perhaps Yaz's own child might be the grandparent of the girl Mali had dreamed of in the time-star's grip.

'Who is she?' Mali stepped closer, ignoring Quell, staring up at Yaz.

Yaz shook her head. 'The real question is why did Agatta bring us here? To this gate? Why a hundred years? It can't be chance. It has to be what's needed. A century.'

'Now you're sounding like them,' Mali said. 'Who is Zole?'

But Yaz couldn't let go of the chain of her thoughts for fear of losing it. 'We know what the years do to the truth: it gets turned into stories. We can't instruct them.'

'Can't instruct who?' Mali asked, exasperated.

'Our great-grandchildren, and those who come after. Lives are short on the ice – there are crises, upheavals, famines. The years will wipe away the truth. For them we're the Ancestor. And you can't tell them, Mali. You're going to live into those times. On the ice fifty years is ancient, but you . . . Anyway, your own Sister Owl said it. Back when Owl was a child Sister Cloud saw the future in her pool – a gate perhaps. She saw Erris: the made man. She said you can't use that know-ledge. If you try you'll change things.' Yaz looked back at the gate. 'So we just have to wait. But then when the time comes, we need to act.' She slapped the runed metal. 'Which is why we're here at this gate. This gift. We need to go through! Come on!' And reaching out, she pulled the star of gold and shadows from its alcove and hurled it like a bolt into the portal in front of her. Then followed it in.

CHAPTER 53

The golden star lit a familiar cavern. The ring through which they emerged no longer had its coating of ancient flowstone, and only the largest of the stalagmites and stalactites remained on the floor and ceiling. Evidence of a great flood lay in the flow patterns set into the thick but thankfully firm mud that had been deposited across the cave floor.

'Where did all the water come from?' Mali stared around, marvelling.

'This is the green lands?' Quell seemed unimpressed.

'We should go up to the convent,' Mali said.

Yaz frowned. 'I think we should use this gate to take us to the one by the ark. We don't know how things are in Sweet Mercy. They put me on trial. Twice. And I know about this Inquisition of yours.'

'I want to go outside!' Quell turned slowly, looking for exits. 'Are we really in the green lands?'

Yaz understood his doubts. The idea that they had covered many thousands of miles in a single step was hard to believe. 'It's dangerous out there. It's not just the Church we need to worry about.'

'It's dangerous just to step out next to the ark,' Mali said. 'That place is directly below the emperor's palace. Seus had control of it a hundred years ago, but now it could be full of the emperor's guards. A place like that isn't just going to be left unguarded. Especially if you're right about this and some descendant of yours with more of the Missing's blood has opened the door.'

'So, maybe we should do what Quell said – go outside. Leave by the Seren Way and go into the city to see what we can learn?'

'Slow down.' Mali raised her hand, speaking with a gravitas at odds with her years. 'You rushed in talking about the need to act. But what are we here to do? If they've opened the ark then the problem is fixed and they don't need us.'

'I think they do need us,' Yaz said. 'Or why would Agatta have steered us here?'

Mali gave an eloquent shrug. 'Because she's insane?'

'Or because the ark wasn't opened to defeat Seus. Perhaps they don't even know he still exists. We're here for a reason even if we don't know what it is yet.'

The discussion rattled back and forth, and Mali reminded Yaz how long it had taken to find the way out last time, but in the end they settled on leaving via the cliff exit, and set out to find it.

For a girl raised on the white emptiness of the ice, Yaz had spent an inordinate amount of time lately wandering through tunnels of one sort or another, from cities beneath the ice, to natural caves, to green-land sewers. She relied on memories of their previous escape when Erris had roamed seemingly at random while claiming to be drawing on his marjal talent for escape. They left markers so they could at least find their way back to the gate should reaching open air prove to be beyond them.

Quell seemed unconcerned about the possibility of becoming lost and instead walked beside Yaz deep in thought, chewing his lip. Eventually he looked up, frowning. 'This descendant of yours . . . that you're assuming has enough of the Missing in her to open the ark . . .'

'Yes?'

'She's Ictha, like us.'

'Yes.'

'And if she's your descendant then you're going to have children.'

Yaz smiled and turned down a new tunnel. Quell hurried after her, Mali following more slowly.

'Have Ictha children . . .' Quell continued.

'So it seems.' Yaz shot him a bold look.

'Oh.' Quell struggled to keep back the emotions fighting to own his face. He paused and looked ahead, something like gratitude in his eyes – perhaps just for the opportunity to change the subject. A deep sniff of the air. 'I smell something . . . new.'

Yaz, her senses dulled by the Corridor's plenty, couldn't smell it yet but she knew what it was. 'I told you we were close. That's the outside. The green world.'

A few more turns of the passage and the darkness ahead began to thin. Yaz caught the scent too, the green, the life, bursting in every breath. Soon they no longer needed the star's light. She eased it into a pocket of her habit where it made a large bulge and tingled against her skin.

Quell stumbled ahead, blinded by the sun, drawn on by the same need that had seized Yaz when she first arrived. She hurried after him, squinting. When he tripped she reached for his arm to prevent him pitching down the cliff side while the green world overwhelmed his senses.

Mali and Yaz guided Quell to the pathway and waited

for him to adjust. Unlike Yaz, Quell hadn't struggled across the ice for months to reach this place. He hadn't believed in it with all his heart, obsessed over it, dreamed of it. He had reached it unexpectedly in a single step and then an hour of hunting through tunnels. He stood, stunned, turning this way and that, his eyes unable to fix upon the endless emerald complexity spread out below them. 'It's so hot!' He'd been pulling off hides since they emerged from the gate and now Yaz slapped at his hand to stop him.

'Enough,' she scolded, worried that he might actually take everything off and stand naked beneath the Corridor sun. It *was* hot though, even for the Corridor, one of the rare sunny days that even the green-landers could enjoy.

'So hot . . .' Sweat beaded Quell's skin. He stopped short of nakedness, however, just baring the musculature of his broad chest, the deep copper of his skin in contrast to Mali's blackness.

Mali touched Yaz's arm and pointed towards the top of the cliff where Sister Owl had waited for them when they emerged the first time. Now two nuns stood there. It was hard to see much detail at such distance but both were young and tall, both in the habits of Red Sisters, both pale-skinned. They were holding hands, Yaz noticed.

'Damn.' Yaz raised her own hand in greeting but it was Mali they seemed to be looking at.

'I'll go,' Mali said, and she started up the path.

Yaz, still holding on to Quell, watched her go.

Both nuns watched the novice intently as she climbed. They exchanged glances and words and then, with gestures well known to Yaz, both began to pluck at the threadscape. Quantals then, but Red Sisters rather than Mystic Sisters. Yaz was intrigued. When Mali approached the top of the path's many hairpin bends, the nuns fell to their knees before her as if she were a God in the Sky. They pulled the coverings from their heads as if unworthy in her sight, reducing themselves to novices, one with a shock of short black hair, the other with long golden waves. Yaz saw Mali reach out her single hand first to one head, then the other. A sense of something profound, almost sacred, reverberated along the thread-bond between Mali and Yaz.

If Mali spoke to the nuns it was not for long. She turned and began to descend by the path once more. By the time she rejoined them the nuns had retreated from view and Quell was back in control of himself, though still astonished and sweating.

'They knew me.' Mali's voice shook.

'There's no wind,' Quell said, as if this were a greater astonishment.

'Are you all right?' Yaz released Quell and reached for Mali.

'I am.' The girl took a deep, steadying breath. 'Let's go.'

Yaz had questions, but she didn't need a thread-bond with Mali to know that this wasn't the time for them. She began to lead the way down towards the forest at the base of the plateau. There *was* a wind of course, a breeze that flapped her habit and stung her cheeks with grit each time it gusted. But she understood Quell. This wasn't the wind that scoured the ice and cut with an edge sharper than any knife. This was a breath of life. A warm kiss. And it still amazed her that the green-landers huddled from it beneath their layers.

Yaz led the way onto flatter ground and into the shadows of the forest. Enfolded in the hot green embrace of an infinity of trees, wrapped in the song of birds, the creak of branches, the rustle of leaves, Quell walked in silent wonder, touching everything, just as Yaz and the others had when they first came to this place. Just as she wanted to now.

The road to Verity was less crowded than Yaz remembered, and the first farmhouse they came to was a blackened ruin, haunted by the memory of smoke. The second lay in rubble too, though a crude shelter had been constructed close by. Quell didn't appear to notice, lacking any idea of how things should look. A horse-drawn cart creaked by, commanding all of his attention.

'Something's wrong here.' Yaz looked out across the fields. Even to her inexpert eye they looked untended, too wild.

'A war,' Mali said. 'The Durns, maybe? I never thought the emperor's enemies could reach Verity.'

They walked on. A mile or two brought a dozen more ruins. Few farms had survived without at least some visible damage. They passed a tavern where travellers drank ale and ate at tables set out in front of the main building. One group were singing drunkenly and for the first time Quell noticed that their language was not the one he knew. Another wonder.

'What are they saying?' He stared, open-mouthed.

'It's a song about . . .' Yaz listened and then translated. 'About some hero, a warrior who died a glorious death. Denam at the Amber Gate.' She turned away: the song had spoken of a red-haired gerant and that brought back images of Kola lying dead in Quina's arms, a hundred years and half a day ago. 'Come on.' But Quell had the scent of their meal now and their beer, and stood sniffing. Yaz allowed herself half a smile, remembering the bliss of her first taste of convent food.

'Yaz.' Mali tapped her arm and nodded down the road.

A rider was approaching fast, his horse throwing up clods of mud. A soldier of some sort, armoured in a breastplate and visored helm, a rich cloak of green and gold billowing out behind him.

Yaz pulled Quell to the side of the road and Mali joined them. Instead of passing by the rider slowed then pulled up, his horse panting and snorting.

'Emperor's guard,' Mali hissed as the man dismounted. He had a sword at his hip and stood taller than Quell.

Yaz braced herself for action, flinching as the man whipped his arms up.

He caught hold of his helmet in one hand, doing something to the chinstrap with the other, and in one motion had thrown it aside. With inhuman speed he caught her in an embrace. 'Yaz!'

Almost before she'd realized what was happening Yaz had been released and the man fell to his knees before Mali, giving her a height advantage of a few inches.

'Erris!' They said it together.

Erris had Mali's hand in both of his and was gazing at her with such peculiar intensity that the girl, clearly embarrassed, tried to pull away.

'I'm sorry.' Erris let her go. 'I didn't mean to—' He shook his head, remaining on his knees. Yaz stared at him in amazement. He'd never paid Mali much attention before.

'Good to see you, Erris,' Quell said, seeming by far the least affected of any of them. 'It's been a while.'

'Months for you, maybe as little as hours for Yaz,' Erris said, never taking his eyes from Mali. 'A century for me.' A century and he hadn't aged a day. He reached for Mali's hand again, and she let him take it, perhaps sensing his need. 'And, Mali, I watched you grow. We were friends for a century.' He stood slowly, a rueful look on his face. 'I had to change my name from time to time, change my looks. Take on new identities.' He managed a laugh. 'You even wrote a book about it, Mali. *The Lives of Lestal Crow.*' Seeing their confusion, he explained. 'At first I just used my true name, Lestal Erris Crow. Currently I'm Orrin Reeveson, captain in his imperial majesty's palace guard.' He executed a salute and then a bow.

Yaz looked at Erris in wonder. He hadn't changed. At all. She understood now what he'd said in the tunnel – back when they had kissed, not without love, but without passion. That had been today for her. A hundred years had passed for him. And in his eyes she could see that no moment of it had escaped him. Questions queued on her tongue. 'When did you last see me?'

'You went through the gate. You never came back.'

'I died?'

He shook his head. 'I can't say. You never came back to me. Or to the Corridor as far as I know.'

'But Mali did?' Yaz asked.

'She did.'

'So what happened here? What do we do next?' She wanted to know. Just for once. She didn't care if it was cheating the gods.

Erris grinned. 'I don't know. Mali didn't know. You can go back through the gate but memory doesn't travel. Not from the future to the past. It's the price of the ticket. I don't know what happens next any more than you do. Except that it would be dangerous to let Mali die.'

'Let's none of us die.' Quell wiped sweat from his brow. 'Unless of course this place gets any hotter, in which case I'm going to melt.'

'Thurin? Quina?' Yaz asked. 'If I don't come back it won't matter what you tell me, and if I do I won't remember so it still doesn't matter.' She tried to keep an edge of bitterness from her voice.

'They stayed in Verity for over twenty years. Later they went west, across the Marn Sea. Quina said she wanted to travel the length of the Corridor and see if you really did get back to where you started.' Erris released Mali's hand and met Yaz's eyes. 'They never did get all the way round, but I'm sure they gave it a good try. And I'm sure they did it together.' A grin. 'Their children stayed in Verity. All dead now. Old age. Not of this.' He waved towards the closest of the burned-out buildings. 'One of their grandchildren went back to the ice when the Ictha came south. One of their great-grandchildren was a novice at the convent. I could see Quina in her. She's a merchant now, very successful. But I'm gossiping like an old man. You're here for a reason and I'm here to help you.'

'How *are* you here?' Quell asked. 'In this spot? It's been a hundred years and we've been here a few hours, and you come up on that . . . "horse"?'

'Ah, well, that's one of the luxuries of time. You can do some preparation. I found another splinter of Taproot. Took thirty years searching, but I found him. He taught me quite a bit. I've learned a lot more about Hayes gates, for example. Including how to set a kind of tripwire that lets me know when two in particular have been used and which gate the visitor came from. When I discovered that the Sweet Mercy gate had been accessed from the Black Rock I have to admit I was surprised. I thought the gate had been underwater for some while. But I came running even so.' He reached back to pat the horse's neck. 'Or rather Zox here did the running.'

Quell nodded. 'So maybe we should go—' He turned towards the nearest dining table, sniffing. 'What is that smell? Is it food? We should definitely eat. I mean, we're not in a hurry, are we?'

Erris picked his helm off the grassy roadside. 'Actually, we probably are. If I know about your visit then we can be pretty sure that Seus does too.'

497

'He didn't give up then?' Mali asked.

'He sent an army that nearly reduced the city to rubble not very long ago. So no.'

'Where did he get the army?' Yaz asked. 'Who would follow him?'

'He doesn't lead, he steers. The people here don't even know he exists. He stirred up the neighbouring states and aimed them at the empire. It's not hard to start a war here; he was just waiting for them to be strong enough to win it. He helped with that too. But wars are easy when the living space keeps shrinking. You can see the northern ice and the southern ice from the Rock of Faith now. The Corridor's only fifty miles wide.'

Yaz wanted to ask where all the people who lived in the miles that the ice had covered went. But she knew the answer. They'd gone into the ground.

'We'd better go before he finds us again then.'

Erris turned sharply, staring back at the Rock of Faith, now several miles behind them. Yaz shaded her eyes with a hand and squinted, trying to see what he saw. She could just make out the lumps and bumps of the convent buildings. 'Is that . . .' Smoke seemed to be rising above the rooftops. '. . . fire?'

'No.' Erris picked Mali up without ceremony and set her on his horse. 'Much worse. Run!'

CHAPTER 54

Yaz was the slowest of all of those running, lacking Erris's Missing-made muscles or the full measure of Ictha stamina that Quell still owned. She saved her breath for running while Mali – up on Erris's horse – asked the most important question.

'What in the hells is chasing us?'

'Many things. With wings.' Erris kept up a relentless pace. 'I'm guessing that Seus sent them through the gate you came out of. He knew you were coming. He must have had an idea of when and where – at least a rough one. He set a guardian on the gate, but the nuns dealt with it. Or rather, the novices did.'

The sight of a guard captain in the emperor's livery racing down the road towards Verity drew plenty of attention, even managing to distract from the novice and the bare-chested man chasing after him. Nobody was fool enough to get in his way though.

The looming walls of the city drew ever closer but Yaz started to pant and lose her rhythm. Erris slowed, eyeing the horse as if he were considering hoisting her up beside Mali.

'I'd fall off,' gasped Yaz.

From the way the oncoming traffic on the road had stopped staring at Erris and was instead watching the skies behind him with increasing concern, Yaz could tell they didn't have long before the flying swarm caught up.

The city gates were close now. The crowd ahead of them was far thinner than when Yaz had last come this way. Many stood aside when Erris bellowed at them to clear the road. Others went flying as he or the horse shouldered them aside.

The swarm had darkened so much of the sky behind them that its shadow fell upon the streets of Verity. The citizens were running for shelter now, some screaming. On the walls guardsmen ducked for cover or raised their weapons.

Once through the gates Erris dragged his horse down a side street running parallel to the wall, then turned and turned again into successively smaller streets which reduced the broad sky to a pale strip hemmed in by dark rooftops, with the swarm's outriders as black dots against the brightness.

'Someone's following us!' Mali's voice jolted with the horse's gait.

Yaz thought they had bigger concerns, though her biggest right now was just hauling in enough breath to keep her legs going. Already she was at the back of the group, watching the swish of Zox's tail as he showed her his hooves. Quell, overwhelmed by the city, just kept his head down and maintained his pace.

A clatter overhead brought Yaz's attention back to the rooftops. Something had landed there, furling long wings, each like a black lace fan. It reminded her of Haydies's demons, all claws and jaws and wire sinews.

Without warning, something hit her shoulder, spinning her to the cobbles, a hot wet pain accompanying the sound of shredding cloth as her attacker tore at her. Yaz yelled and thrashed. A moment later the attacker was gone and she found herself on her back staring up at a man who was leaning on his spear. Ahead, further down the road, the clatter of Zox's hooves slowed as Erris brought his horse to a stop.

'There're more coming.' The man spoke the ice-tongue. He had the deep red skin of an Ictha, his eyes the palest blue, almost white. He leaned more heavily on his spear and twisted it. Yaz, turning her head, saw that the point impaled one of the winged demons, whose struggles now ceased as the spearhead wrecked its metal chest. The thing was the size of a street dog, but looked capable of burrowing through a man in short order.

Two more demons arrowed from the air, faster than falling. The spearman jerked his weapon up, catching the first of them full in the head with the blunt end, but had no defence against the second. Yaz's golden star hammered through that one, launched from her pocket by the force of her will.

'My thanks!' The man's grin was half startled, half excited. Pieces of the second demon rained down around them while he turned to slash at the first one as it landed stunned and graceless.

'Come on!' Quell grabbed Yaz's arm and hauled her up, sparing a surprised glance for the newcomer. 'Let's go.'

A moment later they were running again.

Yaz's star wove around them, twice taking demons from the air. Erris proved to have rebuilt himself well in the years since Seus had nearly crushed the life out of him. He took three more demons out of their path with a black hatchet, once leaping a good ten feet into the air to hack one clean in half. The numbers were building though, the sky above thick with the creatures, hunting for them among the maze of narrow streets. Many of the rooftops were heavy with demons, some vanishing down the largest of the chimneys with writhing motions and a thrashing of their razored tails.

They reached a warehouse district and skirted it to avoid the openness of unloading bays and wagon stops. They were passing a shuttered tavern when the largest of the windows exploded outwards, disgorging a black storm of demons.

Mali screamed above the thunder of wings as some four or five of the demons snagged her habit and tore her from the back of Erris's horse. They hoisted her aloft with frightening speed and for a moment Mali's panic dragged Yaz inside the girl's mind along their thread-bond. She could feel the pain where one set of talons was hooked into flesh rather than cloth. She could see through Mali's eyes too. An ocean of rooftops opened out beneath her as she gained height and in the distance, over innumerable tiled slopes, she saw a sight arresting enough to register even in her extremity. Past the brooding bulk of the emperor's palace a vast hole had been punched through the thickness of the city wall, and some great furrow had been torn into the earth, streaking out through that hole and into the farmlands beyond: a blackened valley, as if a God in the Sky had reached down and swung their spear to wound the city.

Yaz managed to disentangle herself from Mali's terror. While Quell and the other Ictha defended her back, Quell sweeping demons from the air with one of the broken shutters, Yaz sent her star hurtling after Mali. Like a golden comet the star smashed through the wings of the demons holding her friend and the whole mass of them began to tumble towards the ground together.

The demons managed to slow the descent using their damaged wings but Mali still hit the ground with a thump that would have made Yaz wince had she not been wielding her star against a dozen other demons. Erris reached Mali's side at a speed any hunska would have been proud of and reduced her attackers to twisted ruins with a rain of hatchet blows.

'Come with me!' Erris dragged Mali across the street towards a large set of double doors. He released her at the last moment and accelerated into the doors. The impact proved too much for whatever locking bar was in place and Erris crashed through.

Yaz, Quell, and the other Ictha bundled through behind him, scooping up Mali between them.

While the Ictha hastened to close the doors again Erris became a blur of action in the dim space beyond, hacking from the air the handful of demons that had chased them in.

A dozen or more thuds followed as the eerily silent demons hit the closed doors. Quell braced the left one, the other man held the right.

'They'll find another way in.' Erris didn't look up from his inspection of Mali's wounds.

'Is she . . .? Are you hurt, Mali?'

'Yes,' Mali snarled, pulling a knife from inside her habit. 'The bastards.' With her teeth bared and crimson she looked eager for revenge, her usual calm banished.

'She'll live.' Erris pulled her to her feet. 'We need to move.'

'First' – Yaz shook her head, ignoring her wounded shoulder – 'who in the hells is this?' She sent her star to float above the unknown Ictha, bathing him in golden light. He seemed unconcerned by its proximity.

'I'm at your service, Mother Yaz.' He set a heel to the door and stood straighter, drawing a hand down in front of his face in the Ictha gesture of deference. 'I'm Tarkax.'

'What are you doing here—' The noise of splintering from high up interrupted Erris's question. He shook his head, angry at himself for being distracted. 'Quick! Wedge those doors.'

Now that Yaz's eyes had adjusted she could see that they were in a large warehouse stacked with all manner of things, barrels bigger than a man in one section, fat-bellied earthenware jars in another, in several places bulging sacks heaped up high, some trickling grain onto the flagstones.

'I know this place,' said Mali unexpectedly.

'Yes.' Erris began hauling sacks away from part of the floor. The removal of several sacks revealed a large, dusty coil of rope. 'It's where we went down to the oldest sewers the first time and gained access to the ark.' More sacks went flying before he found what he was looking for, a sizeable stone slab, too large for any man to lift, with an iron ring set in its centre. Erris hefted it aside and tied a rope through the ring, tossing the heavy coil into the shaft. 'Get down! Mali last with me.'

Yaz pushed Quell ahead of her. 'You don't have a weapon.'

A crash and an ominous fluttering overhead saw off any argument and Quell vanished down the hole, his Ictha strength compensating for his inexperience in rope climbing. Yaz tried to get Tarkax to follow but the fierce look in his eyes told her it would only waste time. 'I didn't wait my whole life for you so that I could leave while monsters tear you apart.' He lunged and brought down a demon, skewering it through one wing.

Yaz hastened down the rope despite her conviction that she could do more damage with her star than he could with his spear.

Tarkax followed. A few moments later the rope jolted and there was a heavy thumping noise from above.

'I've sealed the shaft,' Erris called down. 'They can't cut the rope now.'

Yaz saved her breath for climbing. She was still not recovered from the run, or from her efforts in the ark which, although technically a century ago, still felt as if they had taken place earlier that day.

She'd made longer descents in Vesta's undercity but the descent into Verity's past iterations, all constructed an age after the Missing's departure, left her arms aching and her feet grateful when a solid floor appeared beneath them, even if it was knee-deep in cold, dark, ill-smelling water.

Quell received her, Tarkax dropped down after, quickly followed by Erris with Mali clinging to his back. The starlight illuminated four faces that turned as one to stare at Tarkax.

'Who are you?' Yaz demanded, wanting more than a name. 'How did you find us?'

'Tarkax Ice-Spear of the Ictha.' He banged a fist to his chest. He was older than Yaz had first assumed, thirty at least, sculpted by the wind.

'Ice-Spear?' Erris grinned. 'Not one of Thurin's descendants?'

Tarkax stood taller, pride showing. 'On my grandfather's side.'

'But who are you to me?' Yaz asked. 'How did you find us?'

For the first time Tarkax's aura of confidence cracked. He frowned. 'I . . .' He looked from Quell to Yaz. 'I . . . came back . . . I was here when she opened it . . . But I came back. I had business in the city. They needed me at the Caltess . . .' He seemed unconvinced by his own arguments even as he spoke them. His gaze kept straying to Mali's missing hand then to her face, puzzled. 'I came back . . .'

'Why?' Erris asked, staring hard at the man.

'They needed me at . . .' Tarkax stopped, as if remembering

505

something he'd forgotten. 'But in Scithrowl I went into the black ice.' He shuddered. 'Why did I . . .'

Yaz understood. 'Theus. You can come out now. I know you're in there.'

Tarkax shuddered, his head slumped, chin to chest. Another shudder and then he lifted his eyes, their palest blue now replaced by a blackness that encompassed both the whites. 'Guilty.' A dark smile spread as he raised his head again. 'Yaz. It's been a while. And Mistress Path – you've changed!' He cast his gaze over Erris and Quell. 'As to how I came to be here, well of course I try to stay close to the ark and have had time to place my own tripwires on nearby gates.'

'But you were out on the ice,' Mali said, 'with this man. In this man. Using him.'

'A little hunting expedition. My last missing piece that Yaz so carelessly lost for me finally returned. I tracked it to the black ice that our friend just mentioned, and recovered it. Your timing has been impeccable. I wait the best part of a hundred years for its return, spend a few more tracking it down, finally reunite, and here you are just months later.'

'Keot,' Yaz said. 'He called himself Keot.'

'And now he's Theus again.' Theus crossed his arms. 'Once more I'm as complete as I can be this side of the gate. All that my beloved kinsmen tore apart and abandoned has been reknitted – ready to return to my kind and seek out the so-called "enlightened" half of myself. After that there will be . . . a reckoning . . . and we will be reborn again as the one they call Prometheus. All I need is access and an open ark. Let's go!' And with that he waded off as though the tunnel they were in was as familiar to him as the back of Tarkax's hand.

'Wait,' Yaz called after him. 'You said the ark was opened? My plan already worked? Why are you still here then?'

Theus looked back at her and spoke as if she were a slow child. 'When they opened it I wasn't whole. I am now.'

Erris made to pass her, trying to catch up with Theus. Yaz held him back. 'Why didn't Seus stop the ones who opened the gate? He's keen enough to stop us!'

Erris flashed a grin and glanced back at Mali. 'Mistress Path and I kept his focus on other things. We weren't idle all these years. And Seus saw you as the threat – he knew you'd crossed the century bound for this city once again. Your "ancestor ploy" – aiming your people at him, breeding a chosen one to open the gate . . . he didn't see that. We made sure he didn't. When the move against the ark came, Seus was busy trying to raze the city around it. His pawn, the battle-queen, was just a few hundred yards from the ark when it was opened.'

Yaz let him go and Erris splashed to the fore, elbowing past Theus. 'You'll find things have changed since you were last down here.'

'I wouldn't be so sure about that,' Theus said. 'I've kept a close eye on the place.'

'Even so, I should lead. Anyone else is likely to get a collection of crossbow bolts through the chest.'

Erris guided the way through a maze of half-collapsed sewer tunnels and ancient voids that might once have been cellars that time had covered over far deeper than originally intended. In places there was evidence of newer digging and efforts to shore up the ceiling or connect different areas with short passages. It took about ten minutes before the first guards challenged them, three men in the emperor's green and gold, albeit somewhat stained. The sight of Erris's uniform eased their fingers on the triggers of their crossbows, and when he came close enough for them to see his face they immediately stood to attention.

Erris offered no explanation for his curious companions: it seemed he carried sufficient authority to pass unquestioned.

Erris took one of the guards' trio of lanterns, lit it from the one they were using, and led on. Once out of sight of the guards he advised Yaz to hide her star and she returned it to her habit.

Soon they were passing along the white-walled corridors of the outer ark, which appeared to have been unchanged by the passage of another century. More guards challenged them and then stood aside.

'It all comes back to this place.' Erris's boots made his footsteps echo in the bare corridor. He put out his lantern. The Missing's ceiling panels mocked its flame with their perfect white light.

Yaz thought of the Pit of the Missing – a portal of a kind – around which her life had seemed to revolve for years. And now it was the ark and its door that drew them all in, exerting its pull whatever the century. Theus aimed to pass through it. She tried to imagine what he might find on the far side. Whatever it was, the Missing had abandoned their lives on Abeth in favour of it. 'Have you seen these golden cities, Theus?'

'No.'

'Do you know where they are?' Mali asked, walking with Quell behind Yaz and Theus.

'I do.'

'Where?' Yaz thought maybe they were in the skies, up where the gods lived beyond the moon.

'Beneath the sea, of course.' Theus scowled, though Tarkax's face seemed unused to the expression. 'Being perfect requires a lot of energy, apparently. There's enough water to burn for millions of years yet.'

'You burn water?' Quell asked, amazed.

'Just the hydrogen. It's all that's needed for fusion—' Theus broke off, seeing their incomprehension. 'Yes. We do. In fact the waste heat from the cities is what melts holes in the ice. Your hot seas. That's all us – the Missing. They don't do it out of concern, of course. They probably don't even know your peoples arrived. The material world is beneath their notice, apparently. Which is horseshit, because they still need it to power their existence. In fact—'

Erris caught Theus's shoulder as he tried to walk past him. 'Careful.'

Yaz realized they were in the final long, straight corridor that led to the chamber where she had struggled and failed to open the ark. Lifetimes ago or earlier that day, depending on which of those who had been present you asked.

Openings to small chambers punctuated the corridor in opposing pairs and the leftmost pair just ahead of them housed the gate she had used several times before.

'Defences are active.' Erris tapped a complicated rhythm on the wall. A hidden panel slid back and he pressed the glowing disc it revealed. 'Safe now. If you'd gone ahead it would have sliced you into pieces.'

Theus scowled, but waited for Erris to lead the way.

Yaz's heart began to beat harder. Her memories of the fight remained raw and unhealed. Echoes of those screams of pain and anger still haunted the air. A strange panic wrapped her. She could hear her own pulse. Or . . . the beat of some other heart.

'There's a shipheart ahead!' Yaz said, puzzled as to why it would be needed. 'I thought the door was open—'

The gate to her left shimmered and something huge broke from it, a figure that could only just fit through.

'Run!'

Everyone ran, sprinting for the door at the far end of the

corridor. Yaz charged, borne on the wings of terror. Seus had found them again. Seus in a new avatar. He'd been waiting for them, waiting behind the gate for Erris to neutralize the invisible blades that filled the corridor beyond.

Tarkax reached the door first and it began sliding smoothly up into the ceiling. Yaz arrived next, with Quell at her shoulder. She turned and saw Mali ten paces behind.

'Erris!'

He had run too, but in the opposite direction, throwing himself at the avatar. Seus had emerged in the shape of a powerfully built beast with two huge curving horns and a great snout from whose flared nostrils smoke billowed. Four sturdy legs ending in hooves supported a horse-like body and drove it forwards at speed. Hopelessly outmatched, Erris had been pinned against the opposite wall by one horn. A shake of the creature's thick neck flung him against the ceiling, horns raised to gore him again.

'Quickly!' Theus grabbed Yaz's shoulders and hauled her through the doorway.

'We have to help him!' Mali started forwards but Quell caught her arm.

'He's buying us time. Don't let it be a waste.'

Yaz tried to find the Path. She felt Mali hunting it too, but it lay beyond them. Even with a single shipheart just ten yards away neither of them had the strength to claim that power so soon after their recent calls upon it. The heavy white door slid down, sealing away the sight of Erris falling beneath Seus's hooves.

'We don't have long!' Theus turned Yaz towards the silver door at the centre of the chamber. A single shipheart had been embedded in the metal, half of it hidden. It was the one Yaz had made from the Watcher's eyes, its light so violet that most of it escaped being seen, making the star appear black save where bright violet lines erupted periodically across its surface.

'I thought it would be open!' Yaz gasped in horror.

'This is how it was left by your descendant.' Theus shoved her. 'Work with it!'

Even through the thickness of the corridor door Yaz could hear the bellow of Seus's avatar. She stumbled forwards, feeling the burn of the star all across her skin, her habit offering no protection at all. Her failure with the four stars had left her less than she was, as if a vital tendon had snapped. Her tolerance for shiphearts had eroded to the point at which even this single example pained her as she closed the last yard and forced her hand to touch its surface. Its light seemed to penetrate her. Her mind started to fragment almost immediately, a multitude of voices lifting from the darkness.

The ark had been changed. Someone with an abundance of the Missing's blood in their veins – one of the Ictha, if Yaz's plans came to fruition – had been here in the chaos of the recent war and opened it. They'd left it closed but not so heavily locked as before. This one shipheart was the only key required now.

Theus ran back to the door to the corridor. He started to move his hands across the wall next to it.

'I can seal this. But—'

An impact made the door shudder. Remarkable given how thick it was.

'But I don't know how long it will hold.'

Yaz took the shipheart in both hands. Even as it tore at her sanity it revealed itself to her, enhancing her skills so that she saw how to unlock the ark. She ground her teeth and began to rotate the star in its silver-steel housing.

Across the chamber a loud metallic squealing started up, underwritten by a deep grating that set Yaz's teeth on edge.

The outer door rose by degrees even as Yaz sought to open the inner one. The star in her hands had been hard to rotate at the start but with every fraction of the necessary circuit it resisted her more. This descendant who the Ictha had bred had seemingly overestimated Yaz's talent. The passage of years had turned her from a flawed example of the species – something to be thrown away and forgotten – into a story and on into a legend. Another century and she might be a myth.

Halfway to Yaz's goal a conviction seized her that yet again the task would defeat her. Never mind that it was a much easier feat than the one that had proved only just beyond her that morning.

Smoke from Seus's nostrils began to blast under the outer door as the bull-avatar wrenched and pounded at the metal slab. Sparks on the wall where Theus had worked to lock Seus out indicated that the city mind's assault on the entrance was not just one involving brute force.

Quell, Mali, and Theus jumped back as two great horns drove in under the door, gouging the floor. Seus started to use them as levers to widen the gap. The horns were smeared with black and it took Yaz a moment to understand that it was Erris's blood, the inner blood that surrounded his vital components. A fire lit in her then. Erris who was nothing but good. Erris who feared himself to be no more than the echo of a dead boy who fell into Vesta millennia ago but was so very much more. Erris who had waited a century for her to return. Seus had destroyed him! The star lit beneath her hands, violet light flooded the room, and with a slight sigh the vast weight of silver-steel began to rise.

'Quick!' Theus ran towards the gap as the silver door opened, revealing a flight of stairs. He fell on his side and slid through the widening slit.

Quell ducked low and hastened after Theus with Mali at his side.

A loud crunch hauled Yaz's attention to the corridor door. Seus had forced it back into the ceiling and now filled the entrance, muscling his powerful body through the opening, smoke snorting from steel nostrils, a feral light shining from his eyes.

Yaz turned and fled. She pulled at the shipheart with her mind and the great door, not yet halfway open, reversed its path. Steel hooves clattered against stone and the avatar accelerated after her, bellowing.

The light dimmed rapidly as the door came down. Seus arrived with a thunder of hooves, horns driving through the gap just before it narrowed towards nothing, their wicked points reaching for Yaz's back. She felt only a sharp sting as one reached her flesh.

The door shut with surprisingly little noise. For a second there was a metallic clattering on the stairs and then nothing, only silence and darkness.

'Let's have some light,' Theus said further down the steps. A white light with no obvious source filled the air.

Yaz found herself standing with a yard of each of Seus's horns lying on the stairs to either side of her. Where the door had sheared them off each metal horn was thicker than her upper arm. She reached to her back and found the small wound where the very tip of a horn had stabbed her before it fell.

'Hurry!' Theus kept going down. 'The ark's still open.'

'But . . .' Yaz followed the others. She remembered that Taproot hadn't entered through the doorway but through the temporary crack her efforts had made in the ark's defences. Seus too would be able to enter the ark in such a manner if the ark's defences hadn't closed as quickly as the silver-steel door.

The stairs led down for some while, terminating in a small circular chamber. They crowded in together, sweaty, panting, bleeding, and stood casting wildly about for . . . something, anything they could use.

The room had no exits, and held nothing but a fragile-looking chair lying on its side. The floor and walls were grimy, the air stale. Yaz stared for a moment then fell to her knees. The price they had paid – the efforts she had taken – for this?

Theus was talking in a language she didn't know. He strode around the room tapping the walls as if he could see something she couldn't. A faint blue ball of light appeared at the centre of the room, hanging there like a shipheart, but it wasn't a star. Yaz could sense nothing of it save with her eyes.

I am Taproot. The voice seemed to issue from the ball of light.

Theus ignored it.

'Taproot?' Yaz asked.

I am Taproot. The voice lacked emotion, like that of someone unable to waken from a deep sleep.

'Seus is outside. We need to keep him there.'

Only the Purified may instruct me.

This wasn't the Taproot Yaz knew, quick-witted, sharp-tongued, and not suffering fools lightly. This was the skeleton of his mind. The needle had held a sketch of him, armed with the knowledge needed to boost the ark's defences against Seus. It had successfully resisted him this past century, but there was little present of what made Taproot the man he was.

'We needed Erris here.' Yaz looked around, hunting for anything that made sense. 'The real Taproot told him how to keep Seus out.' Even as she said it Yaz wondered if there even was a 'real' Taproot among all these copies of the man, each with different fidelity. 'We need Erris—'

'It's done,' Theus said.

'What?'

'It's done. The ark is closed again. On all levels. And I've implemented protocols far superior to Taproot's. Seus isn't getting in here. Ever. Not even if you left the door wide open. It would just be the same empty room for him that it is for you.' Theus saw her confusion and gave her a fierce grin with Tarkax's face. 'Seus crossed me. Me! Some jumped-up city mind thinks it's a god? Tries to kill me?' He shook his head. 'I have things I need to do right now, other scores to settle, but Seus will regret wasting a hundred years of my time.'

Theus stepped back and regarded the floating blue sphere with a level gaze. 'Open the gate.'

Only the Purified may instruct me. Taproot spoke without inflection.

Theus snarled. 'He's bonded with the ark. He thinks he's one of them now. He's become their gatekeeper.' He reached out a hand until his fingers touched the blue light. 'I am Prometheus of the Missing. Open the gate. I demand it.'

Only the Purif—

Theus barked his order in a different tongue, the language of the Missing.

Only the Purified may instruct me.

Theus raced back to the wall and began tapping furiously. Lights and symbols appeared on the stone just as the Missing's script had appeared on the walls in Vesta's under-city. Each time he touched a circle or a line of the symbols it turned red. Yaz saw growing on his face an expression she would never have associated with Theus: despair.

'He's locked me out. He's using his defences against me.'

515

'Can't you—'

'This isn't the Missing's work. I could unlock that. Maybe. This is from the four tribes. What they brought from their ships.' Theus rested his forehead on the wall. All around him the glowing red symbols began to fade.

'What will you do?' Mali asked.

Theus rolled and slid down the wall with his back against it until he slumped at its base. 'What can I do?' He lifted his black eyes to them. 'I can't even get us out of here now. The door controls are locked away from me.'

'We're going to starve in here?' Quell asked. He sounded curious rather than frightened. Perhaps being chased into an ark by the bull-shaped avatar of a self-proclaimed god had made starvation seem rather tame.

'Well, even if you could open the door, it would just let Seus murder us.' Mali regarded her stump in contemplation.

Theus put his head on his knees.

'There must be something we can do.' Mali's eyes had that 'witchiness' about them that Yaz associated with looking at the threadscape.

Yaz joined Mali and together they examined the threads. But the ark had somehow bound the threadscape into itself, almost as if it were woven from them, and where in lesser technology the builders had used wires and components such as those in Erris's body, in the ark those wires were the threads of existence themselves.

Putting the shipheart together from its components had been a puzzle that had nearly defeated Yaz. She didn't have to spend long examining the ark to understand that this was a puzzle so far beyond that one that any attempt to solve it with her own resources would be pointless.

'Taproot.' Yaz faced the blue sphere. 'Do you know me?'

No.

'You must remember me.'

No.

'Just a little—'

No.

'Could you at least open the door enough to see where Seus is?'

Only the Purified may instruct me.

'And this was your grand plan, was it?' Yaz turned to stare at Theus. 'You waited all this time to ask nicely and then starve?'

Theus snarled at that, lifting his head. 'Careful, girl.'

'Well?' Yaz had tired of Theus's threats long ago. 'Was it?'

'Nobody is going to starve.' Theus spat on the ground. 'We'll all die of thirst long before that.' He scowled black-eyed at the ball of light that was Taproot. 'I could have opened the gate, purified or not. I didn't expect Taproot to have become part of the ark, though. Not like this. He's locked me out the same way he locked Seus out, by combining Missing technology with quantal and marjal tricks. There's not enough of him here to reason with. He's just a purpose wrapped around knowledge.'

Yaz found Theus's defeatism more frightening than his threats. Theus was anything but a quitter. He had reassembled himself from discarded pieces. He'd done it through force of will over generations. If he said there was no way to go forward and no way to go back . . . then all hope really was lost. She hung her head, touched Quell's shoulder, Mali's arm, and went to set her own back to the wall. Slowly she slid down to join Theus on the ground. Erris's death dragged at her and it was hard not to feel hopeless. It had been the longest day of her life by far, and exhaustion's teeth were deep in her bones.

'Ouch.' Yaz adjusted her position. She'd sat down on

something uncomfortable – more uncomfortable than the stone floor. She reached down to find what the lump was and discovered it to be in one of the inner pockets of her habit. She pulled it out. Taproot's box. Dull grey and lifeless, mottled with darker stains. She turned it over in her hands.

'What's in the box?' Quell joined her on the floor. Mali, meanwhile, righted the abandoned chair and sat on it.

Yaz continued to rotate the box in her hands, tracing her fingers over its smoothness and the scars where Seus's influence had corrupted it.

'Is it a secret?' Quell asked without rancour.

'All the evils in the world.' Yaz smiled. Seus's madness had filled it and driven out Taproot. The same madness that had torn mankind's knowledge from the hands of the four tribes even as the ice moved to crush them from both sides. The same madness that had wanted to turn the ice tribes into a weapon of war and to take control of the ark with them. The madness that had recently come so close to taking the city with another army steered in from some neighbouring state.

The ice tribes would have been that army, generations ago, if the priests of the Black Rock had been able to carry out Seus's orders. An ocean of blood spilled just to gain access to the small, empty chamber she now sat in, waiting on a slow death. So many lives spent so that Seus could tear the moon from the sky, seal the world in ice, and obey that last command from the Missing as they left for their golden cities. *Let none follow.* That was all they left for their servants. And in time it had become all their servants cared for.

Quell repeated his question: 'What's in the bo—'

'It's empty,' Mali said.

It was empty. It had never held anything physical, though Yaz had not thought to question why it was hollow or what purpose the empty space within served. The ghosts it held, most recently Taproot's, were somehow embedded in the walls of the box itself . . .

She angled the box and examined the interior. Her eyes widened.

'What *is* in the box?' Theus had seen her brows lift.

Yaz turned it towards him. 'Hope?'

There, at the bottom on the inside, a small part of the base remained a pure white.

Theus sneered. 'What's that going to do?'

Yaz stood sharply. She held the box out and reached into the ball of blue light with it.

'Don't!' Theus lunged for her. But Quell was quicker and hauled him aside. 'Are you mad?' Theus struggled to break free. 'If Seus gets into the system . . .'

'Taproot!' Yaz commanded. 'Take what's yours.'

The blue light grew in intensity, bathing the room, making Yaz turn her face away, but she kept her hand where it was. She felt the box crumbling in her grasp, falling to pieces which in turn became dust. A sharp pain made her pull back. And when she looked again the light had returned to its previous level, though perhaps it was a little brighter.

Yaz. You are Yaz of the Ictha. A wilful, stubborn, somewhat troubling girl.

'And you are?'

Dr Elias Taproot.

Theus surged to his feet. 'Open the gate! Open it now! I demand it!'

Only the Purified may instruct me.

'Gah!' Theus turned away to punch the wall.

'I'm anything but purified.' Even now, the voices that the shipheart had tried to split from her muttered in the back of Yaz's mind, just as they always had, her worse selves offering unworthy thoughts, mean emotions, sly suggestions. And, just as she had almost all of her life, she ignored them. She wouldn't be without them though. Every once in a while they said something useful. Every once in a while you had to do something imperfect, even something wrong, to reach a greater good. No path was ever so straight and so narrow that you could keep the world's dirt entirely from your hands, let alone your feet. 'I'm not purified, Elias. But I'm also not instructing you. I'm asking. Please. Can you open the gate?'

Well now – the voice held Taproot's tone now, Yaz could almost see his hands in motion, orchestrating the conversation – *asking is an entirely different matter, my dear. Can I open the gate? Watch me!*

A bright rectangle of golden light appeared, a doorway tall enough to admit a person.

Without hesitation, Theus flung himself at it. And bounced off. He sat down heavily, holding his head as if disorientated. The rectangle shrank, shrank again, became a golden point in the air, and vanished.

Yaz blinked. 'Theus?'

Tarkax raised his gaze to meet Yaz's. His eyes were the palest of winter blues again. 'If I ever see him I don't know if I'll be able to keep myself from killing him.' He stood, shuddering, holding his arms away from his sides as if his whole body had been dipped in something too foul to touch. 'Yaz of the Ictha, daughter of Zin and Mokka, eldest of my ancestors, I pray to the Gods in the Sky and to the Gods in the Sea that this service I have rendered has been for the good of our people. Do not ask me to repeat it.'

Yaz reached out and took Tarkax's hand. 'Theus is an evil that has ridden many of those closest to my heart. But he's also a lesson, and a myth, and a mystery. Sometimes it feels as if I'm in his story rather than my own. And that we won't know what kind of tale it is until the last page is turned.' She turned back towards Taproot's blue light. 'Is there any way out of here for the rest of us? Apart from dying of thirst?'

Only the door, dear girl.

Yaz smiled grimly at the others. 'I suppose we must go out and have our reckoning with Seus then. This place is closed to him. Whether he gets in through the door or not makes no difference. Correct, Elias?'

Correct.

Yaz went over to Mali and took her hand. 'You have to run. You have to escape.' She raised her voice over the girl's objection. 'The witch, Agatta, those old women – or that old woman – she said you had to survive. If what we've done here is to matter you have to go back to the time we came from or it won't make sense and something will go wrong. So you have to save yourself, to save everyone else. Yes?'

Mali pressed her lips into a grim line.

'Yes?' Yaz repeated. And then seeing Mali's stubbornness, she spoke in the green-tongue. *'Run, child. Please.'*

The girl made a slow nod, eyes growing wet.

'Come on then. It doesn't do to delay these things.' Yaz noticed Tarkax's fierce grin of approval and hoped that she hadn't been too much of a let-down when she had stepped out of his clan's stories and into his world. She walked towards the stairs, passing Quell. Stopping, she embraced him, pulling his body into hers. 'I'm sorry. For everything.'

'I'm only sorry I hid the truth from you, back when I thought I was saving you.' Quell pulled his head back so he could look her in the face. 'Everything else . . .' He shrugged. 'It was an honour. I'm glad we could be together again. If only briefly.' He let her go.

With a tightness in her chest, an ache for what might have been, Yaz climbed the steps, Quell at her side, Tarkax behind with Mali. Just below the great door Yaz and Quell both picked up one of the shorn-off horns. Each probably weighed more than Mali and Yaz knew she wouldn't be swinging hers around, but as a lance for an initial charge it might prove a decent weapon.

'Goodbye, Elias!' Yaz called down the stairs, and Taproot began to raise the door.

As the gap widened Yaz could see a dark heap close by. Seus, waiting crouched and ready to hurl himself at them. She exchanged a last look with Quell then braced herself, mouthing a prayer to the gods above and below.

The gap widened further.

'Is he . . .?'

Quell charged out and drove his horn section into the head it came from. The point skittered off Seus's thick skull, leaving a bright line scored in the metal. Seus remained slumped where he was.

Yaz joined Quell, poking at the avatar with her section of horn. Tarkax and Mali emerged behind her.

'Better get away in case he wakes up,' Quell suggested.

The door behind them reversed direction and began to close once more. Taproot's voice reached them faintly up the stairs. *Your friend extended the ark's defences to the outer ark. Seus has lost control of his creation.*

The door closed with a sighing noise.

Somehow embedding the shipheart in the door had significantly reduced its aura. Mali and the Ictha had considerable resistance, but even so none of them wanted to linger near it. Tarkax led the way back to the corridor. Yaz lingered for a moment, gazing at Seus's latest corpse and the door to the ark. They had finally sealed the ark from him for good. The moon was safe from Seus's malice and it would continue to burn its path around Abeth's Corridor, fighting to keep the ice away from untold numbers of empires and kingdoms.

In the end though, it would fail of its own accord, even without Seus's help. In the years since Yaz's last visit the ice had advanced dozens of miles, reducing the Corridor to half of the width it had held when she had first seen it. She turned and followed the others, feeling empty.

A wave of grief surged along the thread-bond she had with Mali, swamping her, bringing tears from her eyes and a gasp of heartbreak from her chest. Mali had stopped a short way along the passage in a place where the white walls were smeared with the black of Erris's inner blood. She was on her knees. Quell stood behind her, head bowed. Tarkax had gone further, spear at the ready, scouting ahead.

As Yaz came closer she saw with horror that Erris's head had been torn free and lay before Mali, black blood oozing around the ragged flesh. At her approach his eyes opened.

'Gods in the Sky!' She took an involuntary step back.

The dark brown of Erris's eyes had been replaced by an unnatural glow, a light that flickered and guttered like a dying flame. His lips moved and though he lacked any lungs his voice came, albeit cracked and broken.

'Go now, Mali. We'll have a lifetime together.'

Mali stood slowly, her shoulders shaking with silent sobs. She reached for Quell's hand and pulled him with her. He paused to set his palm to his forehead, looking down at Erris – the Ictha's sign for honouring a great one.

Yaz fell to her knees where Mali had been. 'Erris . . .'

'Not long now . . .' Somehow he managed a smile. 'I had so many years, Yaz. So many.' His eyes flared brighter. 'It's coming to an end that gives the journey meaning.' The light dimmed and he fell silent. Yaz thought that perhaps it would not return but the eyes flickered and again he spoke. 'These last years . . . here among the people in this final strip of green . . . they carried more weight than all my millennia in Vesta, though you might think them a footnote. It's in the scripture of these people, Yaz. Humanity follow the Path, but each individual is made to cross it, one side to the other. And, fast or slow, that's a journey given value by being temporary.

'I have lived, Yaz. I have loved and I have lived. We both fell into Vesta but only one of us got lost. Escaping was my only talent and still it took you to set me free – to free me from my own fear and make me try again – to take life in both hands and fight for more.' He blinked away a black tear, the light in his eyes growing dim, his voice quieter with each word now. 'Thank you. Yaz of the Ictha. The girl for whom the stars will always shine brighter.'

And he was gone. She knew it, blood to bone. No air would enter her lungs and her heart hurt too much to bear alone. Mali's cry echoed in the passage and when she reached Yaz they crashed together, locked in each other's arms, wrapped in the same wordless grief.

CHAPTER 55

Yaz emerged from the gate and found herself stepping back into the cave beneath the Black Rock she had come from. Mali and Quell stumbled out behind her.

'It didn't work!' Quell turned round to glare at the shimmering circle of light behind them.

'I . . . don't know.' Yaz stared at her hands. For a moment it had seemed they were stained black and she was burdened by a grief so heavy that she almost fell beneath it. Both sensations began to fade. She glanced at Mali and found the girl's eyes bright with tears. 'Why are you crying?'

'I . . . don't know,' Mali echoed her. 'I think it worked though. Agatta said we couldn't bring back memory. We went, we tried, we came back. We can't know if we succeeded. We can't know if the Ictha bred another champion with enough of the Missing's blood to open the Ark. All we can do is keep trying, keep fighting, and wait.'

It hadn't felt like victory when they got Taproot into the ark, and it didn't feel like victory standing there in the cave, her face wet with tears she didn't understand. At best it was doom delayed. The last of the Corridor's green preserved for

525

a few more lifetimes. But perhaps that's all life had to offer – doom delayed.

Yaz looked back at the gate. The light had gone now. It was just a metal ring. The ghosts of memory had fled too, leaving only an ache in their passing. 'We should find a way out.'

'We need Erris.' Mali grinned. 'He can always find a way in or out.'

It took hours rather than days. Quell's memory led them with just the occasional wrong turn. He found them a way to the surface that avoided anyone who might still be living in the Black Rock. It didn't feel like the time for reunions. Yaz wanted to greet the wind and let it cleanse her. And after miles of dark tunnels lit only by Yaz's golden star they saw ahead the brightness of another day on the ice.

Quell led them towards the cave mouth, the light growing each yard, along with the cold. Frost coated the walls and Yaz felt the chill through her convent habit. She and Mali would have to find suitable clothing – and soon – or neither of them would survive half a day in the wind.

Finally they emerged into the teeth of the gale that blew unceasingly across the whiteness of the only home Yaz had known for all but the last few months of her short life. The Corridor's green was just a memory now, images painted in her mind, remembered scent and sound, the feel of grass beneath naked feet. But this, this had its own savage beauty too, an unsullied purity . . .

Only the Purified

. . . the words rolled across her mind.

'This is where I need to be.' The wind stole her voice and she doubted the others heard her.

Quell took her bare hand in his gloved one. 'I'm going to give my jacket to the girl. You're to have my gloves. We'll find the main entrance and ask the Broken to resupply us. Don't fight me on this. You might rule the stars and bring empires to their knees, but the cold is my business.'

Yaz accepted the wisdom of Quell's offer. Mali, shocked to silence by the fierceness of the cold and the anger of the wind, made no argument as she struggled into his hides.

'So.' Quell clapped his hands together. 'We stock up at the Black Rock and then head north to find the Ictha. Your parents . . . they were so happy to have Zeen back and to know you were alive. But now . . .' He grinned. 'And the stories we have to tell. Nobody is going to believe us, Yaz. I mean—'

Yaz turned from helping Mali to fasten Quell's jacket about herself. Something had caught her eye out on the ice. 'What's that?' A bright golden point, like some distant star. The point became a burning line, the line became a rectangle of golden light. And a figure stepped through with hungry flames roaring about him on every side. An armoured figure, a man on whom no inch of flesh was uncovered.

He stepped out of the furnace blast and moved clear. As he emerged from the light Yaz saw that his armour was crimson and black, covering him like the carapace of a beetle. The left side of him was still aflame, fire guttering in the wind's fury, dying down to nothing as he came towards them. The ice melted and steamed where he trod. A helm concealed his head, the visor a curve of black glass. In both hands he carried what looked to be a jet-black star the size of a man's head, though Yaz could sense nothing from it.

He strode towards them and they stood, bound in the spell of his arrival, watching.

When he reached them he set the black sphere down on

the ice between them and then straightened. In his armour he stood a foot taller than Quell and just as broad. He raised a hand to his helmet and somehow the front half of it vanished, perhaps folding away too swiftly to see.

'Holy fuck, it's cold!' The man's long dark hair streamed in the wind. Yaz couldn't tell his age, anything from twenty to forty, sharp-featured, a wildness in his dark eyes, blood smeared across one cheekbone, the other scorched. He laughed, and something made Yaz answer with a grin of her own. 'Well met. I know you,' he said, pointing at Yaz. 'And you. And you. But don't ask me to say your names.' He tapped the side of his head. 'Fractured memories.' He lowered his hand. 'I've brought you a gift. I can't remember why exactly. The gates do that to you if you come back across the years – a dip in the Lethe. And if you knew the trouble I'm going to get into over giving you this . . . Well, fuck them, I say! I'm giving it to you anyway.' He cocked his head. 'You know who I am, right?'

Yaz said it first. 'Prometheus.'

The man sketched a bow. 'They do call me that, yes. A kind of joke, but it stuck. I've had other names.'

'What have you brought us?' Quell asked, suspicion tingeing his voice.

'Ah, well, that will take a little explanation.' Prometheus grinned and spat into the wind, his spittle freezing inches from his mouth. 'Fuck, how do you people even . . . Never mind. I'll show you what I've brought. Then I'll have to close the globe again and it will stay sealed for a little over one hundred years. After that it's yours. Well, I suppose you'll all be dead. But it will be humanity's – property of the four tribes. So be damned sure to find someone more responsible than me to look after it.' He tapped the globe with one foot and the top half vanished, revealing six-inch-thick walls and a small hollow right at the centre in which a dazzling blue-white flame burned. 'I've brought you the gift of fire.'

The three of them eyed him in silence.

'We . . . already know about fire,' Quell said after a long pause.

'Not this fire!' Prometheus squatted down before the half-sphere. 'This is different. Dangerous. Very dangerous. That's why they didn't want me to give it to you.'

'Who are they? And why are you giving it to us?' Yaz asked.

'My people, the Missing, of course.' Prometheus dug his armoured fingers into the ice in a manner that should have been impossible. 'And I'm giving it to you because . . . well . . . I can't bring that knowledge back with me, but you must be my friends, or I must owe you big time, or both. Probably both. Because this is kind of crazy, even for me.' He took the small chunk of ice he'd gouged up and held it to the flame. In a fraction of a second the fire spread to the ice and consumed it. An intense wave of heat struck Yaz and Prometheus's metal-clad fingers glowed red-hot. He winced as the wind cooled them. 'This is—'

'The fire of the gods,' Quell said.

Prometheus shrugged. 'It will burn water. It will burn ice. If you're not damned careful it will burn entire seas, blast away the atmosphere and leave a molten planet. So . . . caution is advised.' He tapped the half-sphere with a finger and it became whole once more. 'Opens again in a hundred and one years. So make sure whoever you pass it on to is prepared. Learn how to use it sensibly and you can reclaim this world from pole to pole. There's enough fuel on Abeth to keep it warm for tens of thousands of years. After that you've got problems. But that's always the way.'

Prometheus stood. 'Better go. I think I left in the middle

of a fight. But seriously. My thanks for helping me pull myself together.' He bowed to Yaz. 'My lady.' And with that he restored his helmet, turned and walked back towards his golden door from which the fire he'd left behind still roared.

Yaz watched as he vanished into the light and the light also vanished.

Quell hugged his bare hands under his armpits and stared at the spot where the door had been. 'What in the hells was that?'

Yaz bent and picked up the black sphere. It wasn't heavy. 'That', she said, 'was victory.'

'What now?' Mali asked the question through chattering teeth.

Yaz looked up from her contemplation of the sphere's midnight depths.

'What now?' Quell echoed Mali, his earlier plans forgotten. He scanned the white horizon.

'Well, for a start you can carry this.' Yaz passed him Prometheus's gift and flexed her hands. The gloves Quell had given her felt comfortable, familiar. Once upon a time she had thought of Quell in those terms. Too comfortable. A familiar seduction that was keeping her from some greater destiny.

She had seen the green world, enjoyed its luxury, marvelled at its many wonders, but still something had recalled her to these empty wastes. Quell no longer seemed safe, and that interested her. They had a people to guide south together. A family to raise against the odds, as every Ictha family was raised. A promise made to the future. A fire to guard. 'What now?' She looked where Quell had looked, at the icy distances stretching away from her. For the longest time all those different directions had seemed the same. Now they felt like choices. She took his hand in hers. 'Time for something new.'

Acknowledgments

As always, I'm very grateful to Agnes Meszaros for her continued help and feedback. She's never shy to challenge me when she thinks something can be improved or I'm being a little lazy. At the same time her passion and enthusiasm made working on the story even more enjoyable.

I should also thank, as ever, my wonderful editor, Jane Johnson, for her support and her many talents, Natasha Bardon, Vicky Leech Mateos, Fleur Clarke and the design, sales, marketing, and publicity crews at HarperCollins. And of course my agent, Ian Drury, and the team at Sheil Land.